The Faraday Cage

Edited by

Steve Turnbull

The Faraday Cage. Edited by Steve Turnbull. Published April 2016.
Anthology Copyright © 2016 Tau Press Ltd. All rights reserved.

'The Haemophage' Copyright © 2016 Robert Harkess. All rights reserved.
'Taking the Cure' Copyright © 2016 Peter A. Smalley. All rights reserved.
'Iron Curtain' Copyright © 2016 Virginia Marybury. All rights reserved.
'Dear Prudence' Copyright © 2016 Katy O'Dowd & Steve Turnbull. All rights reserved.
'The Computationer' Copyright © 2016 Steve Turnbull. All rights reserved.

ISBN 978-1-910342-44-2

This anthology is a work of fiction. Names, characters, places, and incidents are either
products of the authors' imaginations or used fictitiously. Any resemblance to actual events,
locales, or persons, living or dead, is entirely coincidental. No part of this book shall be
reproduced or transmitted in any form or by any means, electronic or mechanical, including
photocopying, recording, or by any information retrieval system without permission of the
publisher. The moral right of the contributors to be identified as the authors of their work
has been asserted by them in accordance with the Copyright, Designs, and Patents Act 1988.

Published by Tau Press Ltd.
Cover by Jane Dixon-Smith (jdsmith-design.com).
Internal art by Maria Oglesby (mariaoglesbyart.com).

To Chris, for the idea.

TABLE OF CONTENTS

The Haemophage

by Robert Harkess

THE HAEMOPHAGE

By Robert Harkess

I

Steam glittered into ice, picked out in diamond sharp detail by the four great arc lanterns surrounding the forward dock. His Imperial Majesty's Space Vessel *Victoria* puffed energetically from her manoeuvring vents as she matched the spin of the station, the stars behind her wheeling six full rotations each minute. Blake tore his eyes away from the star-field, feeling the first stirrings of nausea, and focused on the *Victoria*. She was edging forward now, her blunt nose already out of sight from the observation window. A few seconds later the rail he was holding on to vibrated softly as the ship nudged fully into her berth.

He turned to look down onto the Hub, the vast cylinder that made up the core of the station. Only a handful of minutes passed before a great hissing and a new rumble announced that the inner doors of the main airlock were grinding open. He tapped his hand against the rail he had been holding and let himself float up a few feet, bettering his view. A battalion's-worth of bodies in bright orange overalls drifted through the lock, only to be chivvied along and sub-divided by orderlies. He remembered the drill well, from his own arrival at the station two years ago. He was an officer, and therefore treated better than these unfortunates were about to be. Still, a shiver ran down his spine at the memory of the indignities he had suffered that day. On the other side of the airlock a crewman from the ship, junior but still an officer, hurried over to a mail tube. He saw a flash of red before the cartridge disappeared through the valve. Something for the Commander, and probably from the *Victoria*'s Master.

All the new recruits were male, and nine-tenths of them had shaven heads: miners - or hoping to be. The remaining dozen or so were prospectors. They were all corralled next to a table and a tent. Oh, the things that would be done in the tent. His mind was brought back to the present by a bellowing voice below. Next to the table stood a short, powerfully built man, his scalp shining bald apart from an inch-wide patch at the back from which hung enough hair to form a thrice-knotted plait;

Master Foreman Archer, once a Regimental Sergeant-Major, now a herder of displaced persons.

'This is your induction.' He paused, fixing several at the front of the mob with gimlet eyes. 'You will approach the desk in an orderly manner. You will identify yourself to the clerk, who will record your finger marks. This is not optional.' He gave them a moment to absorb that information. 'You will then go into the tent. Things will be done to you. You will submit, willingly and with good grace. This is not optional. Failure to submit, willingly and with good grace, will result in you being refused entry to the station, and it will then be your responsibility to negotiate safe haven with the master of the *Victoria,* before this area is opened to space after her departure. Is this abundantly clear?'

There was a subdued muttering, with a slight hint of rebellion, then silence.

'Once you are deemed fit to enter the station, you will be assigned crew quarters. You will be Sweepers. You will keep your heads shaved, and you will do as you are told. You will earn your grades. Your previous accomplishments mean nothing here. Your past means nothing here. That is all. First man, come forward.'

Blake's welcome had been warmer, but not by much. Maybe one man in ten was here by choice. He grimaced. Not quite true. Each of them had been offered a choice. His had been to serve on the station, or to be dishonourably discharged from his unit, and his family shamed by a scandal he had played no part in. Now, he was in charge of security and order in a Mining Station in the asteroid belt, trying to keep a lid on more than a three hundred souls as disenchanted as his own.

A flicker of movement in the corner of his eye made him look up, snatched back from his reverie. Someone had exited the hatch of Number 4 Spoke and launched themselves towards him. The railing he had been holding was now just out of reach, so he pulled out his hand-fan, snapped it open, and discreetly wafted himself closer. Moments later, he shook his head in disbelief; the boy was uncanny. No matter where he was, Tommy Stiles, Midshipman and runner for Station Commander Maxwell, seemed to be able to find him. The boy had been on the station only six months, but it was starting to get a little annoying.

'Commodore's respects, Captain Blake,' Tommy said, as soon as he was close enough not to shout. Blake thought it was unlikely, but didn't argue the point. 'Could he see you in his ready room, at your convenience?'

'Understood,' Blake replied, but called the boy back when he turned away. 'How do you do it, Stiles? Know where I am, I mean.'

Stiles had to be sixteen to be on the station, but his grin made him look like a street urchin. He pointed at the observation port. 'Most of the time, I go where I wish I was.'

The door to the commodore's office was ajar, so Blake knocked and opened it in much the same motion. Maxwell enjoyed his position to the full, and Blake was hard pressed not to let his lack of approval show on his face every time he walked into the over-stuffed monument to the station commander's vanity. His real wood furniture, including a full size desk, had been shipped up from Earth at ridiculous cost. Wherever he was getting the money to pay for it, Blake knew it couldn't be from his salary - at least, not judging by his own.

Two people rose from chairs placed in front of Maxwell's desk, turning to face him. A man past the prime of his life, tall and gaunt, his terrible comb-over refused to stay in place in the low gravity of the station. Next to him, a woman. She was more difficult to read; her strictly pinned hair and horn-rimmed spectacles making her appear generic. She was shorter than the man, and her corset did nothing to contain her ample figure. She looked Blake up and down, then her gaze returned to his eyes with a cool neutrality that unsettled him. Both were well-dressed, in an understated way. He wondered how they had bypassed the induction process to get here before him.

'Allow me to present Captain Blake,' said Maxwell, still sitting. 'He keeps things in order on the station. Blake, this is Doctor Fleischmann. The lady is his assistant, Miss Armstrong.'

'A pleasure,' said Fleischmann, extending his hand. Blake was surprised that someone with such a Prussian name would be allowed on the station. The European situation was tense, and the Kaiser was very much out of favour with London. But Fleischmann spoke with no more accent than a slight trace of Celtic, probably Scottish. Miss Armstrong said nothing, but returned his nod. Blake straightened into a sloppy 'attention', and bowed stiffly from the waist, before taking Fleischmann's hand. The flesh was cold and damp, and Blake was uncomfortably reminded of uncooked sausages. He turned to Maxwell. 'How may I be of service, Commodore?'

'Our guests require a workspace, in addition to their personal accommodation. I have assigned them aft hold eight.'

Blake fought to keep his eyebrows where they needed to be. Aft-eight was one of four hangars used for storing and maintaining skiffs when they weren't in use; small shuttles that ferried miners between the station and the mine on the asteroid below them. 'Of course, sir. What...?'

'Really, man, do I have to explain everything. In case you had forgotten, this station is also a research facility.' News to Blake. 'The Doctor is engaged in a project of utmost secrecy, which will bring—'

'Commodore, please.' Fleischmann's reprimand was blade-sharp. Maxwell's complexion darkened but, to Blake's astonishment, the station commander simply swallowed—hard—and jerked his head up and down once.

'Of course. Excuse me.' His eyes flicked from the doctor back to Blake. 'Are you still here, man? Get the area cleared, and post constables at every entrance. Only these good people are to have access, or those they so nominate. Anything they ask for, they get. Am I making myself clear?'

'Abundantly, sir. If I might be excused?' Blake could feel his own face starting to burn, and snapped into an about-turn as soon as Maxwell's hand started its airy wave to dismiss him. As he turned, he caught of flash of Miss Armstrong's face. She was studying him again, her expression speculative and analytical. As the door closed behind him, Fleischmann's voice rose, unintelligible but obviously displeased. Blake rubbed a ruminative hand across his mouth as he walked away.

Blake dropped into his chair. Even at half Earth's gravity, the bare metal seat was uncomfortable. Cold, too. His lips twisted into a humourless grin. That fairly well summed up the station; uncomfortable and cold. He took a pencil and a sheet of paper, scrawled a note to the Hubmaster—keeping the tone as conciliatory as he could—and addressed the p-slug appropriately. Sliding the message into the receiver of the mail tube, he felt the vacuum within suck air around the edge of the seal, and made a mental note to mention the problem to maintenance. With a clatter, the message pod was drawn into the system, destined for Central. He stared at the mail tube a moment longer; Central had been lagging behind for a couple of weeks. He had marked the message as priority, but he would leave it an hour before he wandered down there. Cowardly or not, he wanted the Hubmaster to have blown off at least some of his head of steam by the time he had to confront the man in person.

He still got there before the message.

'You want *what*?'

'*I* don't want anything,' Blake explained. 'I'm just the messenger boy.' He hesitated, just for an instant, surprised by the bitterness in his voice, then hurried on and hoped the Hubmaster hadn't noticed. 'The message is to clear aft-8, and to secure it. No access—not even you—without approval and escort.'

'A week—maybe even ten days.'

'Four hours.' Blake knew he wouldn't get it in four hours but, if he didn't push, it would be closer to the ten days he had just been offered.

'Impossible.'

'Commodore's orders.' Magic words, but how he hated to use them, and he tried not to flinch when he saw the contempt flicker across the Hubmaster's face. He had to take some of it, even though he was only the messenger. It rankled. The Hubmaster turned away from him.

'You two! Get the hangar doors open on A-8 and every other skiff hangar. Move the skiff's where you can. Carefully. And get a detail to move the rest of the equipment out of there to A-1 and F-6.' He faced Blake. 'May I know the reason for this... inconvenience?'

Blake kept his face straight, and rigidly suppressed the shrug primed in his shoulders. 'Sorry.'

One of the ratings ran up to the Hubmaster, tapping a finger to his forehead. 'Your pardon, sir, but I'm to tell you it will take an hour to bring the monties up on all the skiffs, and that *Daisy* is in for a control thruster problem.'

'Then leave two men on the monties, and set the rest to hauling kit. *Daisy* will have to fly. I don't want to try dragging her, not after last time.'

Monties were the reactors that powered the skiffs—and, for that matter, the station. Blake knew the engineers hated the term; to them, they were Monturial Engines, and anything else was a lack of respect. They reacted certain minerals together to generate heat and oxygen without fire, but other than that, he left them to the engineers.

Blake let the micro-gravity in the hub drift him out of the way, but where he could watch what was going on. From the looks being thrown at him by the Hubmaster and his senior staff, it would seem to be that the preferred option was that he depart, but Station Commander Maxwell enjoyed playing the blame game, and Blake had no desire to become one of the pieces. The best way to be sure of that was to stay here and be an irritant.

The first skiff was ready in less than an hour. There were almost as many variations on the theme as there were skiffs but, essentially, they were simply an open framework built around a monty engine, with a small pilot's station atop the monty and either seats or cargo shelves, as required. Designed for outdoor work, the little craft could not have lifted from the half-gravity at the rim, let alone from a planet surface but, here in the hub, they were nimble enough, if noisy. Steam burst in staccato claps and shrieks from control nozzles as the first unit drifted to its new berth.

The rest of the stable moved in quick succession until only one was left, two technicians still crawling all around it. Blake unconsciously leaned forward as a nervous pilot took his position atop Daisy and began edging her cautiously from the hangar. Half-way through the door, clouds of steam screamed from the rear of the skiff, and the stern shot upwards to crash into the top of the door-frame. Metal screeched horribly as Daisy ground herself along the metal, then she was out in the hub, spinning and out of control. Sirens blared, other hangar doors began to close, and interspersed among the cacophony, the Harbourmaster's voice could be heard screaming, 'Dump her, *Dump her.*'

Astonished, Blake saw the pilot was actually gaining some semblance of control, jets at the bow fighting in opposition to those at the stern, until the skiff had almost ceased its wild gyrations. Then a huge blast of steam erupted from beneath the monty, and Blake feared the worst; the engine had blown up.

The steam cleared, and Daisy was hanging in the air, rotating slowly, her pilot still in his chair, hands covering his face. A solitary hand-clap rapidly became a heartfelt round of applause, then lines were being thrown and secured, and Daisy was drawn cautiously into a different hangar. The Hubmaster arrowed through the air towards Blake, his face mottled.

'And *that's* what happens when things aren't done in their proper time, and you can tell the bloody Commodore I said so. No, *I'll* do it, by sending him a copy of my report to the safety board. Have you *seen* the damage to the door frame? We can't even close it, let alone seal it.'

Blake knew the report would never get off station; not unless the Hubmaster somehow smuggled it out. Despite there being no official policy, he knew every item of mail going off the station was vetted, and anything showing the station in a bad light conveniently 'lost'. He had protested, but not too loudly. Pragmatism had to come before one's personal morality. At least, it did here. He looked up at the point where Daisy had crashed into the frame, and saw there was indeed a deformation.

He turned, prepared himself to kick off towards the neared hub door. He turned back to the Hubmaster.

'You have three hours.'

II

The stowaway lying in a crumpled heap at his feet was female, but that was all he could make out with confidence. She was encased in such grime that it was difficult to tell what colour her hair was, or even get a clear idea of the colour of her garment. Then there was the stench, partly of the oily effluvium that seemed to collect in the deeper corners of the station, but he could also detect body odour and even urine in the rancid mix. He wrinkled his nose and wished there was an air mask nearby.

The message had been waiting for him in his office when he got back from confronting the Hubmaster, sitting amongst the half dozen other capsules in the basket under the p-tube. It wasn't unheard of. Perhaps one in five vessels visiting the station brought an unexpected addition to the manifest. Blake felt sorry for them; either they had no idea how bad things were where they were headed, or wherever they had come from was a manifestation of hell he couldn't imagine.

After the first couple of stowaways had led him a manic chase around the station for weeks on end, Blake introduced a number of new procedures; partial lockdown for a number of days either side of a ship arriving, and financial inducements for staff to turn in stowaways. He had tracked this one down in less than forty-eight hours.

He considered his options. He had used his Maxwell on the girl, but had only needed to discharge one of the stunning rounds from the modified revolver. Normal rounds from a firearm could puncture the skin of a space vessel, and the Maxwell had no need for penetrative power, just enough to get the shells, filled with a mixture of charged Faraday Quartz dust, into contact with the target. As a result of the electrical shock delivered by the round, the girl had collapsed like a rag doll. He dragged her out of the service crawl-way and into the corridor. He could cuff her, wait till she woke, and make her travel under her own effort to the jail, but she was showing no signs of recovering. He put the Maxwell back in its holster, his right hand unconsciously resting on the pommel of his sword, and glanced to either side. He was in Miner territory; nothing bad *per se*, but in the maintenance areas, the glows were farther apart, and set to use less gas. In the darkness, things could happen, and he had no desire to sit here, bathed in the girl's miasma, waiting for her to wake up.

He would drag her. She was a slight and slender thing but, in Miner territory, the spin-gravity imitated roughly one-tenth that of Earth. He reached down, grabbed a handful of the back of her bodice, and hoped the unsavoury fabric would hold.

The face of the constable in charge screwed up in disgust as Blake dragged the unconscious woman into the Miners level drunk tank. 'What's that?'

'Stowaway from the *Victoria*. Open number three, and get me a ship-suit, smallest one you can find.'

The constable did his best to keep his distance from the girl as he opened the door, then backed hurriedly out of the way. Half of the cells in the drunk tank had a shower, not so much for the convenience of those who had embarrassed themselves through drunkenness, but more as a consideration to those they would have to pass returning to their own accommodation. Blake hauled the girl into the shower and spun the tap. Cold water pumped out.

She woke, if indeed she had not been feigning unconsciousness, with an ear-splitting shriek. Blake pushed her back as she tried to crawl out of the cubicle, but warmed the water a little.

'Name?'

'Jenny Smith.'

'Real name?'

The girl looked away, catching her lower lip beneath her front teeth, abruptly looking younger than the twenty-five years Blake has originally assessed her age to be.

'Amy Rivers.'

Blake knew it was probably still a lie, but it was a better one. 'Miss Rivers, you are on this station illegally. There are consequences to be addressed but, for now, you must make yourself fit to pass amongst the other inhabitants of this place. You will shower, and change out of those rags into the clothing provided. It will be less than ladylike, but will serve for the moment. At the constable's discretion you will be released, whereupon you will attend sickbay for a medical check. After that, you will present yourself to me at my office.' He saw a crafty flicker in the girl's eyes. 'We know who you are, and what you look like, and you have already seen there are few places to hide on this station. Save us all the trouble of having to search for you again. If you don't... well, stowaways only get one chance here.'

That sobered her up, and the foxy glint was replaced by pallor and fear. The constable returned with a jumpsuit. Blake left it on the bench and backed away from the shower. If they could identify her, she would be accommodated at the station until the employer to which she was indentured could be found. If they were prepared to pay for her repatriation, she would be sent back. If not, she would need to get work, or find a sponsor on the station. Both were equally difficult. Nobody got a free ride.

A blaring klaxon dragged him from sleep. Four long blasts; trouble in the Miners ring. Blake threw off his blanket, and tugged his trousers and jacket onto place, before grabbing his belt and bouncing off the frame of his open door as he stumbled out into the corridor. In the half-gravity of Crew ring, he part ran, part flew towards A-shaft. A small group of Occasionals, akin to Special Constables at home, hovered around the shaft doors, unhappy and unsure of what they should be doing. Blake cursed inwardly that he didn't have a larger, regular constabulary.

'Report,' he snapped to the junior NCO.

'Trouble in Miners, sir.'

'Really? Never would have guessed it. Details, man.'

'Don't know, sir. Just there's some kind of disturbance, and they were trying to get into our shafts.'

That was new. The inhabitants of Miners, which covered everybody who worked the rocks and anybody who supported them, were known to erupt into the odd fight now and then, but Blake couldn't remember anything like this. 'Are they locked down?'

'I think so, sir.'

'You *think* so? Where's the worst of it?'

'Right above, sir.'

'Then get out of the way, man, and send for another squad to defend these doors. And lock them behind me.'

The corporal snapped to attention. 'Sah.'

Blake closed the airlock door behind him, and reached instinctively for a hand-loop on the elevator rope—which, of course, had been shut down for the duration of the emergency. Stairs it was then, followed by ladders as the gravity dropped to the point where stairs became more of a hindrance than a help. The bellow of the klaxon was painfully loud in the narrow, echoing shaft, and Blake was sure it, rather than the riot, was more responsible for his pounding heart.

A knot of men pressed around the small airlock that opened into Miner territory, and though he could not see the door, he could hear people battering on it. By pushing and shoving, he made his way through to the front. 'Does anybody know what kicked them off?' His eyes searched around the group for whoever was in charge. Nobody seemed to want the responsibility. He turned to the door and peered through the distorting lens of the porthole.

The view was surreal. The glass was deliberately shaped to give as wide a view as possible of what was on the other side, distorting bodies and faces into nightmares. Three people stood at the airlock—one he recognised—armed with a metal bar, a chair, and what looked like a hammer. The chair-wielder merely battered ineffectually against the metal door, but the other two were acting industriously on something below his line of sight. Blake looked down and saw the lock-wheel tremble in response to a further fusillade of blows from within. Eye back to the glass, he looked beyond the three working on the door. The mob was serious, jeering and screaming, but giving them room to work.

There was no way he could parley with them through the porthole. At only four inches wide, they would not even see his whole face.

'Anyone in C-shaft?' he called to the crowd behind him. 'Have they done anything? Has anybody tried to reason with them?'

There was no response. When he turned, a sea of blank faces gazed back at him. Irritated, he pointed at a random someone. 'You. Double time, and I *mean* double, up and over to C-shaft. I want to know who is there and what they are doing, and I want you back here in under five minutes or you will be on a charge for the next year. *Move!*

Three of his fellows worked together to give the unlucky rating a 'launch': a traditional leg-up, but with much more force, which sent him flying upwards towards the hub. Blake turned back to the glass, and tried to think of a way to defuse the situation.

The rating did not return within the allotted five minutes, but was only a minute or so over. He looked grave.

'Sir, there are other miners trying to break out at every lock on every shaft. All the doors have been locked. They can't get out, but we can't get anything in. Central says the post tubes have been blocked or damaged.'

A commotion from below disrupted his concentration, and he was just about to bellow for what quiet he could get when Station Commander Maxwell hove into view up the stairs, face thunderous.

'What is the meaning of this, Blake?'

'Riot in progress, sir.'

'Then deal with it.'

Was the man a complete buffoon? 'It's contained, sir. We are just considering options on the best way to bring it to an end.'

'"We"? Don't you think it would have been prudent to involve your superiors when it became obvious you were unable to resolve the situation?'

Blake felt his mouth gape, and pulled it shut by force of will. Maxwell had never sunk to this level before. He took a breath. 'We can't get in. They have enough men at every access point to block any force we use through any door.'

'Well, flood it with that gas the medico uses. Ether.'

'It's explosive, sir.'

'Then space them.'

'Sir?'

'Heavens, man, do I have to explain everything. Open Miners to space. Slowly.'

'But...?'

'It's not like they can't be replaced.'

Maxwell crooked a finger at an adjutant and muttered in his ear. Blake turned to the porthole. Minutes later, the klaxon changed, now only sounding in Miners; the repeating, braying alert of a hull breach. Blake watched. Surprise, realisation, horror, fear. The agitators were torn away from the doors, big men desperately signing everything was under control, and that they would behave. The crowd fell to its knees, hands on its collective head. And still, Maxwell drained the air.

III

Blake had few cells, and they were currently fully occupied by those who had been identified trying to break the doors down, or those identified as being the ringleaders. The rest had been shipped back to the rock, their

R&R terminated prematurely, expensive fines to be garnished from their wages and meagre savings. Station Commander Maxwell had preened himself afterward, strutting around the Officers' Mess as though he had resolved the situation. Blake thought he had only made it worse, storing up even greater discord to erupt later.

Now, he was sitting in his only interrogation room, a burly sergeant behind him, an even bigger miner on the other side of the table. Isaac Rosenthal, or 'Papa', as most of the miners called him. He had been working out of the station since the beginning; five years of breaking dirt to dig out the incalculably valuable Faraday Quartz. The man was as solid as the rock he spent his life cutting through, and Blake had seen him pull a six-man fight apart with his bare hands, then make the pugilists squirm like naughty schoolboys.

'Tell me, Papa,' he said, calmly, quietly.

'Is no point,' Papa replied, his heavy accent thicker than usual, the overtones of Yiddish and Dutch all but obscuring his broken English. 'I see dem. We all for chop. Space us, maybe.'

'What do you think you saw?'

'Rosenthal don't *tink* he saw nothing. He saw. *I* saw. Dey don't need us now.'

Blake sat back. The old miner could be raving. It happened, out here where nothing felt right, where the very laws of nature seemed watered down or distorted, no matter how long a body had been given to adjust. Blake had felt it himself, in the quiet, hopeless hours of the night, smothering him, tempting him siren-like to despair and let go. He suppressed a shudder.

'Not making much sense, Papa.' He leaned forward and rested his arms on the table. 'Or do you not realise how much trouble you are in? How much trouble the whole shift is in?'

The Dutchman nodded lugubriously, an expression of huge sadness and deep anger settling on his face. 'I do, I do.' He sat up in his chair, and squared his shoulders as best he could with his wrists manacled to eye-bolts on the table. 'Sometimes, I cannot sleep. When so much time on the rock you spend, sometime even a little gravity can make the joints hurt and the heart sore. So, I take a wander to Hub. I do this many times. It is soothing to watch the universe spin.'

Blake decided to let the security breach pass, now that he had Papa talking.

'And?'

'I am going back to my bunk. There is a way I know. A door ahead of me is open, for the service, at the back of a hangar. Der is a man shouting, but I don't hear the words. A weak man. As I pass, I look inside, and see the golem.'

'Golem?'

'Mannequins. Robota. I saw them, On Venus. In the—' He broke off, looking furtively to either side. 'They move like men, but are not. They kill without mercy, do not hunger, do not tire. I saw. Machines, without souls.'

Blake sat back again. 'And you got a good look at him? It?'

'Good enough.'

'And this was sufficient to make you start a riot. In God's name, man—why?'

'It wore these,' Papa plucked at his fatigues, overalls in archetypal Miners yellow. 'It wore da miner's helmet, hiding its face. Dey are to replace us.'

'What?'

'No sleep, no food, no off-shift or time on dis station. No pay. The company don't need us. They get rid of us. You tink dey send us home. Only if we can pay, betcha. Der rest? Space us maybe.' Papa's accent sank deeper towards his native tongue the more agitated he became, and his cuffed hands banged on the table. Blake heard a creak of leather as the constable behind him flexed uneasily, and felt a little like backing away himself.

'So you stood at the door and watched this—golem. How long for?'

'A second, maybe five. It moved away. I did not dare go inside.'

Blake laced his fingers behind his neck and arched his back, stretching out some of the tension. 'Some maintenance teams wear orange. Could what you have seen been orange? You were in dim light, the hangar would be brightly lit. And might the helmet have been a welding mask?' Papa was shaking his head, face stubborn, but Blake pushed his point. He had no desire to have to shove this man through an airlock. 'Think about it, man. You were tired, short of sleep, it was late. Maybe a drink or two, or a sniff of *dyne*? Are you sure of what you saw? Sure enough to stake your life on it? The lives of your fellows?'

Stubborn faded to morose. 'Dey kill us anyway. But no. Maybe.' The big man shrugged one then slumped in his chair. Blake stood up and rapped a knuckle on the door. Two more constables waited outside. 'Take him back to his cell. With respect.'

Rosenthal left the room diminished, like a man defeated. Blake stood to the side, thumbs hooked into his belt, finger tapping on the hilt of his sword.

He knew if he went to the Station Commander he would be told to back off. Maxwell would toe the company line, and if it meant a problem with production, there would always be somebody else the commodore would be able to pin the blame on. Blake grimaced as he admitted it would probably be him, for not maintaining station security. A hint of ice chilled his spine. So that was how the miners felt. If Maxwell fired him, and if the bond company he had insured his return fare with failed to pay out, then he could end up looking at space without the benefit of a suit.

There were three entrances to Aft-8. The main door—guarded, the service hatch—which should never have been open, and the inboard personnel door—also guarded. Whether the guards were people he could work with, or Maxwell's men, remained to be seen. He hadn't inspected the arrangements since the day the Hubmaster had cleared the hangar, and now he cursed himself for thinking that an absence of complaints implied everything was in order. He set off for the nearest spoke. There was only one way to find out.

He drifted casually along the corridor and stopped himself with a wall loop right outside the personnel door. 'How is our mad professor?'

He didn't recognise the second man. That wasn't unusual, but it wasn't a good sign. The other was Baker, and Blake had a vague memory the man had been on his team for some time.

'Well enough, I suppose. Haven't seen much of anybody.'

'Well, be a good man and crack the door open for me.'

Baker shook his head. 'Locked.'

'Really?'

'Always.'

'What about when they leave at night?'

'Always one inside, always locked. When they do open the door, like when the kitchen brings food, there's drapes and things to hide anything inside.' The guard's voice dropped to a conspiratorial whisper. 'I heard they're experimenting on corpses.'

Blake had to nip that rumour and quickly. He burst out laughing. 'Wonderful. What's next, undead doxies for the miners?'

'Probably suit them well enough,' said the unknown guard, and the three burst into good-natured laughter.

'Would you mind giving a hefty rap on that door, Baker? I've a mind to speak with our professor.'

'Can always try, sir.' Baker drew his sword, and pounded the pommel against the door three times.

The lack of response was just becoming disrespectfully awkward when the wheel turned and the bolts pulled back from the bulkhead. The door opened no more than a hand's-breadth, and a shadowy face peered through the gap.

'What do you want?'

Blake recognised the voice rather than the fraction of face. 'Miss Armstrong. I wish to speak to Dr. Fleischmann.'

'He is busy.'

'Nevertheless.'

'Commodore Maxwell will be informed of your intrusion.'

Blake managed to get enough of his boot into the gap to stop her closing the door and whispered urgently, 'The very rumour of what you have in there has already caused a riot on the station. Maxwell be damned, but I *will* know what I am dealing with here. Are you so confident of your own protection that you would be safe if I removed mine?' It was a bluff. Maxwell could replace him in a heartbeat. Still, Blake was haunted by the look in Papa Rosenthal's eyes.

The woman looked less certain. 'Wait here,' she said, then closed the door when Blake removed his toe.

He took a step back. She would be discussing this with the doctor. He would be deciding whether to entrust Blake, or report him to Maxwell. Blake felt his palms begin to sweat, his heart to race. It was taking too long. His ears strained for the sound of a squad hurrying along the tunnels to 'escort' him to the station commander.

The clank of the door unlocking made him jump. He looked guiltily from side to side, hoping the two men hadn't noticed. The hatch swung open. Beyond it a cage of medical screens blocked off the view of what was within. Fleischmann stood inside, and beckoned to him with crooked fingers. Blake's hackles rose, but he forced his face into polite interest and stepped across the bulkhead. Behind him, Miss Armstrong swung the hatch closed and dogged it down.

'Your instructions were quite clear, Captain. We were not to be disturbed.'

'Nor would I have done so had you not allowed rumour of what you are doing to leak from the room, Doctor.'

'Absurd.'

'Without authorisation, you opened a service access hatch. While that hatch was open, a passing crew member looked inside, and saw what you are doing in here. The ensuing riot all but cost an entire mining shift their lives, and may still be responsible for the execution of several.'

Fleischmann blanched and spluttered. Blake raised a hand.

'Doctor, my only concern is to keep this station calm and orderly. It seems to me your secret is already at least partly exposed. I may be able to help, but only if I am in full possession of the facts. Otherwise, I must report to my superiors that this project threatens station safety and security.'

The doctor looked over Blake's shoulder, presumably seeking approval from Miss Armstrong, then held aside a section of curtain. 'What you are about to see is so secret they do not have a name for it. Even Commodore Maxwell does not understand the full extent of this exercise.'

Blake nodded, annoyed by how tense his movement must have looked, and stepped through the drapes.

The hangar had been subdivided. He saw space set aside for living and sleeping areas, space for a highly modified skiff, a chemical laboratory, and an equally arcane array of electrical paraphernalia. He walked further in, then stopped in his tracks. Furious with himself for reacting so, he was still unable to take a further step. Hanging limply from racks in the centre of the room were bodies, or rather ship-suits, with boots, gloves and helmets. And yet, whatever was inside the suits was not human. The cloth hung as if draped over skeletons, with strange, sharp bulges where the joints should be. To the side, four more, but these were sitting in chairs, motionless but upright. Pipes as thick as his thumb connected them to a chugging machine set between them. As one, all four helmets turned to look at him, and nausea bubbled in his throat.

'Dear God, he was right,' Blake breathed, then he turned on Fleischmann. 'What are these...?' He searched for a suitable word, then just let the question hang.

'Automata,' said Armstrong, standing at his shoulder. 'And to save time, no, they are not human, and no, you may not know how they are made.'

Blake turned to face the doctor and his assistant. 'And the company is looking to use these to replace the miners.'

Fleischmann looked at Armstrong, his face puzzled, then they both burst out laughing. 'Why would anybody want to replace...? Captain,

seriously. Miners are ten-a-penny, an ocean of hopefuls looking to escape
an old life or make a new one. Either way, they are of little value.'

'Then why the charade?'

'Again, not open to discussion. These units are here for evaluation.'

'Why here?'

'Who leaves, Captain? Our secret cannot be exposed, if nobody leaves
the station to tell it.'

IV

The p-tube rattled behind him. Blake was sitting at his desk. More correctly,
he had his boots resting on the top of the desk, and the chair tipped back
against the wall, drowsing. His feet fell to the floor with a thud as he tried
to stop the chair sliding backwards. He had nobody in the cells and no
crimes outstanding. A quiet word with Papa Rosenthal had—hopefully—
defused that situation and, in summary court, the stowaway girl had given a
guilty plea, although she wouldn't say her real name. She had been given six
months' community service under the sponsorship of the kitchen. He was
less than impressed to have his brief period of quietude disrupted but, when
he flicked an eye in the direction of the basket under the tube, he realized it
was an emergency.

The message slip inside the red- and yellow-striped tube was terse; there
had been a murder.

Once he reached the right quadrant of Miners, someone directed him to
the relevant changing room. The crowd grew thicker as he got closer, until
he was manhandling people out of the way to make progress. There had
never been a murder on the station; at least, not in any record he had seen.
Without precedent or procedure, he was on his own and making it up as he
went along. In a way it was invigorating, stimulating.

A sweet, metallic smell cloyed in his nose, and a cold shiver ran down
his spine. Blood. He shouldered the last two people aside and looked
through the doorway. At least the crowd were staying out of the way.

The room was nothing more than two rows of lockers along opposing
walls, a handful of shower stalls at the far end, and four benches in the
middle. The woman, little more than a girl really, was lying face-down on
the floor between two benches, a rivulet of blood from the floor near her
head trickling slowly towards the showers. For a moment, Blake thought
the body was that of Amy Rivers, then he stepped far enough into the room

to see the victim's face and recoiled. Her eyes were stretched wide open, and her expression was one of unimaginable fear.

'Everybody out, and back to work,' he bellowed. 'Anyone still here in sixty seconds gets docked a half-shift's pay.' He looked into the room again, but turned back when nobody moved. 'I mean it. Fifty-nine, fifty-eight, fifty-seven...' When people started to leave, he grabbed the nearest of them and held him back. 'Not you. I have a job for you.'

'So what do you believe to be the cause of death?' Blake asked.

McEwan, the Chief Medical Officer, gave him a surprised look 'You don't think the raw flesh where her throat used to be might be a giveaway?'

Blake pulled a face, partly in acknowledgement his question had been a little obvious, and partly involuntarily because of the doctor's tone. Blake knew McEwan was from Ultima Scotia, one of the Martian settlements, but sometimes the man's informal way of speaking simply grated. He shrugged, but said nothing.

McEwan gave in after about twenty seconds, turning back to the body, and using a handy surgical clamp as a pointer. 'This trauma was not caused by a blade, or anything with sharp edges. There's evidence of puncture wounds on one side, and the edges of the skin and inner tissues around the hole indicate tearing away from the punctures. Like claws, or teeth.'

'Or *teeth*?'

The medic nodded, then slowly turned his head to look at Blake. 'There is one thing that troubles me, though.'

'Oh?'

'Where's the blood?'

Blake pointed at the gore spread down the unfortunate woman's chest, but McEwan shook his head. 'The body is all but exsanguinated, and yet there was no more than a half-pint on the floor where she was found.'

Blake thought back to the room, then cursed himself for missing something so obvious. He was out of practice, the bucolic herding of miners blunting his skills. 'Killed elsewhere, and left at the scene?'

'Possibly, but I would have expected to see smears on the decking, or droplets, if she was carried. Eight pints of blood makes a hell of a mess, Captain. Try it with a bucket of water one day.'

He let the comment pass. Blake was well aware of the shocking amount of blood that could leak from a corpse. 'Well, let me know if you find anything.'

Subdued, Blake left sick-bay, intending to return to the scene of the crime and trying to do his job this time.

It was, it seemed, going to be one of *those* days. Before he could return to the changing room where the woman had been found, Blake was intercepted by Midshipman Stiles.

'Commodore's respects, sir, and can you please arrange a security detail at the Aft cargo lock?'

'Please convey my respects to the Station Commander, and advise him I will be happy to do so in an hour or so. I have a little job I need to attend to first, Stiles.'

'Beggin' your pardon, Captain, but the Commodore said I was to tell you to snap to it.' The boy looked acutely uncomfortable.

'Why?'

'Cos there's a ship coming in, and it isn't one of ours.'

V

It was inevitable that all the evidence of the murder would likely be washed away by the time he could look for it, but the unexpected ship had to take precedence. Another first. Space vessels did not simply arrive at the station, because only those authorised knew where the station was. There was also the absurd fact the vessel was apparently presenting itself at the aft cargo lock, rather than docking at the front door, as it were. At the observation window, Blake tapped on the shoulder of a lookout with field glasses. 'May I?'

'Right there, sir. Can't miss her.'

Blake raised the glasses to his eyes, scanned the heavens briefly, then gasped. The ship's aetherotors were still engaged, beating hard to kill her speed, sparkling sharply against the dark velvet of the universe. He peered over the top of the field glasses, then back through the lens. Was he going mad? The ship was no more than the size of a cargo scow, and yet capable of interplanetary travel?

Frantic bursts of steam shone in the glow from the aetherotors, some adding to the effort to slow down, others lining the sharp little craft up with the dock. The rotors slowed, stopped, then folded in on themselves and withdrew into the body of the vessel. Blake shook his head. Wherever this vessel had come from, their technology was more advanced than anything he had seen. If there was any hostile intent, he had little idea of what he could do to thwart it. The only thing they could hope to do was contain any threat in the cargo lock; it was designed to protect against runaway scows, so would be capable of withstanding anything up to a 50-calibre round. He hoped the vessel had not somehow concealed any small field artillery.

Half an hour later, Blake was sitting on a bench outside the small airlock that would let him into the main cargo airlock. The modified diving suit bulked him out in a rubberised coverall, and a technician handed him the heavy brass helmet, helping him screw it into the collar ring of the suit. Then the technician heaved a weighty canister—filled with condensed gasses from the station's air—onto Blake's back, hooking the curved supports over his shoulders. He passed Blake the wide leather belt, and while he fastened it about his waist, the technician screwed the hose into the back of Blake's helmet. Blake shrugged his shoulders to settle the mass, then checked his sword and pistol before he stepped into the airlock. He had, at most, thirty minutes before his air fouled.

The technician screwed the viewport into the helmet and spun it closed. Blake felt a tugging as the valve was opened, heard the whoosh as air swept into the helmet, and then felt two solid slaps on the back. The suit was holding pressure. Blake gave the thumbs up to the technician, who turned and operated the controls at the side of the hatch. The door rolled into place.

The outer door of the ship sunk inwards and slid upwards into the curved hull as he approached. He was, it seemed, being watched. He took his time crossing the dock. There were no markings on the ship, but word had come down from on high it was to be allowed into the dock airlock.

As soon as he was inside the ship, the outer door rolled down, and his suit was buffeted by the air being sucked in to fill the lock. He made no move to close the valve of his tank, or open his faceplate. For all he knew, the lock could be filled with poison. The inner door opened, and Blake stepped into the ship proper.

The inside of the ship was spotless. It looked so new Blake felt if he opened a cupboard a cascade of packing paper and sawdust would fall out. The controls and displays were all draped with heavy black cloth. Apparently, the pilot did not want him to see his vessel's secrets.

The pilot's couch turned slowly to face him, and Blake was glad he had the faceplate to cover his astonishment. She was astoundingly beautiful, in a sterile, sculpted way. Her thick, black hair was cut into a sharp bob that curled in just below her chin, and her cheek-bones were almost blade-like in their prominence. Her lips, whether through nature or cosmetic science, were a deep, glistening red that matched the fabric of her blouse. A hint of a smile played around her lips. 'Most cumbersome attire, Captain. May I help you with it, in some way?'

Her voice was thin and tinny, but clear. Blake shook his head before he remembered she could not see him, then gave a thumb-down sign. Fumble-fingered, he grabbed at the handles on his faceplate and slowly turned them until it came free. The woman remained in her chair, and expression of polite attention on her face while he laboured.

'Captain—' he began once the helmet was off.

'You are Blake. Head of Station Security, of whom great things were expected until he was brought low by the scorn of a woman. Girl, really. I could tell you her name, and the lies she told, and why. Would it help?'

Blake said nothing. The woman seemed to be well informed, but that, and the broad, slightly predatory smile, told him nothing. She rose to her feet, and Blake was astonished to see that what he thought was a voluminous leather coat was actually a riding habit and—of all things— trousers. She held out a fold of paper, but Blake simply spread his hands and kept them away from the delicate paper. In his clumsy gloves, he would probably destroy it. She unfolded it and held it up where he could read it, or at least make out the gist. He scanned the text, which was an expected "all courtesy and assistance", but he felt his eyes open wider when he got to the bottom; the signature of Edward and a flat copy of the Imperial Seal Minor, Asquith's signature and seal, and the mark of the Home Secretary.

'Very impressive, Miss—' Blake flicked his eyes to the top of the note, looking for a name, but it just referred to 'the bearer'.

'Quite, Captain. Now, as I have no intention of wearing one of those hideous things, would you make whatever signal you must to have my ship brought into the station, then you may take me to see Station Commander Maxwell.'

'Six-two-three, zero-eight-six.'

'Beg pardon?' Maxwell looked like a mouse confronted by an approaching owl.

'My check code, Commodore. The one you are supposed to use to confirm the veracity of my document.'

'I'm sure we can dispense with such boring technica—'

'No, sir, we may not.'

Blake found something else to look at as a grin threatened to escape across his lips. Maxwell was a womaniser, or tried to be. Blake had dark suspicions that the few comely women who made it to the station either submitted to his flattery or— Blake let the thought, and the surge of self-loathing that he was not man enough to confront the situation, die. The amusement of watching Maxwell squirm under the control of the visitor suddenly lost its appeal.

'I am prepared to take the document at face value, which allows us to take the time to establish—' Maxwell made another, slightly desperate attempt to appear magnanimous and in control of the situation.

'You must. I insist that you fully understand the scope of my authority.'

Face flushed and angry, Maxwell stamped across to his safe—or tried to. The low gravity took his ill-advised ire and mocked him still further by bouncing him almost to the ceiling. He returned a small, red book to the desk, then mumbled over it and the letter of introduction. His face paled, and his whispered the word, 'Ultimax?'

'Indeed. Now, would you please state the terms of my authority aloud, so that the Captain is also made aware of it.'

Maxwell turned several pages of the book, then started to read:

'"Code Ultimax: This person is a directly appointed agent of the crown, personally empowered by the reigning monarch and the highest offices of the Empire, and speaking with their voice and authority in all things at all times, unconditional, without bound or constraint. Said agent is entitled to the unconditional and absolute support of any subject of the sovereign, or any member of the armed forces or government, including any terms material."' He looked up from the book. 'But why? And who are you?'

'You may call me Miss Richards.' Blake caught the minute hesitation as the agent selected a random name for herself, but was certain Maxwell had not. 'As to your first question, that is, for now, my business. I may, from time to time, need the assistance of the Captain, but for the time being, Commodore, I require nothing from you.'

'I see.' Maxwell straightened in his chair and tugged down the front of his tunic. 'Until dinner, then, shall we say—?'

'I think not. I have much to do and little time to do it.'

As they swept through Maxwell's outer office, Blake sought out Midshipman Stiles and hooked him with a look to the eyes. The boy jumped to open the door for them.

'Your office, Captain?'

'Ahead and to the left, Miss...Richards.'

The corners of her eyes crinkled before she turned away.

'What can I do for you?'

'You could offer a lady a drink.'

'Tea?'

'A *drink*.'

Blake kept his surprise to a flicker of his eyebrows. 'Aah, the local spirit is... robust. Perhaps the Commodore...'

Richards shook her head. 'Wouldn't trust anything out of his bottles. I'll take what you have.' Her look became cooler. 'Captain, I do not make a habit of such requests. My journey required certain changes to the air in my ship. A small brandy, or similar, helps dispel the effects, and clears the palate of the somewhat unpleasant aftertaste.'

'Of course,' Blake mumbled, and rummaged for glasses. The bathtub gin he poured into them would probably have eaten through anything metallic.

Richards washed the spirit around her mouth before swallowing and grimaced. 'Robust indeed. Now, Captain, I have a request.'

'Anything, Miss Richards.'

'Stay out of my way.'

Blake returned to his chair propping it, and himself, against the wall. 'And if I don't, the world is going to fall on my shoulders?'

'Something like that.'

Blake studied her openly. Poor manners, but in this context, he considered the usual rules had been at least suspended. 'There's going to be talk.'

'Obviously.'

'So what lie do we spin?'

Richards raised one perfectly plucked eyebrow.

'I cannot obstruct you, Miss Whoeveryouare. I cannot confirm your credentials, beyond the verification my superior has used. I must take them at face value. However, I don't like secrets on my station. They have a habit of coming out, and usually with unexpected results. My best chance of limiting your potential impact is to cooperate with you. So I ask again, what is to be your excuse for being here?'

Richards inclined her head, acknowledging Blake's point. 'What would you suggest?'

Blake opened his hands helplessly. 'You ride in here on an unannounced ship that nobody has ever seen the likes of, and stroll around the station in rather unconventional attire. You may already have limited your options.'

'A survey, perhaps? Something bureaucratic, not threatening to the staff?'

'That might work, but for your attire and the manner of your arrival.'

Richards raised an eyebrow. 'Have you tried managing a skirt and bustle in space, Captain? Even on this station, concessions are made to practicality. Besides,' her lips curled in an impish grin, 'we can just say it's the latest Paris fashion.'

VI

The victim was male this time, crammed beneath a bunk in one of the worker dormitories. Again, the victim's throat had been ripped out, and his face was contorted into a mask of horror that made Blake's stomach twist, and again, there was insufficient blood at the scene with no sign of a trail. Blake had the body moved to sickbay immediately. The mob outside the room was unhappy, and there were whispers of a word he did not want to hear spread.

McEwan called Blake back to sickbay less than an hour after the constable had delivered the corpse.

'It might be nothing,' McEwan admitted. 'I don't have half the equipment I should have for an environment this size, so how I am expected to-'

'Was there something out of the ordinary?' Blake interrupted. "Rumour is starting to spread we have a vampire on the station.'

'Oh, for the love of...'

Blake held his hand up to cut the doctor of before his rant could gather any more steam. 'You called me to show me something.'

'What? Oh, yes. Come here.'

Blake followed McEwan to the table the body of the male had been put on, and was surprised to see it had been placed face down.

'The gore at the front is basically the same, but we found these,' said McEwan, pointing vaguely at the back of the head. Blake looked, but saw nothing. McEwan muttered an apology, and hurriedly handed a magnifying glass to Blake, holding a lamp closer to the table. On the back of the neck, just below the hairline and over the spine, were four tiny puncture wounds.

'And they are?' Blake asked, looking back at the medic.

McEwan shrugged. 'No idea. We missed them on the girl because her hair covered them. Sloppy of us, I know. We're doing an exploratory on her right now.'

'Why not him?'

'He's fresher. He'll keep longer, if we need a second look.'

Blake shot the man a look, but decided not to say anything. 'Very well. Let me know if-'

The door to the sickbay slammed open, and Miss Richards strode in, her fury a veritable thundercloud hanging over her head. Everybody turned to look at her. She pointed at the two orderlies in the room. 'You and you, out. Close the door, and allow no-one to enter.'

The orderlies did not even glance at McEwan for confirmation, but vacated the room with great haste.

'Now look here, Miss—'

Richards raised her hand no more than a foot from McEwan's face, leaving him spluttering, and turned her ire on Blake. 'You do not, repeat *not*, hide events such as this from me, Blake. Is that abundantly clear?'

He held her eyes, fighting down his own fury as being so addressed by a woman, and in front of others. 'I was about to send word when I was called to sickbay, Miss Richards. As you have still to tell me what your purpose is on this station, I have no way of knowing what is of interest to you. If you wish, I can have you so deluged with station minutiae that you cannot set foot through your cabin door.'

'We are not done with this.' She turned to McEwan. 'Doctor, why did this corpse interest you sufficiently to summon the captain?'

McEwan looked over her shoulder, throwing a questioning glance at Blake. Richards clapped her gloved hands impatiently. 'We can deal with the introductions later.'

'We found something unusual on the back of this one's neck.' As with Blake, he handed her the magnifying glass and held the lamp closer. Blake pursed his lips when Richards went immediately to the tiny puncture wounds without being directed. 'How long ago was this man killed?'

'Estimating from his body temperature, between twelve and eighteen hours. It is difficult to be precise on the station, and the estimate may be inaccurate given that—'

'There was little or no blood in the body.'

'How the deuce did you know that?' McEwan took a step back and held the lamp in front of him, as if warding the woman away.

An anonymous shape in surgical scrubs pushed through the door, holding a clipboard out to McEwan. 'Our report, Doctor.' The voice died away as the technician read the tension in the room.

'Summary?'

The scrubs hid the surgeon's face, so there were no visual cues, and even the voice was asexual. 'Something slipped in between the first three cervical vertebrae, two insertions between each. All four stopped in the middle of the spinal cord.'

'Did you do any blood tests?' Richards asked. Blake thought he detected a touch of anxiety in her face, and she appeared quite pale. McEwan took the clipboard and scanned down the report, flicking pages. 'We are limited in what we can test for here. No detectable toxins... Here's something, though. It's a new test. Picks up on a chemical that seems to be associated with emotional states. Could be a mistake, but—'

'The results are orders of magnitude higher than they should be?'

McEwan turned to Richards. 'Yes. How could you possibly...?' His eyes drifted back to the corpse on the table.

Blake was furious, his voice cold. 'You obviously know more than you have told us, Miss Richards. People on my station are dying, and I believe you know why. I would like an explanation.'

A midshipman Blake did not immediately recognise burst into the room. Three voices shouted 'out' in unison. The midshipman blanched, but held his ground. 'You better come quick, Captain. They're at it again.'

'Who?'

'The miners, sir. They're rioting in the hub.'

VII

Miners had blockaded the aft dock, stationing men at the main access points from the four spokes and the secondary service corridors that ran along the back of Aft-8. Through the good offices of the Hubmaster, Blake was shown to the foot of a crawl-way leading up to the back of a service panel that opened out onto a gantry above the huge lock gates. He shuffled through the narrow space, trying to look anywhere but ahead of him. To his annoyance, Miss Richards had insisted on accompanying him, and going first. In order to do so, she had discarded her long coat and now Blake was confronted by a part of the female anatomy, clad in tight leather, that no unmarried gentleman should be looking at.

On the gantry, Richards dipped into a pocket and pulled out a pair of opera glasses. 'What are those people doing?' She handed the glasses to Blake and pointed.

He put the glasses to his eyes, blinked at their unexpected power, and tried again. Whilst the main mass of men hammered ineffectually on the hangar door of Aft-8, a small group had broken away and broken into an equipment locker. Now they were towing a contraption consisting of two large gas canisters and a festoon of piping across the hub.

'Not sure,' Blake replied. 'Something to do with rescue, I think. Cutting metal, perhaps.'

'Fools. That must be a Fouché-Picard cutter. They could turn the station into a bomb.' She held out her hand for the glasses. 'I assume you are armed?'

'My Maxwell, with stun rounds, but there are too many of them.'

'How did you control them last time?'

Blake squirmed for a moment. 'The Commodore ordered their area depressurised.'

Richards raised an eyebrow. 'Brutal, but effective. Would it work again here?'

Blake shook his head. 'We can't be sure we have control of all the bulkhead doors. If just one we don't know about is open, we could vent the whole station before we could find it.'

Richards' hand went to her belt again, this time coming back with a small pistol of a design unfamiliar to Blake. 'Browning 22,' she grinned. 'Semi-automatic, ten-round magazine, modified for Maxwell shells. Doesn't have the punch of yours, but I have two more clips. Shall we?' She lifted the weapon and took aim—not at the crowd around the door, but at the men hauling the cutting gear. Blake threw out his arm, knocking her weapon aside. She rounded on him, eyes flashing.

'How is you hitting a pipe or a tank worse than them using it wrong? A spark might make it explode.'

'Do not judge others abilities by your own standards, Captain,' she snapped, and the moment of intimacy was gone. She turned, aimed, and fired before he could move again. One of the miners around the cutting gear convulsed, then drifted away, motionless. Her pistol barked three times, and the tanks sailed unattended across the hub.

As Blake expected, the crowd around the door quickly realised what was going on and spotted them in seconds. He raised his own weapon, and picked off the two men working most industriously on the door. A group broke off, heading towards them; presumably having heard six shots, they assumed Blake was out of ammunition. Richard's smaller calibre weapon began to bark, and four more men drifted slowly towards the floor. Blake touched Richards on the shoulder. 'Wait.' He felt the tension drain from her, and she nodded. He shouted out to the floor below.

'Stand down. If you do not stand down, this area will be depressurised.'

A howl of protest rose from the miners. Richards reached into her belt, and Blake saw another clip appear in her hand before she raised her weapon. He held his breath. If she opened fire, any chance he might have of defusing the situation would be gone. She glanced at him from the corner of her eye, then gave a jerky nod. She was giving him time. For now.

'You are being fed misinformation. The rumours are not true. A special investigator—' he waved his free hand at Richards '—has been sent to look into these events. It will be resolved.' He paused. He hoped he had some stock with these men. He had always tried to treat them fairly—certainly more so than Maxwell liked. He held his breath. Groups were muttering to each other, and there were only a few angry gesticulations. He played his last card, and the one that would get him in most trouble. 'If you stand down and leave now, no names will be recorded, and no action will be taken.'

The crowd began to disperse. A small group broke away and intercepted the cutting gear, but they were only intent on securing and returning it. The few who still wanted action stood and glared up at them, but eventually turned away.

Blake recorded every face in his memory, said each name out aloud as he recognised them. He would stick to his word, but he would be keeping a special watch on certain people.

'Well played,' said Richards, making her weapon safe and stowing it in her belt. 'Over-generous, perhaps, but effective. Now, perhaps we should discuss what is in that hangar that so incensed the miners.'

'And what brought you here in the first place.'

Alternately pounding on the door and shouting finally enticed Dr. Fleischmann to open the back door of Aft-8. Blake threw courtesy to the wind and barged the hatch open as soon as the wheel had retracted the dogs from the bulkhead, bundling himself and Miss Richards through the curtains and into the main hangar. Fleischmann scuttled after them, squawking in protest, and threatening to call the Station Commander. Once he had reached the middle of the hangar, Blake turned on the scientist, one hand on his sword, the other on his pistol, and glared. Fleischmann's protests stumbled into silence, and his eyes flicked anxiously between the captain and Miss Richards.

'Dr. Fleischmann, yet again, I have just had to disperse an angry mob from your doors. Could you enlighten me as to their grievance on this occasion?'

'I have done nothing to provoke such an act,' Fleischmann insisted, but his eyes flickered to the chairs where previously four of the mannequins had sat. Blake followed the glance, then kicked himself for not noticing there were only three.

'Where is the other one?'

'The other what?'

'There were four. On the chairs.'

'It has been returned to the storage rack.' Fleischmann waved at the frame where more of the monstrosities hung limply, but Blake saw the sheen of sweat on the doctor's forehead. He made a quick count. 'There is one missing. At least. I don't know how many there were, but I know it was an even number. Now there are only nineteen.'

'You are mistaken.'

'Then let us be sure. If you will do me the courtesy of not moving, sir, I will summon a number of my staff, and we will turn this hangar and your private quarters inside-out until I find—'

'You will do no such thing. Your orders from Commodore Maxwell—'

'Have been superseded by a higher authority.'

'What higher authority?' He seemed to take in Miss Richards for the first time. 'And who is this woman? This environment contains state secrets.'

Richards shot Blake a disapproving look, but stepped forward. 'Hardly, Dr. Fleischmann. Secrets they may be, but I would suggest commercial rather than state. I really would co-operate with the captain.'

Blake threw a look at her. 'Commercial? Maxwell told me—'

'Whatever lie he had been fed. We know of this man. Would you care to tell the captain who you really work for, Herr Fleischmann?'

Fleischmann looked from one to the other, then his shoulders drooped. 'This morning, there was a disturbance. A number of men burst in, overpowering your guards, making the most outrageous claims. We keep the test units draped at night - the eyes can glow in the dark, and it is disconcerting. There were too many to throw them out, so I pulled the drapes off to show them. I did not know it was there. More of your men arrived and dragged them from the room, but not before they saw...'

'Saw what, man? Out with it.'

Fleischmann waved for them to follow him, and moved heavily to the farthest corner of the hangar. A heap of tired cardboard boxes formed an untidy pile, and Fleischmann pointed to the bottom. 'Under there.'

Blake cast a look towards Miss Richards, then started throwing the empty boxes out of the way. It took him only moments to uncover a shrouded, huddled form at the bottom. The captain felt Richards move closer, and sensed her excitement as he reached out for the shroud, pulling it aside. He couldn't stop the gasp; underneath was one of Fleischmann's mechanical men, its coverall, hands, and helmet drenched in blood.

'And I tell you, it cannot be.' Miss Richards was beginning to get rather heated. The mannequin had been taken, in extreme secrecy, to the sickbay, and was laid out on one of McEwan's examination tables. Fleischmann and his assistant had been asked to remain in their quarters, until told otherwise. McEwan had taken one look at the device before throwing his hands in the air and declaring he was a doctor, not an engineer, and that he would have nothing more to do with it.

'Ms Richards, the—thing has blood down its face, everywhere. It's covered in it. It's no wonder half the crew are running around muttering about monsters and vampires. If not this, then what?'

'Captain, have you considered how this thing might move? Did you not see the cables connected to the others?'

'Yes, but—'

'These are inferior. I have an idea who Fleischmann is working for, but I assure you again, it is not His Majesty's government.'

'What? Why?'

Richards drew a deep, exasperated breath, glared at both men, and exhaled. 'I tell you this only to allow us to focus on the real issue here, and because it would be all but impossible for the information to leave the station quickly enough to be of use to... well. The situation at home is fraught, gentlemen, and it is almost certain at some level Britain will be compelled to engage in conflict. I would imagine that an outside agency is desperately trying to develop these automata for sale to the highest bidder, or bidders. We, of course, are developing our own solution. Which is why I know these puppets are of little use to man or beast.'

'I am still—'

'They are pneumatic, sir. Examine the actuators here, and here, and follow the connection back to the regulator here. This is where the hoses were connected, providing the pressure required to motivate the device.'

'But that would mean...'

'They cannot leave Dr. Fleischmann's laboratory, unless the pump goes with them. Exactly.'

'So why the blood? I find it difficult to believe we have a vampire on the station.' Blake and McEwan laughed, but became silent when Richards did not join in. She looked troubled, indecisive. 'Miss Richards?'

'I think it may be a diversion.'

'By whom?'

'An excellent question. Perhaps the time *has* come for me to lay my cards on the table. I have been sent here directly from the colony on Venus. The same facility, incidentally, that discovered the rather obscure organism used to lend a small semblance of intelligence to these things.' She waved dismissively at the mannequin on the slab. 'The problem with poking around in dark corners to discover things is that sometimes, the discovery bites back. I don't suppose you gentlemen are aware of the bizarre actions of certain examples of the Gypsy Moth caterpillar?'

Both men shook their head, bemused.

'In noticeable fractions of the population, the caterpillar does not moult to become a moth, but eats continuously before climbing high into trees and dying. It is surmised that some form of infection perverts the creature's mind, such as it is, and that the death and putrefaction at height spreads the infection to other caterpillars. There are other examples, such as the fearless rat, and the parasitic wasp *ampulex compressa*, which hijacks a cockroach to use as an incubator. Such an agent has been discovered on Venus.'

'In the name of sanity, who would develop such a terrible thing?' cried McEwan.

Richards raised her hands helplessly. 'Not my area, Doctor. All I know is that it is no longer confined to Venus. We have had a report of a case on Mars.'

'What exactly are we talking about here?'

'They call it, "Haemophage." Those infected behave almost normally, often concealing themselves in plain sight. When they are not hunting, they have no knowledge of their ailment, and deny everything they do while feeding.'

'How many of these are there that you can know so much?' asked McEwan.

'We have no idea. I am told this is what has been gleaned from the very few victims who have been taken alive.'

'And how do they... hunt?'

'Again, the facts are few and the supposition plentiful. We know they physically overpower their victims, and we know they have some modification to their bodies which produces the pin-pricks in the neck. From blood tests, we know the concentration of stress and fear related chemicals is astonishingly high.'

McEwan looked sick. 'They terrorise their victims, then drink the blood to extract these chemicals as nutrients?' Richards nodded. 'And why are you here?' Blake felt bile burning at his throat. He already knew.

'One pattern of behaviour is to travel, as far as possible. We know they have stowed away on space vessels. We thought one might be trying to get to this station. It seems we were right.'

VII

The station was in lockdown. Blake's entire team had been tested, as had two-score hastily sworn in Special Constables; blood drawn and a full body examination. Then every major bulkhead door had been dogged shut and a guard placed. Despite Station Commander Maxwell's howls of protest, all the on-shift mining crews had been recalled to the station, too. The place heaved with bodies, and the air was stale and heavy.

This was the fifth section to be processed, and there were six more to go. A posse of constables had herded the group to sickbay, while another carried out a nuts-and-bolts search of the area thus vacated. McEwan's staff were looking harried, McEwan himself, furious.

'I still don't see the value of this. We cannot be sure what we are doing will expose the creature. You said yourself it is a parasite.'

Miss Richards, several strands of errant hair indicating her own fatigue, took a deep breath and seemed to make an effort not to snap. 'Then tell me your superior strategy, Doctor, or be quiet. We do not want to have it repeated that we have no faith in these tests.'

Blake drifted away from the conversation. He could understand both positions, but had no intention of taking sides. He ambled to the door, smiling, occasionally nodding to a half-recognised face, until he could see out into the corridor. The line had no visible end, and he barely suppressed a sigh. This had to be done in one action, without respite or opportunity for anybody to slip through the net.

A slight figure, animatedly chatting to somebody next to her, stepped a little away from the line. When she saw Blake she froze, fear on her face. Blake smiled at her. He hadn't seen Amy Rivers for some time, but it was good to see she was apparently settling in to station life. He turned back into sickbay and a hand of ice clamped around his heart. Her?

'Your identification, please,' he heard a bored medic mumble, then the word was repeated in a sharper tone. Blake strode across the room, intent on telling Richards of his suspicion, but the raised voice distracted him. A burly – but then, weren't they all – miner glared down at the orderly behind the desk, then raised his head, eyes flicking from side to side, narrowed. Blake's hand closed instinctively around the butt of his revolver, his thumb pulling the hammer back for the quickest possible shot if it was required.

The miner roared, and threw the table into the orderly's face. Pandemonium broke out behind him as everybody tried to get out of the room at the same time, completely blocking the exit. The miner began to pull bodies out of his way, tossing them negligently aside as though they massed no more than children. Bones snapped audibly as people crashed into walls and furniture, and the screams took on a more desperate edge.

Blake drew his weapon, but before he could raise it, he heard *pak-pak-pak* from his right as Miss Richards shot three rounds from her Browning. Blake held fire, waiting for the miner to drop, but all the brute did was flinch. Blake raised his revolver and added two of his more powerful stun rounds. The miner stiffened, shuddered, but did not fall. He turned, glaring at Blake, then leapt towards him.

Blake was still pulling the trigger long after the revolver was empty. A part of his mind registered the sharp sounds of the Browning. He ducked, and the miner sailed over his head, crashing into a cabinet and throwing supplies and equipment out into the general chaos. Blake dropped his revolver back into its holster, drawing his sword as he turned. The miner, head weaving groggily, was extricating himself from the cabinet. A moment later, he launched himself again. There had been just enough time for Blake to see that Richards was fumbling with her Browning, trying to reload. He was out of options. He turned slightly, let the miner come to him, then drove his sword through the madman's heart.

The room was cleared, not that most inside needed much encouragement to leave, and guards posted on the door. McEwan was crouched over the body, hacking at the clothing with surgical scissors. By the time Blake had made sure the room was secure, McEwan was grinning like an idiot. He was holding the miner's hand and, when he pushed against the base of the thumb, four thorns extended from the hand.

'Got him.'

VII

Blake woke, fully alert by the time his eyes had finished opening. Subconscious alarms let him know that something was not right, and told him he should stay put, lying on his side, until he knew what it was. They played him false. A weight landed on his back, turning him face down on the bed and pinning his right arm underneath him. He flailed with his left, but whomever or whatever was on top of him was out of his reach. Something cold touched his neck, and there were pinpricks of pain. In seconds, his whole body went limp. Not numb, though. If anything, things felt more intense, but he had no muscle control.

Fear started to freeze his gut, building towards panic. He tried to shake his head, to clear it, but he could not move. He tried to rationalise it. This was not like him. He had never felt despair like this, even when his suit had developed a leak during a training exercise. He sank deeper and deeper into the terror, his heart hammering in his chest and his muscles starting to tremble. His breath rasped in his throat, and he could hear the soft shriek as his lungs laboured to drag in air. A hand gripped his shoulder, heaving at him, trying to turn him over.

He rolled part way onto his back. In the dark, a shaped loomed over him, indistinct, invisible. A hand that cupped the back of his neck like a lover, felt small and cold. He knew that should mean something, but he couldn't understand what. The hand pushed up gently, but with implacable strength, easing his head back and his chin up. The body shifted, and cool breath tickled his skin before he felt a pair of dull points start to press down with an exquisite agony over the right side of his neck.

There was a crash, then another. Blake wasn't sure where the noise came from as the terror raving through him distorted his perception. The scream and the shout, neither his, were simultaneous, and still he could not see what was happening behind him. He was pushed roughly onto his side as pain ripped across his neck and his whole body spasmed. His brain slowly reasserted its ownership of his body, jerking and imprecise, but he managed to get his left hand under his pillow. Blake gripped the revolver he kept hidden there and dragged it out, trying to roll over at the same time.

Night-shift illumination from the corridor glowed weakly yellow through the outline of his door. In a shadowed corner of the room, he saw two figures struggling, but his eyes refused to sharpen the image. They looked of a small size, and neither as bulky as a man. He tried to raise the revolver for a quick shot, but his muscles were still shaky, and he was too late. He switched it to his right hand as bodies swept back into the corner and all was again confusion.

Belatedly, Blake reached to the console next to his bed and opened the valve that brightened the lantern above his bed. When he turned back to the fight, Richards was locked in the embrace of Miss Armstrong. He tried to lift his arm long enough to get a clear shot, but his muscles still had no strength, and the combatants were too entangled to shoot one without risking the other.

Richards was thrown from the fight and flew across the room to crash into the wall. Blake managed to track the revolver across the room and, halfway to where Armstrong should have been, the sights lined up on her as she took the fight back to Richards; Armstrong's hands were bent into talons, nails like claws, and her mouth opened in a gaping snarl. She was too fast and too strong for any woman—or man, for that matter. Blake fired. Armstrong sagged as the round discharged into her, then turned back to Blake. She hissed, and Blake felt his gorge rise as he saw her canines extended a good half inch longer than they should have. He fired another round, and another. Armstrong did not stop. She flinched again, but kept drawing closer to him. Blake fired again. The woman stopped, but she did not fall.

The room erupted in a coruscation of actinic light. Armstrong stiffened and fell to the floor. Behind her stood Richards, a short baton in her hand.

'Is there anything you think you ought to be telling me?' Blake asked, once he had caught his breath.

Richard leaned against the wall, then slid down until she was sitting. 'Of course. But can I suggest you first summon enough people to incarcerate this creature?'

'Lock it up? You saw how strong it is.'

Richards nodded. 'Please. It is important.'

Blake looked at her, then pressed a button that sounded a signal in the nearest guard room. A squad arrived in minutes and, in short order, Miss Armstrong was restrained by almost every suitable device on the station.

'Have her taken to my ship. I have a holding area within that can contain her.'

Blake shook his head. 'An explanation first, I believe, or she goes to my cells.'

Richards gave him a long, speculative look, obviously weighing him against something. 'Very well. It is extremely difficult to capture live Haemophage specimens, and without them, we cannot progress in our efforts to contain or destroy them.'

'And that weapon you are holding?'

'An experimental device. Not actually authorised for use. It is a prototype for a baton that has a similar effect to a stun round. Unfortunately, the discharge tends to be—overenthusiastic.'

'Designed for use against these Hem...Heem...?'

'Haemophage. No, actually, they are intended for crowd control.'

'And you just happened to bring it to my room because...?'

'I couldn't sleep. The excitement of the day, I suppose. I needed to talk to you anyway.'

'About what?'

'You are wasted here, man. I wanted to offer you a job.'

'Lucky me.' Blake placed his revolver carefully on his pillow, then dropped backwards across the bed.

~ end ~

Living just north of London with a wonderful wife and two attention-seeking cats Robert Harkess shares his writing time with his real-world job as an IT manager.

His stories often refuse to fit neatly into pigeon holes, as he prefers to blend genres. His favourite flavours are science fiction, urban fantasy and Steampunk.

As R.B. Harkess he writes YA fiction from "Aphrodite's Dawn" to the Warrior Stone series (starting with "Underland") which can only be described as 'contemporary urban steampunk'. Meanwhile his novel "Maverick" is a blend of Fantasy and SF. Others of his stories have appeared in various anthologies.

You can find his on Amazon at:
http://www.amazon.com/R-B-Harkess/e/B0070CCSFG

Social media:
Twitter: https://twitter.com/RBHarkess
Facebook: https://www.facebook.com/rbharkess/
Google+:
https://plus.google.com/u/0/114351001736513757578/about

Taking the Cure
by Peter A. Smalley

TAKING THE CURE

By Peter A. Smalley

I

'Good morning, sir. Welcome aboard. Good morning. Watch your step, ma'am. Welcome to the *Palladion*. Good morning, miss, sir. Welcome aboard. Good to have you aboard the *Palladion*...'

It was a routine duty, but Midshipman Jasper Stokes enjoyed the ritual of welcoming passengers coming on board at the start of a voyage. There was something cheering and almost hopeful in greeting each fresh face setting out into the void. It was especially true for this particular journey. Currently docked at Victoria Void Station and thus hovering in geosynchronous orbit many miles above Ceylon, the *Palladion* was not only the largest civilian voidcraft ever built, but it was also carrying some of the most wealthy and influential citizens of the British Empire on its maiden voyage to Luna. It was, as all the British papers would have it, history-in-the-making: a veritable pleasure cruise for the well-bred, the well-off, and the well-to-do.

'Good morning, my lord, my lady. Very good to have you aboard. Welcome, sir. And a very good morning to you as well.' Stokes kept his expression and tone carefully professional. It was important to make a good impression on every passenger who had booked aboard the *Palladion*, but even more so here on the upper deck where only the extremely wealthy and the aristocratic could afford to berth. *Port out, starboard home* had little meaning on a void steamer, as the vessel was required to spin on its axis to maintain internal gravitation, but 'posh' still accurately described the majority of those with accommodations here on the A deck. Stokes was fairly certain the pair who had just passed him on their way up to the first class cabins were Lord and Lady Holmwood, the current Home Secretary's brother and sister-by-law. There were many equally important passengers already enjoying the lavish accommodations on the uppermost passenger deck, and surely more to come. All were here to *take the cure*, as the saying went.

'Welcome, madam. Tea will be at two o'clock sharp, ship's time. Thank you ma'am, good to have you aboard.' He nodded respectfully to an older man in an impeccable black frock coat, accompanied by two very large men bearing two steamer trunks apiece. The trunks bore a red cross insignia; the midshipman was glad to see the medical profession would be well represented aboard.

A seemingly endless stream of passengers followed, but before he knew it Stokes caught sight of Lieutenant Brickham and acknowledged the officer's glance with a respectful nod of understanding. The midshipman realized time had flown, and it was now very nearly the hour for the *Palladion* to cast off from its moorings and begin steaming toward Luna at a slow and stately pace.

For the duration of the voyage—a fortnight for the round trip—the ship's passengers would enjoy luxurious accommodations, gourmet foods, and the latest in scientific treatments designed to relax, re-balance, and restore both body and spirit.

A rejuvenating spa experience unlike anything on Earth! So the voyage had been billed by Aleister P. Doolittle, the man behind the *Palladion.* As a mere midshipman, Stokes had yet to encounter the great man in person, but the scuttlebutt aboard ship was that Doolittle was eccentric in every sense of the word. Not least of his personal legend, to Stokes' mind at least, was Doolittle's ability to obtain loans for the unheard-of sums required to finance the building of his voidship-spa. Stokes shook his head as he closed the hatch behind the last of the first-class passengers and made it fast. He was still more than a little uncertain about the concept of a craft designed to pamper well-to-do passengers on a round trip through the void of space, but competition to serve aboard the *Palladion* had been fierce and Stokes was all too conscious of how many of his fellow Naval Academy graduates had been passed over for the post he now enjoyed. He felt fortunate in his berth as the ship's most junior officer, and had privately vowed to let nothing mar the ship's maiden voyage.

A distant whistle blew twice somewhere below, and a palpable shudder went through the deck. Stokes quickened his pace. The engineers were disengaging the ship from Victoria Station and making ready to cycle the engines in just two minutes. His presence as a junior officer was required near the bridge should anything go wrong—a practical impossibility according to the finest voidship designers in the British Empire, but regulations were regulations. Stokes jogged rapidly down the corridor, making his way toward the aft deck hatch—and stopped. A furtive figure had just slipped around a corner of the corridor and withdrawn into a side passage some distance ahead. Though he had not seen the person clearly,

Stokes was certain it wore neither the dark blue uniform of a crewman nor the whites of an officer. *A passenger?* It had to be, though at this point all passengers should be safely in their cabins or seated on the observation deck for departure. Most irregular.

Weighing his conflicting duties to appear at the bridge and also to ensure the safety of every passenger aboard the *Palladion,* Stokes hesitated momentarily before setting off down the corridor. Slight tardiness could be overlooked given the circumstances, but an injury to a passenger could mean reprimand, even a black mark on his service record. It certainly would do no good to the ship's reputation, and that outweighed even his own record as a junior officer.

Hastening his steps, Stokes quickly arrived where he had last seen the errant passenger. There was no sign of him. Every cabin hatch was carefully shut, as per regulation before an imminent launch into the void of space. Stokes peered carefully down each direction of the intersecting corridor in some relief. Clearly his eyes were playing tricks on him. It was nerves, surely; the importance of the *Palladion's* maiden voyage had kept him from sleep the night before, and this was simply an overactive imagination at work. He was about to head for the bridge when the hatch of a nearby cabin opened and a beautiful woman backed slowly out. She half-closed the door with some care and turned—then started violently in surprise when she saw someone in the corridor.

Stokes gave a quick, almost automatic bow. She was obviously someone of quality, not someone who had strayed to the first-class deck from one of the lower areas of the ship. Her hair and eyes were dark, her skin pale enough to show a fine tracing of bluish veins at her high brow and cheekbones. She wore a dress of dove-grey silk with soft, elbow-length gloves and dark brown leather boots. Her expression as she gazed at him fell somewhere between startled and haunted. She raised her hand to her face.

'I beg your pardon, miss, I did not mean to surprise you. The ship is about to get under steam, and for their safety and comfort all passengers are to be either in their cabins or on the upper observation deck. I would gladly escort you there if that is where you wish to be…' He let the question trail off.

She lowered her hand from her lips and let out a shuddering breath. 'You startled me,' she said in a soft contralto, forcing a nervous smile. 'An escort is not necessary, sir. I can find my own way easily enough. Please, do not trouble yourself.' She spoke quietly, as though not wishing to be overheard, and edged away from the door as she spoke.

Stokes opened his mouth to reply when a confident male voice boomed over her shoulder. 'The lady will be quite safe with me, crewman, I assure you.' Stokes looked behind the now even paler woman as the half-closed cabin door opened wider. The man who stood there was of slightly larger than average height, but obvious strength; his brawny shoulders filled the doorway. He was bald, with a fierce black beard and mustache, and wore a copper-colored waistcoat under a severe black evening jacket. A gleaming stethoscope hung loosely about this thick neck.

'Lady Alethea, as your doctor I really *must* insist that you wait until after takeoff to explore the ship.' His eyes were dark brown, almost black, and burned with a palpable intensity. Stokes felt for a moment as if he were standing too near one of the *Palladion* boilers at full steam. A moment later the man turned his gaze away from the woman and pinned the midshipman with a heavy, pointed stare. 'My apologies, crewman. I'm certain Lady Alethea had no intention of interrupting your no-doubt pressing duties.'

The implication was thick, and Stokes inclined his head. 'Of course, sir. Madam.' He turned to go, but as he did so, the midshipman caught a glance between lady and doctor: his, stern and admonitory; hers, caught between hope and anguish. Embarrassed at being privy to so personal an exchange, Stokes hastened down the corridor even as he heard the pair conversing in low, urgent tones. It was certainly none of his business.

Stokes hoped he could make it to the bridge before Lieutenant Brickham noticed he was late for the official start of the ship's maiden voyage. One long blast of the ship's whistle and the bass thrum of the Faraday Device engaging somewhere deep in the metallic bowels of the ship told him it was probably too late for that. He kept running, each step sending him further as gravity's shadow lengthened and the *Palladion* slipped free of the clinging grasp of Earth.

II

'A toast, ladies and gentlemen: first, to His Majesty and the government of the British Empire, for their support and continued patronage of the *Palladion!* Second, to all those whose far-sighted generosity made this historic voyage possible! And third, but certainly not least: to your *very* good health!'

Aleister Peabody Doolittle raised his glass high, and a murmured chorus of 'good health!' rang out from genteel throats around the room. Glasses were raised not only to the toast, but in part to the toastmaster, for 'Doctor' Doolittle was not merely Chief Medical Liaison aboard the *Palladion*, but also its technical owner-of-record. If this well-heeled voyage succeeded and became, as the hyperbolic London journalists at *The Times* would have it, *quite the done thing,* Doolittle stood to become one of the richest men in the Empire.

Midshipman Stokes, possibly the lowliest guest at this upper-crust soiree, sipped quietly and looked around at his social betters, wishing not for the last time he had had the opportunity to see a tailor before leaving England. The cut of his uniform was generally good, but the collar dug interminably at his neck like a teetotaler determined to keep good honest ale from passing his parched throat. His gaze took in the elite gathering from the safety of a corner near the door closest to the passage leading to the crew's quarters. While all off-duty officers had been extended an invitation, he was one of the few who had taken it. Now, he was uncertain if it had been a wise decision. He felt adrift and five fathoms out of his depth.

'Undersecretary! I am so pleased you could accept my invitation to attend this little informal party...' Doolittle pumped the hand of a thin, tuxedoed man with ginger hair and mustache who somehow managed to look down his nose despite being of modest stature. Undersecretary Gladstone bore the look of the polite but faintly bored as Doolittle continued effusively. 'It is so very good to have Their Majesties' government so well represented aboard the *Palladion*. Everything has been arranged to ensure a safe and healthful first voyage through the void...'

Stokes hid a grimace behind another sip of ale. Aleister Peabody Doolittle, at least, had relatively little to do with the safety of the voyage. He was the owner and chief fundraiser, and had involved himself deeply in the many health-enhancing aspects of the ship, no doubt of that. The actual operation of a complex voidship such as the *Palladion,* however, was left to men such as Stokes—for which Stokes was intensely grateful. The idea of 'Doctor' Doolittle at the helm made his palms sweat. *If his so-called 'medical treatments' are as exotic as I've heard, I can only imagine what his ideas on engineering might be.*

The ebb and flow of the party continued apace, the tide moving slowly back and forth between the twin gravitational pulls of Doolittle and the champagne flutes at the open bar. Stokes was far from an experienced socialite, yet he was not a complete novice either. Any self-respecting

Englishman planning a naval career knew the social dance was a prerequisite for advancement, and Stokes knew enough of the steps to see them being made here tonight. Doolittle wanted to ensure the Undersecretary continued to support his civilian voidship cruise venture, and once that assurance had been made he was on to Lord and Lady Holmwood, and then to others with whom he could curry favor, solicit money, or both. It was all quite expected and pedestrian—

Stokes paused mid-drink. A slender, graceful woman in a dark blue satin dress had entered the room on the arm of a heavy-set bald man wearing evening dress. He knew them, though he had not seen either at the observation deck or about the halls during the eight or so hours that had passed since departing Victoria Void Station. Her eyes looked no less haunted, nor his any less dark and smoldering. Involuntarily, Stokes moved toward them, drawn into their orbit as surely as the ship's Faraday Device pulled the vessel steadily toward the heavens.

'Harrowgate, Dr. Ulysses Harrowgate,' the burly man was already introducing himself to a pair of genteel Londoners. 'And this is Lady Alethea St. John.' The slender, dark-haired woman inclined her head slightly as their interlocutors smiled.

'Your wife?' asked the gentleman of the pair, expectantly, hand already raised to offer her a courtesy.

'One of my patients,' said Harrowgate softly, almost warningly. The man froze for a moment, the potential for social impropriety showing in worried lines around his eyes. Harrowgate smiled broadly, showing more of his teeth than Stokes thought strictly necessary. 'Do not be alarmed, sir, she is under excellent care, and properly escorted—as are all of my patients who have come with me aboard the *Palladion*.'

'With you…?' said the female Londoner, one hand held protectively to her throat.

Harrowgate was all charm and bonhomie now. 'Indeed yes. I am something of an expert on nervous conditions of all kinds, and when my esteemed friend Mr. Doolittle requested some advice on which medical professionals to include on his ship's maiden voyage, I was pleased to accept his kind invitation.' His gaze fastened on Alethea, who had turned away to look at the blue-green curve of Earth visible out the nearest brass porthole. 'A condition of my professional presence aboard this ship was the inclusion of certain of my current patients whom I felt would most benefit from the voyage. Lady St. John and others have already found the *Palladion* most...restful.'

The Londoners seemed to have recovered their aplomb. 'Ah, that explains it. What a stroke of good fortune that Mr. Doolittle asked you to join the ship's staff, Doctor. I'm certain your expertise will be of great benefit to many aboard who suffer from nervous conditions.'

'*Hysteria.*' Dr. Harrowgate and both of the Londoners started at Alethea's sudden vehemence. So did Stokes. She still stared out the window with rapt attention, but a bluish vein on the near side of her pale throat beat with a fluttering pulse. '*Hysteria periculosus* is one of the nervous conditions Dr. Harrowgate hopes to alleviate. Something about the effects of reduced gravitation on the circulatory system, I'm told.' The Londoners stared at her with open mouths, utterly flummoxed, but Stokes could not look away from the woman's dark, haunted eyes. Harrowgate's expression was an odd amalgam of censure and elation as Lady St. John broke away from the trio and walked quickly toward the buffet, hands pressed down on her dress near the bottom of her corset as if to prevent them from shaking. Stokes found himself drawn after her, a drowning leaf in the wake of a powerful undertow.

Her hand visibly shook when she attempted to reach out for a flute of champagne. 'Please, allow me,' he said quickly, and lifted a glass to offer her. She forced a thin, tight smile and followed him to a nearby table. Stokes put the glass down and drew out a chair for her, but she did not sit. Instead she stood beside the table, closer to him than was entirely proper, and stared at him as if seeing him for the first time.

'Do not,' she said softly, so softly he had to duck his head to catch the words over the convivial din of Doolittle's soiree. '*Do not pursue me,* sir. Our encounter in the hall must remain the only time Dr. Harrowgate sees us conversing.'

Stokes drew back, confused. 'Your doctor? But surely he must approve of you being here, being out in society, if he was the one to bring you aboard the *Palladion*—'

Her eyes were dark pools in the pale landscape of her face. 'Sir, I implore you. No good can come of it. For either of us.' Her voice rang with terrible urgency, for all that she still spoke barely above a whisper. Her hands rested on the lower portion of her bodice once more, and he saw they were pale as snow and trembled.

Stokes straightened. 'Madam, forgive me for intruding. Please, enjoy your evening. Excuse me.' With a slight bow, the young officer retreated a half-step before turning on his heel with naval precision, charting a course straight towards the nearest egress from the party. It was clear to him this was not a fête for the likes of him; the other officers had been right not to attend.

He did not see how she watched him go, did not feel the weight of her dark eyes pressing at his back with a strength approaching madness. He did not hear her whisper, so softly it might have been meant only for her own benefit, '*Especially for you.*'

Harrowgate, however, did.

III

'Stokes! Blast it, man, where in blazes are you? Stokes!'

'Here, Lieutenant.' The midshipman raced out of the crew common room and snapped to attention, breathing hard and trying just as hard not to show it. He couldn't swear to it, but he was willing to wager that a winning poker hand did not show under the concealment of his duty uniform—just as he had wagered moments before, with that self-same set of cards. Lieutenant Brickham eyed him with the air of a man unwilling to admit the last broken-down horse in the stable would, in fact, do. 'Sorry, sir, I was just—'

'Belay that,' Brickham cut him off sharply, and Stokes fell silent at once. 'We can deal with the sad matter of your complete moral dissipation later. I have a situation on the medical deck that requires an officer to resolve. You're it. Congratulations.'

'Medical deck, sir? But isn't that— what I mean, sir, is wouldn't that be a matter for Mr. Doolittle or one of the doctors aboard?'

'It would be, midshipman, except that this is not a medical matter.' The lieutenant shook his head, causing his ginger muttonchop-bedecked jowls to wobble alarmingly, like meringue atop an especially gelatinous slice of lemon chiffon pie. 'And as to why it is you and not one of your fellow dissipated crewmen, I can only say your name was suggested by the captain.' This intelligence was accompanied by the elevation of one wispy eyebrow, implying polite concern for the mental equanimity of that fine officer.

Stokes saluted sharply. 'Aye, sir. I will go and see to it at once, Lieutenant.'

'See that you do. Now cut along, midshipman. I shall expect a report when the matter is settled.' He narrowed his watery eyes and dismissed Stokes with a wave.

Requested by the captain! It was far better than Stokes could have hoped for. Captain Haversham was well-regarded by the men and his good regard could do wonders for Stokes' career. His heart jigged a merry hornpipe as he hurried through the forward hatch and scrambled quickly up to the next deck. His fortunes might well be going up in the world if he had already come to the attention of the senior officers. It was common scuttlebutt that Brickham was the oldest lieutenant ever to serve aboard a voidship, and would not be promoted for anything less than single-handedly saving every life aboard the *Palladion*. But not so for Midshipman Stokes! His fortunes were already rising, and the ship had not even reached Luna yet!

He slowed as the hatch leading into the medical deck neared. This part of the ship was given over entirely to the health and relaxation of the esteemed passengers. It would not do to barge in puffing and blowing like a bellows and expect to impress anyone with his handling of the situation. He took a few calming breaths and straightened his uniform.

What might be happening in there that could possibly require a member of the crew? Stokes had been distracted by other, more immediate concerns until this moment. The thought sobered him like a dash of cold water after a nice hot shave. The rich, well-to-do passengers taking their ease on the medical deck might not take well to a mere midshipman being sent to untangle whatever knotty problem had arisen. They might even try to overrule him, and that would be a black mark for his service record. Officers were expected to be able to control disobedient passengers, as a rule, or they were not of much good to the vessel. Could this have been a put-up job? Some other officer setting him up to fail and so rid himself of a rival for promotion? Surely not. The captain had suggested him personally, or so Brickham had said. Perhaps it would not be so very difficult a matter after all.

Stokes stepped inside.

A double line of tall Corinthian columns marched away from him in stately order. Each pair framed the veiled doorway of an individual treatment room, he knew. The design was intended to create an intimate atmosphere where the latest in modern medical treatments could be individually tailored to each first-class passenger. Stokes advanced carefully, wondering if the situation he had been sent to address would be obvious or not. Would he have to poke his head into each and every treatment enclosure? Surely not. But to be on the safe side, he leaned close to the first room on the left and drew the heavy brocade curtain aside so he could see inside.

Steam obscured his vision at first: billows of puffy white steam like he
was accustomed to seeing in the boiler room, rather than in one of the most
elite medical treatment spas. Four large boxes, two pairs on each of the
facing walls, stood chuffing out steam from holes in their tops—from
which the mustachioed heads of four gentlemen also protruded. Their faces
were red and ran freely with a mixture of sweat and condensation. The
noise of whatever mechanism it was that produced the steam was terrific,
and none of the gentlemen so much as looked up, but an attendant in white
gave Stokes a reproving stare. He retreated.

So it went down the hall. Stokes saw no sign of any disturbance at first,
though he himself was somewhat disturbed by a number of treatments he
encountered. What was the use of twirling the human body about in endless
circles like some kind of whirligig? Watching the turning of that horizontal
wheel with men strapped along its spokes head-outermost made him feel
quite queasy. Then there was the enclosure where elevated buckets of cold
water slowly filled and then dumped their frigid contents onto men in
bathing suits strapped to chairs just below.

What ailment was this treating? Oddest of all, perhaps, was the slapping
room. What earthly good could come from standing between two rotating
pillars from whose sides projected endless leather straps to whip the patient
standing between them? Stokes' father had used his leather belt on his son
when discipline was called for, and Stokes remembered it quite clearly. He
was hard pressed to believe there was actual therapeutic value in it, unless
perhaps the man being whipped had some sort of moral failing.

Stokes was nearing the end of the corridor defined by the double row of
Corinthian columns. He had peeked into about half of the curtained
enclosures and not yet discovered the disturbance he had been sent to
resolve. Was it possible, he wondered, that the fracas had resolved itself
before he arrived? Then he heard raised voices and hastened to the last and
largest enclosure. Its entrance lay at the far end of the colonnade and took
up the entire width of the room. Pushing aside the brocade curtain, Stokes
beheld a sight that put all the other treatment enclosures well inside the
medical establishment in comparison.

Armatures of steel and wood enclosed six human figures draped in
white sheets, lying slack and recumbent on structures reminiscent of
dentists' chairs. The principal difference lay in the myriad coils of copper-
colored wire descending from the armature to affix themselves to various
portions of human anatomy beneath. Every few seconds one or more
coiled wire would spark, and the individual to which it was attached would

jerk and spasm. The scent of ether was redolent in the air even from where Stokes stood. Stokes had heard of these modern treatments with electricity. They were all the rage.

An enormous wooden waterwheel stood to one side of the recumbent figures, supported by a heavy gantry. Inside, a red-faced gentleman was contained in clear distress; though Stokes could not see him clearly, it was from thence the first raised voice had originated.

Before him stood Dr. Harrowgate, a white laboratory coat over his herringbone waistcoat. His reply was a brusque bark of command. 'I tell you, sir, you must continue! Your health and sanity, to say nothing of that of your fellow patients, depends upon on it!'

'Let me out! *Out, I say!*' came the reply, and Stokes was appalled to recognize in that wail of despair the voice of Undersecretary Gladstone.

Harrowgate grated, 'You will be the ruination of your health, sir! Your nervous system requires complete exhaustion before it can be restored. But where the water treatment and colonic pneumatics have failed, I assure you, repeated Faradization can and will succeed. Now,' he growled with thunder in his voice and eyes like storm-clouds, '*Run!*'

At first Gladstone merely cringed before the black-bearded doctor; then, weakly, pathetically, the man began to pace at the waterwheel. It creaked and turned, slowly at first, then with growing rapidity. As it did so, the rate of electrical sparking from the copper coils affixed to the six recumbent figures accelerated in time with its turning. Spasms shook those figures and the smell of something burning intermingled with the heavy odor of ether. More sparks came from somewhere inside the wheel; some clearly contacted with Gladstone, who cried out pitifully with each shock.

'Dr Harrowgate, what is the meaning of this?' Stokes spoke loud enough to penetrate the sound of sparking electricity and the groaning of the waterwheel.

Harrowgate's head swiveled to regard the young officer, but Gladstone immediately ceased running and clung to the wooden bars enclosing him within the wheel. 'Help! Help, this madman has me running on this blasted contraption of torture and shocks me if I can't keep up!' The wheel slowed to a crawl, and the spasming figures went slack once more.

'Midshipman,' Harrowgate said with icy civility, 'what is the meaning of this intrusion on my work? I was assured by Mr. Doolittle I would have the complete cooperation and support of the staff and crew of the *Palladion* before I agreed to assist him in his enterprise.'

'Begging your pardon, Doctor, but I was sent by the captain after a report of a disturbance.' Stokes stifled an exclamation as Gladstone touched something inside the wheel and cried out in pain. Involuntarily, Stokes took a few steps into the room, then stopped at a sharp glare from Harrowgate.

'I assure you, midshipman, nothing untoward is happening here. Certainly there is no 'disturbance.' I cannot think who would have reported such a thing. Faradization treatment is a safe and effective therapy for the management of numerous nervous conditions, to which both Mr. Gladstone and several of my other patients are sadly subject.' His gaze took in the recumbent figures with an expression Stokes felt crossed over from professional pride into something closer to proprietary glee.

'Midshipman! Get me out of here!' panted Gladstone breathlessly. 'He's a lunatic, I tell you! A lunatic!'

Harrowgate spun in his tracks and stalked toward the wheel and its occupant. Unsure of exactly how far his mandate extended, Stokes hesitated. Gladstone clearly needed help, but there might be consequences if he interfered with the doctor. He took a few steps toward the draped figures and noted the constant drip of ether onto the cotton cones they wore over their faces. All were in varying states of anaesthesia, but the smell of burning hair was much stronger here. Stokes was turning away when he heard a voice say his name.

He turned and saw one of the sheeted figures shakily removing its cotton cone. It was Lady St. John. 'You should not be here.'

Ignoring the doctor and Gladstone for a moment, Stokes felt drawn to her bedside. Paired copper coils dangled from the armature above to disappear beneath the drape somewhere near her hips, and another set ended in a metal band on which her head had been resting. She had risen to one elbow, struggling with the effort. He began to speak but she interrupted.

'Please, you must go. *Now*. He won't tolerate interference. You are in danger the more you are near him.'

'What about Undersecretary Gladstone? I have a duty to protect the safety of all our passengers, even more than my own.'

'You must get out of here. Please. Just stay away; you don't know what he's capable of...' Her voice rang with urgency and concern.

'I'm sorry, but I can't do that,' he said quietly and, placing a hand on her bedside in consolation, he rose and strode more confidently toward the waterwheel. Harrowgate was busy with the set of controls manipulating the current generated by—and in, Stokes saw—the wheel. Gladstone was banging weakly on the wooden bars. His face was grey.

Stokes approached the wheel and removed the heavy wooden bar holding the entrance shut. 'If you please, Undersecretary,' he said softly, and Gladstone all but fell out of the wheel to collapse upon his arm. Stokes supported his weight and shifted it up to his shoulder, then turned to convey the quietly weeping gentleman from the room. He left the wooden bar leaning against the wheel and transferred both hands to supporting Gladstone. As they reached the curtained exit from the enclosure, he cast a glance backwards. Behind him, Harrowgate stood next to the gantried waterwheel. His dark eyes burned into Stokes' with a look of fury and pure malice. Then without blinking or looking away, he stepped into the wheel and began to trudge methodically forward. Bluish sparks rose from the twitching, etherized patients.

Stokes fled.

IV

It had been a tense eight bells.

Stokes' service to Undersecretary Gladstone had not gone unnoticed. Halfway through his watch the day following his confrontation with Harrowgate, Stokes had received a brief note of thanks from Gladstone's secretary by way of the great man's personal valet. He had been warmed by the Undersecretary's official attention, though part of him wondered if the man truly remembered anything from that ghastly scene. It would be a mercy if he did not. Lieutenant Brickham had also taken notice, though his response to the midshipman's report was a grunt and an order to stand to for further duties.

He had slept poorly that night, and his shift the following day had seen him growing increasingly uncomfortable. Stokes felt unaccountably watched throughout the day. It was nothing he could put his finger on, not precisely: a stray glance here, a too-long stare there, and always that feeling of an itch between his shoulder blades. He told himself it was nothing, just a case of nerves—then hastily amended that thought, remembering Dr. Harrowgate's assertions regarding the efficacy of electrical shocks for the treatment of nervous conditions.

Though he did the best he could to put it from his mind, the events of the preceding day continued to haunt him. The sickeningly sweet scent of ether intermingled with the stench of burning hair and flesh in his memories; to his senses it seemed to permeate everything, from the tea and biscuits he consumed before watch to the exotic perfumes worn by ladies of quality passing by his station. Disconcerting did not begin to cover it. By the time his watch was almost over, Stokes felt well and truly on edge, with the cut of his jib well down at the mouth.

It did not help that he had seen Lady St. John not at all that day. She, too, had haunted his thoughts at odd moments. He told himself it was merely concern for a passenger, but knew himself for a liar even as he thought it. She had captured his imagination and there was no use denying that. It was a mystery to him what a lady of quality like her might be doing with Dr. Harrowgate. Surely she was not foolish enough to believe his 'treatments' would help. Stokes was no medical man, but anything that burned the skin was no kind of medicine in his books.

Given the number of those aboard who were taking the cure by the more customary means of Turkish baths, Swedish-style massage, and hot or cold hydrotherapy, he wondered why some few felt the need to be whirled about like tops, slapped by leather belts, or shocked with jolts of electricity. He simply could not see Lady St. John as one of the latter. He hoped desperately she would not be hurt by her association with that villain of a doctor. *A right bad'un,* as his aged grandfather would have said.

It was that thought which propelled him uppermost after eight bells called an end to his watch. Stokes nodded to the relief duty officer and went below to a meal of beef and red lead—stewed tomatoes—followed by a crumb of pudding. He passed the time weighing his options. The lady had been nothing if not clear. His offers of aid had been met with warnings, both about her and about Harrowgate. Stokes was too much the gentleman ever to force his help on a lady, but Harrowgate was another cask of rum entirely. He'd run afoul of the man twice now, and that itch between his shoulder blades crept back each time he thought of the doctor. But what could he do about it?

Pushing back from the mess with a nod to the other crewmen still eating, Stokes bussed his kit and made for the crew's quarters. It was high time he took the initiative. He might be the lowest of the officer class, but he was still an officer and held certain prerogatives aboard the *Palladion.* Among those was the ability to go more or less where he chose, within reason. Much as he wished, however, he could not enter a passenger's cabin without an utterly compelling reason. Dr. Harrowgate's personal effects might be deeply revealing, but he would have to look elsewhere before he could force an entry without being broken of his rank.

Aboard a vessel the size of the *Palladion*, 'elsewhere' was a dauntingly large space to search. Stokes began methodically, eliminating first the passenger cabins and crew quarters. He also marked off the medical deck, for now; no sense returning there any sooner than necessary after yesterday's harrowing experience. He began by seeking out Harrowgate himself, whom he quickly found in the first-class dining room, surrounded by a table full of the well-dressed and well-to-do. From the sound of it he was holding forth on the latest medical treatments and their indications, fashionably re-imagined for the genteel client in need of therapeutic electrocution. He scanned the doctor's rapt audience anxiously, but Lady St. John was not among them.

Having made certain he was free to roam without encountering the doctor unawares, Stokes next made for the lower decks, where passengers were of a different class and cut. More at home here, the midshipman found himself relaxing a trifle as he nodded and smiled at the families on holiday and the young, adventurous blokes hoping to make their fortunes on Luna. He'd been little different on a fine spring day some years before when he first entered the service.

A bit of quick reconnoitre and shaking of hands gained Stokes the intelligence that while such a refined gentleman as Dr. Harrowgate had not so much as set foot in the lower passenger deck, several individuals of his entourage had. He listened with great attention as two men in dark coats and bowlers were described—big toffs, necks like trees; hard to miss. According to one young adventurer, a likely chap just working into his first pair of ginger muttonchops, the pair had been overheard to use the doctor's name to gain access to the boiler room service entrance: an area normally off-limits to passengers. Stokes thanked the earnest young man with a clap on the shoulder and set off to see why a boiler room should be of any interest to a medical man.

It did not take him long to find the place. It was, as the ginger had said, a service entrance leading down into the lowest reaches of the vessel. Stokes hesitated. There was little save stowage and engineering down there, and only rarely did any of the crew need to access it. Even less so should any passengers have reason to go below. Something was clearly amiss. He resolutely opened the hatch and stepped into the dark, humid space, ignoring the itch between his shoulders as he did.

Lit only by infrequent sodium lights that burned a sulfurous yellow in the gloom, the passage was clear of anything save rivets in the sheet metal. Stokes made his way carefully, ducking his head low to avoid bulkheads in the narrow space. It was noisy and claustrophobic, and the heat and humidity of the nearby boiler room made sweat quickly stand out on his forehead. Stokes tried to imagine a pair of big chaps navigating the narrow passage and shook his head. It seemed far-fetched now that he was himself trying to squeeze his way through the restricted access.

Abruptly he paused. *What was that?* A clank, almost rhythmic but not quite, resonated in the passage above the bass rumble of the boilers. It came from somewhere near, reaching him more through his shoes than his ears. *Conducted through the metal, likely,* he thought. Which meant the source could be a deck below. Moving slowly ahead, Stokes had a moment of regret that he had not a single bit of defense about his person, not so much as a wrench or a belaying pin. It had seemed an unnecessary precaution aboard a pleasure cruise; it seemed so no longer.

Ahead, a dark hatch loomed into view. Taking a deep breath that savoured of damp coal and combustion, Stokes stepped forward as quietly as he could and pushed the hatch open just enough to peer inside.

It was a stoking-room, one of several accesses to the furnaces powering the boilers that kept the ship's rotational gravity constant. Only here Stokes saw a row of several figures slumped against the wall. In the flickering light that escaped the edges of the furnace chute he could see they were bound and gagged.

What in the name of…? Midshipman Stokes could think of no honest reason why anyone should be trussed up in the bowels of the *Palladion,* and the officer in him immediately shifted into high gear. He pushed open the hatch and made his way over to the nearest, a white-haired older man in a dirty white shirt and black cravat who seemed to come to only as Stokes' shadow cross the fitful light.

At first he flinched back and strained away wildly, but as the midshipman's face was framed by the furnace glow he went wide-eyed and made entreating sounds from behind his gag. Stokes reached around his neck and worried the knotted fabric until it loosened enough for him to bring the slack around the man's jaw and down to his neck.

'My god, you cannot imagine how good it is to see you,' came the elderly man's voice, weak and hoarse with disuse. 'We were yelling for help for days, until they gagged us.'

Stokes leaned back slightly in confusion. 'Who gagged you, sir? What is going on here?'

'The blackhearted fiend Eliphas Graves, that's who!' came the grated reply. 'My patient, until he turned on us. I'll have his ears for this—'

'Pardon me, but did you say *my patient*? Who are you?' Suddenly, the older man's features began to look alarmingly familiar to him.

'I,' the bound, rough-shaven man pronounced with slow and terrible gravity, 'am Dr Ulysses Meriwether Harrowgate, administrator of Broadmoor Criminal Lunatic Asylum in Crowthorne, Berkshire.'

Stokes' mouth dropped open. 'But how can that be? I saw Dr. Harrowgate not half an hour ago in the first-class dining room. If you are Dr. Harrowgate, then who…'

'Listen to me, midshipman,' the older man interrupted urgently, *'there's no time.* I accepted a position as medical officer on the *Palladion* so I could examine the effects of reduced gravity on the insane mind. Graves and several of my other patients set upon me and my staff unawares just before launch and hid us here the first night of the voyage, before any of our faces were well-known aboard ship. He's a criminal lunatic and god alone knows what he's planning! Untie us and take us to the captain at once. There might still be time to avert a disaster. Hurry, man!'

Stokes bent over the doctor and began to fumble with the restraints. He and the other prisoners were bound at the wrists and ankles around a stout metal pipe, putting them in a kneeling position that made it awkward to reach the knots. He was forced to bend fully over in order to have any access at all, and then only by all but draping himself bodily over the doctor. He had almost succeeded in loosening the first knot when a sudden shadow blotted out the light. He heard Harrowgate shout a warning and reeled back just in time to see a fist the size and consistency of a nine-pound hammer strike him full in the face with the force of a steam engine, and his vision went black.

V

He woke certain his soul had been condemned to perdition.

Red light seared his eyes. Agony pounded at the back of his skull. Every part of his body felt as if one of his superior officers had worked it over with a cat o'nine tails.

Stokes groaned softly and did his best to sit up. And failed. Something held him down where he rested against the wall. His eyes struggled to focus. Something bound his wrists together, something coarse and tight.

Rope. Grey tendrils of fog began to lift from his mind. His wrists were bound behind him with rope passed around a metal pipe. In the stoking room. *The stoking room...Dr. Harrowgate!* He sat up as best he could in his confined position and scanned the room wildly. He was alone. *The others? Where are the oth*—

His eye caught on wisps of fabric, then grey worsted wool fabric as if from a waistcoat or gentleman's coat. They were caught on the edge of the metal grate through which coal was shoveled down into the furnace that kept the *Palladion* under steam. Stokes closed his eyes and tried not to imagine what might have happened to Dr. Harrowgate and the others.

His own predicament was quite as bad. After straining mightily but ineffectually against his bonds again, Stokes slumped back against the wall. He was caught. The criminal lunatic posing as Dr. Harrowgate was no doubt enacting some form of malefaction even now, whether against a hapless guest like Gladstone or some even more vulnerable passenger. And there was nothing he could do about it. Nothing at all.

Stokes sagged. Unexpectedly, his fingers touched cool, smooth metal instead of the rougher surface of the stoking-room floor. Carefully, he began to feel his way along the slim length of the smoother surface until sudden pain made him almost cry out. He could feel blood slicking his left hand now, but he gritted his teeth and moved more slowly with the right. It was the handle of something sharp...

Stokes gripped it carefully and experimented until the blade dug into his bonds, rather than his hand. Cautious at first, he rapidly felt Harrowgate's urgency pressing at him. He sawed faster. Though it could only have taken minutes, it felt as if hours had passed when the rope suddenly parted and he all but fell away from the wall.

In the flickering light of the furnace, Stokes brought the blade around where he could finally see it. It was a scalpel.

There was no reason on earth for a scalpel to be in a stoking-room, none whatsoever. Had Dr. Harrowgate—the real one—somehow managed to push it across the floor to the midshipman while he lay unconscious? It was the sort of tool only a doctor might reasonably have. But if he had had a scalpel all along, why had he not used it to cut his own bonds?

Still too foggy and unstableto think his way through that mystery, Stokes got to his feet and took stock. He was badly bruised and still somewhat shaky. His wrists were chafed and raw, and his left hand was bleeding lightly from where he had sliced it open trying to work the scalpel. He felt his face with his right hand and winced in pain. *That punch felt as if it took my head off. No wonder if I'm black and blue.* Still, he seemed more or less capable of action.

But what? With the real Harrowgate no longer there to ask, he was not certain where to begin. Should he confront the impostor? Tell the captain? Eliphas Graves was a criminal lunatic, Harrowgate had said, and remembering the feverish intensity of that dark-eyed stare, Stokes was more than inclined to believe him. What was such a man capable of, unchecked? The thought made him shudder.

It was straight to the bridge, he decided. Captain Haversham would know best how to apprehend a lunatic hiding in first class—and maybe even how to do it without alerting the genteel passengers to the extraordinary danger they had unwittingly endured.

Palming the scalpel, Stokes cautiously put his head back into the corridor. All clear. He quickened his steps and was soon jogging, albeit painfully, toward the hatch to the second class compartment. Yet when he arrived there a painful minute later, he was taken aback. It was locked. That would not normally have been an issue for the midshipman, who had access to most parts of the ship, but there was something about the heavy metal bar and thick chain affixed to the wheel operating the hatch that implied his officer's key would not avail him much. But why would anyone go to the effort of barring the second class passengers from this level? Stokes pondered the question fruitlessly as he set off down the shaft toward an access panel he knew would lead to the medical level.

En route, Stokes came to pass by the boiler room and stopped so abruptly he almost fell. Unable to believe what he was seeing, the midshipman stepped slowly into the boiler room. It was deafeningly loud and filled with myriad riveted pipes, most of them too hot to touch without heavy leather gloves, which lead to both the steam turbine that kept the ship in rotation and to the central heating needs of the various decks. But that was not what had attracted Stokes' rapt and horrified attention.

The flue of the furnace duct had been wrenched from its riveted moorings, curling like a question mark up from the floor. The furnace exhaust was venting directly into the room.

Even as he drew an aghast breath, he felt the choking hand of carbon dioxide grip his throat. He put a reflexive hand to his mouth and staggered from the room, his thoughts dimming to all but the need to find fresh air to breathe. Managing to reach the corridor, Stokes drew a ragged breath and tried to comprehend what he had seen. *Sabotage.* It was the only explanation. It would take not one but several strong men armed with crows to prize out the heavy metal flue like that. And they would have to know what they were about in order to work quickly so as not to be overcome by the furnace exhaust themselves. And these saboteurs—he could think of no other word—clearly intended to fill the second-class compartment with choking, unbreathable gas from the furnace exhaust. Suddenly the new bar and chains locking the access hatch took on an even more sinister cast; these men were not mere saboteurs. They intended mass murder.

If he had been jogging before, Stokes all but flew down the corridor now. He had to reach the medical level and warn the captain, the crew—good lord, even the passengers if need be. Nothing short of an engineering team could repair the damage in the boiler room, and even they would have difficulty now the room was filled with gas, but perhaps there was a way to vent the furnace exhaust into the void instead of the second-class compartment. It was the best he could hope for.

A metal ladder set into the wall brought him to a metal grate. He wrenched at it with increasing agitation before realizing it had swivel-locks on each side. Hastily, he pushed them aside and let the grate fall to the deck below as he scrambled up into the medical level. The contrast could not have been greater. Instead of drab steel and rivets, the luxury of Doolittle's vision for a voidship-spa met his gaze. The treatment rooms were empty now, however; he saw not a soul.

His eyes found a ship's clock and made the time: ninth hour. First-class passengers would be in their cabins if they were retiring early, or else socializing in one of the many withdrawing rooms, tea services, smoking parlours, and music halls. Stokes ran for the double-door exit. He had to warn someone!

But there was no one. Outside, the hall was as empty as the medical wing had been. Each room he peered into was devoid of life or activity, even though all were lit and ready—as if they had been populated minutes before and their occupants had merely wandered away *en masse*. But Stokes felt sure it was not so. If nothing else there should be crew and other staff about manning their duty stations at this hour. They, too, were utterly missing. There was skulduggery about, no question.

There was only one place so many people could be gathered all together at once. He made for the ballroom at a dead run.

'Ladies and gentlemen, a toast!'

The clear, ringing tones of a knife tapping fine crystal penetrated the indistinct chatter of many small conversations filling a large room. All around the many white-clothed tables of the grand ballroom of the *Palladion*, glasses were raised. Some of the arms that held them were tuxedo-black. Others were clad in long satin gloves, and still others were bare save for the sparkle of jeweled bracelets. Some even bore the pure white of dress uniforms with embroidered gold bars of rank. But one and all, they raised champagne flutes as the man before them proposed a toast.

'Ladies and gentlemen, I am a simple man at heart, and my toast is therefore simple also. You came aboard the *Palladion,* whether lord or lady, sir or dame, gentleman or gentlewoman, as my patients. You came aboard with nervous conditions; mental afflictions; palpations of the heart; pleurisy; enervation; and many, many more of the various manners in which the human machine can dysfunction. But! You had the wisdom and good judgment to entrust your health to me! And I have shown you how good diet, rigorous exercise, and the application of heat, cold, percussion, and Faradization in a reduced gravitational field can and has cured you of your ills!'

There was applause, a bit hesitant at first, but quickly spreading throughout the ballroom. But the speaker was not yet done.

'And so, my very good friends—for though you came aboard as patients, I so name you now and for all time the very best of companions!—I thank you for joining me on your journey into the void on a quest for perfect health. I hope you have enjoyed the voyage as much as I have—although to be perfectly honest, I am not certain if that is truly possible.' His dark eyes glinted, and his broad smile held just a little too much tooth. There was chuckling and more scattered applause. 'And so without further ado, ladies and gentlemen, I raise my glass to you, my patients and friends, in one last and final toast: to your very good health!' Dr. Harrowgate raised his glass, and two hundred glasses were raised in answer.

Stokes peered through the round window in the swinging double-doors of the grand ballroom and weighed his chances. Harrowgate—*Graves,* he reminded himself sternly—sat at the head table surrounded by the rich and powerful, London's elite. Behind him stood two large men built like sides of beef, dressed now in white waiters' jackets almost ludicrously too small for their muscled frames. He remembered one of them all too well and rubbed his aching jaw with a wince. He fingered the scalpel with which he had freed himself and tried to imagine incapacitating one of them with it before—what? He could think of no plan in which he subdued both bodyguards and yet might still be in any condition to confront Graves.

He had pushed one of the doors slightly in that he might hear some of the conversation going on in the ballroom, but was still taken completely unawares when a whispered voice came to him through the crack. 'Midshipman Stokes, is that you?'

He almost faltered in relief. 'Lady St. John! Yes, I'm here. But you must leave at once, you are all in terrible danger-'

'There is no time. He has drugged the crew and the passengers are next. The ship is lost. You must get to one of the life-rafts and take it to Luna. Perhaps you can find help there. Now go, quickly, before he hears…'

Stokes' mouth worked silently. 'You know about Graves?' His mind felt torpid, unable to keep up with the import of her words.

'I told you I was Dr. Harrowgate's patient,' she said softly. 'I was at Broadmoor Asylum when he brought several of us to Victoria Station for an experimental medical treatment. Reduced gravitation. A voidship. I was hopeful…' She trailed off. 'Graves counterfeited being ill just after boarding, and when the doctor took him for examination, Graves attacked him in his own cabin. That was just before you and I first met.' Her voice trembled. 'I did not know what he planned, then. At first he told me we would take the cure for the two-week trip and escape in the crowds when we landed back on Victoria Station. We could go anywhere in the world, he said.'

'But then…he started pretending to be a doctor. He tortured people in the guise of medicine. And he so clearly enjoyed it…' She swallowed hard. 'I told him I didn't want to go with him after the voyage, but he just laughed. I…I do not believe he means to return to Earth. Not anymore.'

Stokes pushed the door slightly further ajar. 'He's sabotaged the boiler room, and all the second-class passengers will asphyxiate in a few hours if I don't do something. Come with me, Lady St. John. I'll send you off in a life-raft to get help while I find the captain-'

'He poisoned Captain Haversham,' she whispered, and it was all Stokes could do not to sag in despair. 'Almost all the crew are here, and will soon be unable to help anyone—he's just given them a surgical anaesthetic in their champagne. And the passengers below are very likely beyond our help by now. I overheard Graves saying he was removing the supplies of the chemical used to make fresh air on that level, and you were unconscious for hours…'

'*You* left me the scalpel,' he breathed.

'I had to do something. You wouldn't wake up and I could not stay. I could not bear to think of him pushing you into the furnace like the others. Not after…you were so kind.'

Stokes swallowed his horror. 'Lady St. John—Alethea. Come with me. *Please.*'

'I…' He felt her hesitate for an interminable moment. 'I will try to break away.'

'Meet me by the forward port escape hatch as soon as you can. It's at the end of the corridor outside the ballroom, follow it left until you see the warning sign for—'

There was a loud thump from somewhere inside the ballroom, followed by a muffled scream. 'Alethea? Alethea, what's happening?'

'The anaesthetic is taking effect,' she whispered hurriedly. 'You must go! Now! I will join you as soon as I may.'

'Alethea,' he said urgently, but already he heard the receding swish of her full skirts as she left the door and moved back into the ballroom. Stifling a curse, Stokes slumped with his back to the wall and pounded his fist on his leg once, twice. It was all coming apart at the seams. The captain, dead. Passengers drugged, even gassed in their sleep. It was not supposed to happen like this. Not to a ship like the *Palladion*.

With a supreme effort, Stokes rose above his own anger and regret and took one last look inside the grand ballroom. It was chaos. Half the room seemed slumped on tables or sprawled on the floor beside their overturned chairs, many with champagne flutes still grasped in limp hands. Others seemed to be trying to flee without success toward the elevated stage and its broad exits. Both were sealed shut, despite the frantic pounding of many well-manicured hands. Even among these panicked throngs there were those losing consciousness and slumping to the floor.

And from the head table, Graves watched them fall with a smile no longer constrained by the dignified propriety of the medical profession. He sipped from his own champagne glass and laughed long and loudly as his aristocratic guests succumbed to the anaesthetic and trampled one another like animals in their panic to escape, and in that laughter even Stokes' untrained ears heard the sound of madness.

Then, through the glass in the ballroom door, their eyes met.

Instantly Stokes dropped from sight, but the damage was already done. Above the panicked shouts of the drugged elite of the Empire, Stokes could hear Graves shouting for his muscled minions. He surged to his feet and ran pell-mell for the life-raft.

His heart was in his throat, and his feet could not seem to move as fast as his mind. He had just reached the corner at the end of the corridor when he heard the doors of the ballroom slam open and heavy booted feet pounding toward him. Stokes redoubled his pace and moments later kicked out the glass in the waist-high wall unit labelled IN CASE OF EMERGENCY in bold black print on a small brass plaque. He thrust his hand inside, not caring about the shards of glass still clinging to the frame, and pulled the metal handle inside it with all his might.

There was a heavy mechanical groan, a hiss of air, and as Stokes almost danced with impatience, a heavy hatch opened in the exterior hull of the ship. Squeezing through even before the hatch was fully open, he mashed the control to retract the door and began readying the life-raft to separate itself from the ship. It was designed for exactly that, but still the controls were slow, maddeningly slow, to obey. He had to lock the hatch until Alethea could reach him—

'*Oi*, you! C'mout, we wanna talk ta ya,' came the grating of a rusty bucket kicked along a gravelly riverbank. Stokes threw a glance over his shoulder and saw one of the muscled ruffians had pushed himself partly into the life-raft, and now his tree trunk of an arm was preventing the door from closing! With a yell, the midshipman spun and slashed wildly with the scalpel Alethea had given him. Bellows of pain erupted from the ruffian. Stokes kicked him as hard as he could, and the bull-necked man jerked his arm back toward the hallway; red streams gushed from it in several directions. Stokes advanced on the hatch to deliver more remonstrance, but it was already closing to with a metallic locking sound. A low, insistent alarm began to sound.

Suddenly he realized what he had done and tried frantically to find a way to stop it, but the life-raft had only one purpose: to propel itself away from the ship as quickly and safely as possible. Wheels turned, louvers angled, and fuel cells ignited with automated precision. Even as he searched feverishly for a way to shut down the sequence, the life-raft's small rockets caught fire and thrust it away from the *Palladion* with a sudden sharp kick of propulsion.

Stokes screamed and pounded on the hatch, to no avail. Through the heavy glass porthole he saw the *Palladion* begin to recede. Its own great engines were at full burn and angling away from Luna toward the vast, uncharted emptiness of the outer solar system.

It was only his imagination, he was certain, that gave him a last glimpse of her still, pale figure at the port observation deck, one hand pressed to the glass as she watched a small, frail sphere of pressurized metal bear him away into the Void.

~ end ~

Peter A. Smalley was not so much born as he was the object of a suitably ominous origin story. If only Marvel had been more attentive, "I, Writer" might even now be a successful comic and movie franchise starring Billy Connolly. So it goes.

Peter was raised in Seattle, Washington USA. In 2011 his picture appeared in the New York Times for something that had nothing directly to do with writing but, coincidentally, his first self-published work also came out in 2011: the speculative fantasy novella "The Burning Times".

This was quickly followed by the full-length fantasy novel "Grimme". He co-edited and contributed to the acclaimed anthology "20,001: A Steampunk Odyssey". His Steampunk novella and Shakespearean-homage "Full Fathom Five" appears in the anthology and as a stand-alone ebook. "Disbelief," his first Paranormal Romance thriller, came out in Summer 2012, followed by the Hardboiled Detective Noir tale "Emerald City Blues" in 2013. His latest work, "The Eagle and the Wolf" is a Historical Fiction novel with Urban Fantasy elements set in Paris during World War 2.

You can find his work on Amazon:
http://www.amazon.com/Peter-A.-Smalley/e/B0055QE0MS

Twitter: https://twitter.com/Peter_Smalley
Facebook: https://www.facebook.com/peterasmalley/
Google+: https://www.google.com/+PeterSmalley

The Iron Curtain
by Virginia Marybury

THE IRON CURTAIN

By Virginia Marybury

Up and Down

The *ting* of a telephone sounded, somewhere deep within the Club. Iffy noted the brevity of the sound: the Up and Down employed utterly efficient staff, who would not suffer a telephone to remain unattended.

There was always the possibility that a telephone call might be about him, but even a few seconds after the sound, no-one had come to shame him out. Perhaps this morning's eight shillings and fourpence had been a sufficient bung. It had to be: he had given up his lodgings to settle all his accounts. A man in his position could not afford to have debts.

In the shining leather chair opposite, Mr Joshua Addington was now fastidiously pursing his lips within his beard to sip his coffee. Then he gave a rather forced clearing of the throat.

Still half-listening for a Club official, Iffy glanced back at the letter in his lap.

'Hm. Well, they're based in Manchester, which indicates ambition and a desire for proximity to the Stock Exchange. However, without even knowing how the car is powered, and whether it carries a Faraday device, I really couldn't say how good the investment–'

'Come with me to their show room this afternoon, then!' Mr Addington gripped his tiny *demi-tasse* with both hands. 'I do appreciate your counsel. Why don't you come to lunch with me beforehand? I understand there will be roast beef from the Argentine today.'

Shifting in his own leather chair, Iffy straightened his spine and settled his shoulders into a pose suggesting prosperity. 'I'm afraid I shall have to decline the luncheon. Now that Young Mr Deede has moved up to Manchester, I have my own schedule of appointments at the show room.'

'But can you not be anywhere in London in a flash, with that splendid motor of yours? It would mean so much for me to turn up with you.'

It was time to escape, lest his empty stomach—teased by mention of Argentine beef—enter the conversation. Even chicken was off Iffy's menu card until his next sale commission—hopefully today. 'Perhaps another day.

I am now *chargé* at the London office, so have my appointments, and shall also be putting on a theatrical programme in Greenwich this Thursday. Er… perhaps I might send you a ticket?'

Mr Addington also straightened up. 'A theatrical programme!'

Iffy sank back in his chair. Allowing both the shiny leather wingbacks and his confidential tone to muffle his words, he said, 'A spectacle of inventions by Henry Deede's House of Patents. These are some of the latest we have acquired. Some items have not even entered commercial production.'

'But that sounds splendid! I've always wondered what your business was, where you got all your gear from. I hadn't a clue that you were so... plugged in!' Mr Addington was goggling now. Trade was rarely spoken of in the Up and Down, even by a fourth son to a fourth son. The portraits on the walls of the Naval and Military Club depicted men just as often as they depicted ships and battles, but the men were always navally rigged: that was 'gentleman's attire' here.

'I shall leave you a ticket at the Club, old chap.' Iffy slid neatly out of the chair, and grasped Mr Addington's hand. 'Don't trouble to see me out.'

In the cold mid-day sunlight of the courtyard, his smooth-lined, gloss-black motorcar reflected his lean figure.

His stomach ached with hunger.

Tea for Inwood at two o'clock, he reminded himself, *and sandwiches*.

He mounted the 'car and ignited the engine. Driving out of the courtyard onto Piccadilly, he watched the winged bulk of the Club building—with the naval air-dinghies tethered above, like the 'cars parked below—warp and slide towards him over the polished bonnet.

An ornithopter flickered, bird-like, over the edge of the reflection: no doubt hastening off on some war-mongering errand for the glory of the Royal Navy. Iffy made a face.

The showroom was in Mayfair, not far from the Club, in a substantial, stone-fronted building, which the Deedes always took care to keep clean of coal-grime. The steps and wide black door could have accommodated an Indian elephant and, indeed, Iffy hoped they would one day have such a spectacle of a client. That would be a phenomenon to excuse mentioning Trade in the Up and Down!

Iffy's eyes travelled his office, but apart from the two boxes of his own papers—which represented thousands of contacts and all the scribbling he could do for money—it was all scenery left behind by Young Mr Deede. A thick blue carpet and curtains of woven white fleur-de-lys on a cobalt background husbanded the warmth of the gas fire. Against such a background, he *could* make a living, even enough money to marry, but it would take time, and he must never *appear* to be in want.

He carefully hung his coat on a stand, and set to work laying out the wide, convex automobile mirrors on his desk, ready for Mr Inwood. Then he went out to loll against Mrs Moody's desk, in approved gentlemanly fashion.

With the company's trunk telephone at her right hand, Mrs Moody was typing out what looked like a bill. She poked her white correction pencil back into her wicker-neat nest of grey hair—unused, of course: she was a very competent typist—and looked up at him. 'Yes, Mr Pearson?'

'Has Mr Inwood telephoned?'

'No, Mr Pearson. However, Mrs Farthing is awaiting a client, and the lady prefers not to be seen.'

'Perhaps I should wait outside for Mr Inwood, then, so they don't cross.'

The bell jangled, and Iffy surged across the room to open the front door for Mr Inwood.

This was no dilettante of gadgets like Inwood. Nor even a mere gentleman, but nearly a lord... a lord of industry, or perhaps of the merchant navy.

The tall, black-bearded man occupied almost half the width of the doorway. He wore a Russian boyar's hat, its leather dome trimmed with rich black fur. Behind him, two ladies were approaching from the street, one in a pale green coat, clutching a cane and veiled and muffled such that it was impossible to see her outline. However, from her hat, a wide, white froth of ostrich feathers, one could see that she was young, and wealthy. The older lady wore a darker shade of green, with a narrower, much less wealthy silhouette. The ladies moved in step, the older lady supporting the young lady's left elbow.

Carefully, Iffy retreated, holding the door open and bowing them into the space, then he ceded to Mrs Moody and escaped to his office, chiding himself for the indiscretion of seeing the young lady who preferred not to be seen. His guts were now churning properly, like the twin propulsion screws of a dreadnaught.

There came a knock at his door.

Again, not Inwood, but the unknown man, with Mrs Moody. Despite the Russian affectation of his winter hat, and the now-visible French style of his tie knot, the rest of his dress was English, his beard Edwardian. Iffy rose to greet the man.

Mrs Moody began with the agreed fiction: 'Sir Thomas, Mr Pearson is now the manager of the London—'

'Mr Deede wrote to me about the changes,' the gentleman interrupted, looking at Iffy instead of Mrs Moody. He did not extend his hand. 'I must admit I had forgotten the matter until today.'

Iffy inhaled deeply and began to speak. 'I'm afraid my two o'clock caller is late, sir, or we would not have crossed. Mr Deede always decreed—and I agree—that Mrs Farthing's clientèle shall enjoy whatever degree of privacy they desire. In fact, now that I am to manage this office, perhaps we might arrange for a separate door? Our mews entrance might be redecorated, and a sitting room added, do you think?'

The gentleman seemed surprised, and actually smiled within his beard. 'By Gad, young man, you may be fresh, but you're not green. I wouldn't have expected such old-fashioned gentlemanliness in a... a... den of modernity.'

Iffy inclined his head in acknowledgement. 'I am a Cambridge man, sir, but read engineering, so I understand these contradictions. Those who truck with modernity do also long for quaintness and tradition. That is how this House will continue to do its business in London.'

The man nodded, too. 'Mrs Moody will inform us when the new entrance is ready.'

'Yes, sir!' she chirped, smiling at Iffy behind the gentleman's back.

Inwood was a more cheerful and flattering client, a Cambridge contemporary. He accepted Mrs Moody's offer of refreshments, as Iffy had known he would, and the two young men left the building supplied with tea in patent flasks, and sandwiches in a rubberised bowl.

Taking two triangle-cut sandwiches from the container on the Little Siddeley's bonnet, which was shaped like the lid of a steamer trunk, Iffy circled the 'car, fitting one of the mirrors and then the other, nibbling at the sandwiches all the while.

His friend sat in the driving seat, twisting this way and that. 'That was a frightful gale last week.' He waved his hands above his head, striking the canopy. 'The roof was quite useless. I almost lost it.'

Iffy took another sandwich and popped it in whole, then swigged tea from the flask. The refined white bread dissolved in the flood, and he swallowed, keeping the thin, savoury ribbon of ham in the centre of his tongue; then he swallowed that, too. Accepting the gift, his stomach gave a tiny groan of relief.

Setting his hands on the left mirror, Iffy instructed, 'Tell me when you see mostly road and just the edge of your car, to give you a point of reference.'

'Yes, yes. Tell me, have you any goggles in stock? I've lost a pair. Oh, and scratched another.'

'I'll get Mrs Moody to send you three pairs of Andrews goggles when she despatches your bill.'

Behind the motorcar, a hansom carriage emerged from the mews behind their building.

'That's it!'

Startled, Iffy looked up into Inwood's delighted, toad-like face. His friend was bouncing slightly in the seat. 'You... you can see the road in relation to your car, can you?'

'Excellently. Now the other one.'

Now standing in the street, Iffy manipulated the second mirror. The hansom slewed at the corner, and bowled off with a rattle, towards Regent Street. Iffy frowned at it. *They ought to have a motorcar. That poor girl!*

There was no point thinking about a girl; he was still hungry. Iffy mounted the running board and began examining the struts which held the canopy over the driver. 'Let me check your canopy, make sure you didn't damage it in that storm of yours.'

'Thanks, old chap. I wasn't sure the wind hadn't bent all the little bits holding it on, and you know I'd be no good fixing them if it had.'

Now Iffy smiled again. Inwood always knew the right thing to say. He had dragged Iffy out of his funk after the fourth class degree; and it was true: Inwood was a fine engineer, but no mechanic, as Iffy was.

'There. Splendid. Now, old chap, here's ten shillings' payment towards the bill—Pa likes me to be honourable about these things—so send me those goggles and the rest of my bill. I'll treat you to supper after your programme on Thursday.'

'Thanks, Inwood.'

Iffy regained the pavement, and gave the Little Siddeley's rump a slap, causing Inwood to laugh and honk, before driving off into the light evening traffic.

Iffy grasped his Gentleman's Tool Case and the refreshments, and ran lightly up the steps to the office.

'Have they gone, Mrs Moody?'

'Yes, Mr Pearson. They wanted to leave by the back entrance.'

Iffy surrendered Inwood's shilling note, which Mrs Moody stowed safely in the cache-and-chute. 'You'll need to bill him for the mirrors, the fitting and also three pairs of Andrews goggles.'

She looked up, her face alight with a smile. 'Well done, indeed, Mr Pearson! I shall type that up directly.'

Iffy lingered by the desk, waiting for his *de facto* employer to emerge from her office.

The hall's second door opened on Mrs Farthing. She was wearing a neat white blouse and violet corduroy waistcoat, which followed her fashionably pinched-in silhouette before flaring over her brown cotton-twill skirt. Her white hair was dressed in a modest *chignon* at the back of her neck. In her eyes, voluminous hair-dos were for the young ladies.

She closed the door behind her, preserving her private, sacred space. Old Mr Deede's daughter was a perfect chaperone. She had nursed her late husband long enough, and had employed enough of her own domestic staff, to navigate blindfolded in both medical and domestic waters.

'I hope your appointment went well, Mrs Farthing?'

She glided closer. 'Yes, Mr Pearson,' she answered, with a hint of severity in her eyebrows.

'Your client's father—or uncle—came in to see me, and I happened to mention the rear entrance.'

'Her father. I had wondered how he suddenly came to think of that.'

'Well, Mrs Farthing, I think it would benefit your clients in particular if we were to make formal arrangements, ensuring the mews entrance is respectable, and providing a string of sitting rooms for waiting: one for male relatives, one for ladies and maids. Ordinary visitors who want the show room but who have no appointment may continue to enter by the front door.'

'Mr Pearson, surely that will be very expensive...' ventured Mrs Moody.

Mrs Farthing said nothing, but waited, her dark eyes unmoving beneath the gentle swags of her discreetly powdered eyelids.

He shook his head. 'They will not be real rooms, but partitioned spaces, and they will serve as tiny show rooms. A fireplace with the asbestos hearth guard, electric lighting softer and more subtle than anything they've ever seen, soda siphon and whisky—in short, everything we put in the sitting room for the Greenwich theatre programme.'

Now Mrs Farthing spoke. 'Remember, Mr Deede and I must approve expenses.'

Iffy made a slight bow. 'Although they were not introduced to me, I am sure you know whether your visitors are clients worth keeping. I assume you were fitting the young lady–'

'Training her new maid.'

'Another excellent service. However... such a family could be persuaded to buy more. A carriage is a high climb for a crippled girl, and an uncomfortable ride: they ought to have a motorcar.'

'We have no motorcars on our books.'

'We carry patent products for motorcars. I sold a set of convex wing mirrors this very afternoon, and Mr Inwood also paid us to fit them, and ordered new goggles.

'Also, presumably the young lady has patent insoles, or patent shoes, as well as... whatever orthotic garments you have provided for her, but she also ought to have a Verity Spring Cane, orthopaedic cushions, warming cushions, possibly a massage device.'

Mrs Farthing was smiling at him now. 'My brother would never be so forward as to present so many recommendations to such a client.'

Iffy smiled back. 'Young Mr Deede is in Manchester now, and the old capital is yours, Mrs Farthing. Would you send a catalogue with their bill, and tickets for the show on Thursday? Make sure they know the *finale* will be a ballet.'

Still smiling faintly, Mrs Farthing said, 'We mustn't over-reach, Mr Pearson. Now, have you made any new contacts to-day?'

'Someone at the Club asked me to look over an investment prospectus, and finally asked me 'what I did' so I promised him a ticket to the spectacle. He may be good for gentlemen's gadgets and presents for his womenfolk. However... apart from Captain Wemyss this afternoon, and the theatre on Thursday, I don't believe I have any appointments until Monday....?'

From her pose by the desk, Mrs Moody leaned toward him to pat his arm. 'Oh, don't be despondent, Mr Pearson! Christmas is coming, and that is our busiest time of the year.'

Iffy looked back to Mrs Farthing.

'Yes,' she agreed. 'My brother has high hopes for you this Christmas-tide, and with your new contacts, we need never over-tax any single client.'

'Yes, Mrs Farthing.'

'See that you are on hand at the theatre, during the spectacle, and remain in the show room all of the next week–'

Their door-bell jangled.

'–to welcome in the new clients,' she finished, firmly. She turned to go back to her office, and waved for Iffy to do the same, as it would not do to have the ostensible managers of the establishment waiting on their clients.

Captain Wemyss had carried his rank into retirement, along with a loud, hoarse voice which spoke of a career of shouting. However, when he presented his gout-swollen feet for the shoe-fitting, he made no bluster at all, just as though he were submitting to his steward.

Thinking of the crippled young lady, Iffy bent to his task with great care and gentleness.

'Do you have children, sir?'

'Yes, indeed!' the man rasped. 'Two boys in the Navy and a granddaughter in-waiting up at Court in Manchester!' He leaned back in the armchair, and tilted back his balding head, the better to project his voice to the ceiling. 'Such a shame to be without my little girl, but that's the best place for her to gain a respectable establishment. Why are you not in the Navy, young man?'

Iffy kept his head bent, and offered the appeasement he always used with his father's friends. 'I would be of neither use nor ornament, sir. I try to serve the Empire through her inventors instead. Patents bring thousands a year to His Majesty's Treasury, not to mention the income taxes paid by the inventors themselves.' He sat back on his heels, and stood up. 'Will you try to stand now, sir?'

After his appointment, Iffy took a change of clothes—cunningly folded—and a stock of the new radium chocolates, and went out to perform a round of the clubs of Mayfair. He accepted several offers of drinks, a cigar and smoked salmon canapés, and in turn offered the chocolates around, advertising the warming effect.

At last, to his relief, advice to a Mr Selwyn—about not investing in shipping lest the vessels be commandeered for war—produced an invitation to supper, and it was late enough that Iffy might decently manage to stay the night, rather than creeping back to the office.

In St James's Street it was sky-dark and smog-dusk. The freezing mist preserved the savoury tang of coal-fire exhalations, like salted meat in aspic. Iffy, Mr Selwyn and a crowd of Selwyn's friends surged along the pavement together.

At Selwyn's flat, conversation turned back to investments and war, and Iffy repeated a tale he had sold recently to a magazine, about a family of patriotic British émigrés on the Continent, whose glorious hotel so distracted a Johnny-Foreigner admiral that the planned naval invasion of Britain had to be cancelled.

The fee from the story had only relieved the author of his debt to his landlady, but had not allowed him to keep his lodgings.

It was time for Iffy to start his pretence of tipsiness, which would lead to a bed for this night. Yet, with the conversation moving back to war, the feigned pain in his head began to develop—genuinely—in his guts.

Zero Degrees of Longitude, and Love

The Crystal Palace Meridian Theatre lay east of the old Naval College. Iffy always approached the theatre from the front, so he could enjoy the spectacle Harald Denman had created. The naval authorities and bourgeois inhabitants of Georgian Greenwich had been pleased to see an ugly Woolwich warehouse being plastered with elegant false fronts and a triangular pediment, until Denman also illuminated the façade and added more signs than on an Oxford Street shop. In fact, it was more like the frontispiece of a novel with several subtitles.

Crystal Palace Meridian Theatre
located on the Greenwich Meridian, the Birthplace of Time
Sunrise Half a Second Before the Royal Naval College,
and Two Degrees, Thirteen Minutes Before the New Houses of
Parliament.

Moreover, on either side of the front doors were ornithopter wings, in the ancient Greek style of Daedalus, bearing the words: *Fully Electrified: The Light of the Modern Day never sets on our Modern Theatre!* and: *Tonight: Tableaux of Modernity, and a Classical Ballet Reinvigorated by Modern Invention.*

Grinning, Iffy completed his circuit of the building and entered by the rear door.

Once in his boiler suit, his first task was to check the Faraday grid under the stage floor. With the growling generator trickling a tiny current through the metal mesh, Iffy picked up the yoke—equal weights suspended on either side of the scales—and hooked it onto the pulley, which would take it across the grid. When the scales entered the lower-gravity shadow of the Faraday area, they wobbled in the air. Iffy touched the bar to steady it.

Methodically, he wound the weights forward and back across the vast space, alert to variations in gravity.

Inwood arrived in the middle of this exercise, but watched silently until the end. He was already dressed for the theatre.

Iffy unhooked the plumbing scale, and handed it to Inwood, then went to turn off the generator.

In the silence, he was suddenly aware of sweat in his hair and under his arms. His neck and shoulders ached. He let out a sigh. 'Thanks for keeping your trap shut, Inwood. Denman's promised to skin me alive if one of his dancers turns an ankle.'

Inwood's face relaxed into his friendly toad's smile. 'Do the naval Johnnies have to go through all this folderol every day they're at sea?'

'I doubt it. *We're* worried about fragile human bodies, but from the way Pa and Arthur talk, I gather they just turn on the Faraday and bash through the waves.'

'D'you think there might be time for me to try it? I've never had a chance at more than Faraday theory. The brass have got it so sewn up these days that a civvie can't get his hands on it unless he buys a 'car, but all I could afford was the Siddeley.'

Iffy sighed again. 'Sorry, old chap. I've got to vacuum clean it now, and in any case I can't turn it on again till the *Swan Lake*.'

Inwood clapped him on the shoulder. 'Rather you than I! I thought I had set you up for an easy job, but it seems not!'

'Oh, no, it's splendid... thanks to your invaluable advice, of course! You know I'm not up to scratch with the Alpha and Omega of ampères and ohms. But come back after Christmas and I'll smuggle you backstage, so you can hop about in the wings when the Faraday is on.'

In Denman's box, Mrs Farthing occupied the front row by virtue of her age and wealth. Mr Denman perched next to her, but he was in constant motion, nodding to patrons and acquaintances, checking the stage, examining the theatre chandelier.

Iffy stood behind them.

His words about the Faraday and fragile bodies were still bothering him. Would the young lady and her protectors accept their tickets?

The box he had offered them was still dark, and remained so as the theatre lights dimmed.

The stage curtains swept open to reveal an elegant gramophone pedestalled on a tall table of shining dark wood. Its trumpet iridesced like mother-of-pearl. Iffy's shoulders dropped slightly, in relief. Mr Denman's lighting was offering the correct flattery to the goods sold and promoted by Henry Deede's House of Patents.

The gramophone seemed to wait until it was assured of its audience, and then music strode out of the horn: Jeremiah Clarke's Trumpet Voluntary.

As the next trumpet part entered the music, it seemed to be coming from stage left.

Mrs Farthing leaned toward the edge of the box to see and rocked slightly back in surprise when a second spotlight illuminated another mother-of-pearl horn, with no body.

Anticipating the next cadenza, Iffy tilted his head to look stage right, and... yes, a third gramophone horn received its lighting cue.

'Curious, but very effective, Mr Pearson,' Mrs Farthing murmured.

The three lily-like horns serenely conducted their procession unto its climax and then fell modestly silent. The curtains swished over them and the theatre lights swelled to allow the audience to read the programme. Denman and Iffy had instructed their friends in the audience to begin the clapping on this cue. The prompt worked: the applause sounded almost natural.

The curtains re-opened, on a domestic scene. There were fifty-nine patented articles in the *vignette*, but Iffy counted on wealth, comfort and Christmas sentiment to camouflage them. Generously pleated green velvet curtains screened high windows, while all inside was prosperous cosiness: a Christmas tree, a clean, cheerful gas fire warming two small children playing with blocks and a tin motorcar. A well-dressed lady was knitting in deep brown wool. A lamp shed its warm stained-glass glow over it all.

In the sketch, a naval father returned from his ship at Greenwich, and greeted his children with oranges, silk scarves from India and a small box of cloves. He had a Whiting's Magnetic Hair Brush for his wife.

In their turn, the girls and lady of the family presented their gifts: a patent safety razor— 'for shaving on the rough seas, Papa,' —and a Magnetic Foot Battery.

The man kissed his womenfolk. 'I am sorry to have missed Christmas itself, but let us light these sparklers while we sing *Joy to the World.*'

The lights were dimming, and the curtains moving across the scene, even as the players sang their carol.

When the lights came up again for the interval, Iffy supported the applause with energetic clapping, but he was looking sideways at the box opposite.

They were there, and she was unveiled. Her hair was dark, like her father's, but she wore it in abundant coils, as wide as a hat. She was not pretty, though if she had been a man, and if she had been robust, like her father, she would have been handsome... and strong: she was strong. The physical strain—visible through her fixed, intense expression—was like an orthotic, artificially bracing her body.

She turned, too. Iffy instantly acknowledged her, with a deep bow. When he straightened up, she was veiled again.

When the curtains re-opened, the Swan Lake had been rendered in black and grey, under dim blue light. It was silent.

The phonograph sang again, in triplicate, relaying the quivering, balancing music of Tchaikovsky's overture, as the swans entered, glowing with phosphorus paint. They moved with a lightness extraordinary. This was the Faraday Floor, transforming human bodies into wildfowl.

In the theatre box, the young lady's own torso rose in her seat, in a column of involuntary power. She turned to look across the theatre, and saw Iffy, too. This time she did not veil herself.

The glowing, dancing bird-maidens circled the lake lightly and hurried their princess up into the air, away from Siegfried, who remained heavy, bound to the earth by the magnets on his dancing shoes.

Iffy had programmed for the theatre lights to come up very slowly, a lengthy twilight to protect the dream state. During the long rise of the light, he scanned the box, trying to see her face. At last it was light enough again to see her for a moment.

He was startled when his hand was suddenly seized in a masculine grip.

Mr Denman was wringing his hand, with emotion. 'My dear boy, that was extraordinary. The future of the theatre is assured!'

Iffy responded with a squeeze which allowed him to free his hand. 'Yes, sir. I hope so, sir.'

She was gone.

Iffy unloaded two armfuls of newspapers onto Mrs Farthing's desk with the picture pages of the Illustrated London News on the very top: the pictures of the swans in flight had been taken at the dress rehearsal.

Mrs Farthing looked over the pile at him. 'I will read through in the course of the morning. I believe Mrs Moody has only one appointment for you today, after lunch, so you may go out and show yourself in town before then, if you like.'

Iffy felt his excitement—which had impelled him through his early rising at Inwood's house, and in the long 'car journey from Richmond—ebb like a turn of the powerful Thames tide, and he answered, 'I have some personal correspondence and a story to write. May I stay in my office?'

'What is the story about?'

'An amateur spy story. A fisherman with a new Kodak Brownie camera spots invading German Zeppelins over the sea.'

'Will it be in print by Christmas?'

'It should be in print by the end of this week. Certainly in time for a camera to be considered as a Christmas present.'

She smiled. 'Stay in your office, then. I don't know how you think of these things.'

Iffy lifted his chin. 'I was living on my wits even before my father stopped my allowance, and it really is no trouble to think of stories. You know how our valiant fishermen were lately fired upon by mistake, by the Russian Baltic fleet. This is simply a more sinister tale.'

He bowed and returned to his office to start clipping reviews for his letter to his father and mother, with a shipping map propped up in front of him, so he could consider the geography of his story.

Telegrams came throughout the day. Most were simple congratulations, but there were two orders. He copied all of them, and gave the originals to Mrs Moody.

The last telegram of all was a hurried request from Mr Denman for Iffy to come to the theatre before the afternoon rehearsal to turn on the grid for a very special client.

He stared at the squat letters of the telegram. *She* was the one who should enjoy the grid, but was it she, or had someone else decided to be forward?

It might be someone old and gouty and aggressive, like Captain Wemyss, he told himself, grimly.

The 'car was almost out of petrol—and not his vehicle anyway—so he left it in the mews behind the show room, and went by omnibus, arriving at three o'clock.

When Iffy arrived, Mr Denman dragged him into the building and thrust him toward the backstage doors. 'Connect it, sharpish!' he hissed.

'Sir, I'll need to test and clean it for the performance!'

'Marcus has cleaned it. You can test it later. Go!'

In the confines of the crawl-space, not wearing his boiler suit, Iffy moved carefully. He skirted the edge of the grid to the power lever, then braced himself to grasp and slowly push it to the 'on' position.

This done, and unable to resist the chance that it might be her, he pushed himself up through a trap-door, and hid in the wings.

With the curtains drawn, the space was like a tiny ballroom, bounded by draped velvet. At the other side of the Floor, the young lady approached the edge of the grid. She was unveiled now. In the theatre lights, her dark hair was slightly reddish, and her skin pale as fish flesh.

They've probably given her rickets, too, by her seclusion, he thought, with sudden fury.

Each left step was performed with two 'legs': her own weak limb and that damned solid cane. The ferule was probably rubber-tipped, but a spring cane would make the shock of each step so much softer.

She stepped onto the Floor–

–and flourished upright, like an unfurling flower. After a moment's silent joy, she strode forward, poling with her cane, as though she were a giant of a man, punting at Cambridge. She paced to the other edge, near Iffy—though she gave no sign of seeing him—and then she whirled.

It was clearly an unpractised move: she staggered, but recovered her footing, and laughed aloud.

She seemed to have forgotten her body's deformity, but he could not ignore it. Her left arm was entirely withered, and the crumples in the green, ivy-patterned satin of the left side of her bodice showed that half of her body was withered, too. No doubt only the support of her orthotic garments could keep her straight and upright. Cut by the joy which sprang from her, unbroken, Iffy could not bear it. He fled, back through the rat-walk tunnel, and into the auditorium.

Only the front lights were on, warming the velvet front curtain of the stage. There were two male, unhatted figures in the front stall seats.

Donning his frock coat, Iffy walked along the aisle toward the front row, where Mr Denman and the girl's father were sitting, smoking, then waited.

Mr Denman stood up, and gestured for Iffy to approach. 'Sir, may I present Mr Godfrey Pearson, who put the Floor together for me? Mr Pearson, may I present Sir Thomas Burchett.'

Sir Thomas stood up slowly, holding the younger man in his gaze. He accepted Iffy's bow with one of his own, then raised the Russian cigarette to his lips once more. In the enamelled Fabergé holder, the glowing cigarette could not endanger the man's thick beard. Speaking through a tide of smoke, he commented, 'My daughter was delighted with the ballet.'

'I am glad, sir. Mr Denman's ballet and dramatic troupes are very fine.'

'Tell me, how much does it cost to install such a Floor?'

'Sir, it is not the installation, so much as the electrical requirement. Mr Denman was obliged to install a separate Tesla generator for the Floor alone, lest the surge in demand knock out half of Greenwich on ballet nights. I believe the Faraday Floor has a fine future, Sir Thomas, but mostly for institutions, for example the theatre, and certainly spas and nursing homes... perhaps the grandest of ballrooms.'

'Ballrooms!' The man's thick eyebrows rose expressively. 'Do the dancers not simply spin off, and stagger about drunkenly? Whenever I am underway, by rail or sea, or in the air, I must walk carefully. Surely not everyone can dance in Faraday lightness, as those dancers did on stage last night. They have trained for this.'

'The matching centrifugal force of a pair of dancers creates a kind of gravity between them, Sir Thomas. No-one is flung anywhere.'

'Hm.' The bear-man glanced at the stage curtain. 'Before she fell ill with the infantile paralysis at thirteen years of age, my daughter Cosima loved to dance. She danced with all her older sisters, and all of their friends, as they were preparing for their Seasons. Now she can scarcely hold herself upright, so she has not danced since. Would you dance with my daughter now, Mr Pearson?'

Her name was Cosima. Order. Cosmos, not a damnable Void which every country wanted to capture.

Iffy's heart throbbed painfully. 'I would be honoured, sir, if she agrees.'

The three men climbed onto the stage and pushed through the curtains. Cosima Burchett was still in motion: striding energetically across the expanse. Her gait stuttered as she saw them emerging from the other side of the curtain.

She met Iffy's gaze for a moment, without shyness, as though to say, 'Look at me, then,' and then turned her head to listen politely to her father's introduction. She curtsied correctly, even lightly, a movement which ought to have been exquisitely arduous.

Iffy bowed deeply.

'Thank you, I would love to dance,' she said quietly.

Hypnotised, Iffy approached her, and bowed again.

The strains of a Viennese waltz thrummed across the stage, and he clasped her in the correct waltzing pose, then sprang lightly into the steps of the dance.

The waltz made them whirl, but as he had promised her father, they were balanced on either side of the turning fulcrum, and never lost one another. Underneath Cosima's skirt, her mis-paired legs wove invisibly fast, matching Iffy's momentum. She held his gaze, as though connected and drawing Tesla power from him. The stage lights shone brightly on her perspiring forehead and cheeks.

When the end of the music approached, Cosima's eyelids began to quiver. She blinked rapidly, as though she were calculating her landing.

At the final note, Iffy unwound their last whirl and set her down gently.

'It is finished, isn't it?' she asked quietly.

Iffy nodded, stepping back. 'For now. Everyone here in the theatre will soon be preparing for the show.'

'And you?'

'I am on call here a few nights a week until just before Christmas, to ensure the season gets off to a good start.'

He glanced at the side of the stage, where her father was standing, expressionless, beside the lady's maid. 'Shall I fetch your cane, Miss Burchett?'

'Yes, please.'

He took the cane from the lady's maid and brought it back to her as she stood upright in the centre of the stage. Then he accompanied her, lifting her gloved hand just slightly, as she strode toward the edge.

On the brink, she looked at him. Inside the glove, she was trembling; yet, rather than have the machine turned off underneath her, she stepped off.

Iffy watched Sir Thomas muffle Cosima's warm body in Russian fur, and turn her to leave the stage. Her father handled her gently, but as though she were a puppet.

For all of Iffy's twenty-three years, people had generally teemed around him, yet some inscrutable Faraday-like force had lightly repelled him from others. With Cosima, that force was switched off, and it was an effort to climb out of her gravity, when all he wanted was to fall to ground. Even a distant, chaste orbit would be *something*. It was madness, but he loved her.

Home Harbour

December passed. As the nominal male head of the London office, Iffy signed three hundred and seven Christmas cards from the Company to clients, including a card to Sir Thomas and his family in Manchester.

His Christmastide sales at Deede's brought relief from his tailor's debt and Club dues, accumulated in the several months since he had left university. He also sold his tale of the spy-camera to a magazine in early December, and was paid on the 20th, meaning he could pay for the presents he had ordered, and could also buy his ticket for the trip home.

On December 21st, therefore, he left the company motorcar at Euston for transport to Manchester, then followed himself, by atmospheric train.

His carriage, though Third Class, was comfortable until the pneumatic doors closed, the Faraday engaged and the floating train was punched out of Euston by a ram of compressed air. The tunnel was blessed with daylight from the glass panels, but thick glass and the curved surface distorted the view. Shearing and squashing images of city and countryside, the jerks of acceleration after pumping stations, wobbling in the Moon-like Faraday lightness, and the air-pressure in the cabin were all making him feel somewhat sick.

The man opposite him hid behind a giant spread of The Times, such that Iffy could see nothing of the man, but everything of the report on how the Russian Baltic Fleet was faring in its long voyage around Africa towards the East and the war with Japan. In a marginal column, he could just see the headline about strikes elsewhere in the Russian Empire.

He closed his eyes. War never came alone. With it always came the high-ranking cowards, the political schemers, the profiteers, and they nourished all the discontentments which they had long ignored.

He opened his eyes and looked at his watch, trying to calculate how long it would be before he was delivered from pressurised purgatory.

It was after three o'clock when the atmospheric reached Manchester Piccadilly. With his rucksack strapped to his back, Iffy alighted into the young capital's air of commerce, coal smoke and confident, flat-vowel speech, and headed along the platform towards the cargo warehouse.

'Iffy!'

He halted. The acoustics of the place were baffling, and it took him some moments to spot his brother Arthur, who had become entangled with a family group mobbing another prodigal son redeemed from London in time for Christmas.

Iffy circled the group and extended his hand to his brother. 'I did wire that I would have the 'car. There was no nee–'

Arthur shifted his grip to Iffy's shoulders. 'Francis was nearly killed last week.'

Iffy stared at his brother. The square face, straight dark eyebrows, well-trimmed beard, frank hazel eyes: all were just the same as ever, yet Iffy could not put them together into a face.

Arthur shook him for emphasis. 'Last week, at Way High.'

Iffy blinked.

'It's very close to Port Arthur.'

'I know that, but he's a… a… civil servant!'

Now that Iffy had finally answered, Arthur dropped his arms. 'There's plenty of rattle when a siege is going on over the water, even for a civil servant drinking tea miles away—*if* that's where he was.'

'Oh, God!' Iffy said violently, shoving at his brother, and staggering a little himself, as his rucksack pulled at him. 'I don't want to hear of anything else he might have been engaged in.'

Arthur sniffed. 'Well, Mr Mufti, you'll be ashamed when the whole world is in uniform and you're still playing lily of the field.'

'The Empire needs money,' Iffy snapped. 'Who's going to make the bloody money which pays for all of your dreadnaughts? Now, is Mother at home?'

'Ye-'

'Then let's get my motorcar and I'll drive you.' He twitched away from Arthur's hands, and set off at a fast pace, weaving through the crowd.

Arthur sulked while Iffy uncovered and checked over his motorcar. Finding everything in order, Iffy got into the driver's seat and free-wheeled it off the ramp into the cargo aisle, then got out to push it along to the fuel station.

'New fuel, please. Five gallons.'

The cargo station manager frowned at him. 'New fuel's tenpence t'gallon. Stuff from t'siphon's eight.'

'I don't know what stuff other people put in their 'cars, so I'd like new fuel, please.' Arthur climbed into the passenger seat and folded his arms across his dark grey civilian wool overcoat. His silence was not patient: he was frowning hard, as though willing his brother to question him.

Overseeing the refilling of his motorcar, Iffy examined his brother out of the corner of his eye. Even brooding like that, Arthur's face looked something like Francis's, but it was still a different face, a less dear face; hard to look at without wanting to rearrange it: tweak the ears out a bit, make the mouth smile and the skin around the eyes crinkle.

Iffy drove slowly and carefully out of the warehouse garage.

'Another new 'car, then?' Arthur said finally.

'It belongs to Deede's. The company, that is.'

'Oh, yes, the shop girl in the show room.'

Iffy ignored the opportunity to repeat the official lie about managing the London office. 'I'm not often in the show room. Mr Deede wants me to show how modern products look on a young man about town.'

Arthur smirked. 'A mannequin, then.'

Iffy pressed his lips together and drove.

Navigating the edge of Manchester—where seething pumping stations punted the atmospheric trains along their viaducts—Iffy remained alert to the traffic, a dangerous mix of pedestrians, motorists and horse-drawn vehicles.

They penetrated the neighbourhood of Victorian and new 'Edwardian' villas built in the last decade, and found the decorative red and black brick façade of 'Wisteria Lodge' behind its box hedge.

Iffy reached down into the green Chesterfield armchair to embrace his mother, whose lavender halo also smelled faintly of laudanum. Iffy kissed her on both cheeks and took his own seat on the end of the Chesterfield sofa. Arthur had already taken the only other armchair.

They were all silent, apart from the grandfather clock behind Iffy's mother. That giant wooden column, which stood between two of the darkening windows, showed them nearly twenty-five past four. Some Christmas cards had been strung up across the fireplace mantel, beneath the woven evergreen boughs, but tucked under the left-hand edge of the garland was an untidy collection of unopened letters, cards and telegrams.

His mother lifted her head, and looked at him directly. There were Francis's eyes again, only swollen with tears. She sighed and twisted her handkerchief in her lap.

Iffy felt heavy. Christmas-tide in the naval soup would be bitterer than ever this year.

True to family form, all conversation was nautical, and communication between the four men was as terse as telegraphy. Their father formed the brooding low-pressure point, to Arthur's stormy gusts. Iffy and Horatio tacked away from them as much as possible, and their mother remained secluded, as though in dry dock, lifted away from them all, with a terrible gash in her heart and hull.

On the morning of Christmas Eve, before breakfast, Iffy went out to the back terrace, where the Christmas tree was waiting in a bucket of frozen water. He knocked the light snow off the tree, wincing at the jauntiness with which the hanging boughs bounced up. The snow-powder sparkled slightly in the early light which planed through the garden's back hedge. In the few years she had lived here, their mother had worked hard to create order: there were low, clipped hedges, and lawn-edges as neat and right-angled as a naval husband could require, yet they formed the frame for softer lines of lavender, whose scent perfumed the house and also the teas and jams which she made every year.

Movement in the house caught his eye: a hand behind the glass of the morning-room window, beckoning. Iffy raised his own hand in acknowledgement and went back into the house to join his eldest brother.

Horatio was seated in front of a most un-naval collection of sweet pastries. 'Morning.'

'Morning.'

Iffy preferred the savoury viands of breakfast: bacon and kippers, with scrambled eggs and toast. Everything had been left in chafing dishes by their servants, so they were alone.

'How are you faring?' Horatio asked. 'Are you in funds, or parched?'

Iffy shrugged. 'Things were a bit tricky when I came down from Cambridge, and I sold the 'car, but I have plenty of wit to live on. Still no need for Pa's allowance.'

'How is the new job? Manager? Deede's is well known in Manchester and London. I even know a Woolwich man who went to them for a patent.'

'If that was Captain Jervis, I heard about it from Young Mr Deede. Jervis ended up selling the damned thing directly to the War Office and Deede's got nothing. It's a state secret now, so no-one will earn a penny from it, not even the Crown. Mr Deede hasn't touched a naval inventor since, and has forbidden me to do anything but pass the details on to the War Office directly. We get kudos, rather than money, but don't waste any effort. But, listen, I don't want to talk about money. I want to know how Mother and Father are.'

Horatio shook his head. 'As you would expect. Ma's holed below the waterline, but Pa's bearing up, and expects us to, too. He's been saying he's proud of us.'

'Even of me?'

Horatio coughed.

'… given that he thinks I'm less likely to die in battle than to electrocute myself with an iron,' Iffy finished off, smiling slightly. 'Or so he thinks. Not only am I a modern gentleman, with a trouser press rather than an iron, I deal with plenty of more dangerous gadgets than irons. I suppose you haven't seen the clippings—they would have arrived a few weeks ago, and... well, we have other things to think about now—but I recently installed a Faraday Floor for a theatre. *That* current would electrocute the crew complement of a dreadnaught, yet here I am.'

Horatio straightened up. 'Faraday devices are dangerous?'

'No, no. Of course it's always dangerous to connect electricity, but once in the grid, everything flows smoothly enough.'

Horatio's lips tightened, as though he were trying to hold back a comment—no doubt about a fourth-class degree—then he said, 'We'll bring the tree inside before lunch.'

Iffy nodded.

'Mother wanted us to take down all the decorations.'

Iffy found himself unable to soften his tone. 'Why are you surprised?'

'This is a naval family.'

'She never expected it to be Francis. What actually happened to him?'

Horatio sipped his hot chocolate, and blotted his moustache. 'He lost an arm.'

Iffy's guts turned over. These pangs of cowardice were becoming stronger. 'That's a hell of an accident for a civil servant! People seem to be losing all self-restraint. We kept the peace—or kept the wars small—for so long, but now there are wars and strikes left and right. Peace won't last.'

'Why do you want peace so desperately?'

'Why do you want war?'

Horatio shook his head. 'Iffy, you would be a fine naval man if it were a matter of sunny patrols in Indian waters, with your brass buttons spiffed and all equipment working, but–'

'Yes, that's exactly it! I like equipment when it's working. I like making equipment work. I don't like equipment which kills and wrecks. I like....

'I met a young lady recently, Hortie. She's crippled, but she holds herself upright, *and* walks, thanks to invention. When she stood on that Faraday Floor in the theatre, she– *she could dance!* I danced with her, and—my God—*that* is a modern miracle. *That* is what I love. *That* is what peace is for, so that we can save our money for life, and health, rather than destroying all of our wealth and invention with warfare.'

Iffy stopped speaking abruptly.

Horatio shook his head. 'The British Empire has *suppressed* war through the sheer size of her naval and Void fleets–'

'Threatening war to keep the peace isn't working anymore. We've had war with the Boers–'

The door opened, and Arthur came in. Under his tan, his face was sallow and puffy and, when the morning light hit it, he showed the weather lines of a naval man's face.

"Morning,' Horatio greeted him, then turned back to Iffy. 'How long do you think our vast Navy and armed forces will enjoy keeping the peace? There *has* to be a war.'

'Exactly! Why build up the forces so that there *must* be a war? It's perverse, and too many people will suffer for the enjoyment of those–'

Arthur interrupted. 'When the Forces expand, they bring more and more men into the fellowship of patriots.'

'And lose them again when they're killed!'

'Will you still be cold-footing it when the rest of the country is in uniform?' Arthur retorted. 'Francis having his arm blown off is proof there's no hiding behind the lines.'

'Or will you still be waltzing with your *young lady* on a poodle-faking Faraday dance Floor?' Horatio put in.

Iffy swallowed. Even his eldest brother was angry now.

'Young lady?' Arthur repeated.

Iffy felt himself flinch. He pushed himself out of his chair and picked up his plate, coffee cup and saucer.

'Go, on, then,' Horatio told him. 'If you even run away from an argument, you'll be of no use in battle.'

'I *know*,' said Iffy, through gritted teeth. 'But I can make things work, and help people make money, so why not just leave me in peace to do that, for God's sake?'

'Don't you dare go and repeat any of this to Ma,' Horatio warned.

Iffy shook his head. 'She and I have got other things to talk about.'

'Why not tell her about *your young lady* instead?' Arthur gibed. 'A young lady. Really!'

When Iffy closed the door, it was with a slam.

Iffy entered his mother's room with a tray of coffee. The room was bright with daylight and orderly, and she had dressed for the day.

As his mother gazed quietly at her garden from her dressing table chair, Iffy watched her sideways, arranging the china and vacuum flask of coffee by touch. The streams of coffee and milk steamed, twisting down into the cups from the flask.

'Ma,' he prompted gently. 'You shouldn't be alone with Pa and...bloody Arthur. Why has no-one visited?'

'The FCO said we weren't to tell anyone yet, and even though he survived, I simply can't hide something like this.'

'Ah. So... he *was* doing something dangerous?'

'I don't know. It's a terrible thing to be a mother of men, Godfrey. Men make ridiculous secrets of their plans, and of their mistakes.' She pressed her lips together and blinked.

'Come on, Ma,' he said tenderly. 'Let me take you for a drive. The Deedes are At Home today, and their house is a damned sight more cheerful than ours.'

The Deedes had built their house long before the Court had brought its train to the city, and it was proudly Victorian, without any new 'Edwardian' flourishes of stained glass and Art Nouveau mullions.

A jumble of motorcars blocked all the kerbs nearby, so Iffy parked a street away, and walked back with his mother to the front door. Just before

Christmas, it was adorned with the soft, sinuous ever-green of ivy and the sharp, glossy ever-green of holly. The electrical sconces flanking the front door blazed through the afternoon dusk.

The whole family was At Home, from Old Mr Deede to the great-grandchildren, whose toy boxes in the parlour overflowed with the richness of British industry, and even some German toys offered by some of the family's well-to-do friends. The *plinking* of metallic music from the wind-ups mingled with the more musical tinkling of a player-piano in the parlour and the cheerful conversation of some thirty guests: ladies, gentlemen and their children.

Iffy settled his mother in a chair next to the player-piano, and went to fetch her some punch. When he returned, he saw that her head had begun to nod in time to the piano's lively arrangement of *The Holly and the Ivy*.

She took her glass of punch and sipped it.

Seating himself next to her, Iffy spoke. 'There are ridiculous secrets, and there is discretion. Now, Ma, let me pull my veil of discretion around you and tell you a nice secret, for a change. It's about a young lady I've met.'

She sat back abruptly. 'Really? Who is she? Have you declared yourself? Oh, Godfrey, what will you live on?'

Iffy put his hand on hers. 'No declarations. You're quite right that I'm too poor yet to marry, but I *am* beginning to make money.'

'If your father hadn't cut you off–'

'–I still couldn't afford to marry. An allowance isn't an income. All fathers understand that, hers included. Don't worry, Ma, there's money in this world. Look at what the Deedes have, from selling the best of British industry. I'll make my way.'

She gave a distracted glance away from him, around the parlour. 'How did you meet her?'

'I first saw her at work, when she was a client of Mrs Farthing, and then she went to the theatre to see my programme–'

'Is there a *Who's Who* in the house?'

'Not here and now, Ma! I have looked up her father, though. Sir Thomas Burchett, of   Rossiya-Vostock Metal Import, and Burchett & Orme-Philmey Wiring.'

'Where do they live?'

'Manchester and Stoke, but in London Sir Thomas is a member of the St Petersburg Kensington Society, the Travellers' Club and the East India Club... unfortunately where I have no entrée.'

His mother's white brow crinkled. 'Oh, Godfrey, you'll need quite a bit to support a wife from such a family. But you needn't go into the Navy. A young man like you could be of great use to… to… why won't you go and see Harry at the War Office? He needs–'

There was that watery feeling in his guts again. Quickly, Iffy plucked up her other hand and kissed it. He glanced around the room for their hosts. The player-piano was covering their conversation, now with *I Saw Three Ships*. 'Please don't say such things. I have given my word to Mr Deede and Mrs Farthing, and will stay where I am.'

'Will I meet them today?'

Iffy nodded. 'They will come through, or we might join them in another room.'

His mother set down her punch glass and held out her hand. 'It's over-warm in here, with the fire and the punch. Let us find them.'

In the drawing room, Mrs Farthing greeted Iffy with something approaching warmth, and smiled civilly at his mother. 'Mrs Pearson, your son has brought us some new orders from an old client. Mr Pearson, Sir Thomas said Miss Burchett did require a Verity cane. He also thanks you again for your kindness in helping her to use the Faraday Floor.'

Young Mr Deede approached from behind his sister. He clapped Iffy on the shoulder and bowed to Mrs Pearson. 'Is this your mother? We are pleased with your young man, madam. Now, tell me, when do you lose him to London again?'

Iffy answered quickly, 'Right after Christmas. I want to travel before the Tubes are mobbed.'

'Wait until New Year for the Russian ball,' said Young Mr Deede. 'Thanks to their calendar, their Christmas comes afterwards, *and* they've got money to spend.' With a playful smile for his sister and Mrs Pearson, he added, 'When my sister returns to London, let her come back to a list of new orders; in fact, don't wait: wire us with every new order.'

'A wire message for every order, sir? I could not presume to tax our profits like that!'

Mr Deede laughed. 'Perhaps one day you *will* be our manager, with that care for the pennies.'

Feeling the gentle squeeze of his mother's gloved hand, Iffy smiled.

Even in the swarm northwards to the new English capital, the Russian Empire had secured a fine palace for its embassy, outside Heaton Park.

Iffy left home as early as decently possible, and parked the company's 'car beside the Embassy. Wind gusted along the street, zig-zagging between the pale neo-Kensington stucco façades, and then the deep-throated sound of a cannon-shot ricocheted. Iffy checked his watch. It was eight o'clock, well before the fireworks he had been told to expect at nine and twelve—midnight in the two Imperial capitals, St Petersburg and Manchester.

The palace had been built around its gardens, and the ballroom lay at the centre of the two curving wings. Iffy entered the room to a lilt of chamber music and a cry of 'Mr Godfrey Pearson!'

The garden wall was all window. Behind the musicians' stage, on the left, a green-house was green indeed, with vines and flowers all vividly coloured in the warm gas lights.

'Mr Pearson, welcome!'

Iffy turned to the speaker, a man in his early thirties, dressed in the blue and red uniform of the Czar's Life Guards.

'May I introduce myself? Lieutenant Ivan Ivanovich Kizhé.' Someone had taught him not to wallow too much in his Ls and Rs, and his accent was very slight. The light brown mutton-chop whiskers were likewise remarkably un-foreign, bushy enough to be respectable even on a middle-aged Englishman. Otherwise, his triangular face could have been any man's, framed with pomaded waves of hair. Only the uniform made him splendid.

Iffy bowed to him. 'Good evening, Lieutenant. How do you do?'

'Please come. I shall present you to the ambassador now.'

They found Count Benckendorff amongst the ice-sculptures, looking up at the façade of a church. On the square-bodied, encrusted Baroque foundation, the onion domes sat oddly.

Kizhé performed the presentation with élan, and Iffy had only a moment to formulate a polite question for the ambassador, as to which church was represented.

The diplomat's deep-set eyes travelled over Iffy's face. 'It is the St Nicholas Naval Cathedral.'

The church was breathing a cold draught. Iffy shivered, as though he were at sea. 'What an extraordinary feat of engineering.'

The ambassador nodded. 'You will see more ice at our ball this night, Mr Pearson. Lieutenant, please remember that I rely on your help for the fireworks.'

'Yes, Your Excellency.'

Kizhé steered Iffy away, into the right-hand corner of the ballroom, an enclosure entered through an enormous, meltwater-sheened triumphal arch of ice. Kizhé swept his hand grandly at it as they passed underneath. 'The Narva Gate, celebrating the victory over Napoleon's *Grande Armée*, a victory completed by Russian winter!'

Wild yells lanced out from the wedge-shaped block of ice on a table, with a channel ironed down the face of it. The bottom lip, where young men in dress uniform clustered to lap the flowing vodka, was already worn into a bowl. The raw, slushy air dampened the smell somewhat, but there was vodka being liberally spilled.

'The *Samogon* Luge! A favourite winter entertainment.' Kizhé slapped Iffy on the shoulder. 'We will meet again after the fireworks at nine, since I have a commission to discuss with you.'

Kizhé's released his firm grasp on Iffy's shoulder and marched off.

Another young Regimental approached the base of the ice slope and shouted for the pouring to begin.

'The bottle's empty!'

A red-coated Northumberland Fusilier made a grab for one of the bottles lined up on the table, but missed, toppling three onto the marble floor.

'Oh, dear, trust a rifleman to be cockeyed,' sang out another, who shouldered his way to the front and seized another bottle with a sure touch. 'We grenadiers can lay our hands on any cylinder even when our blood is more than half whisky!' He bustled up the ladder to the top of the Luge.

A martial trumpet cut across the chamber music, and the men around Iffy all came to attention.

'Fireworks!'

They buffeted him in their eagerness to make their way outside. Iffy let them go. Young Mr Deede would forgive him for shunning young bucks who could be kept amused with trifles as un-patentable as a block of ice. And it wouldn't do to be drunk when Kizhé came back to discuss that 'commission.' He scanned the crowd.

The solid older men, eating water biscuits and black caviar at the buffet table, were officers, too, but at least they weren't drinking, and the Royal Engineer was wearing a fine—and decidedly civilian—gold watch. Iffy approached, nodding politely to them.

Just then, the first crack of fireworks came, and the ballroom's glass windows lit up in a brilliant gold light. The three officers abandoned the table, too, hurrying to the French doors.

To hell with them, Iffy thought, and drifted that way.

There, in the warm orangerie, seated in one of a pair of comfortable wicker armchairs, was his young lady. Cosima Burchett.

Feux d'Artifice, and True Love

The brilliant firework colours flickered over her dark hair and pale skin. She sat with her right hand braced on the chair-arm and her withered left arm in the hand of an elderly lady, who sat bolt upright, facing the garden window, completely consumed by the display which filled the air with cracking, fizzing thunder.

Cosima's head dipped as she looked at her brooch-watch. Iffy found himself checking his own wrist-watch. It was five minutes past nine. She did not look back to the window, but set her shoulders back and gazed into her lap. Iffy stared at the tender curve at her neck. It was so delicate, yet it supported the weight of her head, with all its abundant dark hair and her woven crown of wired silk apple blossom.

There was no telling how long the display might continue. Judging from the enthusiastic wailing which could be heard in between fusillades, the Embassy's guests might revolt if the display were cut short.

Iffy approached.

She raised her head. In the heated, perfumed air of the orangerie, her cheeks showed pink against the pallor of her thin, sharp-featured face.

'Mr Pearson!' she exclaimed.

'What's that?' asked the old lady, without looking. The reflections of the fireworks danced in the soft pale hairs of her faded blonde *chevelure*.

'Aunt Anne, this is the gentleman who created the Faraday Floor!'

Now the other lady turned around, though with some difficulty, and, plunging past the question of introduction, beamed at him. 'Cosima and I spoke of your Floor in our Christmas cards to the Imperial Family, and now here you are! They must have sent for you!'

'Oh, no, madam,' he demurred. 'I am more humble, having benefited from my employer's invitation to attend the ball.'

'Of course you were invited. Cossie mentioned you most particularly. I was in waiting to Princess Helena, and we went to Russia in '97, you know! I still exchange cards with the Empress every year!'

Iffy's eyes widened. *Who's Who* had indicated Sir Thomas's business interests in Russian ores and metal, but Iffy had thought the gentleman's Russian fur hat an affectation.

'I told Her Imperial Highness of dear Cossie's troubles—Her Imperial Highness has her own health troubles—and how the Floor had worked, and Her Imperial Highness was most interested. Of course, it would be an extraordinary ballroom floor, and a mere *bagatelle* for the Romanoffs, but the value for dear Cossie is much greater than that!'

'Aunt Anne, please!'

Cosima turned back to Iffy. The blush had sunk back into her pallor, leaving her greenish-pale—or perhaps it was the glass-house flora. Faint circles showed up under her eyes. She was not one for powders and rouge. 'I have not–' she began, then paused, as Iffy came closer, leaning toward her.

'I am sorry, Miss Burchett, I could not hear.'

'Sit with us for a bit,' Aunt Anne directed. 'The show will be over soon, and Cossie will take me home. I cannot wait for English midnight, so we always say that Russian midnight will have to do!'

Iffy hastened to fetch another chair and drew it up on Miss Burchett's side, further from her aunt.

'As I was saying, I haven't been indiscreet, I hope. I'm no-one to them, really, just a story, as in the illustrated papers, about a poor crippled girl, but I–' Cosima cast a swift glance at her aunt, who had turned back to gaze at the spectacle '—write to them for her sake. She spent so many years in various courts, and was so distressed when her heart trouble meant she could no longer wait at Court. She has only her correspondence left, and I think that she sometimes writes more words in a day than she utters. However, words clearly have power. They brought you here.'

Her gaze was straight and penetrating—though why should she be demure? She could not seek a husband, so need not care about propriety.

'After all,' she continued, 'her words helped her half-sister—my mother—to a good establishment–'

Now she did blush, and falter. The fireworks seemed to be ending now, too. Miss Burchett took a deep breath.

'It is a relief to have that over and done with,' he said quickly.

She nodded. 'They've been firing every hour since yesterday, marking off midnight in every time zone of the Russian Empire. There was even a shot for Alaska, though that has not been a part of the Empire for a decade! Then they put on a fusillade in the afternoon, to indicate midnight sweeping over the war with the Japanese.'

'Very brave,' Iffy blurted out. He stopped speaking abruptly, as the green-house doors clashed open.

Iffy and Cosima watched the guests shedding the borrowed fur cloaks, which started to form a pile under a small fan-palm tree. Diamonds and gold braid caught the light, and a variety of European languages sparkled in the air. Aunt Anne seemed entranced by the new, impromptu spectacle.

Holding fast to his position in the wicker seat, Iffy murmured, 'I knew that the Russians were fond of their uniforms, but it seems as though there are scarcely any gentlemen here tonight.'

Cosima inclined her head slightly. 'Russian nobles and gentlemen are almost always in uniform in public, thanks to Peter the Great's Table of Ranks, but... yes, it's true. I've never seen so many of the European guests in dress uniform.'

'Even the diplomats,' he agreed.

'You move in diplomatic circles?' she asked, in a murmur.

Iffy shrugged. 'I make my living on my wits, Miss Burchett. I haven't an establishment yet, but I am always around those who have. Some are very fine establishments.'

'And that is what you will make your living on?'

'Yes. My post at Deede's is... more solid than anything else I've done, and I will stick it, so I can afford to marry.'

She smiled suddenly, then realised what she had admitted, and dropped her gaze for a moment. Then her head was up again, level, and she was facing him directly. 'Mr Pearson, would you write to me?'

Words clearly have power. They brought you here. He felt a thrill of warmth, that she could answer his own indiscretion with one of her own.

'If... if it will not cause trouble for you,' he faltered. 'I would not for the world cause you any unpleasantness.'

She was speaking more softly now, as well. 'Father knows my likely future as a spinster, and allows me to correspond widely. Not just paying my respects to Aunt Anne's correspondents.' She glanced sideways at her aunt. 'She looked up your father.'

'*Did* she?'

'Ernest Michael Edward, R.N., Commander. Four sons, the youngest Godfrey Douglas, born 1881... Faraday College Chatham, New College Cambridge, Engineering. Yet you didn't go into the Navy.'

'That isn't what Cambridge engineering is for. That isn't what life is for.'

The account of his life from a book, from an aunt who had also taken an interest in him, was beginning to make him feel drunk.

When she nodded, he continued, in a rush, 'That's why no-one calls me Godfrey. As fourth son, I was permitted a name suitable for the Church, just in case. However, no-one really wanted that. They expected the Navy, and I'm known as 'Iffy' because I was... unpredictable, unreliable. It is simply inexplicable that I don't want my head blown off, as happened to a great-uncle, and now that my only brother not serving under arms has *lost his arm*, I am apparently unreasonable to want to stay even further away from the front line!'

'And even if you did take holy orders, they might still suggest you be a chaplain to one of those ghastly dreadnaughts,' she chimed.

She had uttered one of his own fears. He exhaled deeply. 'You don't like war, then?'

'I hate it.'

He took her hand, the withered one. It lay so lightly in his grasp that he wondered whether she could feel him at all.

Yet she leaned closer. 'I know that I would have been safer if I had been kept at home by warfare, rather than travelling with Papa as he traded, since it was in Egypt that I fell ill. Something in the water, apparently. However, I cannot help but feel pity for anyone who is crippled by war.'

'Or killed,' he added.

'Yes. I have my life, and I am grateful for it.'

'What- what would you do with that life, if you could?'

She looked directly at him. 'I would marry a man who is kind and gentle, and bear him children, for us both to love. Of course, I... cannot have children, but... I still long for kindness.'

She paused for a moment to breathe. Her breath trembled on Iffy's cheek, like the fore-echo of a sob.

However, her voice was steadier as she concluded, 'Your domestic tableau at the theatre was what I would do with my life.'

He kept hold of her hand. 'That is... not quite what I want. I wouldn't be the father returning from the sea only for Christmas—that was to please our patriotic audience, and that is the only sort of Christmas I know. I also wouldn't leave my gifts in my place... However, those gifts do represent money, and... I would clearly need money to marry.'

'My father—'

'Your father keeps you, of course. However, it's not right and proper that he should keep you *and* your husband. I must be able to offer my own establishment.'

They fell silent. The crowd had left the green-house, and had been subdued by the music of the ball room. Aunt Anne had fallen asleep. Finally, Cosima slipped her hand out of Iffy's and leaned over to touch her aunt gently on the arm. The lady stirred, but did not wake.

'It's too late for her,' Cosima whispered to Iffy. 'I was meant to escort her home at nine, after His Excellency wished her a Happy New Year in Russian.'

'I can support her, but that would leave you without assistance.'

With a smile, she shook her head. 'You have already offered me far more than... assistance. And I have the spring cane you recommended.'

She allowed him to take her elbow and gently lift her to her feet. Then she stepped away to give him space to wake and assist Aunt Anne.

The elderly lady swayed a bit, so Iffy tucked her against himself as though they were promenading upon the dance floor. He caught Cosima's dark-eyed gaze on the tiny figure of her aunt, and he felt warmer, imagining Cosima there instead, her greater height bringing her ear within reach, so they could converse while he held her upright....

'My mother and father should be inside,' said Cosima.

She turned to stalk slowly—really, she used the spring cane with wonderful grace—toward the French doors.

In the ballroom, men in the dress of gentlemen were few indeed, and Cosima easily found her father, conducting her mother in a genteel *polonaise*.

Everyone else had noticed, too. The group of young Regimentals had reunited by the Luge and appeared to be challenging two civilian gentlemen to a relay race of spirits.

Sir Thomas led his wife away from the floor and joined Iffy with Cosima and her aunt by the French doors.

Cosima's mother took hold of her sister with a physical robustness belied by the soft pink and gauzy drape of her silk dress. Like her daughter, she looked directly at Iffy, as though assessing him. He bowed correctly, and waited to be introduced.

'My dear, this is Mr Pearson, who put together that famous Faraday Floor. Mr Pearson, this is my wife, Lady Charlotte. I see you have already met Miss Gordon.'

The half-sisters were both golden—Miss Gordon somewhat silvered—leaving Cosima to her dark-haired, dark-eyed father. He slipped his arm into hers on her withered side, underpinning her, and he turned back to Iffy, examining him again.

A voice sounded from behind. 'Ladies! Sir Thomas! Mr Pearson!'

It was Lieutenant Kizhé. He clicked his heels, an insistent sound.

Sir Thomas bowed. 'Good evening, Lieutenant.'

'A Happy New Year to you, Sir Thomas!' returned the other, mirroring the bow. 'Please forgive me: I must abstract Mr Pearson from you to discuss his commission.'

'By all means.' Sir Thomas smiled, and Iffy's heart leaped.

Does he know?

Lady Charlotte waved indulgently. 'Mr Pearson must do his business. We shall take leave of Count Benckendorff then depart for home and bed.'

Still supporting his daughter, Sir Thomas bowed to both young men.

As the officer drew Iffy away, he felt a tugging against his heart and spared a last glance for Cosima. *That gravity again, a force that can cross the Cosmos.*

We will come back together.

The puddling foundations of the icy naval cathedral were deserted. Iffy's shoes sloshed against the floor. 'Yes, Lieutenant?'

'I had not time to speak of this earlier, and it was a confusion that you came alone, without Mr Deede to sanction our request. However, I have spoken to him by telephone, and he agrees to your trip to St Petersburg, where you will be introduced to Court and society.'

Iffy blinked. 'St Petersburg?'

Kizhé flourished a paper telegram. 'Mr Deede's acquiescence. He is assembling a collection of toys and gadgets and catalogues, which he will send direct to the docks.'

Catalogues. Commission. Cosima.

'How did all this happen? Mr Deede cannot have known; he told me to come in his place!'

Kizhé raised his elegant eyebrows. 'You have seen the Misses Gordon and Burchett. They must have told you about the correspondence.'

'Lieutenant Kizhé, be serious! Many gentlefolk write to royalty, but it rarely results in anything more than a picture card reply!'

Kizhé smiled tightly. 'The Romanoffs... exist on a different plane. You will see. Although they are aloof with many, they permit themselves some surprising intimacies.'

Correspondence with a former lady-in-waiting of another royal guest was perhaps a *surprising intimacy*, but making contact, through Miss Gordon, with an utterly unconnected young man was a matter for fairy tales.

Or spy stories.

How long have they been planning this?

It had been a mere month since he had danced with Cosima on the Faraday Floor. Autocrats were impatient, but could all of this really have been set in motion in such a short time?

'Let us away!' cried Lieutenant Kizhé. 'Mr Pearson, your carriage awaits. We drive to the docks tonight.'

Over the Horizon, Then Below

When they halted, it was too dark inside the motorcar for Iffy to see his watch. Lieutenant Kizhé, his brilliant uniform concealed by an English overcoat, sprang out of the closed compartment and beckoned.

Unlike the officer, Iffy was stiff and aching. He slid out of the 'car and had to dance aside as Kizhé flung the door closed.

Waving down the dark, deserted quay, the officer exclaimed, '*S balá na korabl!* The hero of *Oblomov*, of Goncharov... Goncharoff, I mean, goes "from the ship to the ball"! You are doing the opposite!'

Iffy smiled placatingly. 'That does sound very literary.'

All the lights stood behind them, stretching their shadows along the dock. Iffy peered at the only vessel moored here, a tiny tug. Quiet, steady streams of steam rose from the funnels, mixing with the darkness and the faint glow from the navigation cabin. Out in the dark channel, two cargo vessels were passing.

'You really mean we are to go to sea now?'

'Everything is packed—'

'*I* haven't packed!'

'There is a full wardrobe for you abroad... I mean to say *aboard*. Ha! From *aboard*, you will go *abroad*! Ha ha!'

Iffy shook his head. *That Goncharoff again.* 'Sir, are you drunk?'

'You agreed to go, and your master permits it. Why not now? No time like the present, as you say.' Again, Kizhé produced the telegram from Young Mr Deede, and waved it. 'Look what he says: 'Sending toys gadgets catalogues direct to docks. STOP. Awaiting many Russian orders. STOP. Don't hesitate seek represent Russian engineers. STOP. Nothing political. STOP. Best from all Deedes. STOP."

He seized Iffy's hand with a force that was closer to violence than enthusiasm, and towed him toward the tug, where the grip moved painfully to Iffy's upper arm, and Kizhé's body became the engine propelling them both to the edge of the quay.

Harsh electric light suddenly flooded the dock.

'Here is your whale, Jonah!' exclaimed Kizhé, holding Iffy straight to see the submersible low in the inky water behind the tug. A man in naval uniform, half-concealed in the forward turret of the vessel, saluted.

The sea was quiet, moved to mere ripples by the weak breeze. However, the air was sharply cold and cut at Iffy's hands and face. His eyes watered. He freed his left hand from Kizhé's hold, to wipe at his eyes, but with the water undulating shallowly across the broad, dark body of the strange vessel, lapping lightly at the open forward turret and the closed aft turret, its lines were difficult to make out. Newspapers portrayed these new terrors of the seas as darting eels, or balloon-like underwater Zeppelins, but Iffy knew sub-mariners from his father's acquaintance and the Up and Down Club; this would be a dark, stale space, and as narrow as a tomb.

Iffy's coat presented no defence against the chill. He began to tremble.

The man in the turret ducked and two other crew-members bustled out, levering a gang-plank into position between the deck of the submersible and the dock.

An intensification of Kizhé's grip gave warning that they were about to board.

Iffy's legs failed.

He slumped to the dock, momentarily hot with shame, before a cold flash of relief followed.

'*Chiort vozmi!*' Kizhé hissed, disentangling himself.

'C-can we not continue our journey above water?' Iffy stammered, gripping himself across the chest.

This damned cold!

Kizhé bellowed with laughter. 'Mr Pearson, do you not come from a naval family? Are you afraid?'

'Y-y-yes, why do you think I didn't go *into* the Navy? I *know*!' Iffy flung a glance at the whale-like back of the vessel in the black water. 'As b-b-bad as a Voidship for suffocating or drowning. N-no *thank you*!'

He kicked his legs out, shoving himself away from the officer, and fell against the leeching cold of the dock. The two seamen stared at him. Kizhé smiled, and took a single, deliberate step forward.

'I—' Iffy coughed, and tried again. 'I shall need very strong spirits to undertake such a voyage.'

Kizhé's grin became triumphant, and he gave a string of orders in Russian to the two sailors, who saluted him and set off at a run down the quay toward the silent motorcar.

The two sailors returned, swiftly carrying three trunks, and posted them through the hatch into the submersible. Kizhé said nothing.

Now shuddering uncontrollably in the cold, Iffy fixed his eyes on the back of the submersible, where stillness was slowly effacing the ripples, as though they were melting while he froze.

When Kizhé lifted him, Iffy could scarcely direct his own limbs. Nor did any sensation reach him from his legs. His transfer to the submersible was a mystery, and he cast his eyes up at the night's sky for a last moment's communion before that sense too was closed off.

Sealed, the vessel was as dark as the harbour, with only feeble strings of reddish light hinting at the secret forces which animated it.

Iffy found himself in an almost lightless berth. Kizhé was there, and strapped Iffy firmly into his seat. 'The tug will take us out. Drink quickly before we dive. We must descend, as your Shakespeare says, 'full fathom five'.'

The officer unlatched a trunk, pulled out a clear bottle from a bed of ice, and handed it over without a cup.

Iffy's stomach felt queasy at the sight of the spirits, sliding down the sides of the bottle's glass, as though they were a ring of transparent mermaids, all clinging to a single beloved. However, these sirens were the only ones who could save him from this place, and so he drank.

Kizhé was not drinking. 'Would you truly be less afraid to travel visibly, in the Imperial yacht *Shtandardt*, than to travel underwater, in a discreet submersible?' he asked.

'Yes!'

The other man shrugged lightly. 'As a consequence of the unpleasantness with Japan, Russia has no navy at her disposal in Europe, for the moment, at least. However, no one is prepared to lose such a treasure as the Imperial Family's yacht, and so money was found for a submersible.'

Feeling somewhat steadier after the mention of money, Iffy ventured, 'Can a submersible act as an ice-breaker? I understood the Baltic Sea was ice-bound.'

'Yes, indeed! Scabbed with ice, while all below swarming with German submersibles like maggots.' Kizhé was looking at him with a smile, as though mocking his cowardice. Iffy suppressed a shudder, but was unable to break that humorous, challenging gaze.

'However, we are not travelling to St Petersburg, but to *Romanóv-na-Múrman*.' The officer's crisp English pronunciation faltered over the name. Then his grin seemed to turn savage, and he added, 'Would you like to see the map?'

He drew an oilskin packet out of an inner pocket, and held up a thick curl of paper in the dim light. 'We travel north until the Nordkapp, then bear east into the Barents Sea. Though over six hundred miles further north than St Petersburg, Romanoff is ice-free – by sea, at least – and then we travel south overland some six hundred and fifty miles. Not ice-free.'

'I see-ee,' Iffy murmured, peering at the outlines of northern coasts, which seemed to ripple like currents. He took another gulp.

The officer flipped the folds of the map together, and slipped it neatly away. 'I imagined you more excited.'

'I–' Iffy straightened his posture and held the Russian's gaze. 'I am playing the rôle of an adventurer in a new market, but I am no soldier, Lieutenant. I am in business. I want to make a living so I can marry and live decently.'

'There is much money in Russia. You have met the father of your *inamorata*, have you not? Sir Thomas founded his fortune in India and the Mediterranean, but his daughter caught ill in Egypt, as you know. So, he returned to England and built a second fortune importing metal from Russia, for all the Faraday devices which you English make and break. He also exports English goods now and then, when he can supply something we desire.'

'*Vniz!*' called out one of the navigators.

'We plunge now,' Kizhé translated.

There was a gargantuan voiding belch from the tanks of the submersible, and her body tilted.

Iffy glutted himself directly from the bottle. The tiny vessel careened around him – the submersible was veering as she dived – and he struck his head and shoulder against a bulkhead.

The acidic spirits did not last long and Iffy unstoppered his mouth with a gasp while they were still in descent. Still he could not open his eyes. 'My God,' he whispered, 'are we being pursued?'

Somewhere nearby, Kizhé spoke calmly through the chaos. 'Only above the waves. Below, we shall escape detection a little while longer, and I hope as far as Romanoff. We are all anxious, are we not, about the fleets of Imperial Germany, plying the sea and the Void. Not peacefully like the English, but with insatiable desire to snoop and gobble up!'

The very idea of Imperial gobbling made Iffy feel sick again. He retched.

Seventy Degrees of Latitude, Ten of Frost

They saw no light of day at Romanoff-na-Murman, but the sensation of a sky beyond their own dimmed lights gave him breath again.

Iffy teetered unsteadily on the turret ladder – though Kizhé had ensured he would not be drunk for the disembarkation – but climbed out onto the gangplank himself and walked almost steadily down to the sailor on the dock, who was holding a light.

A sharp wind was blowing, but beside the man Iffy could smell hot metal from the shutter-lantern, and could see other sailors emerging from the underwater vessel, bringing out the trunks of samples from Deede's. Kizhé came last, moving lightly and wearing his ferocious grin.

He stopped on the dock next to Iffy and said casually, 'I must make arrangements, but Filip Petrovich will take you to meet me at the railhead.'

The light here was worse than at Liverpool, but the wind was stronger, and uncovered something new: there was a jagged edge to Kizhé's left ear, at the bottom, as though someone had once torn at him with bare hands. A little lower on his jaw, his mutton-chop whiskers were pressed open on the seam of another vicious scar.

'You have come back in time, Mr Pearson,' the officer continued calmly. 'Not only thirteen calendar days, but a century or more in some ways. You will breathe history. Our train in particular will please you.'

Numbly, Iffy nodded.

Kizhé strode along the dock, out of the circle of light, as though he were a wolf following his nose.

The railhead was just a fan of tracks with half the ribs missing. The main track ran southwards into emptiness, where a delayed Arctic sunrise was filtering through freezing mist. In the yard, there were no buildings except for the antiquated English passenger train-carriages of pre-Faraday vintage – neatly removed from their bogies and set up like cabins on the port side – and the scaffold-built control tower on the gate side, controlling the main line. Between these two elevations was the jumble of tracks and a capsized and burnt-out coal wagon.

One of the sailors had given Iffy a stick: he gripped it hard, jabbing it about in the snowed-over trash in front of his feet. The snow was piebald: grey ice here, soot-slush there, while around the shell of the coal-truck, the bones of the yard were bare and black.

'Come, Mr Pearson! Come!'

Iffy glanced up, but could not see Kizhé. Treading warily – for in spite of the new galoshes, he could scarcely feel his feet in the thin dress shoes from the ball – he followed the other sailor around the side of the wagon where the sun suddenly seemed warmer. Iffy blinked, trying to make sense of the bas-relief in black before him. Gigantic exposed wheels. A long, black cylinder, its seams studded with bolts...

A J15 steamer!

Such engines belonged in museums and engineering textbooks – *and, clearly, in backward countries.*

He started calculating the money someone must have recouped from the mass British scrapping after atmospheric trains were introduced, and that warmed him, even as the engine radiated heat from its boiler. Iffy found himself moving less clumsily as he made his way to the front carriage.

Two sets of doors baffled the cold and kept in the warmth from the stove. Kizhé had already doffed his coat and seated himself in one of the pistachio-silk striped Art Nouveau armchairs. 'Your trunks are in your cabin, one carriage back, Mr Pearson. There is no food aboard. We will collect provisions at Petrozavódsk.'

Awkwardly, Iffy began pulling off his outdoor clothes. Gloves. His useless dress overcoat. The galoshes were the most difficult to remove. He braced himself in one of the armchairs, then wedged his cold, insensible thumb under the rubber seal and shoved.

Peeled off, the galosh slumped to the floor, shedding slush onto the chequered plush carpet. Iffy hesitated over the mess, but tackled the other one. 'H-how long will it take to get to P-p-p–?'

'It depends on the state of the tracks, and whether we need to… negotiate tricky territory.'

Iffy looked up. 'Tricky with snow and ice? Or do you mean the strikes I've read about in the newspapers?'

Kizhé chuckled. 'You are a well-connected young man; you need not read the newspapers, but – yes, that may be.'

Iffy's gaze travelled around the saloon. All the lights were lit, both the bronze sconces on the walls and the table lamps in their silk shades.

The chuffing of the engine was becoming more insistent. Iffy sloughed off the second galosh. As the train jerked forward, he grabbed for the arm of the chair.

'It is unlike your atmospheric trains. I told you, did I not, that you would be travelling back in time?'

'Er… yes.'

'Of course there are glimpses of the future, even here. This track runs on pontoons across the tundra – the investors were most insistent on that.' Kizhé rang the bell, and a person emerged from the front door of the carriage, a new individual, austerely moulded in naval uniform, but so slight that it could have been male or female. Iffy's gaze was riveted on the faint sheen of the pistol at this person's hip.

'Tea,' the officer said, blandly.

'*Khoroshó*.' The newcomer met Iffy's eyes for a second, then pivoted in place and left.

'Is it – necessary to be armed?' Iffy asked.

'Always necessary. I am always armed. I am permitted to arm you, too, if you like. We must deliver you safely to Petersburg. Thanks to the intercession of *Mesdemoiselles Gordonne et Burchette si charmantes*, the Imperial Family has undertaken to protect you.'

'It is too generous of them to offer protection to someone who comes to Russia to sell goods,' Iffy ventured. 'Is there not another purpose? You mentioned a… another commission for me.'

'Of course there is a favour for the Imperial Family, but your *entrée* to society must nevertheless seem to be the purpose of your journey here.'

The androgynous individual came back with a tray bearing a delicate white teapot, teacups for two, and a small *samovar* urn. He or she placed the ensemble on the mahogany table between the two men, and adjusted the tea-light under the shining belly of the *samovar*.

Kizhé waved the youngster away and then flicked his hand, for Iffy to serve.

Handing the teacup over, Iffy managed to hold the other man's gaze, but that discomfiting, fierce energy was under generation again: some scarcely retained force with no outlet. Or, worse, an outlet unknown.

Stretching into a prouder posture, Kizhé emptied his teacup in one draught, then set it down precisely. In this Imperial setting, his uniform no longer looked gentlemanly. Blue wool strained across his broad torso, allowing the electric light to flow brightly over his gold braid and spark aggressively off the diamond-edged decoration.

'I will inform you when we get to Petrozavódsk.' He rose, and clicked his heels with a bow, then strode forward towards the engine.

The hangover of two days drunk at sea had made him terribly thirsty. Iffy gulped the hot, spiced water gratefully, and poured more, adding sugar and hot water from the *samovar*, savouring the heat and taste. Despite the stove, the carriage was still cold. Beyond the windows' striped silk drapes, the landscape was a mere white undulation. The sky was almost as featureless.

Curious now about his quarters, he left his teacup at the table, and made his way aft.

The cabin he had been allocated occupied nearly a whole carriage, and was a dream of English wealth: studded leather cushioning on the wall – as though that side of the room were simply an enormous Chesterfield sofa in some club – and a desk.

Felt had been laid down to protect the mahogany from 'his' trunks, but the trunks themselves were locked, and presumably Kizhé held the key. Iffy left them, and went to lie down on the leather sofa-bunk.

With his eyes closed, he lifted his hands slowly to push his thumbs against the tragus of his ears, and went gently deaf. The cabin was not cold, but cool, and the pleasant heaviness of his body, weighted by the thrust of travel, soothed him. If Cosima could be here, stretched straight on the bench beside him, the pressure of gravity and momentum might align her, open her rib cage to ease her lungs and her heart. The cabin wavered slightly under him, with a regular, repetitive *thunk* which must have been the pontoons. He was no longer cold: in fact, around his groin, he was quite warm, even moving slightly, easily, with the percussion of the track. What if Cosima were pressed not beside him but under him? Could his own weight and momentum align her bones, make space for her to breathe, and her heart to beat?

Abruptly, a rattle of deceleration and a jostling of coaches announced a halt. Iffy's cabin door slammed open on its runners, and Kizhé darted in, holding two bottles in his left fist. He flung them on the bunk at Iffy's feet.

'A 'spot of bother,' Mr Pearson,' he announced, with an almost seductive smirk. 'Not to worry. Take your medicine and stay quiet.'

Iffy scrambled into the corner of the bunk and brought the bottles into his lap, twisting them back and forth until he heard the first gunshot; then his tic became an ineradicable nervous tattoo in the jeering rhythm of a popular song:

There once was a man with no cou-rage,
Who hid from both horse and gun car-riage.
The young ladies sneered!
The old ladies jeered!
Of white feathers he had quite a plu-mage!

There was another gunshot. Iffy's heart jerked, and his grip moved to the stopper of the bottle.

Then, slowly, the train started to move again, so gradually that the carriages did not jostle. If there had been a man on the track, Kizhé had cleared him.

Time passed, before a small blink of day, and then the Arctic darkness resumed for a lengthy night of chaotic shadows and the light of burning somewhere inside a city.

A new member of the train crew entered the cabin several times to bring tea and resupply his coal stove. This one was definitely a girl, whose haughtiness and physical frailty made her boiler suit and closely cropped hair seem a mere disguise. However, she carried coal like a boy, and ignored the passenger.

When it finally became light again, Iffy was sober, but hung over, and hungrier than he had ever been in London. Peering blearily through the window, he could make out only that trees had softened the barren severity of the northern landscape: winter-white frames of silver birch. The pace of the train slowed again.

The train was entering a Baroque toy town of smooth stucco façades in soft colours. Iffy's eyes widened as he felt for the first time the softness of colour after the strain of whiteness.

Finally, there came the halt which lasted.

Kizhé appeared at the door of Iffy's cabin.

'Tsarskoë Selo. The Czar's Village,' he announced. 'We are here.'

King of the Mountain Hall

Iffy stared, appalled, across the silent, chilly lustre of the Mountain Hall, where he was to install the Faraday grid.

The electric chandeliers had been illuminated for his inspection, revealing a two-storey polished wooden platform and ramp, crowned with untidily draped bird-cages. The structure occupied the greater part of one wall, carelessly disfiguring the pattern of the shining marble floor. Antique tables stood against every panel of the marble-veined wall, holding treasures from the last two centuries, all cheapened in a theatrical store-room jumble.

By contrast, at his feet, the modern wealth of electrical copper wiring was in impeccable order. The wire had been tightly and perfectly spooled onto the flat bolts, creating a surface like luminous copper silk. Iffy grasped one by the cardboard end and hefted it out of the trunk. The oval end-cap was inked with the legend: 'Burchett and Orme-Philmey Wiring. One hundred Imperial Feet, 30.48 Continental Metres.'

Burchett. A dowry from Cosima's father?

At last, he found his voice. 'What will happen to the marble floor? I would have expected it to have been taken up.'

'It is too heavy, and there is no need,' Kizhé said. 'The Faraday Floor must be made in sections which may be transferred to other palaces.'

With a surge of anger, Iffy spoke quickly. 'Truly? Even given the astonishing cost of getting me here, when an airship journey might have achieved that object in a day or so, is the cost of making separate Floors for different palaces truly so great?'

Kizhé slapped his thigh with his gloves. 'Time is more essential than cost. The Imperial Family removes several times a year. It will take time to equip all households.'

'A doubly false economy, then, to not supply me with wire-grids already made up!'

'Made-up wire grids? Mr Pearson, be serious. Napoleon called you 'a nation of shopkeepers', but there are some things a foreign power cannot buy in England, for any money. Kindly make your calculations and start planning your work. Here is the key for your trunks of wire, which you must keep here in this hall. The case of samples has already been taken to your room. I will conduct you now. It is three in the morning, you understand.'

The officer handed over the trunk key, attached to a fob-chain, then moved into his now-familiar position slightly behind the young Englishman, and gripped his arm.

Iffy wriggled. 'Lieutenant, I–'

'You will ring when you wake, morning or not, and will be conducted back here after breakfast. Let us go.'

The corridors of the Alexander Palace were wide enough for a carriage, but the guest room was of human size: a small, cosy corner of middle-class England, opening onto a softly gleaming, white-tiled private bathroom. Iffy felt his strength ebbing as he considered the luxury of bathing.

The door was shoved firmly into its frame.

Iffy half-turned, but he had no will to argue. He stumbled across the room to the bed, where he let himself fall.

He rubbed his face into the thick, red, English counterpane, inhaling the scents of lavender water and cedar. His mother had always packed up their bedding in herbal preservatives, and his own bedding would smell like this one day, in his own home, with Cosima.

O God, Cosima.

He longed to write to her now, but no letter would get to her, and certainly not unread. They were not parted by mere clothes and space and walls and fathers, like a normal courting couple, but by thirteen calendar days, over two thousand *versts* and innumerable spies and borders.

A Second Christmas-tide

For a day and a half, Iffy saw no one but servants, Lieutenant Kizhé, and two other officers – Gendarmes in pale blue who stood guard in turn in the Marble Hall. When Iffy demanded tools and the materials for rigging up a wire-mesh loom, it was the officers themselves who brought everything, and assigned a silent pair of palace servants to work the loom while Iffy built the frames, starting in the corner furthest from the gigantic wooden slide. As pieces of mesh came off the loom, he laid them over the frames to await the provision of a generator.

A brief afternoon was giving way to electric dusk again, although it was probably only three o'clock. Iffy lay braced under a frame, soldering two meshes together.

Away behind him, he heard someone at the door, talking in soft tones with the Gendarme on duty.

Self-consciously, he continued working, loath to appear lazy in the sight of the Imperial household. In his hands, the soldering iron conjoined two wires with the pleasantly acrid smell which always reminded him of assembling circuits with Inwood – in truth, *for* Inwood – who looked over his deft friend's work with a broad, amphibian smile...

Then came the Gendarme's shout, distorted by the marble echoes of the hall. Hastily, Iffy pushed himself onto clear floor, and went to present himself.

The young woman was just out of her teens, he judged, and far from a Court beauty – with a stout waist and round puffy face – but she was in expensive English costume, and carried herself with great assurance.

'My name is Anna Taneëva. I wait on her Imperial Majesty,' she declared.

Iffy offered her a bow. 'Good morning.'

'Mr Pearson, you are invited to afternoon tea with finest toys, and entertain Their Imperial Highnesses, Grand Duchesses. The Gendarme will help you with trunk and bring you.' She nodded in conclusion, and departed.

The Gendarme's English was not as good as Kizhé's, but was sufficient to allow for a derisive, 'Have bath and change clothes before you go, good chap.'

Like Iffy's room, the Imperial Family's suite seemed like a cosy dolls' house inside the Palace, where all was for the use of humans, not giants or royalty. The nursery was large, but it boasted a ceramic stove and the tiny furniture of a children's room: even the fir-tree in the centre – trimmed for Christmas in the 'Victorian' fashion – seemed like the centrepiece to a model. The proud dolls stood there, a half-circle of white-clothed girls in a row, end-stopped by their nursery-maid.

The Gendarme placed the chest of samples on one of the tables and withdrew, leaving Iffy alone in the presence of the Grand Duchesses, with only the nursemaid and two shy *domestiques* for propriety. In the silence, Iffy performed a full Court bow, which the dolls returned with civility.

As soon as the contract of courtesy was complete, the youngest girl, the Grand Duchess Anastasía – whom he judged to be about three years old, skidded out of line, her light brown hair flying, and into a corner, from where she returned pushing a polished wooden toy-trunk. She scrambled around in front of it and opened the lid. The second-youngest sister, the rounded, sweet-faced one – Marie – now joined her to help, burbling: 'Baby had so many christening presents this summer.'

'Our ships!' squealed Anastasía, setting up a naval line on the floor beside a table and yanking the tablecloth askew to create a white-bluffed harbour. 'This is Golden Horn Bay,' she explained. 'Papa showed me pictures.'

The two older girls leaned nearer, politely silent, though the younger of the two, the Grand Duchess Tatiana, seemed to wish to be on the floor as well, creasing her white dress.

Iffy studied the fleet presented him by the two youngest Romanoff girls, and then reached into his trunk for the model airship, of which Deede's had sold two hundred before English Christmas. He tore off the packing paper and lifted it through the air towards the youngest Grand Duchess, who gazed open-mouthed for a moment, then roared an artillery barrage from her ship. She leaped up to seize the airship out of Iffy's hands, and spun it away, down into the waves.

Marie answered her cue with a celebratory volley, piping, 'Horrid little Japanese!'

Anastasía resurrected the toy for a new dive from a different angle, and capsized Marie's ship. The older girl groaned and sprawled on the floor, calling on God to save her sailors from drowning, and cursing the Japanese again.

Iffy looked to the two older girls, who had now primly seated themselves at the white-covered table. However, they offered their sisters no rebuke, and he dared not speak. The eldest, a grave girl of nine or ten, with dark blonde hair and blue eyes, beckoned to him.

Iffy crossed the floor to seat himself at the table in front of his trunk and accepted the cup of tea offered by the Grand Duchess Olga. They drank in silence while warfare between the two youngest girls grew fiercer.

'Will you show us your things from London?' Tatiana interrupted suddenly.

He obeyed, opening the chest top completely and turning the box to face the two girls.

Grand no longer, Tatiana climbed onto her chair and delved in the trunk, removing packets and boxes, turning them this way and that to see the labels, which she read aloud in a soft voice. Her dark brown hair fell across her shoulders in heavy, well-cared-for locks.

'Miss Burchett wrote to Mama about the special Floor,' Olga said. 'Are you really making another one for us?'

'Yes, Your Imperial Highness, it is downstairs in the Marble Hall.'

'Will our 'mountain' go on top of it? It would be so very nice for Baby to slide safely.'

'The area of the Floor is very small still, and I… have not been told to extend it under the… 'mountain'. Forgive me, Your Imperial Highness, I believed it was for dancing.'

Tatiana interrupted, 'Miss Burchett said it was like a fairy ring, where a girl could dance all night and not tire. Look, Olichka, a hair-brush for dear Miss Eagar!' She held up the Whiting's Brush. 'Miss Eagar was our dear nanny. We are so very sad, Mr Pearson, that she went home.'

'Our dear people should not leave us,' Tatiana agreed, handing the brush to her sister and diving in again. 'Oh! What a dear little rattle for Baby!'

She laid the silver toy aside, and continued exploring the contents of the box. Young Mr Deede had packed almost the entire Christmas scene from the theatre, so dolls and dolls' tea-sets, trains, and playing-cards joined the safety razor and Foot Battery – *for Papa!* A pneumatic rubber ball fell off the table and rolled into the sea of battle, striking one of the fine Russian ships. Little Anastasía took the cue to send it to the bottom of Golden Horn Bay.

Olga retrieved the ball and returned to the table, remarking, 'When our Baltic Fleet arrives in the East, I hope it will kill all the Japanese; not leave even one alive.'

Across the Time-Zones

The carriage clock on the table nearest to him told him that it was nearly eleven o'clock on the day after Orthodox Christmas Day: time for the first presentation of the Faraday Floor to the Romanoffs. Beside the small, makeshift platform, the generator was already in operation, feeding electricity into the grid.

At eleven o'clock prompt, the Imperial family entered the hall without a guard or any servants, led by Nicholas II, Czar of all the Russias, and the Empress Alexandra, carrying the Czarevitch, who was still in skirts, in the

English fashion. The four Grand Duchesses followed, dressed identically in white.

Iffy waited for the strange, silent procession to approach the Faraday grid, and then he bowed deeply. The Czar dropped his chin slightly, but his face remained impassive behind the tidily trimmed brown beard.

Straightening up, Iffy offered his hand to help the Grand Duchesses climb onto the platform, in order of age. Olga showed no reaction to the strangeness of reduced gravity, and stood quite calmly, extending her hand to Tatiana, who mounted second. Marie came up next; her blue eyes grew wide and she gasped, but she obediently took Tatiana's hand. Finally, Anastasía came, but she seemed unwilling to submit to anyone's grip until Olga seized her from one side and Marie from the other.

The girls now in a ring, the youngest giggled suddenly, and tugged at her oldest sister's hand.

In the lightness of the Floor, the girls' excitement flourished, and they began to circle until they were spinning in a wheel of joy, all four sisters united as Iffy had never been with his three brothers.

At the edge of the Floor, the Czarina, too, seemed hypnotised.

Then her husband moved behind her, cradling her and his son, and spoke above the laughter of his daughters, shooing them away to their 'mountain' for their brother to have his turn.

The girls flew off the platform like a string of white birds, and circled the wooden 'mountain' before climbing. With a whining crescendo, an organ began to play, and one of the girls slid down the ramp with a cry of delight.

Iffy turned his attention back to the Imperial couple and offered his hand to the Czarina.

She took his hand with a cool, soft-gloved grip. Her red-gold hair had been dressed with all modern style in a glossy pompadour, but she wore no powder. There were shadows under her deep-set grey eyes. She inclined her head to him, and he eased her over the border of the Faraday influence, before releasing her hand.

Czarina Alexandra bent down and cautiously placed the boy down, feet first.

With a murmur of interest, the boy wound around and around his mother's arm, then abruptly lunged away and toppled into a slow, rebounding tumble. His mother's voice rose in a shriek, but the Czarevitch completed his roll and faced them, squealing with laughter.

Nervously, the Czarina joined in. Iffy climbed onto the platform, picked the child up and set him on his feet. The boy shouted again, incoherently, jigging up and down in Iffy's grip.

Smiling again, Iffy took the boy's hands and gently spun him about.

The tiny Grand Duke laughed again, wriggling with pleasure, and fell over, bouncing gently.

The Czarina's breath hitched in a sob.

Tactfully, Iffy looked away from the giggling, rolling Czarevitch towards the Czar. 'It is an extraordinary and pleasant effect, Your Imperial Majesty.'

Then the Czarina spoke, her voice low and trembling, 'It gentles the world for Baby.'

Her husband climbed onto the Floor and stood behind his wife, like a bulwark. 'Mr Pearson, do examine our 'mountain.' It was built for the children of the first Czar Nicholas. When the Faraday Floor is extended far enough, my son will benefit also.'

Accepting the autocrat's hint, Iffy retreated to the wooden structure, where just then the three younger Grand Duchesses were careening, shrieking, down the polished ramp on a strip of carpet. Olga remained at the top, static, despite the lively, pumping organ music.

Chubby Marie rolled into Iffy's legs and gasped out an apology in English, before running after her two sisters to climb up again.

A small troop of the blue-uniformed Gendarmes was filing into the hall. Distracted, Iffy stared as the officers encircled the small Faraday grid and the Czarevitch. None of them were watching him, so he followed the Grand Duchesses up to the top of the platform. There, he caught Anastasía looking across the hall. She flung a quick, anxious glance at him, then hurled herself down the slope, crashing into her eldest sister, Olga.

Suddenly, Tatiana was with him, holding his attention with her wise, widely spaced grey eyes. With grave politeness, she offered him a small square of exquisite silk carpet.

To his right, the tableau of Imperial inheritance – the Gendarmes with the Czar of Russia, his wife and his Heir – had become a double vision: a game of Blind Man's Buff played in the park by a well-bred couple and a group of uncles, fending off their little blond boy whenever he rolled too close to the edge.

Iffy yielded to Tatiana's invitation and rushed down the ramp on the rug, landing in a spin at the bottom. His elbow ached from the fall, and as he got to his feet he rubbed at it.

The officers shouted encouragement at the Czarevitch.

The boy would be a general one day. Given the boy's naval 'godfathers,' he might already be an honorary admiral.

It gentles the world for Baby.

Iffy frowned. An Imperial heir was certainly not destined to gentle the world.

Anastasía slammed into his legs. 'Sorry!' she shrieked, and scrambled back toward the stairs.

Iffy rubbed at his shins absently, then checked his elbow again. The bump was in an awkward place. He hoped it would not bruise.

At the top of the slide, Olga and Tatiana were watching their brother on the Faraday Floor. Anastasía reached the top, and also became still for a moment, watching.

He stared at them, too. That was no mere curiosity, nor even jealousy for their brother's monopoly of the Floor.

The Czarevitch had the bruising disease.

The Measure of a Short Life

Facing his troop of new apprentices – young engineers from the Gendarmes – Iffy had the sensation of a cordon, a wall more substantial than the mere iron railing which was all that separated the Alexander Palace from the village of Tsarskoë Selo.

'These are the finest engineers we have in the Gendarmerie. We are police; we protect the state; we protect the Imperial Family,' announced the Gendarme captain.

Despite the man's enormous physical bulk and sonorous voice, Iffy felt himself relax slightly. Not soldiers after all. 'I see, sir.'

'They will learn to lay out and solder grids, so the Floor may be built more quickly.'

'Yes, sir. Er… they do all understand English, don't they?'

'Of course, Mr Pearson.'

'And… forgive me, what is your name?'

The Gendarme gazed down on Iffy with cool hazel eyes. 'Captain Ludorff.'

'I… see, sir.' Iffy cleared his throat. 'I will make a start, then. Er… gentlemen, please observe.'

Iffy climbed crablike across the wooden frames, instructing the young men, each with a uniformly clean-shaven chin and a small moustache.

Remembering the time at Cambridge when his whiskers had taken a singeing, sparing his face, he was just wondering whether he should make a joke about beards as a safety measure for engineers, when Ludorff's voice rang out again.

'Mr Pearson, may I present General Biely-Kalinin, who answers for security at the Palace. Your High Excellency, Mr Godfrey Pearson is the Faraday Engineer.'

Carefully, Iffy transferred his weight back onto his haunches and dismounted from the grid. On the marble floor, he faced the General – silent, magnificent and bald, in the pale blue and white of the Gendarmerie – and bowed.

The General inclined his head slightly, then spoke to Captain Ludorff in Russian.

Iffy waited.

'It is after ten o'clock,' said Ludendorff finally. 'I am to choose shifts, then accompany you to your room for correct food and rest. Have you identified at least two engineers competent to turn on the grid?'

Iffy felt his hands turning cold. 'T-turn it on? Why should they need to do that, when I will be back here in the morning? May I not at least spend just a bit longer with the engineers, to judge who may be trusted with the delicate operation?'

Both officers were studying him. Though Ludorff had not translated Iffy's refusal, his square face was expressionless, and the General appeared to understand, for he, too, was stony-faced.

'I would not like to have sparks and see the grid melted in a fire,' Iffy added. *And a small, vulnerable boy left without a place of safety.*

Still neither Ludorff nor the General spoke.

Do they wish to build something else? How bloody typical of the brass to see their advantage in something therapeutic.

'I would not like to answer for that,' he persisted.

Where the hell is Kizhé?

The Lieutenant was outranked by both the General and his adjutant, but he was a Life Guard with a direct line to the Imperial Family, and someone had been sure enough of his wolf-like fierceness to send him thousands of miles to England to fetch someone who could save the Czarevitch's life.

The General muttered something to his junior officer, then turned on his heel to walk away, across the hall.

'You are stubborn, Mr Pearson,' said Captain Ludorff.

Was that exasperation? Hard to know, with these military types. All that habitual obedience.

Iffy took a deep breath. 'Sir, I... acknowledge that I should not be the only one possessed of an engineering secret which benefits the Imperial Family, but I must be sure of the people I entrust it to, lest someone be electrocuted, or a fire break out and endanger everyone! If you want me to go now, I will go. Then I will be back in the morning to continue work, and if your engineers have more mesh ready for me, I will show them how to test it.'

Ludorff shrugged. 'Very well. Come with me now. You must remain fresh for your work.'

'Yes, Captain.'

Yet there were no Gendarmes the next morning. Iffy's breakfast was brought to his room by servants, and he ate at the dressing table, as he would with Cosima, at some point in the future. Perhaps even by next Christmas. Iffy closed his eyes to imagine her smiling across a morning room table at him, braced comfortably in some sort of patent chair, celebrating a year since he had brought relief to the Imperial Family.

You take care of me, Godfrey, she would tell him. *You are the only man in the world who takes such care of others, rather than wrecking.*

With his eyes still closed, he reached for her withered left hand, and brought it to his lips. She sighed softly, and then dissolved. Iffy let his head fall back and opened his eyes. The ceiling was blank and white with the room's electric ceiling lamp, and he was alone.

Light careened across the curtains, like an accelerated blink of day.

He sat up. That had been artificial light.

Stiffly, he hobbled to the window, to make a crack in the curtain. He made out a sleigh travelling fast away from the Palace, flanked by officers on skis, all illuminated by two beams of electric light from the opposing wings of the Palace.

Shivering in the halo of cold around the window – despite the double casement – Iffy watched until the sleigh passed out of view into Tsarskoë Selo.

He glanced at the clock: now nine o'clock, an hour and a half after he had first got out of bed and rang the bell .

The hands moved slowly around the clock face, and the sun slowly rose outside, but it was not until past ten o'clock that the door was unlocked again.

It was Miss Taneëva. Iffy offered her a bow. 'Good morning.'

She made an arrogant flourish with her hand, still holding her châtelaine, so that Iffy could see the cascade of keys and the bottle of sal volatile, all hanging from a Romanoff eagle in silver.

The master jewellers of Birmingham would salivate at the very idea of supplying the Russian court. *What a pity the Russians already have Fabergé.*

As they made their way back to the Marble Hall, Iffy studied her, yet she swept along quickly and without looking at him. At the doors to the Marble Hall, she again produced a key from her châtelaine and unlocked the room.

The two Palace servants who had been assisting him were already weaving, and had left a quantity of made-up mesh for him to place today. Iffy quickly hung up his frock coat to resume work. He heard an exchange of soft women's voices at the doors, and then quick steps toward him.

Miss Taneëva had remained. She took a position beside the grid, and waited.

Iffy paused in the act of lifting one of the meshes. 'May I assist you, madam?'

'I come to watch the work, Mr Pearson. It is so important for the family, and Baby.'

He scanned her face for signs of ulterior meaning, but discerned only avid interest. Her eyes roved across the sixteen frames Iffy had put together.

He made a little bow to her and took the grid over to the edge of the Floor, where empty frames were waiting, then knelt to begin work.

Miss Taneëva remained by the door, silent.

Below Iffy's hands and soldering iron, row after row of shining copper threads found their alignment with the rest of the mesh. Order advanced across the frame, not like the untidy borderline of a tide, but a strong, metallic edge, fortifying the Czarevitch's field of safety.

Not looking up from his work, he asked, 'Do you know where the Gendarmes are, the engineers who were helping me?'

'Something is happening in the capital. Someone stirring things up.' The lady-in-waiting's voice was flat and unmusical.

'It must be something special, to keep the Gendarmes away from this important task which benefits the Imperial Family,' he ventured.

'My holy angels are ill-served by many of their people,' Anna Taneëva retorted. 'The foreigners are one thing – they have their own heathen emperor – but our own people have been swayed... There was a riot. It is an ungodly disgrace.'

Miss Taneëva departed after the servants brought his dinner, but returned at eleven o'clock to escort him back to his room.

She returned the next day at nine, and watched him for an hour, then left for the rest of the day.

Outside, new snow had muffled all sound from outside, and the Imperial children were all quiet somewhere. The servants were called away, but had left five meshes beside their loom. Iffy lined them up and soldered them into place, increasing the area of the Faraday influence square by square. The area was now larger than that at Mr Denman's theatre.

When the light faded from the windows that day, no one came to illuminate the chandeliers. Iffy squinted at the mesh for as long as he dared, but at last – it was three-thirty by his watch – he could not see to work.

Restless, hungry and thirsty, he paced the borders of the Faraday Floor. It now covered half the hall and would give the Czarevitch more than enough space for now, small child that he was. He could now learn to walk in complete safety, and play with his sisters.

Iffy went to peer out of the window at the new snow, then left the scene to go and sit on the end of the 'mountain' ramp.

Suddenly, automatically, light flooded the chandeliers.

No one had come, yet they had signalled to him nevertheless.

He returned to his work.

Where are all the officers?

At four, palace servants entered, to close the curtains and bring him a samovar for tea, with *zakusski* of salted cucumbers and open-faced *buterbrody*, which he devoured, before carefully wiping his hands clean of grease.

There was more noise that afternoon, many footsteps in the hallways. However, no one called him, so he returned to work until, abruptly at nine, the moon-faced Anna Taneëva was heralded by the sound of the door being unlocked.

'Please come,' she said, without ceremony.

The study was illuminated in warm pools of lamplight, which sank into the fine-grained leather and reflected brightly off the rows of picture frames on the Czar's desk. Each a different royal relative, and each round frame shone like the muzzle of a gun prepared for parade. Iffy blinked away the dazzling effect of the array and focussed instead on the long, pensive face of the Czar, enclosed in its own frame of neat beard and well-barbered hair. He was smoking a cigarette, and his free hand rested on an enamelled cigarette case. Alexandra sat at his side.

Having ushered Iffy to an armchair in front of the desk, Miss Taneëva sat down modestly by the door.

The Czar spoke abruptly. 'The Faraday Floor is a modern miracle which you have arranged for us, Mr Pearson. I must confess that I was sceptical when my dear Wifey brought the news to me of the fairy tale in Miss Cosima's Christmas card. However, if Baby is not to be carried everywhere like a degenerate Roman, he must have it, or something like it. Moreover, it is right that a Romanoff should walk lightly across the land which he rules, by grace of God.'

He broke off at an irruption at the door, but merely raised his eyebrows at Lieutenant Kizhé.

'How is Petersburg?' asked the Czar.

As Kizhé strode into the light by the desk, his uniform buttons glinted fiercely. 'Unsettled. The crowds remain angry about the way their riot ended yesterday. There is talk of a Bloody Sunday.'

Nicholas sighed and waved his cigarette indolently. 'The sound of gunfire may wake them up. They will come to their senses. Without agitators like this Father Gapon, they will remember who their real 'Little Father' and 'Little Mother' are, will they not, Wifey?'

Alexandra swelled. 'They will, and then they will humbly beg you and God for pardon!'

'Oh, yes, Your Imperial Majesty!' interrupted the lady-in-waiting, now leaning forward.

On Kizhé's right side, Iffy spotted the officer's glare at the woman. Inhaling deeply, she seemed to be adjusting her posture for a counter-attack. 'Lieutenant Kizhé, I–'

'Miss Taneëva, it is also connected with the military situation, and it is not right that a woman should treat on such matters, save Her Imperial Majesty.'

'The military situation, Kizhé?' Nicholas asked softly.

The officer shook his head. 'I cannot discuss military matters in the presence–'

'Your Imperial Majesties, he already knows one of the Empire's greatest secrets. *He's* not officer, or even Russian!' cried out Miss Taneëva, flinging up her arm to point at Iffy.

The Czarevich. Iffy shrank into himself.

'Mr Pearson is a man and an engineer,' Kizhé retorted. 'He may discuss war.'

Iffy hastened to deny the Czar's attention. 'I am not one to analyse such things. My father is a naval man, but not I...'

Miss Taneëva made a sound of disgust and stormed out, shutting the door with a bang.

Kizhé resumed, 'Your Imperial Majesty, the war and the unrest in the empire are intimately connected–'

The Czar roused himself with a pugnacity which seemed somewhat artificial. 'So the Japanese are behind the strikes and riots and assassinations! What better can one expect from a race which does not even make a decent, Christian declaration of war, but simply attacks!'

Kizhé coughed, firmly interrupting his Czar. 'The ability of all foreigners to cross our borders, Your Imperial Majesty. In the East, Port Arthur has just fallen. The Japanese navy has given us a good thrashing, but the aerial harassment is worse. Meanwhile, on our Western border, Britain and Germany have fleets of the sea, the air, and of the Void!'

Iffy pushed himself back into his seat. *Oh, God, not that again. Little wonder that the belligerence penetrates even the nursery–*

Nicholas's mouth had fallen open.

'Yet there is a way to become inviolate.'

The Imperial couple stilled, facing Kizhé.

'The Faraday mesh provides a safe, small platform for the Czarevitch. Let it also enforce a border which will keep us safe from agitation and war, both foreign and domestic. Let us tumble the invaders as they try to enter holy Russian land and air. We shall give no ground.'

'I must... I must secure the Empire against them and... any other nation which would attack us...' said the Czar, slowly. 'Mr Pearson?'

Iffy hesitated. 'I– I am no naval man, like my father and brothers, but from what I know of Faraday forces, it will certainly scatter infantry, cavalry, motorised invasion...'

Alexandra's expression and tone grew unexpectedly savage. 'If only we had had this Iron Curtain at the beginning of this war, we would have held our border strong against those nasty horrid yellow people and preserved our ships! We would have mined our Eastern possessions with these Faraday grids and blown their Air Force out of the sky. Never mind: we shall do it now. Russia will no longer be vulnerable. We would not have others overlook us.'

'Bravo, Your Imperial Majesty!' cried Kizhé.

'The expense, though,' murmured the Czar. 'My ministers keep trying to tell me that–'

'Put off work on the Trans-Siberian Railway,' Kizhé urged. 'Simply write me an order for whatever men and money I need, and I shall send out Mr Pearson to make a start. The Gendarme engineers can complete the Faraday Floor for the Czarevitch.'

In motion again, Kizhé reached across the desk for the block of paper, and pushed it in front of his sovereign.

The Czar nodded, and transferred his cigarette to his left hand. He wrote a few words, then offered the sheet of paper to his Life Guard.

Without knowing quite how it had happened, Iffy found himself again in Kizhé's grip and moving towards the door.

Out in the corridors, they moved swiftly, leaving the Imperial apartments and returning to Iffy's rooms.

Kizhé cast Iffy inside and tucked the precious commission inside his jacket, speaking quickly. 'What a stroke of luck, eh? A proper commission, not like selling knick-knacks and toys! You will marry your Miss Burchett and live happily ever after, eh?'

Iffy tried to catch his breath. 'I will need to consult a friend in England... he is a greater theoretician than I! And the materials–'

'Oh, the materials are all here, in this piece of paper. Materials, engineers and all the money a project could need. Do not worry, Mr Pearson, you will be back at home in England and married in no time!'

Iffy shook his head. 'It's too soon for me to leave this Floor. I must ensure the engineers are trained...'

'I will take care of all of that. The Czar has written, and he will be obeyed. You may depart tomorrow.'

'You seem to have planned all of this.'

Kizhé laughed gaily. 'Indeed, it has been discussed on... not quite on the highest levels, but on a level below that of the Czar. This is the way autocracy works. The autocrat is presented with useful ideas, fully formed, with which he may benefit his people. It will benefit you, also.' Kizhé's hand found the now-familiar bruises on Iffy's arm. 'Now, you must pack your things for the journey tomorrow.'

'But- what about the strikes and riots in St Petersburg? Did His Imperial Majesty not say there was shooting?'

'No one will be shot who obeys the Czar.'

'Really, Lieutenant Kizhé, I cannot simply go to work on an outside grid... a grid in the field... without–'

'We will draw the border for you, and you will install and test the line. 'Tis scarce beyond the wit of man!"

'But what line?' Iffy insisted. 'Will it be on the railway track, or through wilderness? Where will my electricity come from?'

'Ask no more questions.'

'No engineer can work without these answers. Let me at least consult with my good friend Mr Inwood, who understands Faraday forces. Without my books, or him, I don't even remember the formula for determining the height of a Faraday field by width and breadth. This Iron Curtain of yours might be too thin to disrupt flight, like… like a vessel passing over the beam of a searchlight: no more than an updraft of hot air. And I don't know who has ever created a Faraday grid wide enough to reach the Void.'

'Shut your mouth!' Kizhé struck him, hard.

Holding his face, Iffy gasped.

The officer's triangular face had turned savage again, like the muzzle of a wolf.

Iffy stepped back. 'You mean… you already knew this? How can you suggest such a thing when you know it won't work? That… isn't that *treason*?'

Kizhé grinned. 'So you are a patriot after all! However, you are wrong at the last moment. None of this chaos is about patriotism and warfare. You have been right all along. Money really is the most important thing in the world. You know that. You know money could have given you your Miss Burchett, your freedom from your father, her freedom from hers.'

Iffy shook his head. 'I can get money – and Cosima – without treason. I am a coward, Lieutenant, as you know, but I didn't go into a safe Ministry job, either.'

Kizhé snorted.

'Does- does Cosima's father know any of this?'

Kizhé grimaced, then reached for his firearm.

'What will happen to her, without me?'

When the officer's giant body filled his horizon, Iffy realised he had fallen to his knees. He called upward, desperately, 'What will happen to her?'

In the shadow of Kizhé's uniform, his buttons were like faint stars. Then the muzzle of the pistol rose, like a dim moon with a metallic halo. 'Nothing unexpected. Spinsterhood, probably. Unlikely she will marry anyone else, if that's what you're worried about.'

Yes, her father would keep her safe: safer than Francis had been; safer than the Romanoff children, who would think they were sheltered by a useless Faraday field. Then the wolves of the world, like Kizhé and Sir Thomas, would devour undefended Russia and then, enriched, would turn on France and

Britain. On his mother, too, if the other men of the family could not stand in the way, with their ghastly, aggressive, finally necessary dreadnaughts...

Within the muzzle, a comet flashed out, and bowled him away. Iffy tumbled, but not across Cosmos – this was not order. This was Void.

Epilogue: Zero

Early the next morning, when it was still sky-dark, but snow-bright, a young man emerged from the Alexander Palace. The driver who put the small travelling trunks in the *troika* tutted to himself at the young man's absurdly thin English woollen overcoat and lined felt hat.

Some of these courtly types and their English mania. Why won't they dress like proper Russians? thought Afanasy. This one wasn't even in fashion. With those too-perfect whiskers, curled in waves above the jawline, and his pointed chin, he looked like that unfortunate *Prins* Albert of theirs, who must have been dead for a hundred years.

'I'll get you some furs for the drive,' grumbled the driver. 'Get in, Excellency.'

The young man gave an exaggerated flinch, and stammered something – something in English.

Afanasy looked at him more closely. So it was a foreigner, after all? He spotted the jagged bottom of the young man's left ear, and his annoyance increased. *English whiskers will never cover that sort of deformity. He needs a proper Russian beard, the fool.*

'Afanasy Nikiforovich!'

The driver's heart jumped. This deep voice echoed with authority and Russianness.

It was the deputy of the Gendarme General who answered for the Imperial Family's security.

Wearing no winter coat, the Gendarme captain marched down the steps into the snowy driveway, picked up Afanasy's chin in his great paw and growled in the driver's face, 'Stop staring stupidly and get our guest to the station. He has an important job to get on with.'

Despite the chill – ten degrees of frost – the man's hand was hot and strong, and he seemed utterly unconscious of the weather... and not simply out of ignorance, like the foreigner.

The foreigner had not been looking at the Captain, but at Afanasy. He caught the driver's quick glance at him and instantly dropped his eyes, muttering something in English to the officer.

Captain Ludorff dropped Afanasy's chin and gave him a little shove toward the driver's seat of the *troika*. 'Get him to the station, then come straight back and see me.'

'Yes, Your Right Highly Born,' the driver mumbled.

Captain Ludorff helped the foreigner into the seat of the carriage and clapped him on the shoulder, with some encouragement in English, then pulled fur robes from the box under the seat. The foreigner took them gratefully, and even wrapped a fox-tail around his head, the barbarian.

Now warm in his seat with the furs, he looked up at his driver with a new grin, vicious and vulpine.

Afanasy hesitated, then turned his back on the man and whipped up his horses, as though the devil were behind him. The *troika*, with only one passenger and his inadequate luggage, lightly gained the path of packed snow, and all but flew toward the station.

After the *troika* had gone, Captain Ludorff whistled out, and a second sleigh emerged from behind the Alexander Palace, bearing a long, awkwardly bundled object. A parcel as long as a man.

At the reins of this conveyance was no lowly Afanasy, but a muffled-up General Biely-Kalinin himself. He exchanged nods with Captain Ludorff, then drove the bundle away from the Imperial village, into the birch forest.

~ end ~

Virginia Marybury read Russian and French at university, and wrote her M.A. dissertation on corruption. As a journalist, she is scrupulous about not fabricating facts but, in fiction, history often turns toward the alternative. "Iron Curtain" is Virginia's first story in the Voidships universe, but she is working on an alternative history resulting from climate cooling. Her short stories are often near-fantastical, and even the name Virginia Marybury is imaginary.

In Russia, she has lived in St Petersburg, and also spent time in Krasnoiarsk and Vladivostok. She now lives in exile outside London, and her books are in exile in the loft.

Through her background in shipping and commodities journalism – as well as event management – Virginia has been on many business trips and trade missions, but none so dangerous as the one depicted in Iron Curtain. She's a much luckier coward than Iffy.

Twitter: https://twitter.com/VMarybury
Facebook: https://www.facebook.com/VirginiaMarybury

Dear Prudence
by Katy O'Dowd
with Steve Turnbull

DEAR PRUDENCE

By Katy O'Dowd with Steve Turnbull

A Matter of Prudence

Dear Prudence,

My wife, while we were courting, never minded my preprandial cigar. Now we are married, she says that she cannot abide the smell of it and urges me—strongly—to step outside to the garden to partake rather than from the comfort of my button-back chair by the fireside. Can a man not do what he chooses in his own home? Who is this harridan?

Dear Prudence,

My husband believes himself to be a great poet, yet the doors of every publishing establishment in London bar their doors against him. How can I tell him honestly—without causing damage to himself and our marriage—that he should find another occupation? What would the neighbours say?

Dear Prudence,

While at a ball, I saw my best friend sally forth boldly to talk to a young man who has stolen my heart. Now I find I have a very close acquaintance who has shown herself to be a hussy—who knows all of my secrets. I am afraid for my marital chances.

Dear Prudence,

My husband does not like my spaniel, complaining that he sheds his fur all over our Turkey carpets. He huffs and puffs and generally makes a nuisance of himself. My husband, that is, not my darling little Spencer.

Temperance O'Rourke—Tempy to her friends, and indeed anyone else, since she disliked her given name—rubbed a hand over her tired eyes like a small, irritable child and sighed mightily, blowing away a dark curl which had escaped from its moorings and dangled across her nose.

Mr Darcy, the fawn-coated black-muzzled pug, snorted and snuffled and then opened one eye to see what all of the fuss was about, before burrowing back down into his basket and promptly falling asleep again, snoring enough to rattle the sash windows.

'Honestly, Mr Darcy, I have no idea what scraps Cook is feeding you, but you are not fit for polite company!' Tempy left the small writing desk at which she was sitting, kicking the modesty panel as she did so. 'There,' she said in pained surprise. 'See what you have made me do?' She hobbled over to open the window to free the eau-de-pug from the room.

Putting her hand at the small of her back, she bent backwards, turned her face towards the ceiling, and stretched. Then she stood up straight and raised both arms above her head in a most unladylike posture to relieve the tension from the hours she had spent at her desk giving advice to her desperate correspondents. Realising the risk of being seen, she lowered her arms. Given the number of people that frequented Court View in Swains Lane, the probability of someone entering the room unannounced was not insignificant.

The truth of it was that, even after several years, she was quite unused to such restraining clothes. But her corset felt particularly tight today, the wide brown leather belt annoyed her waist, and her bustle irritated her coccyx.

Tempy smiled at the thought. A padded bustle was not something she was used to wearing. In the place she had been brought up diaphanous gowns were more in vogue, night and day. Up until a few short years ago, she had lived with her mother at The Cloister, a high-class brothel in Dublin.

It was just like some upside-down fairy tale where the happy ending occurred at the start. She had been very content at The Cloister but her mother had acquired a secret benefactor who enabled them to make an altogether new life in London with their pasts left firmly behind them.

Unfortunately the benefactor's grace did not cover the running costs of the house her mother had bought and, since 'respectable' was something she and her mother would never really be, every penny helped. With this in mind, Tempy's alter-ego, a Lady of Quality known simply as 'Prudence', wrote a self-help column for *The London Leader* newspaper. Agony uncles and aunts were all the rage since a few betterment books for the common man had been published.

Tempy's mother, Mary O'Rourke, ever the business woman, had cast an eye over the burgeoning trend for spiritualism in London—no longer the capital of Great Britain and Ireland, an honour that now went to Manchester, but still the biggest city in England—and had recreated herself as 'Madame Lacroix'. The house's proximity to Highgate Cemetery provided a never-ending supply of grieving relatives looking to make contact with their loved ones.

In addition, the recently opened Hampstead Air-dock, near Kenwood House, was almost literally on their doorstep. One end of its field bordered on the house's gardens; indeed Tempy had, from the privacy of her rooms, seen the workmen looking with what she could only call impatience into their land as if they intended to invade. Another section of the air-dock's perimeter bordered the cemetery, and there had been jokes about that. With appropriate advertising, said her mother, it should bring plenty of passing trade as visitors, no doubt gasping for a cup of tea and knowledge of their future, caught their first glimpse of London.

Though the ships were noisy and a pall of smoke from coal and steam coloured the air, Tempy loved to watch them rise from the ground and then take off at great speed, crossing the world in as much time as it would have taken her to catch a tram to the new dock at Victoria Embankment where one could see the barges bring tea, silks, and spices from the Faraday boats recently arrived from China.

But to be aboard one of the flying machines was what she really wanted. How she pined to be a passenger, to strap in, and watch the earth recede underneath her as they became nearly weightless.

An Unfortunate Occurrence

Tempy decided to clear her head and took Mr Darcy's lead from her desk. She called to him softly, and on seeing that a walk was imminent, he turned his head from her, pretending that she was not there. 'Mr Darcy, you are already a butterball. Come, boy!' The pug turned his head so far he fell on his back, short legs sticking up inelegantly.

Laughing, she scooped him up and fixed his lead to his collar, ignoring the reproach in his fathomless black eyes.

In the hall Tempy pinned her hat in place and the maid assisted her into her coat. The door shut after her as she stepped out into the damp air of the early autumn. The wide yellow leaves of the London Plane trees made a thick carpet on the stone slabs of the pavement. She raised her fur collar around her cheeks.

She took one of her usual routes, crossing the road and entering Waterlow Park. It was a pleasant area of green, and from the south side one could look out over London. On a clear day—not today—it was even possible to see the Houses of Parliament, no longer occupied by those damnable politicians, and St Paul's Cathedral, which was majestic even if it was Church of England.

She wandered along a path towards one of the small lakes and kicked at the leaves, which was oddly satisfying, while Mr Darcy snuffled through them, forcing her to travel at an excruciatingly slow speed.

There were a couple of children, a boy and a girl buttoned up against the cold, at the water's edge with a sailing boat. There was no wind but that didn't stop them from pulling their vessel along with a string. A woman sat on one of the wrought-iron benches nearby, reading a book and occasionally glancing up at them.

Tempy was not sure that she wanted children. At The Cloister there had been no shortage of pregnancies, births which often went badly, and little children running about the place; in truth she was one of them. Women in the oldest profession could hardly avoid the problem.

But to have children she would need to be married. The closest she had come to that, so far, was Elbert Kimperton. What a disaster that had been. At the thought of him she turned abruptly and headed home, quickening her pace much to Mr Darcy's disapproval.

Elbert Kimperton had been a miniaturist, not in art but in engineering. Always he was attempting to construct smaller and smaller devices. He was not very good at it.

They had met at an exhibition at the Royal Agricultural Halls where he had been exhibiting a mechanical hoe, half the normal size, to be deployed in city gardens. It had run amok destroying both Elbert's stand and the one next door before Tempy had grabbed a tablecloth and pushed it into the air intake where it had choked off the engine's air supply. Elbert had suffered contusions to his legs, as well as a gash on one arm. The exhibition manager was unsympathetic and had ejected him. Tempy had felt sorry for him and tended his bleeding wound.

And that was where they had started, though she had done most of the work in their relationship as he was shockingly shy. Despite that, he jumped on her friendship with fervour since he had devised a plan for a miniature Faraday mesh for the personal use of ladies with, not to put too fine a point on it, extensive bosom. Tempy's experiences at The Cloister were of considerable value to him, once he had got past the embarrassment of her candid answers to his hesitant questions.

It was the day he had over-enthusiastically attempted to force her into his device that spelled doom for their otherwise entirely chaste relationship. He had caught her unawares and she had responded in a manner taught to her by the ladies of The Cloister. It had stopped his attempt to disrobe her but also permanently damaged their bond.

And so it was, with her head full of thoughts of Elbert and his *Lightening Corset for the Generously Proportioned Woman*, that she failed to notice the approaching funeral party. She was on the verge of crossing the road when the first of the professional mourners was practically on top of her. Snapped from the turmoil of her thoughts, she jumped back to let them go. All would have been well if it had not been for Mr Darcy.

The hearse was pulled by a matched team of four magnificent black horses with sable plumes on their heads nodding in time with each tread of their muffled hooves. While Tempy kept her respectful silence, head bowed, she felt Mr Darcy pulling. His lead slithered from her grasp. Then he was jumping up and down, barking at the strange feathered thing on top of the lead horse's head. The horse tired of that game all too quickly. It aimed a hoof at the small dog, and kicked hard.

Mr Darcy let out a high-pitched yelp, and tumbled into the gutter where he lay unmoving. Tempy screamed, and ran to his side, kneeling on the road, not minding the dirt that stained her striped skirts.

The funeral procession passed on, and Tempy looked up from the dog, her gloves covered in blood with her tears silently streaming. She picked up his little body and held it to her, feeling his heart slow down. Smelly of the nether regions though he might be after something had disagreed with his internal workings, Mr Darcy was her constant companion and one true love.

Tempy gathered herself together and bolted for home, nearly colliding with the last carriage full of mourners, its wheels perilously close to her buckled boots. She staggered back almost senseless of what had interrupted her flight of mercy. A man (that he was both young and handsome did register in her mind) leaned his head out and called to her to watch out for her safety. Observing the dog in her arms, and the blood that already stained her clothes, he rapped on the carriage roof to signal to the driver to stop.

He pulled his head in. Tempy heard a woman's protesting voice from the interior of the carriage and him speaking in response. Then the carriage door was flung wide and the fellow leapt down onto the road. In long, firm strides he came up to her. Tempy looked up at him through her tears. So distraught was she that she only just noticed his kind eyes and generous mouth. He had brown, somewhat untamed, hair that invited one to try to tidy it, and a nose that while straight was not too stern; his clean-shaven chin had a delightful cleft in its centre.

Tempy became breathless for quite another reason than Mr Darcy's injuries as the stranger towered over her, and the tempo of her heart accelerated so that she could hear the blood whooshing in her ears. Heat rose to her face as he removed his topper and held it loosely in his grey-gloved hand. An unruly lock fell forwards across his cheek.

'I'm so sorry about your dog, miss.' He brushed back the rebellious lock and ran his long fingers through his hair in some vain attempt to tame it. Instead it made him look as if he had just risen from his bed.

She was blushing scarlet now, she knew it. What was she thinking? She needed to get Mr Darcy home and mended as soon as may be.

'Look.' He reached into his pocket, withdrew something and offered it to her. 'For your dog.'

His hand brushed hers, and she felt a jolt like electricity as their fingers touched, even though they both wore gloves. Then she saw the folded paper that he was passing to her. She jerked back her hand, and kneaded poor Mr Darcy's fur.

'Money?' she fairly screeched, and gave the man such a venomous look he stepped back in shock and astonishment. In Tempy's experience, a man offering coin to a woman meant only one thing and it had nothing to do with dogs.

Tempy turned her back on him and hurried away with anger, desire, and worry all rolled into one, crushing her.

Denton Lester climbed back into the carriage. He paused, clinging to the door frame to watch her retreating back.

'What was that all about?' said Mrs Tushingham, the younger (and only remaining) of his late mother's sisters; they were burying the elder. Her daughter, Catherine, sat quietly beside her. She barely spoke a word in her mother's presence—it was never required since Mrs Tushingham was perfectly capable of speaking for both or, indeed, anyone else.

'Apparently we ran over a young woman's dog,' he said, finding it difficult to remove the image of said young woman's face from his mind, not that he had much desire to do so. Indeed, for the sake of desire he wanted to keep that image in his mind forever.

'What young woman?' Mrs Tushingham's tone was sharp and demanding.

'A remarkably handsome one,' he said and resolved to look her up once the business of burying was done. He interpreted the frown on his aunt's face to be annoyance at the delay.

A Doctor is In

'Mother, Mother!' Tempy tripped over the welcome mat in the front hall, barged into a potted fern in her haste, and sent it flying with a tremendous crash.

'Mother!'

'Child, hush, I am communing.' Madame Lacroix wafted down the stairs seemingly on a stream of aether, turbaned, be-ringed, be-jewelled, heavily made-up, and wearing some kind of Chinese gown of her own design.

'Mother, Mr Darcy has been in a most terrible accident.'

'Now Tempy, you know not to call me Mother when there are people around.'

'What people?' Her mother was hardly dressed for receiving guests and there was no séance scheduled until the evening. The dark was more effective. Madame Lacroix reached the bottom step and raised an eyebrow at the state of her daughter and the dog.

'We will talk of that later,' she said. 'Fear not, my dear, there is a doctor in the house who may be able to help the animal.'

Tempy looked stern. 'Doctor? Mother, did you have a gentleman in your room last night?'

'A gentleman?' said her mother and waved her hand as if to dismiss the comment like an unwelcome ghost.

'Are you up to your old tricks, *Madame*? I thought that was behind us.'

'Temperance O'Rourke, you know nothing of *l'amour*. So do not speak of that which you do not understand.' Her mother's hurtful words only served to remind Tempy of her lack of success in that arena. 'Come, the good doctor should be able to help your smelly hound.'

Dr Mayfield pushed his spectacles to the top of his bald head, not quite believing that having taken off his jacket, rolled up his shirtsleeves and unbuttoned his waistcoat, he found himself tending to a dog—and one with an unpleasant odour at that.

If any of the ladies he treated for their various humours could see him now, he would lose their patronage in an instant. However, for Madame Lacroix, he would examine the dog. There was nothing he wouldn't do for Madame Lacroix, and that had been true for all the many years he had known her.

Dr Mayfield noted Tempy's pale face and agitated demeanour, so typical of the weaker sex when they became overwrought, and asked Madame Lacroix to fetch a small tipple for her.

The girl held up her hand to defend herself when her mother offered the cut-glass tumbler and the amber liquid rolling around in it. 'I'm sorry, Doctor, but I drink nothing stronger than tea,' she said by way of protest.

'I must insist, Miss O'Rourke,' he said kindly. 'Your humours are out of balance. This is but a simple calming draught.'

'But, Dr Mayfield—'

'Precisely. I am a doctor of medicine,' he said with a little more metal in his tone. 'I have prescribed it. You must take it.'

She sighed, very sweetly he thought, and raised the glass to her perfect lips. She winced as she swallowed it. He popped out his pocket watch and checked the time. He did not need to be about his rounds for another hour or so.

The doctor turned his attention to the poor dog that remained in a state of blissful unawareness. It was just as well; his patients did not normally bite—apart from Mrs Jenkins-Smythe, of course, but with her it was simple playfulness—and he did not relish the prospect of dealing with one that did.

Mr Darcy, it would seem, had been very lucky. Two of his ribs were badly bruised but not broken, and the prodigious amount of blood that had poured forth came from a wound that needed only three stitches.

'There,' he said as he washed and dried his hands. Quite a new thing to do that, but sanitary measures were all the rage—and long may that continue, in his opinion. 'Your dog should be quite fine, Miss O'Rourke. He must undertake no strenuous exercise, such as chasing after sticks and balls, for at least'—the doctor wondered how quickly dogs were able to mend, but he had no idea, so he guessed—'six weeks.' That ought to be enough.

Tempy stood too quickly and had to steady herself by putting her arm on Madame Lacroix's shoulder.

'Thank you, Doctor. I am indebted to you, but,' she said as she stood up straight and wavered only a little, 'my name is Tempy, please be sure to use it in future.'

The older man blushed, for the young lady with her dark tumbling curls, blue eyes and pale skin, was quite beautiful though she seemed not to know it.

'Of course, Miss—Tempy, you may pet him but do avoid lifting him as much as possible for two of those weeks. Otherwise the stitches may tear and you may hurt his ribs.'

Dr Mayfield was horrified as tears coursed down Tempy's face, and he fumbled in his pocket for a clean handkerchief. Tempy took it and blew her nose noisily.

'Now dear, come with me and we shall have a nice cup of tea. Nothing is a surer comfort.' Madame Lacroix smiled at the doctor as she walked forwards to take the girl in hand. 'Dr. Mayfield, perhaps you would be so good as to return Mr Darcy to the basket in Tempy's writing room?'

The doctor smiled his acquiescence.

Just Another Letter

Several days later, Tempy sat at her writing desk once again, rubbing her eyes, though her mother had told her she would get bags, sags, and wrinkles if she continued to do so. Her mother was full of such advice. Tempy had the idea that perhaps half of what her mother said was just nonsense, which meant the other half was useful. The difficulty was in deciding which was which. That did not stop her from incorporating large amounts of her mother's words into her advice to her correspondents.

She growled and threw down her pen. Stupid people.

Mr Darcy lay in his basket looking up at her pathetically as dogs are wont to do, even though the good doctor had been kind enough to leave some laudanum to ease his pain. Dr Mayfield had also passed on a warning that Mr Darcy should not be given too much lest he become addicted. Tempy was in full agreement; the last thing they needed was an opium-eating pug in their lives.

Tempy had answered any number of inane letters from the whinging public at large that morning, everything from best tips on weight loss from a woman whose daughter refused to take even the slightest walk to a man who was worried about hair loss and which treatments he should use to a lovesick boy who was being spurned because of his bad skin.

But no, not even that could plunge her quite into the foul humour in which she found herself. The ultimate cause was the *other* letter that she had received at breakfast.

Dear Miss O'Rourke,
I hope you will not find this too forward, but since Wednesday morning last, when we went to bury my dear Aunt, you have been on my mind.
It was you, was it not, with the small dog who was trampled by the horse's hooves? My man had your name from another resident when I sent him to enquire.
I apologise for not being able to stop and offer proper help at the time, but hope that you understand, given the circumstances. I trust that all has been brought to a satisfactory conclusion.
Please do let me know if there is anything I can be of assistance with.
Your servant,
Denton Lester

Her mother had, of course, demanded to know who the letter was from and the look on her face when Tempy had read the name. Well! That had put her mother in quite the spin. Mr Darcy had been run over by the funeral cortège of none other than Minnie Lester: an irascible, hateful old gossip who just happened to be one of London's wealthiest women. She had come into her money by way of her deceased husband and, because of that, she owned the Hampstead Air-dock. Or rather, it was owned by her estate, since she too had passed on.

'You will have nothing whatsoever to do with the spawn of that she-devil!' her mother had cried when the content of the letter was revealed to her.

'He's not her son, Mother, he's her nephew.'

'Bad blood, Temperance.' Her mother always insisted on calling her by her full name, much to Tempy's annoyance, but that was a mother's prerogative. 'And bad blood always runs true. Every one of those three evil witches came from the same sire and dam. The whole family's tainted.'

'How can you possibly know that, Mother?' Tempy was remembering his handsome face and the fine figure he made even in mourning black. Just the thought of his features made her heart flutter and her pulse race.

'The spirits are never wrong,' said her mother. 'I forbid you to see him. I forbid him entrance to this house.' It sounded as if she were casting a spell, or more likely a curse.

'Oh really,' said Tempy in a desperate attempt to save the situation. 'Let's be quite clear about this, Mother. The only spirits you hear are the ones calling from the bottle. And they are the ones that speak to your clients. You are a fraud, Mother, don't pretend it's anything else.'

'And you're turning into a harridan of a spinster, my girl. It's high time you found yourself a good Irish lad to teach you the real way to make love. Not like some jumped-up English lordling who could not find his way out of his trousers without help.'

'What would you know about love, Mother? What happens in your bed is not love'—Tempy took a deep breath—'you don't even know the name of my father.'

Her mother stopped short and for a moment Tempy thought she had won. However, Mary O'Rourke might have taken a heavy blow but she was not out for the count. 'I might not have known his name, my girl, but at least he was Catholic.'

A Message From Beyond

Madame Lacroix sat at the round table opposite the door, so she was the first person each guest saw as they entered. She kept her eyes closed, her hands flat on the heavy embroidered tablecloth, and breathed in the incense-filled air. She'd have to have a word with the maid, Lily. She had set too much burning in the pot and it was almost overpowering. It made her quite light-headed.

The guests filed in. Madame Lacroix could hear them breathing. Almost all had that quickening of breath in expectation of the excitement and the thrill of the séance. Whether they were believers or not, they always felt the tension. Some of the more modern practicing mediums used the new phonographic devices to add atmosphere, whether it was music playing in the next room, or sounds of the other world created especially for the occasion. Mary O'Rourke preferred the traditional approach; there was too much that could go wrong with those new-fangled devices.

The carpet had a very thick weave so the chairs made no sound as the guests settled. They barely even creaked. Madame Lacroix heard the door close, which was the signal for her to open her eyes. She rolled her eyeballs back and slowly revealed the whites. There were several satisfying gasps. She closed her eyes again and reopened them to look at the audience.

That she had her clothes on, and there was a group, did not mean this was any different to the old days. It was always a show, and she gave the best performance she could. The first person on the list was the husband of Mrs Juniper, a nervous woman who would be easily satisfied with some kind words from beyond the grave. All her life Mary O'Rourke had seen herself as a provider of solace and comfort. Nothing had changed.

'Henry, we call thee, Henry!' Madame Lacroix' eyes were closed in seeming ecstasy. She swayed in her seat in an expression of joy. The table tipped and the ladies and gentlemen seated at it let out a variety of shrieks and screams.

There was a flare from behind her, and the air became nothing but incense. The crown of Mary's head felt as if it were about to break free. Why had she not told Temperance the truth?

She coughed and lights seemed to explode behind her eyes. She tried to focus on the sort of thing Henry would say to his wife. But, as she opened her mouth, a crotchety, wavering voice scratched its way out of her throat.

'You whoring baggage! The decrepit sailor will not fail me! He will tell her everything.'

Tempy sat with her mother as she tossed and turned. Her mother's fiery red hair highlighted the paleness of her fevered skin, and she looked old. Tempy turned to Dr Mayfield. He had a genuinely concerned expression, and Tempy realised his eyes were the same hazel as her own.

'How is she, Doctor?'

'She has had a bad fright, my dear. It seems that she really can commune with the dead.'

Tempy frowned at that but said nothing. She knew her mother's performance was just an act.

'Or, your mother was overcome by the fumes of the incense,' he added with a gentle and sympathetic smile.

'How did you know she is my mother? She has never told anyone since we came to London.'

'Why, you look so alike only a fool would not know.' He smiled at Tempy. 'Your hair alone, the same colour and the same waves, would be enough to mark you.'

A cold hand clutched at Tempy's wrist and any further question she might have had for the doctor was forgotten. Her mother's eyes were open and she looked so very tired. Worn out.

'Tempy?' Her mother's other hand clutched at Tempy's wrist. 'forgive me.'

'Forgive you, Mother? What in the world for?'

Her mother hesitated and glanced at the doctor. She almost looked as if she was going to say nothing more. But then she looked back at Tempy.

'The good Lord punishes me for sins,' she said. 'A package came for you from Denton Lester. I hid it away.' She gripped Tempy with hands like claws. 'But, Temperance, you must not start a relationship with him. Minnie Lester has made our lives very difficult. It was by her word that we have struggled to be accepted into London society.'

'Oh, Mother, why did you not tell me?'

'Somehow she had learnt of our past,' again her mother hesitated, 'and I was ashamed.'

Tempy recovered the package from the chest at the foot of her mother's bed. It was wrapped simply in brown paper and string. It bore no marks from the Post Office, so must have been hand-delivered. Settling on the bed she held it for a long moment, fearing—without understanding that fear—what she might find inside. Her heart felt as if it fluttered within her breast.

She opened it with trembling hands. Within the paper was a cardboard box, and pulling off the lid revealed a small blue Indian rubber ball accompanying a red leather collar and matching lead for Mr Darcy. The note with it simply read:

Forgive me for any distress caused. It was not my intention to pry or to hurt, but when I was shown the door at your house I feared that the incident must have wounded you more than I thought.

Denton.

Tempy's hand went to her throat where her pulse beat much faster than it should. She had thought of nothing but Denton's handsome features since the day of Mr Darcy's accident. She sighed in annoyance at herself. What a lovelorn fool she was to moon over just one man, whom she had met only once. Yet her heart raced at the image her mind so helpfully supplied: he was, quite simply, the most gorgeous man she had ever seen.

She paced the room, annoyed with herself. Was she, Tempy O'Rourke, really falling head-over-heels in love like some waif-like heroine in a romance story? She feared to admit the truth to herself and, worse still, her mother was unshakable in her belief that Tempy must have nothing to do with him.

It was all too much, really it was.

A Sensation in Society

'It goes on to say that even Mr Conan Doyle is interested in meeting the famous Madame Lacroix,' said Catherine Tushingham, running her finger along the lines of the newspaper as it lay beside her on the breakfast table.

'Well,' said her mother. 'I am quite sure he will find her out to be a fraud.'

'But a visit to her parlour is the thing, Mother, everybody who is anybody is doing it.'

The autumn sun was barely strong enough to light the room, and all the gas lamps were glowing. The fire's embers warmed the breakfast room at 32 Kensington Square Gardens—formerly the London address of Minnie Lester, now the property of Denton Lester and temporarily occupied by his aunt and cousin.

Lester's attention was fixed on a copy of the previous evening's *London Leader*.

'What are you reading, Denton?' Catherine asked abruptly, spoiling his concentration.

'Oh, nothing,' he said and turned the page.

'You were very absorbed.'

'Nonsense, what were you saying?' He gathered a forkful of kedgeree and chewed it. Truth be told he disliked the rice and fish combination, though at least his deceased aunt's cook did the best she could. He supposed that it was now his responsibility to deal with such things that were not to his taste. How much simpler it would be if he had a wife to manage such things. He had no idea how to ask the housekeeper (a forbidding woman at best) to change the menu to something more appetising. Chances were his attempt would cause ructions in the household.

Simpler to just put up with it.

'I saw in the paper about this Madame Lacroix,' said Catherine. 'There's gossip all over the country about how she had a true vision at a séance. Apparently all the ladies fainted and the gentlemen were quite unsettled by the incident.'

'Your Aunt Minnie, God rest her soul,' put in Mrs Tushingham—Aunt Dolly to all those of Denton's generation—'very wisely shunned the woman. She is most certainly not a lady.'

'Lady or not,' continued her daughter, 'it says that the strain of the contact with the dead rendered Madame Lacroix senseless and she has not been seen in public since, though all enquiries are being replied to by her associate Miss O'Rourke.'

Denton jerked his head up. 'Temperance O'Rourke?'

Catherine scanned the newspaper again. 'Oh yes, it says that. Temperance O'Rourke. Why do I know that name?'

'Wasn't that the name of the woman who threw her dog in front of our carriage at Minnie's funeral?' said Aunt Dolly.

Denton looked across at her. There was a strange hardness in her eyes that he did not understand. Abruptly the look disappeared and was replaced by a smile; at least it *looked* like a smile. Sometimes, with Aunt Dolly, it was hard to tell. As far as Denton could tell she lacked a sense of humour.

'She did not throw her dog in front of the carriage, dear aunt,' he said. 'It was an accident. However I think I should send my condolences.'

'Goodness me, Denton,' she said, still with the enigmatic smile. 'That would be quite improper. You cannot be sending condolences to someone you barely know.'

That he had already sent a gift, even if for the dog, was probably something he should keep hidden from his aunt. 'Well, it is not as if we are entirely unacquainted,' he said, hoping to stay on safer ground, 'after all I have sent a letter apologising for the behaviour of the horse.'

Catherine burst out laughing. 'You apologised for a horse?'

When she said it like that it did sound ridiculous. But then he had not precisely used those words, and perhaps it would be better if Catherine and her mother were diverted by that than consider how much he felt for the woman he had barely even spoken to. His heart pounded like an engine as he thought of her beautiful face. It had been with him ever since that fateful but wonderful instant when they met.

'I have a much better idea,' said Mrs Tushingham.

Denton, in a moment of childlike enthusiasm, thought she was going to suggest he visit.

'I shall invite her to afternoon tea at Lyons in Piccadilly next week,' she said. 'And I will extend all our condolences.'

Denton's hopes were dashed to smithereens. All he could do was nod.

There was no atmospheric tube train running from Hampstead into the city. The Charing Cross, Euston and Hampstead Railway Company had plans to construct one, but it would not open for several years yet.

Tempy did not, however, object to riding a steam omnibus. The day was not wet and she was fully clothed to protect herself from the cold so she climbed to the open top deck and paid the conductor tuppence for the fare. She would have liked to ride at the front, but that was not what a lady did. Instead she squeezed herself onto the wooden bench (glad she had not had Lily tighten her corset excessively) three from the front so she could observe the glories of the ex-capital as they were paraded before her.

Mr Darcy would have enjoyed the journey since he would not have had to walk, but he was not yet well enough to take the stress.

The omnibus's descent of Hampstead Hill was breathlessly exciting, even though she knew they did this journey every hour of every day, as the slope was so steep she felt as if she might fall out the front of the vehicle. It was as good as a fairground ride.

They proceeded into the city, descending Primrose Hill with the Regent's Park Zoological Gardens in the distance. Along Marylebone Road and then Gower Street. They passed through the theatre district and entered Oxford Street, lined with all manner of shops and offices.

There was a traffic jam at Leicester Square where there appeared to be an altercation between a bicyclist, a steam-hansom, and a goods truck carrying fruit. It took twenty minutes and the arrival of several policemen before the vehicles began to move once more. She always marvelled at the sheer quantity of people and vehicles on London streets.

But as they turned down Shaftesbury Avenue, only a few stops from Piccadilly, she wondered at the invitation from Mrs Tushingham. The letter had mentioned Denton and explained that she was Minnie Lester's sister.

Tempy's mother had recovered quickly when she realised that her 'attack' had potentially increased her business tenfold. And, now that Minnie Lester was no longer spreading rumours against her, she fully expected a much better quality of client. And by quality, she meant well-heeled.

It had taken all of Dr Mayfield's efforts, and those of Tempy, to prevent her from heading directly back to the tilting table. Tempy had also pointed out that her mother must refuse any request from Conan Doyle, since the man was notorious for unmasking fraudulent spiritualists. (Though he claimed a genuine desire to find the real thing.)

'Then he should see me,' declared her mother.

'Mother, you are a charlatan.'

'I had a vision.'

'You were sick from incense fumes.'

'I received a message from beyond.'

'That called you a whore. It is just as well they aren't mentioning that in the papers.'

Her mother only acquiesced when Tempy pointed out that disappearing for a few days would increase her mystery, and hence the demand for her services.

Then came the letter from Mrs Tushingham. The feeling of excitement and fear had only grown over the last few days. Tempy tried desperately not to hope this was an opening gambit in allowing her to enter London society and thus win the heart of the man she adored. She was terrified she would be disappointed.

The omnibus came to a halt just before Piccadilly Circus and Tempy alighted. The fountain in the centre of the Circus splashed in the late autumn sunlight. The statue stood at its heart, erected to commemorate the good works of Lord Shaftesbury. She looked with longing at the young Greek deity with its bow and arrows: Anteros, god of requited love and the avenger of those unrequited.

'Bless me, Anteros, so my love is returned to me in full measure,' she muttered under her breath. The Lyons Tea House stood on a corner a little way down Piccadilly itself: a temple to delicious food, open all day and night except Sundays.

The ground floor was given over to the direct sales of the excellent fare of J. Lyons, so she headed up two flights to the floor reserved for ladies and gentlemen of quality. She was relieved of her outdoor clothes and escorted to the table of Mrs Tushingham.

The woman was so thin one might assume she had the consumption, but her gaze was sharp, clear and certain like a bird of prey. One to be careful of. Introductions were made and a waitress brought a fresh pot of tea and a plate of sumptuous-looking cakes. Good manners forbade Tempy from taking more than two on to her own plate, though after the hour in the fresh cold air she was ravenous.

'I would like to offer my sympathies to Madame Lacroix,' said Mrs Tushingham after Tempy had eaten her cakes delicately and sipped her tea.

'Thank you, it was a fright for everyone.'

'I imagine the spirits can be very strong.'

'Not usually.'

There was a pause. Tempy knew she was not being helpful in the conversation but she was certain that Mrs Tushingham had not been referring to ethereal spirits. There had been a very definite edge to her voice. Tempy's upbringing had fully acquainted her with malicious innuendo.

'You know my nephew.'

Oh Denton! 'We met briefly.'

'How is your dog?'

'He is on the mend.'

Mrs Tushingham glanced around, leaned forwards and placed her hand on Tempy's wrist. 'My dear, I felt it important to speak to you directly as there is a matter of grave importance.'

'There is?'

'It is Denton.'

Panic made Tempy's heart beat faster. 'Denton?'

Mrs Tushingham hesitated. 'This is a difficult thing to say, particularly of one's own flesh and blood.'

Tempy held her breath. Was he ill? Dying?

'He is a man of low morals, my dear.'

Tempy blinked in surprise. 'He is?'

The older woman nodded, released Tempy's wrist and sat back. 'He is known for leading young girls on and *ruining* them.'

The image that the word 'ruin' conjured in Tempy's mind made her catch her breath. It was most certainly not the picture Mrs Tushingham had intended. Tempy's skin flushed hot as she tried to concentrate on Mrs Tushingham, and not the image of Denton completely unclothed. Tempy was familiar with male anatomy and its function.

'Quite so, my dear, horrifying.'

Tempy was confused for a moment and then realised Mrs Tushingham had taken her reaction as disgust, rather than with a most unladylike thrill which coursed through her veins.

'I strongly recommend you stay away from him.'

'I see.'

'I certainly hope you do, Miss O'Rourke,' said Mrs Tushingham. 'For your own sake.'

And somehow Tempy could only interpret her words as a personal threat.

The weather had turned colder and it rained for three solid days. Living as they did at the top of Hampstead Hill, they were not much affected, but below them, in the city, the recently constructed sewers overflowed and life was miserable. It was reflected in the letters that *Dear Prudence* received. Then again she never received happy letters; she did, after all, provide advice for the lovelorn and otherwise helpless.

The postman had delivered another package of letters from the newspaper for her to answer. Her task was not simply one of answering all the letters. There were column-inches she was required to fill, the same each week. And it was a matter of choosing those letters that best filled the space; from her viewpoint long letters with short replies were ideal, as it meant less work. However, her editor had made it clear that he preferred more and shorter letters.

So she needed to select the typical and most frequent questions and answer those in a way that might help more than one. Also there should be variety, though that was hard to achieve since the letters she received tended along the same lines: a man who wanted to know how to speak to a woman; the woman who wanted to rid herself of the affections of an unwelcome suitor; husbands or wives who did not listen; difficulties with staff or neighbours.

Tempy went to the drawing room where she did her writing. Mr Darcy lay in his basket, looking quite forlorn as usual. He wore the new collar Denton had sent. She would have replaced it with the old one, after Mrs Tushingham's words, but it had been disposed of. The sight of it made her heart flutter again, as it always did when she thought of the handsome lines of his face.

In a rush she went to the window and looked out to the gate in the park. Just in case. Tempy was sure she had seen Denton Lester from her window, flowers in his hand, shoulders slumped as the rain dripped from the brim of his top hat the day before. Perhaps he was there again.

She cursed herself for being a fool. Not only could she not be in love with him, his aunt had made it quite clear that he most certainly was not in love with her. After all love at first sight was ridiculous, was it not?

Somehow that did not stop her from searching for him on the street, and as far into the park as the dim light would allow. There was a movement in the shadow beneath a tree. A man stepped forwards. She held her breath. Could it be him again? Was his aunt wrong about him? Was Tempy the woman to make him honest and decent?

But it was not him. Instead it was a surly fellow in a leather overcoat, with a matching hat that looked vaguely nautical. He stood in the half-light, water running from the oiled surface of his coat. It may not have been Denton, but this man was looking directly at her with a gaze that did not waver. Tempy held his eye for the count of ten, then shuddered and turned away.

The room looked ghostlike in the half-light of the fire and the gas lights. It was almost unreal, as if the spirits her mother pretended to conjure had taken up residence.

She sighed deeply and shook herself. This was no time to become maudlin; she had work to do. Tempy strode across to the writing desk, sat in the chair and took a sip from her teacup. She unfolded the first letter of the day and nearly spat out said tea—terribly unladylike, but when one has a shock, one has a shock.

Dear Prudence,
I find myself in a difficult situation.
I was witness to an accident in which a young lady's dog was injured by a horse that was pulling a carriage. That it was a funeral cortège should make no difference.
Having found out that the lady lives just doors away from where the accident occurred, I sent a note to which I have had no reply. I then, feeling braver, came with a package that was accepted but I was turned away from the house.
Just yesterday, I stood like a fool with flowers outside her home again, afraid to knock for fear of being turned away again.
Please advise me on what to do.
Lost in London.

Tempy realised she still had a mouthful of lukewarm tea. She swallowed it and then eyed the decanters of spirits as being something more appropriate to the situation. However, her previous experience with hard liquor had not been a good one.

She was in a quandary. She must decide whether to ignore the aunt's words and pursue him, or cut him dead. She thought about her mother's words about her understanding of love. She considered her relationship with Elbert.

Dare she encourage Denton? She lifted her Birmingham-manufactured fountain pen and pulled a fresh sheet of paper from its pile. What was the worst that could happen? That he would 'ruin' her? Sad to say she was already there—not that she had had relations with a man, but she knew exactly what that entailed and desired it from Denton. Truth be told, if anyone were to be ruined, it would be him.

That decided her. With a trembling hand, Tempy scratched out a reply.

Dear Lost in London,

Has it occurred to you that there may be some impediment to the young lady entering into correspondence or indeed meeting with you?

Perhaps there is someone within your family, past or present, with whom a member of the young lady's family has a grievance.

My advice would be to do some research, give it some time, and then approach the young lady again when you have more information at your disposal.

Prudence.

The Personal Perambulator

The following day dawned bright and clear. It remained so through the morning though a raw wind blustered through the skeletal trees. Tempy was muffled against the coarse elements on a walk through the park. Mr Darcy, resplendent in his red collar and lead (though he clearly did not appreciate their quality),snuffled at the remains of the leaves.

If he had been doing his job as a dog, thought Tempy, he would have chased the leaves as they ran and spun in the wind. Her cheeks were cold and she knew they would be bright red. She looked into the sky above the air-dock but with the wind this strong it was unlikely any ship would take off.

The great sky-liners could ignore the wind but they flew from Croydon far to the south beyond the Thames. Why could her mother not have found them a house there instead?

But if she had, Tempy would not have taken Mr Darcy for his walk and they would not have encountered the funeral. And she would not have met Denton.

The morning post had not brought a letter to Prudence from *Lost in London*, but her reply would not have been printed until this morning. Then, if he truly wanted to win her, he would take the advice of *Prudence* and investigate. That might take another day, perhaps two. And then he would write again, or call. She sighed and felt the cold penetrate her ample clothing. She should return home and write her replies.

On the lake a toy boat in full sail scudded across the water, splashing in the ripples that on its scale were big waves, while the children that owned it raced around the edge to meet it on the far side.

Mr Darcy dawdled as they made their way back along the paths while Tempy became uncomfortably chilled. Finally she scooped him up and set off at a brisk pace to warm herself. She imagined he had been going slow on purpose simply to make her carry him. He was most certainly back to his old self, even if not fully healed.

Tempy stopped short at the park gate as she was greeted by a most extraordinary sight. The door to her home was open and something was emerging. Not truly understanding why she did so she withdrew back under the trees, much as the fellow she had seen on the previous day had been.

Mr Darcy wriggled. She calmed him by rubbing his neck.

A mechanical contrivance emerged through the arch. It resembled a bath chair though it had four sturdy wheels like a carriage. There was a steam pipe that rose a little way at the rear, but it was not emitting smoke or steam. In the middle of the vehicle sat a man; he was huge—not of stature, though it was hard to tell, but his clothes hid fat that stretched from one side of the bath chair to the other. Despite his size she could see the cut of his clothes indicated someone of fortune. But his face, under his hat, was fixed in an unfriendly scowl.

A whirring sound reached her ears and she deduced the machine must be running on electricity. The vehicle descended the two steps at the front of the house and sped up, making good time along the path. Lily, the maid, scooted ahead, though she was not dressed for the cold, and opened the gate to allow the machine to pass through.

The steam engine puttered and thumped into action as he moved out on to the street and headed away at a good pace. The bath chair part bounced languidly on its suspension.

Since her mother was not yet accepting clients for spiritual consultations, Tempy was very curious as to whom this visitor was.

Lily directed Tempy to the lounge to find her mother, though following the marks the rubber tyres had made on the parquet floor would have been sufficient.

The door was ajar, and Tempy did not knock; she was an adult and lived in the house on equal terms with her mother. More than equal, since Tempy considered she had a much more sensible head on her shoulders.

Tempy was not entirely sure what to expect. Perhaps her mother lounging on the sofa with a glass in her hand. Perhaps sitting with the newspaper, for The Cloister had been very advanced and taught the women to read and perform arithmetic. It even employed a doctor who visited regularly to ensure they were free of diseases.

However, she did not expect to find her mother leaning forwards and wiping her eyes with a kerchief.

All of Tempy's questions flew from her mind and she rushed to her mother's side. She sat and put her arm around her shoulders.

'What is it? What has happened?'

Her mother sniffed in an unladylike manner, then blew her nose.

'It is nothing, Temperance.'

'You're crying. Why?' It was all the more shocking in that Tempy had never seen her mother cry before. Not here and not in all the years at The Cloister. Anger, yes. That was a favourite emotion. But never this.

'No, I'm not,' she sniffed. 'It is nothing, merely a reaction to that fellow's contrivance, can you not smell it?'

It was true there was an irritating sort of smell, something like the chemicals in cleaning liquids. But it was not strong nor had Tempy ever known her mother react to anything in such a fashion.

'Are you sure?'

Her mother sniffed again. This time she raised her head and turned it towards her daughter. She put a smile on her lips; it even spread to her eyes. 'Yes, of course, I am sure,' she hesitated and then added. 'I have been more sensitive to such things since my turn. See, it is wearing off as we speak.'

Tempy saw her mother's eyes were red and swollen. Her cheeks were damp with tears. But it might be true.

'Who was the man?'

'Which man?'

Tempy blinked in astonishment. 'Really, Mother, do you take me for a complete fool?'

'He was a client.'

'You are not receiving clients.'

'He wishes to be a client.'

'And he came to the door?'

Her mother escaped Tempy's enclosing arm by standing up. She waved her kerchief dismissively. 'I might have had a letter from him and invited him.'

'When?'

'Yesterday, the day before, I really can't recall.'

Tempy stood up and went to the door, where she paused before leaving. 'Have it your way, Mother. But you are not well enough to start seeing clients.'

'Yes, dear.'

If her mother thought Tempy was satisfied with her answer then she was quite mistaken. Tempy cornered Lily in the drawing room and got the truth from her. The man was one Giles Mackenzie who had arrived and insisted his card be presented to Mrs O'Rourke (not Madame Lacroix). He had been invited through immediately.

Of his card—and Tempy searched quite thoroughly—there was no sign at all.

A Moment of Revelation

The weak winter sun had certainly brought out the toffs and hoi polloi, thought Denton as he brushed through the crowds in the Cremorne Pleasure Gardens. The wind was strong but the large numbers of people made it tolerable. Even so his coat, scarf, and gloves were hard put to protect him from the elements.

Catherine Tushingham's tight grip on his elbow and the pressure of her body against his kept his left side warm, however.

'It's very bracing,' she said conversationally.

'We're lucky to get a good day this time of the year,' he replied. 'It will be snowing before you know it.'

'Snow makes everything very pretty.'

'And brings life to a halt.'

She poked him in the side. He really disliked it when she did that. 'Don't be so out of sorts.'

He sighed. This outing had not been his idea. It was his aunt's and he knew precisely why. She continued to throw her daughter at him in the hopes that an engagement would be forthcoming. All his aunt was doing was attempting to mimic the nobility; it was not something he wanted, even if he had liked his cousin.

They edged their way around a crowd watching a juggler with knives that flashed in the sun as they spun above his head.

The occasional ragamuffin ran through the crowd. As long as they were moving fast he could be sure that someone else had been relieved of their possessions. It was important to keep one's wallet, watch, and other precious possessions safe.

'Let's have a pie!' exclaimed Catherine. Denton eyed her fawn coat; if she spilt gravy on her it would be very obvious. Anyway it would be her mother's decision. To be honest he could do with a break; his arm was aching from the constant pulling, and the cold weather did make one hungry.

Denton stopped and detached Catherine. She grabbed at his hand to hold it but he deftly moved it out of the way, to rub his cheek. He turned to Mrs Tushingham.

'Catherine would like a pie, Aunt.'

Catherine took off through the crowd towards a stall that was belching smoke from its ovens, with a gaggle of customers around it. She might be nearly seventeen but she acted like a child of twelve, and Denton would not have considered her as a suitable wife even if he did not have someone else in mind. His heart thrilled as he thought of the beautiful and strong Miss O'Rourke. However, he could not let Catherine run about the crowd unattended.

He set off after her but not before his aunt had attached herself to his arm.

'Is she not a delightful creature?'

'Oh yes, delightful.'

For some reason Mrs Tushingham was walking slowly, forcing him to match her pace. Catherine was already out of sight. He worried but this revealed itself as an ideal moment to speak of a matter that had been bothering him.

'You have not said what transpired when you met Miss O'Rourke, Aunt Dolly.'

She hesitated. 'That is because I did not want to hurt your feelings.'

'Why would my feelings be hurt?'

'Because she was quite indifferent to your solicitations, Denton,' she said. 'If there is a word I would use it is that she was cold.' She paused to let that sink in and then said, quite casually. 'But that really comes as no surprise.'

Denton felt an anger turning inside of him though he did not know in which direction it should be hurled. 'I don't understand. Why is it not a surprise?'

'Because of her stock, of course.'

'Because she is Irish?'

'Oh no, if only that were all it was. Your aunt, God rest her soul, knew the truth of it. She told me though I am not sure I can even bring myself to say the words.'

Denton stopped and faced his aunt. 'Tell me.'

'Here? In public?'

Denton glanced at the people milling about them, not a single one interested in their conversation. 'There is no one here that listens; it is more private than any room with a door. What is it you want to say?'

'She is the daughter of a prostitute.'

'I don't believe you.'

'The woman, Madame Lacroix, was a whore in Dublin. She is the girl's mother, though they try to hide that fact. You think you have your heart set on her, but she is the lowest woman you could ever encounter. I doubt the mother even knows who sired the child.'

Denton felt his world spinning. He staggered back and then turned away, heading into the crowd not even knowing where he was going.

A Relationship Undone

The day after the visit from the man with the self-propelled bath chair, Tempy took her usual morning walk with Mr Darcy—or rather her morning 'carry' as she assisted him across the road.

'Perhaps,' she said to him, 'we should arrange for a self-propelled basket for you.' She looked down into his eyes, upturned in a look of sorrow towards hers. 'Yes, I imagine you would find that most amenable.'

Once she had entered the park she set him down gently on his paws and he proceeded to investigate the new smells that had accumulated since yesterday.

The weather continued cold as if winter had arrived and decided it would stay. The park was almost empty as she and Mr Darcy made their slow way through the trees towards the lake. Tempy had not given any thought to the man she had seen watching her from the park but, in the distance under a stand of trees, there was a figure again. Just a shadow among the trunks.

She told herself she was foolish and simply imagining things. But she kept her eye on him just the same, ready at any moment to grab Mr Darcy and head home as quick as may be.

There were no children playing by the lake today. Its surface was free of ice but Tempy imagined it would not be long before it formed. A man sat on one of the green-painted wrought-iron benches which dotted the path around the lake. His head was down and cradled in his hands though all she could see from this angle was his voluminous coat and homburg.

He looked familiar—though not Denton, who was taller—as she reached the lake path she saw the doctor's bag at his feet. She still could not see his face with his collar pulled up tight around it against the cold.

'Dr Mayfield?'

He must have been completely unaware of her approach as he jumped and stared up at her in astonishment.

'Miss O'Rourke.'

'Tempy.'

'Tempy, yes, apologies, my dear.'

To save him the necessity of standing she sat on the bench next to him. Mr Darcy looked up with his eyes even more full of sorrow than the good doctor. She took pity on him and brought him up into her lap, wrapping her scarf around him. 'Are you well, Doctor?'

'Of course, I am quite fine.' He was completely unconvincing. His voice broke as he spoke and while it would be most improper to suggest that a gentleman might have been crying she could see the redness in his eyes. The eyes that resembled hers.

Perhaps it was just the cold. Perhaps not. 'Forgive me for being contrary, Doctor, but it seems to me that you are quite upset about something.'

He smiled a sad slow smile. 'You are as perceptive as your mother, Tempy. It is true, I am out of sorts.'

'Well there's no need to sit here,' she said. 'I'm sure a visit with Mama would cheer you up.' After all, even if Tempy could not have the man she desired so strongly, there was nothing to forbid her mother from making love with the doctor—in private, of course, as all that lovey-dovey talking was enough to turn one's stomach.

However, the words she intended as a kindness caused him to turn away and bring his handkerchief to his eyes. He hid the action by blowing his nose.

'Goodness me, Doctor,' she said. 'You are behaving like one of those lovesick puppies that write to Prudence asking her to solve their problems.'

'And do you?' he said, so vehemently she was taken aback.

'Well,' she said. 'I do not really know. They never write back to tell me if they've been successful.'

'Do you think Miss Prudence would be able to help an old man like me?'

Tempy blinked twice. 'I, um, suppose she might.' The doctor did not respond so she continued. 'But only if she knows what the problem is.'

'If a body, that is, someone who had formerly been very close, turned about unexpectedly one day and declared a relationship to be over.'

Tempy felt as if she had become a frozen cavern, empty of all substance except cold. Her mother had rejected Dr Mayfield? She turned away and stared at the ripples as they proceeded across the water and lapped at the far bank. The doctor's words pierced her mind and there hung like icicles.

'But if the rejected person wanted to continue. What could he do? What would Prudence suggest as the best course of action for such a sad individual whose heart had been so misused?'

It was so different listening to a person say the words directly to her. When they were written in letters she could separate herself from them, but now she realised that those correspondents were all real people with genuine troubles, even if their concerns seemed trite and trivial. What strength did it take to write a letter spilling their souls on to paper?

A gust of wind curled around her feet and whipped some leaves into a turmoil, one chasing another. Mr Darcy scrabbled to be let up onto her lap, and she stroked his fur absentmindedly.

She realised she had been silent for a long time when the doctor said, 'What do you think Prudence would say, Tempy?'

'I will speak to my mother on your behalf, Dr Mayfield,' she said. 'At the very least I will determine why she has done this. I will see what can be done to mend it.'

'You are a good girl, my dear,' he said. 'Any father would be proud to have you as his daughter.'

For some reason his words scared her to her marrow. She jumped up and bade him goodbye, promising she would be in touch, lifting the pug when he refused to budge from where he had spilled from her lap.

Mary O'Rourke was drinking in her bedroom when Tempy found her. Like the doctor, she appeared to have been crying. The bed itself was in complete disarray. It was not the mess of a liaison; rather, the sheets, blankets, and pillows were scattered across the room. More a sign of someone having had a tantrum.

Her mother glanced at Tempy as she entered but returned her attention to the glass and bottle in her hands.

'What have you done, Mother?'

'I don't know what you're talking about.'

'Why have you broken off your affair with the doctor?'

'I thought you didn't approve of him staying the night.'

'Don't you dare make this about me,' Tempy's voice increased in volume and she could feel the anger growing. 'Why have you sent him away?'

'That's my business.'

'Is Dr Mayfield my father?'

Her mother was halfway through refilling a glass but Tempy's words stopped her. She returned the bottle to its upright position. There was barely a splash of gin in the bottom of the glass. She was not far gone with the booze, thought Tempy; her gaze was still clear and strong.

'No.'

'No, he isn't, or no you won't tell me?'

'No, he is not your father, Temperance O'Rourke.'

Tempy's heart fell. She had hoped he was, and believed after the last thing he said that he must be.

'But our eyes…'

Her mother nodded. 'I know.'

'Are you sure he's not?'

Her mother's faced flickered with anger, which subsided as fast as it manifested. 'That is a fair question, daughter,' she said, 'but the doctor never availed himself of the ladies at The Cloister. Though I believe every one of us, myself included, would have given ourselves to him free of charge.'

'He was there? I don't remember him.'

'For a time, when you were younger. He was engaged to examine and treat the girls for disease.' Her eyes became unfocused and she smiled. 'I remember how embarrassed he was at the start. And even after he became skilled he never lost his kindness.'

'But he's not my father?'

'No, Tempy, I'm sorry, he is not.'

'Then why have you hurt him like this?'

Her mother sighed heavily. 'Because the time has come for us to move on. I think we shall go to New York.'

And Tempy was so shocked she did not even question why her mother expected her to go as well.

Navigating Stormy Seas

The rest of the day passed in a strange daze. Her mother did not come down and Tempy assumed she had drowned her sorrows to the point of complete insensibility.

The following morning she realised she had already resigned herself to leaving London and travelling to the United States. It would be exciting, she told herself, and her mother would undoubtedly do very well there with her spiritualism and séances. Not only that but there would be many young men that would fall at Tempy's feet, and with so many Irish there she could no doubt satisfy her mother's demands and find a good Catholic lad.

She opened the post and went through the letters, sorting those that were banal or repeats from the ones that would interest and titillate the dedicated readers of Prudence. Did they have advice columns in the American newspapers? Well, if they did not then she was sure she could interest them in the idea.

Dear Prudence
Your previous advice to me has become a chain around my neck.

Tempy gasped. What was this?

You advised me to make enquiries to see whether the impediment to my relationship was, in truth, between the family of the one I admired, and my own.
Your advice was sound in that I discovered that the object of my adoration is far more low-born than I imagined.

'Low-born? You blithering great buffoon!' she cried out loud. 'Why did I ever think you might love me?'

But I don't care.

'Oh.'

My family is against the connection in all ways, and I cannot deny that I am upset at the deceit.

'Deceit now is it? How many words have we spoken? A score? A dozen? Less? Tell me, where have I deceived you?'

But that is not the fault of my love. And I will do anything to be with her but I do not know how I can make this work.

'Your love,' she smiled at the letter, 'he called me his love.'

The course you advised carried the ship of my love through some terrible shoals and almost I was sunk. But I believe I see the shore of bliss on the horizon.
Dearest Prudence, tell me what course I should steer now so that I may reach port safely and be with my heart's desire.
Not-Quite-So Lost in London

She clutched the letter to her bosom and wept with pleasure.
'Well, Mother,' she said to the mirror as she wiped at her cheeks, 'there is no way I'm going to America now. And neither are you.'
She sat down, pulled out paper and pen, and prepared to answer the letter.

Dear Not-Quite-So Lost in London
Bravo for being such a bold sailor in stormy seas. The path of true love seldom runs smooth, as the great Bard said.
In this modern age, true love supersedes any thought of station, so do not fear on that count. And a man, or a woman, can be the master, or mistress, of their destiny.
But do not think all troubles are past you. There may be sand bars hidden just beneath the waves, and rocks may block the way before you reach that hidden harbour.
Yes, that was good; the editor liked a little salaciousness. And, in this instance, so did she.
Keep your course and resolve steady. The object of your desire must find her way to you as well and there may be difficulties in that quarter, but rest assured that if she returns your affections—and I am certain that she does—she will also find her way to you.

Tempy made a point of completing the correspondence for the day, even though she could barely contain her excitement.

Her mother's change of heart had occurred after the visit from Mackenzie. Before that she had had no intention of leaving London, and subsequently it was her only thought even to the extent of rejecting the doctor. The knowledge that that fine gentleman was not her father still pained Tempy when she thought of it.

So her course was clear. She must track down this Mackenzie.

The previous day's newspaper was always sent with the packet of letters for Prudence. Tempy liked to read over what she had written and note the errors made by the typesetters. Sometimes she thought they did it deliberately.

But instead of reading her page she started at the beginning and scanned the advertisements. The man had a motorised bath chair. He had bought it from somewhere, so all she had to do was locate the manufacturer then persuade them to reveal Mackenzie's address.

There was nothing. She sighed and turned back through the paper, barely looking at the text. The word 'perambulator' caught her eye in the middle of an article in the financial reports. The word before it was 'personal'. Then she saw 'Elbert Kimperton' and read the article in detail.

It seemed her former gentleman friend was looking for backers to launch his new Personal Perambulator for ladies and gentlemen of stouter proportions. Exactly what she had seen.

She smiled to herself. Either Mackenzie was already a client or Elbert would know who else was building machines like his. Either way, her ex-beau was about to receive a visitation from his past, and whether she was an angel or a harpy would depend on whether he was willing to give up the information she desired.

She noted down the address from the newspaper and called for Lily to prepare her for battle.

The Inventor

On this occasion she took a hansom cab, but found one that was horse-drawn, because they were cheaper. If she was going to make everything right for her and Denton she needed to deal with this Giles Mackenzie, and why her mother felt she needed to leave London, as soon as may be.

The address of the company in the newspaper was south of the river, in Vauxhall. Much further from Hampstead than she had ever been since coming to London. They had not even taken the train to Southend or Brighton for a day by the sea.

However, the route was surprisingly direct, at first following the same route as the omnibus through South Hampstead and St John's Wood. Right at Lord's cricket ground, then south again passing along the edge of Hyde Park, past the now seldom-occupied Buckingham Palace—their majesties now resided at Heaton Palace in North Manchester—and finally through Pimlico to Vauxhall Bridge.

The Thames was grey and sluggish. All manner of vessels plied the river but all were relatively small save the great strings of barges that wound their way beneath the low bridge arches. No boat with a fixed funnel or mast could make it past Blackfriars Bridge.

The difference south of the river was obvious. The wealth of the north bank was replaced by the relative poverty of the lower middle classes. As they moved off the main roads those were replaced by rows of terraces for the lower classes. Tempy had seen plenty of poverty in Dublin. This was no different.

Finally they arrived in an industrial area where the buildings were warehouses of various sizes. They even passed a space where airships were sitting waiting for cargo: an unofficial air-dock. It was exciting to think she could have stopped the cab, and walked onto one of those flyers and simply left the country.

The cab trundled slowly along the narrowing streets until it finally stopped outside a smaller warehouse with the words 'The Personal Perambulator Company' painted in small red letters on a board, above another that read 'South China Imports'. Someone had pasted a piece of paper on the door with a faded note saying 'PPC up one floor'.

Tempy instructed the driver to wait. It would cost more, but she was not happy with the idea of walking through the back streets of Vauxhall on her own as the evening came on.

The door hinges complained as she pushed through. The air was fragrant with an unfamiliar perfume. Stairs to the right led both up and down. She followed the directions of the sign and headed up. Her heels clicked on the stone steps, and the iron banister, though it looked flimsy, was solid under her hand.

She did not knock but pushed open the wooden door. A bell jangled just above her head. Immediately inside was an office of sorts with pieces of machinery scattered about. On the far side, by a dirty window, was a desk piled high with papers.

'I will be with you in a moment!' called a voice from beyond another door. She instantly recognised it as Elbert's and butterflies let loose in her stomach at the sound. Tempy had never expected to encounter him ever again. She realised that she was scared but did not know what of.

She kept her back to the door and faced the desk and window. She resisted the urge to check her makeup. Her mother called it gilding the lily but Tempy felt that a little rouge on her lips and something to hide her freckles improved her looks.

Her fear reached a peak when she heard the door open, and a shiver ran up her back.

'Sorry about that, oh, excuse me, madam.'

She could not bring herself to turn round. 'Hello, Elbert,' she said to the wall.

There was a pause. 'Tempy?' His single word communicated the same astonishment that she was feeling. Now that communication was established she felt she could turn. She kept her gaze down in a demure fashion until his shoes, in need of a polish, came into view.

Tempy allowed her gaze to travel upwards. He was clearly doing better as his trousers and shirt were not ragged. She finally reached his face. Elbert Kimperton was not a handsome man, not like Denton. His nose was a little too large, his black eyebrows too bushy and his left eyelid tended to droop.

Not that she was shallow enough to judge a man purely on his looks, at which point she thought of Denton who she had barely said a word to and was hopelessly in love with because he was utterly handsome. Elbert's problems went deeper than that.

He sniffed and cleared his throat. Tempy resisted the temptation to purse her lips and frown at him.

'Why are you here?' he asked.

She felt somewhat offended by his tone but had to admit he had some justification in being short with her, after all it was she who had rejected him.

'You make the Personal Perambulators?'

'I do.'

His words were cold and his face was as unmoving as iron. And as if in silent accusation she noticed a version of the 'lightening corset' in the corner behind him.

'You attacked me, Elbert.'

'I was forced to stay abed for five weeks.'

'If you had not jumped on me.'

'If you had not done what you did.'

'It was not my fault.'

'It was your action.'

'Yours first.'

Tempy took a deep breath; she had not come here to argue with Elbert. Nor did she wish to renew any form of friendship with him.

'You have sold one of your perambulators to Giles Mackenzie'—she saw the flicker of something in his eyes at the name—'and I need to know his address.'

He continued to stare at her for a long moment, almost expressionless as if he had not heard what she said. Then: 'No.'

'No, you haven't sold one to him?'

'No, I will not give you his address.'

'Out of spite?'

'Perhaps a little of that, Tempy, and Lord knows you deserve it.' He seemed to straighten and an unpleasant grin emerged on his face. 'However, even if that were not the case, it would be improper of me to reveal the address of any of my sponsors.'

'If you let me explain—'

'No.' He held up his hand to emphasise the word. 'No, your reason is not relevant to me. It has nothing to do with me. I cannot give you the address. If that's all you want from me I will bid you good day and you can be on your way.'

Tempy could not quite believe her ears. This was not the Elbert Kimperton she had known.

'What do I need to do, Elbert?' she said. 'I need that address.'

The grin returned. 'It must be serious if you would offer me anything.' He paused and she guessed he was giving her time to run a number of unpleasant options through her mind. Her eyes flicked to the corset.

'You cannot bribe me, Tempy,' he said. 'The answer now and always is no. There is nothing you can do that will persuade me otherwise. Goodbye.'

And with that he turned his back and went back through the door to do whatever he had been up to. 'You can show yourself out,' he called back to her.

Tempy stared after him. Had she done this to him? Had she made him so callous?

She shook her head and forced her feet towards the door. She opened it so the bell jangled, waited for a moment, and then slammed it shut. Hardly daring to breathe she stood by the door holding the handle. Sounds of metal work started up on the other side of the inner door. Tempy crept to the desk.

She stared at the mess of papers and journals. It was difficult to know where to start.

One pile on the left had an accounts ledger with letters and envelopes sticking out from it. She opened it and saw it contained the necessary columns for income and expenses. The dates started nine months ago.

There were not a great number of transactions and most of them involved money going out to a greater or lesser degree. She turned the pages covering a total of three months and there she saw it. The income column, previously having been filled with sums of ten or twenty pounds every week or so, suddenly contained an amount of seven hundred and fifty pounds.

Eagerly she looked at the entry beside it: to her dismay it had simply 'G.M.' and nothing else. She gave up on the ledger itself and extracted the letters from the back. Most had typewritten addresses on the envelope and contained bills. Then she reached one of a much higher quality of paper. She turned the envelope over and there, on the back, was the return address. One G. Mackenzie Esq, 37 Cheyne Way, Chelsea.

She placed the ledger back where she had found it and crossed to the door. The bell was too high for her to silence with her hand, so she opened the door as far as she could without setting it off and attempted to squeeze through. Unfortunately she was too well proportioned for the gap.

Taking a moment to gather herself, she pulled the door that little bit further and pushed through. The bell rang but she was already flying down the stairs as fast as she could.

The cab was still outside, thankfully, and she jumped inside. 'Chelsea as fast as you may!' she cried. The driver was surprised by her sudden appearance, and it took a moment for him to gather the reins but he cracked his whip and the horse jerked into motion.

Tempy did not dare look back. And she pretended not to hear Elbert's angry voice shouting after her.

The Secret Sponsor

The hansom pulled away with the horse's hooves clopping on the cobbles leaving her standing on the corner of Cheyne Way and Cheyne Street. Number 37 was an impressive Georgian building, and lights shone behind the curtains.

She breathed deeply, almost panting with trepidation. She had reached this point, but what was she going to do? If she did not enter now the fellow would be warned of her coming by Elbert. She panicked for a moment and studied the house in the failing light. There were no wires leading to the house that indicated it had a telephone. But Elbert could have dispatched a telegram. Or called a cab himself.

A shadow rolled smoothly across a ground floor curtain of one of the bay windows. No, the deed must be carried out now. She must know the nature of the hold this man Mackenzie had over her mother.

Tempy went through the gate up to the door and pulled on the bell rope. She could not hear it ring.

There was a short delay before the door was opened by a rough fellow whom she recognised immediately: the one who had been watching her from the park. She barely had a moment to gasp before he reached out, grabbed her arm, yanked her into the house, and slammed the door behind her.

She aimed a kick at his groin but he turned and it landed on his thigh. He grunted in pain but back-handed her, knocking her to the floor. Her head struck something very hard with considerable violence and she knew no more.

'Headache? Shouldn't wonder.'

Tempy opened her eyes and looked around her. She was lying on a chaise longue in an over-warm drawing room. The curtains were closed and the lamps lit, not that it mattered what time of day it was. The place smelled of disinfectant and there was no sound save for a mechanical whirring. She pushed herself up on her elbow but was forced to shut her eyes against the pain that shot through her head.

'I'd lie back down if I was you, Miss Tempy O'Rourke.'

Tempy stiffened, but did as she was told. The pain eased and she opened her eyes. All she could see was additional furniture, good quality but not exceptional. The sort one might expect to find in a ready-furnished home of good quality for rent.

The whining of the motor increased and an ancient man with a plaid blanket covering his lap and driving a Personal Perambulator came into her field of vision. The same man she had seen leaving their house. The only other noise in the room was the ticking of the grandfather clock. Then the old man cleared his throat to speak.

'See here, Miss O'Rourke. I do apologise for the roughness of my man. Once a sailor always a sailor, I say.'

Tempy did not trust herself to speak, so inclined her head and winced again as the pain struck afresh.

'The thing is, dear, that I am old now. Not that long to go, I shouldn't think. You'll let me say my piece now, girl, for it has been a while in coming. No interruptions.'

He picked up a glass of water from the table beside him, on which also sat a small bell, and drank, wiping his mouth on the back of his hand. Tempy winced at his deplorable manners.

He saw her face and smiled.

'That is the least of it, young lady, and were it the only bad thing that I had ever done I could go to meet my Maker with a clear conscience. I am hoping that my talking to you, telling you, will enable me to do so anyway.

'Mackenzie is my name, Giles Mackenzie.'

'I know who you are.'

He laughed then coughed. 'You may know my name, girl, but you do not know *who* I am. So you mind your manners and listen.'

Tempy said nothing.

'I was stationed aboard a ship with one Daniel Lester. Best friends we were, but things happened, things that I am not proud of. And I know your mother of old. I heard she had left Dublin and moved to London, and Swains Lane.'

He eyed her shrewdly.

'You are, what, twenty? No, nineteen I should think. Image of your mother—except for the eyes, of course.' He took another drink of water.

Tempy's stomach sank; she didn't like where this was going, not one little bit. Woozy as she was, though feeling better, she climbed to her feet and paced the floor as Mackenzie continued to talk.

'Many years of good living and the gout have left me too swollen to leave this blasted chair. I paid an inventor an extortionate amount of money to build me a personal perambulation platform, that I might not be confined to these rooms when there is nobody to push me. Come here, Tempy O'Rourke, let me see you.'

Against her own will, Tempy felt herself walk across the floor and look down at the old man.

He reached out and gripped her hand. She was surprised by how strong it was. He pulled her close and she could see his eyes were just like hers.

'Always a bad one, me. But it looks like something good came out of my life. You.'

Tempy yanked her hand from his grasp, shaking her head, tears in her eyes.

The old man cackled.

'Come for a kiss, daughter.'

Tempy felt sure that she would swoon, and started to make her way back to sit down, black spots swimming across her vision.

'Old Daniel Lester wasn't a bad man. That wife of his is another story though. I shan't bore you with the details, but once she found out your mother owned the house on Swains Lane that was such a disruption to her plans for the Air-dock, she paid me to try to get you out of the house. I am not proud, but your mother gave me short shrift. What a woman. Nothing worked, nothing. Not money, nor even the vilest threats. Until I said I would tell you who your father was.' He grinned. 'Hard to imagine a woman like that being ashamed. But she was, Tempy, she would do anything to keep you from knowing.'

'And now you've told me so your threat has no more power, Mr Mackenzie,' Tempy said with more confidence than she felt. 'So I will be taking my leave of you. My mother and I will be remaining in Swain's Lane, thank you.'

Mackenzie rang the small bell. Tempy supposed that would summon his man to let her go.

'Sadly, Miss O'Rourke, I think you may be spending some little time with us. I'm sure your mother will be most agreeable when she learns who controls your destiny.'

'But what were you saying about meeting your Maker?'

Mackenzie shrugged. 'I find the lure of money to be far stronger than the threat of the hereafter.'

'But who is to pay you?

'Oh, you can let me worry about that, Miss O'Rourke; I know exactly who will pay to see you alive again.'

Tempy sank to the ground with the old man's laughter ringing in her ears.

The Wrong Head

That Tempy was the daughter of a prostitute had come as something a shock to Denton Lester. In all his imaginings of what woman he might one day come to have affection for and perhaps, if he was lucky, to love, the illegitimate daughter of a whore had not been part of any scenario.

It had been improper of him to abandon his aunt and cousin at the park. On the other hand, the delight with which his aunt had imparted the information was equally improper. More so, it made her no more than a common gossip. In many ways, no better than the woman she sought to discredit. Perhaps worse.

He returned to Kensington Square Gardens but instead of going to the house he strode into the square itself and took a seat at one of the benches. The trees in the middle of the square were like skeletons with their black fingers reaching for the grey sky.

Cold crawled through his clothes and seeped into his bones.

What should he do? How did he truly feel about Tempy? The thought of her made his heart race and drove the cold back. Though he had seen her for only a moment she had been like a fire, like no woman he had ever known. She had not had her rough edges worn away by society and etiquette. She said what she thought. She was independent and strong.

He could put her on a pedestal and worship her from now until the end of time. Except he did not think that was what she would desire. Tempy would not want a man to crush beneath her boot. She wanted an equal.

But she was the daughter of a common whore.

He thought about her mother and what she had said to him, turning him away when he came to the door with the gifts for the dog. Perhaps she may have been a whore but she was most certainly not common. And now she was Madame Lacroix, the highly sought-after medium. True, that was not a great uplift in society but better than a prostitute.

And it was not as if he were a noble. His father had been born the son of a blacksmith. He had built his empire through hard work and shrewd business decisions.

It was true he had married far above his station, due to his wealth, but even the family he had joined was only upper middle class. The most pretentious of all classes: his aunts were testimony to that.

So he could ignore whatever his aunt thought. Which left only his own feelings. What if Tempy were to be taken from him? A wave of sorrow and emptiness rolled over him and he gasped.

'Sir, are you well?'

The voice came from a shortish fellow with a bowler hat and a doctor's bag standing nearby.

'I'm sorry?' said Denton.

'I asked if you were well. You appear to be in some distress.'

'Thank you for your kind words but I am quite well. It was a passing thought and I was merely caught by surprise.'

'That is good, Mr Lester,' said the man.

'You have the advantage of me, sir,' said Denton rising to his feet. He topped the man by several inches and did not feel threatened.

'Please, let me introduce myself. I am Dr Mayfield.' He raised his hat for a moment. 'I was seeking you, sir. I believe we are in the same boat.'

'Boat?'

'Yes, sir. We have both set the course of our heart for a woman by the name of O'Rourke.'

Denton flushed with anger. 'You are in love with Tempy?'

The doctor laughed. 'Oh no, sir. While my niece is a delightful young lady, let me assure you I have no designs on her future, except to see her happy. It is her mother whom I find myself drawn to.'

'Your niece?'

'I believe your house is nearby; perhaps we can withdraw to its warmth and I will explain everything, such as I know it.'

Tempy was woken by the sound of the key turning in the lock. A glance to the window told her it was still night, and a flickering candle flame showed beneath the door. She had been closeted in one of the smaller servants' rooms on the top floor of the house. Tempy had looked for escape but the window was nailed shut.

She pulled a blanket from the bed and waited behind the door. The door creaked open.

Tempy flung the blanket over the intruder's head and threw herself at him screaming. She grabbed his arms as tight as she could, though she could not get her arms around his body, and pushed him back. There was a short landing and then a flight of stairs to the lower floor.

The fellow staggered back under her onslaught. He teetered on the edge and she shoved him over. Still clinging to him she rode him down the stairs like a mat on a helter-skelter. Every step knocked the wind from him as well as striking his head and the bump at the bottom made him groan terribly.

She picked herself up and kicked him in the head before speeding off along the passage, as fast as her skirts would let her go. A door ahead of her opened out, partially blocking her way, and the whirring of the motor heralded the emergence of the Personal Perambulator. It skittered out, surprisingly fast, and blocked the passageway completely.

Tempy, unable to stop in time, collided with it and found herself lying across the front. She could feel the lightness caused by a Faraday mesh that must be woven into the machine. It made its occupant lighter so there was less strain on their muscles and organs.

'Not so fast, Miss O'Rourke.' Mackenzie grabbed her arm and held it twisted across her back. She could not move. 'No, daughter, you will not disobey your father,' he said in a venomous manner that betrayed his utter contempt for her and her sex.

Looking down over the far side of the machine, Tempy spotted wires coming out from the lower part of the mechanism. They would carry electrical power to either the motor or the mesh. She reached out and found she was shy an inch or two, but tried to gain those inches by stretching further.

'Still trying to escape, miss? I should beat you raw for disobedience.' This apparently amused him and he shook like a jelly with laughter.

Tempy ignored him and wriggled forwards. She got her fingers around the wires and pulled. They would not budge. Elbert had never been a bad engineer, just one for bad ideas. She sighed then reached into her hair, she extracted a long metal pin.

Mackenzie was still laughing as she jammed it into the hole where the wires entered the body. A strange pulse went through her that stopped almost immediately. Her normal weight returned. Mackenzie's laugh became wheezing as he fought for breath.

His strength deserted him and she escaped his grasp. She fell on the other side of the perambulator and had made one more step towards freedom.

As she took the stairs she heard a faint cry of help from Mackenzie. She ignored it.

There was a light coming from one of the front rooms and the sound of fighting. Tempy did not pause but ran for the front door.

Within a minute she was on the Cheyne Walk and had hailed a mechanical hansom. Less than an hour later she had crept into the house and crawled gratefully into her bed.

Tomorrow she would settle it all.

'Dear Prudence'

'Tempy! Tempy, darling girl, wake up.'

She heard her mother calling to her as if from the end of a tunnel and forced her eyes open. On seeing her mother's troubled face, pretty and cosmetic free, Tempy burst into tears.

'Now, now my darling girl, you must not worry yourself!'

'I met my real father. He told me the whole story. I know everything.'

'Oh Tempy, darling girl! That Minnie Lester was ever a vicious woman. She had it from Giles Mackenzie that Daniel Lester was sweet on me, and so plotted her revenge against me. What a laugh that is! I never even met him. When he was stationed in Dublin aboard one of his ships he never came to The Cloister. But your father was always greedy, always, and he was a bad man. Oh, my love.'

Tempy sat and let her mother hold her close, the comfort of her presence driving out the badness of others.

'Can we stay in London, Mother? Please.'

'Yes, my darling girl, we can. So much has changed. Now you must mend your face, dress and come down stairs. There is work for you.'

'Work?'

'Letters from the lost and confused to be answered.'

With that her mother swept from the room leaving a very confused Tempy. She realised she was not even sure what day it was.

It was five to ten when Tempy entered the day room where breakfast had been laid out. And she discovered her mother in a tender embrace with Dr Mayfield. Tempy was quite embarrassed particularly as they seemed oblivious to her presence and the doctor's hand was in a most inappropriate location.

Tempy cleared her throat and the two of them broke apart with the abruptness of young lovers. She gasped; the doctor's face was terribly bruised, and she wondered that he could tolerate the kissing.

'You should let the doctor make a respectable woman out of you, Mother.'

Her mother did not reply but deferred to the doctor. 'That is the intention, Tempy, if you have no objection.'

'Why should my opinion make any difference?'

The two old lovers glanced at one another as if some secret communication passed between them. Her mother came to her and took her hand. 'Because, dear heart, Dr Mayfield is brother to Giles Mackenzie. Technically he is your uncle.'

Tempy took a moment to absorb that information. She wondered for a moment whether her real father had any say in it, whether he could forbid it, but no. She herself was the product of a paid service that her mother had provided. Mackenzie did not own her. But still.

'Won't my father cause trouble?'

'He is beyond any ability to cause any more trouble,' said the doctor sadly. 'He is dead.'

'Dead?' said Tempy. 'But I saw him last night.'

'Sadly his machine failed to work and the strain on his heart was too much.'

'But how do you know?'

'Because I was there.'

Tempy blinked once. 'Oh.'

'Oh indeed, my dear,' said her mother, who pulled an envelope from her bodice and offered it to Tempy. 'This letter came for Prudence.'

Tempy took it barely understanding what was happening. She broke the seal and pulled out the letter.

Dear Prudence

'What does it say, Tempy?' asked the doctor. 'Read it to us. Out loud.'

'*Dear Prudence, Thank you for all your advice. I kept my course steady but you were right, there were more difficulties. Quite painful both to my soul and also my body.*'

Tempy looked up and frowned. 'His body?'

'Keep reading.'

'*…also my body. But now we have both arrived safely at harbour so I believe it is time for proper introductions and conversation.*'

'It just stops,' said Tempy. 'I don't understand?'

A voice she dreamed of came from behind her. 'Temperance O'Rourke, my name is Denton Lester. I am delighted to make your acquaintance.'

'It's Tempy,' she said, turning. Then she saw his face was as battered as the doctor's and he walked with a limp. She glanced at the doctor who gave her a smiling nod. Realisation swept over her. 'Oh goodness, did I do that?'

Epilogue

Well, this was uncomfortable. He was finally here, for a proper visit this time, and he couldn't get the words out. Mrs O'Rourke and Dr Mayfield had left the room to let the two young people talk. He and Tempy sat in chairs that faced each other. Clearly she was going to have to lead.

'I am so pleased to finally meet you properly,' she said. 'I saw your letters in *The London Leader.*'

'You saw it in the newspaper?' He seemed surprised by her words.

'Yes.'

'But you are Prudence,' he said.

She felt her cheeks redden. 'How did you know?'

'My man was very thorough in his investigations.'

'You had me *investigated*?'

Her anger must have been obvious because he raised his hand as if to fend off her emotion. 'It was the only way I could communicate with you since your mother barred every other route.'

'She is quite formidable.'

He could only nod. 'I feel as if I've known you forever. And I'm so sorry about your dog.'

'Mr Darcy? It was hardly your fault.'

On hearing his name, the pug made his way over to sniff at Denton's hand, wagging his curly tail.

'There's a good boy, did you like your ball? You look quite fine in the collar I chose for you.'

Mr Darcy waddled back over to his basket, returned, and deposited the ball in Denton's hand. Denton smiled and tossed it across the room where it bounced against the wall, rolled back a little, and came to rest. Mr Darcy looked at it in disdain.

'Not a great fetcher, then?'

'Not a great fetcher,' Tempy agreed.

'Well, then, it is very nice to have everything cleared up.'

'Very nice indeed.' She hesitated and then added. 'I am sorry for hurting you last night.'

He touched his strong fingers to his ribs. 'You were not to know.'

Silence.

Denton glanced at the window where the low winter sun shone through. 'Lovely day, though, is it not?'

'Indeed,' she said in a measured tone. 'Lovely.'

Neither spoke again for a very long minute.

'Oh, for goodness sake, this is ridiculous.' The words seemed to burst from him. Denton Lester stood to his full height, blond hair falling over dark eyes, perfectly cut clothes outlining a wonderful figure. He strode over to Tempy and pulled her from her chair into his arms.

She did not resist. Holding his head—gently, given the damage she had done to it—she drew his face to her for him to kiss her. And so he did, softly at first and then with a growing intensity, holding her so close that their bodies melded.

Denton stepped back suddenly and looked at her. He was breathing quickly. Some of her hair had escaped from its elaborate updo. 'You are so beautiful.'

Tempy was breathless, the heat rising and making her knees tremble.

'Forgive me, Miss O'Rourke, what bad manners. I have wanted to do that ever since I saw you nearly get run over by my carriage. But I have behaved quite improperly.' He stepped away from her while Tempy stood mute. 'I do apologise.' Then he turned away from her and left the room. She felt as lost as a sinking ship abandoned in a storm.

'Tempy O'Rourke! If you are any child of mine, you will go after that man, at once!'

She jumped as her mother's sharp voice cut through from the next room.

'Were you listening, Mother?'

'I was, but we have no time for that now! Go, child, go! Manners be damned!'

And so it was she ran to the front door without coat, muffler, gloves, or Mr Darcy. She pulled it open and found him standing there his hand poised above the knocker.

He took her bare hand in his. The touch of his skin was a lifeboat for her heart.

'Miss O'Rourke. Temperance. Tempy. If I might start again?'

He looked down into her eyes and must have seen her unspoken assent written there.

'Your mother mentioned that you always wanted to take a trip in an airship. Since I find myself in ownership of a whole fleet of them, I was wondering if you might like to go on a journey. A short journey. A visit to the Air-dock, just to see them?' he rambled on.

Tempy flung her arms around him.

'Oh, yes, please!'

Looking over her shoulder, Tempy saw her mother giving her the thumbs-up, Mr Darcy at her feet, and Dr. Mayfield beside them. Winking at him, she turned back to Denton.

She raised her head with the refrain 'manners be damned' dancing through her mind, and she kissed Denton Lester surely and sweetly.

~ end ~

Irish-born Katy O'Dowd, in addition to writing, is a reader, mother of two boys, a puppy socialiser, cat wrangler, and is owned by Christopher Lee, the pug. She is an arts and entertainment journalist who has worked for Time Out, Associated Newspapers and Comic Relief with her articles appearing in The Times (London), Metro (London) and many other arts and entertainment publications, paper and online.

With her father, using the pen-name Derry O'Dowd, her first book "The Scarlet Ribbon" was chosen to launch the History Press Ireland's fiction line. Under her own name she has published two further novels "The Lady Astronomer" a whimsical steampunk fantasy based on the first woman to be paid to work in Science: Caroline Herschel. She followed this up with "Memento Mori", a novel set among the crime gangs of early Victorian London.

Katy reviews for the *Historical Novels Review* and the British Fantasy Society.

You can find her work on Amazon:
http://www.amazon.com/Katy-ODowd/e/B006292ELG

Twitter: https://twitter.com/katyod
Facebook: https://www.facebook.com/katy.odowd
Google+: https://plus.google.com/u/0/109100749123016978303/about

The Computationer
by Steve Turnbull

THE COMPUTATIONER

By Steve Turnbull

i

Gilda put down the pencil and rubbed her eyes. The oil lamp made barely enough light for this sort of number work, but neither of her parents could do it and Dieter was too young. That was part of Gilda's problem.

The corrugated iron roof rattled in the wind. She pulled the knitted wool jumper tighter around her shoulders. It wasn't really cold but there was a draught from the chimney. She sat back and flexed her left hand, trying to uncramp it; she rubbed the wrist with her right. Her parents were seated around the bigger light, mending one of her father's fishing nets.

"I made it add up, Papa," she said. She had to forego her visit to the library this afternoon but tomorrow would do.

"You're a good girl, Gilda. You take the books to Mr Aronson at the bank tomorrow."

"Yes, Papa."

They might only be fishermen—not ones that braved the open sea, as Papa fished the Swan River just like the natives—but a business was still a business and the bank liked to have its yearly report of income and outgoings. Her father's profit was not a big one, but it was enough that perhaps she could persuade her parents to let her go to Sydney to study at the university.

"You go to bed now, Gilda."

"Yes, Mama."

As she moved to get up, her chair scraped across the wooden floor boards.

"Lift it, don't push it."

"Yes, Mama."

Gilda slid sideways out of the seat. Her behind had gone numb from being seated for so long and she walked awkwardly for a few steps. She leaned over her mother's shoulder and gave her a peck on the cheek, and then did the same to her father.

"Goodnight, Gilda."

"Goodnight, Papa, Mama."

She gathered up her loose skirts, lit a candle and went into the short corridor that led to the bedrooms. Gilda remembered what it had been like in Switzerland where they had just the one room in the log house her father had built with his own hands. Here they had five rooms but each was small.

Back in the homeland Papa had worked hard and saved all he could. Then a distant relative Gilda had never met, Papa's great aunt Hilda, had died and left them some money. Papa said it was because she thought Gilda was named in her honour. He had smiled when he said it.

Gilda was not sure why Papa had been so keen to leave the beautiful lakes and mountains—although things were always difficult in the winter—but his heart was set on that course. It was in the summer of 1899, when Gilda had just turned thirteen, they set off with their meagre belongings.

That was four years ago and she found her memories of the journey's details to be fuzzy. There had been the cart to Zurich, then a train to a city in Germany. Followed by days in a Zeppelin that set down in strange and exotic places. Finally they had disembarked in a place where everyone's skin was dark and they spoke a language that sounded like singing.

Then the sea voyage. Two weeks in a steamer being tossed back and forth—that was just the good days. There had been storms and high winds. Until finally, escorted by dolphins, they reached the Australian coast, passed through a gap in the reefs, and docked at Fremantle harbour which was the port for Perth.

Why Perth? She had never asked. It was almost as if Papa was trying to find the most out-of-the-way place on the whole planet. She had seen maps; often, Perth was not even on them.

She pulled off her clothes, put on a thick nightdress, and climbed into bed, sitting with her back to the wall. Through the window she could see a full moon had everything shining silver. She divided her long, loose hair into two handfuls, one on each side, then picked up her hair brush and ran it through the right-hand section. Once all the tangles were out, she plaited it loosely and then set to work on the left, more awkwardly since she was left-handed—something which never seemed to please her mother or her teachers.

It was so flat here. Sometimes she missed the mountains. A few miles inland was the Darling Scarp that rose above the coast, stretching north and south hundreds of miles. But it wasn't mountains. A strong wind blew in from the Indian Ocean almost constantly, bringing huge waves with it.

It was hard to imagine, when she stood on the sand and stared out facing the islands, that beyond them there was nothing but ocean for thousands of miles. And when she turned around with her back to the waves, there was nothing but desert for thousands of miles.

Then, in the east, mountains—more mountains than in all of Switzerland, and higher too. Then Sydney, on the distant east coast, where she could study mathematics and science. Or she could go to Melbourne, which had a good university too. Perhaps better.

She sighed and threw her arms around her knees. If only she could persuade her parents. She could imagine all their arguments and some of them even made sense—but there were always ways around them. If they were willing to look.

She wet her finger, snuffed out the candle and then lay back. As she closed her eyes she thought about taking an air-ship to Sydney.

She jerked awake. For a moment she had an idea she was on an air-ship, because she could hear the low throb of a powerful engine. Her mind cleared, and she realised it was not the shred of a forgotten dream. She really could hear an engine.

A glance at the window showed it was still night. Nobody flew at night; it was too dangerous. In a trice, she was out of bed and across the room.

She reached the window and stared up into the sky. A dark form, moving slowly, blotted out the stars in sequence as it floated like a bird. It had two pairs of stubby wings sprouting from a slim body. She couldn't tell how high up it was so the size could be anything. Dieter would have known what it was immediately. He knew them all.

She pushed open the window and leaned out. The cold wind off the sea went straight through the thick flannel of her nightdress. The air throbbed with the rhythmic thumping of the air vessel's engines that mingled with the roaring of the waves on the beach. She could almost feel it.

As the vessel turned inland, the moon caught on its side and she thought she could see portholes. That made it big enough to carry perhaps twenty people. She jumped when a great explosion tore out its side in a cloud of steam. It seemed to stagger in the air. Its direction did not change, nor did it fall from the sky, but the sound of the engines was altered and it trailed steam and smoke.

Why did they not turn back to land near the city?

The sound of the explosion, like a huge wave breaking on the rocks, reached her ears. A chorus of dogs set up their barking across the city. Closer to home, she heard someone shouting at their animal.

Was that four seconds? During thunderstorms she loved to watch the lightning and count the seconds to the thunder. The speed of sound in air was one thousand feet per second, so five seconds was a mile. They used kilometres in Switzerland, but the British used their own scheme.

She watched the ship descending and made mental notes of the major stars it obscured as it did so. She marked its position in relation to the roof when it finally went out of sight and then pulled her notebook from under her mattress. Working quickly before she forgot, she made a sketch of the roof showing where it disappeared, marked significant stars, and traced its position back to where the explosion happened.

Back in her bed, by the light of the candle, she turned the drawing she had made into a series of geometric diagrams. She drew triangles and labelled their sides, then calculated distances and made guesses.

She knew there was a lot of room for error and did not have a map of the local area to hand, but she could pop into the library tomorrow.

She wondered if anyone else had seen or heard it.

ii

Everyone was talking about it. Over-the-fence gossip travelled faster than the telegraph. But the tales varied from a shooting star to a monstrous Zeppelin—and that was only over the breakfast table.

"A shooting star doesn't make any noise," said Gilda. "And it wasn't as big as a Zeppelin, only a twenty-passenger vessel. No balloon."

"How do you know?" said Dieter, pausing with his spoon of porridge halfway to his mouth.

"Because I saw it."

"No need to make things up, Gilda, dear."

"I'm not making it up, Mama," she said. "It woke me up."

"Well, I don't know," said her mother as she cleaned her father's dishes in the sink. "Mrs Baxter says we'll all be murdered in our beds by sky pirates."

"It was crashing, Mama."

"Crashing?" said Dieter with an excited gleam in his eye. "Can we go look? Maybe there are dead bodies."

"You will do no such thing. If it crashed who knows what will come out of it," said Mama. "Gilda, you keep an eye on your brother. He must not go up-country on his own or with anyone else, do you understand?"

Gilda sighed. Keeping an eye on her brother was the last thing she needed, with everything else she wanted to do. Even school was unnecessary. There was almost nothing they could teach her anymore—well, nothing she wanted to learn, at any rate—but she had to set a good example for Dieter, who did not study so well.

Nor was today a good day for her at school. There was very little science or mathematics, not even arithmetic: just poems written by British men who were dead. She preferred the language of numbers. Speaking English had come to her easily enough, though they still spoke *Züridütsch*, the main Swiss dialect, at home.

Her parents were much slower to pick up English. Gilda thought they should make more of an effort, partly for their own practice but also for Dieter. The schoolteacher for his class did not punish her brother for not understanding, but the other children made fun of him and his accent. They called him the Kaiser's puppy because they thought he was German.

So, he did not like going to school—and who could blame him?

In school the stories about the crashed air-plane were ridiculous. By the end of the day it had been piloted by monsters from Venus who had come to Earth to eat babies (or possibly maidens).

"They're going to eat all the black fellas," shouted Evan Green to his clique of hangers-on, who erupted in vicious laughter. 'Black fellas' is what they liked to call the natives. "Save the government a job."

Gilda wanted to say something, to wipe their nasty little faces in the dirt. Perhaps she should be grateful they weren't attacking her this time. But somehow it did not make her feel any better. Just angry. She turned away and headed for the other end of the school where Dieter would be waiting.

On the way home, in the midafternoon when the sun was still high and warm but the wind from the ocean blew cold, she told him about the ship she had seen.

"Four short wings with rotating engines on them?" he said. "That's a Brunel design usually, but it's been copied." She let him speak in *Züridütsch* for two reasons: She didn't want to upset him by forcing him to use English, and she did not want anyone else to understand what they were saying. There were advantages in being foreign.

She stopped outside a general store where a newspaper seller stood on the corner, shouting about the mystery ship. But she gathered there was no real news; there hadn't been enough time to find it yet.

The bank was on the opposite corner. The accounting books from her father weighed heavily in the school bag over her shoulder. Just a little further along the road was the Mechanical Institute. Inside its hallowed halls was the library with so many science and mathematical books, it was like heaven to an engineer or a computationer.

She glanced back at the bank and then at Dieter. She could get into the Institute library; Gilda had managed to demonstrate her genuine desire to learn to the librarian, Mrs Holman, but the woman would not let her brother in.

Between the bank and the Institute stood a building housing the local power generator, also owned by the bank manager, Mr Aronson. Power cables hung across the dusty streets, supplying the local businesses. The Institute was fully equipped with electric lights, and the bank had its own Babbage Analytical—which she would dearly love to get her hands on.

They crossed the street easily; at this time of day traffic was limited to a few horse-drawn carts and the occasional mechanical. Most Perth machines were steam because diesel fuel was hard to come by, while wood and water were plentiful.

The bank building was brick-built. Only the major municipal buildings in the centre of Perth were made from stone. The factories that made the bricks lay to the south of Fremantle. And that was where she would end up if she couldn't get herself to university. Dieter would take over the fishing from their father, as would his son after him.

They pushed through the main doors, oak with leaded stained glass panes depicting the story of Midas—which she did not think was in very good taste.

Of the five places for clerks, only one was staffed. The others were only fully manned first thing in the morning during the week, and all day Friday. The floor was wood and well worn. It creaked as she and Dieter walked across to the one clerk on duty.

"Afternoon, Gilda," said Mr Prescott. He was in his fifties, with thinning hair and a round face. He always had a smile and Gilda liked him.

"Good afternoon, Mr Prescott. I have my father's books for Mr Aronson."

"Well, just pass them over, my dear," he said, putting aside the journal he had open in front of him.

"Papa said I should give them to Mr Aronson," said Gilda. It was not that she didn't trust the clerk, but when Papa asked her what had happened, as he most certainly would, it would be easier to be able to tell the truth.

Besides, there were other reasons for going into the back. One of them being the analytical.

Mr Prescott beamed. "Of course, Gilda, just take a seat."

She pushed Dieter in the direction of the chairs that lined the wall. Gilda sat but Dieter pulled some paper and a pencil from his bag, and then knelt on the floor. He used the chair seat as a desk on which to draw his pictures.

Mr Prescott disappeared through the door with the frosted glass and the word OFFICE neatly lettered on it. The whole of the wall above waist height was the same glass and she could see distorted dark shapes moving around on the other side.

To the right, on the far side of the building, loomed something large and yellowish. The thing that she most wanted to see. A figure moved around in front of it; Gilda could imagine Lemuel collecting his Extended Hollerith cards into a neat pile and depositing them into the hopper. She saw him move to the operating station and reach out his arm. There was a pause before the room was filled with the clattering music of cogwheels and connecting rods.

Gilda could have prepared the cards for the machine when it came to processing her father's accounts, but, even if Mr Aronson had permitted it, she knew Lemuel was very picky about what went into "his" machine— even though it wasn't his at all.

The volume increased as the door opened again and Mr Prescott gestured for Gilda to enter.

"Stay here, Dieter, I'll just be a little while."

He didn't respond. She glanced down and saw him drawing something that looked remarkably like the vessel she had seen last night.

iii

Gilda had been into the inner sanctum of the bank on two previous occasions. The first time she had been accompanying her father. The second, she had been delivering last year's accounts.

This year was especially important because the profit meant they would be able to get a loan to pay for a better boat. If Mr Aronson agreed, that is. She was sure he would; the figures were quite positive.

She stepped through the door. Mr Prescott held it open for her, smiled, and then went back out into the main hall. "I'll keep an eye on him," he said quietly as he passed.

Gilda always thought a banker ought to be a big fat man smoking a cigar, but Mr Aronson did not fit that description at all. He was almost as short as she was, and he was thin though his suit was a perfect fit. She thought he must be at least forty, but his hair was still thick and dark.

Mr Aronson did not smoke and did not like the smell of stale cigarettes, so the air in his office was clean. She knew this because Lemuel had complained about it to her. She glanced across at him. He had his back to her but she could tell by the way he was standing he was listening to the way the cogwheels interlocked and the rods bumped one another. Every computationer knew the sounds of their coding sequences when executed on their machines. They could monitor the condition of the analytical itself, at the same time as listening to the progress of their computations.

Gilda had once suggested to Lemuel that one might create a set of computations that wrote themselves depending on their inputs; then you wouldn't know how it was going to sound. He had scoffed and derided such a ridiculous notion. She had acquiesced at the time, but she had kept thinking about it.

If only she could get her hands on a decent analytical—but that was impossible. They cost far more than all the money her father made in a single year, even if they didn't have to spend any on food.

"Please sit down, Miss Dettwiler." Always courteous, Mr Aronson even slid the chair under her as she sat. She opened the flap of her school bag and pulled out the two books. She passed them across and he placed them down in front of him.

He smiled at her, opened the first, and ran his eye down the columns.

"You have a very neat hand, Miss Dettwiler."

"Thank you, sir."

He flipped to the last page and nodded. "Good, good, entirely up to date I see. You are a credit to your family."

He closed the books and placed them to one side.

"Are you still keen to be a computationer?"

"I am, sir."

"Strange occupation for a woman."

Gilda went cold inside. It could have been either of her parents saying the same thing.

"Miss Ada Lovelace was the very first computationer, sir."

"That was a long time ago and she was a mathematical prodigy," he smiled. "You're not suggesting you are her equal?"

Why not? "Of course not, sir, but it would be an honour to follow in her footsteps."

"Well," he said, climbing to his feet. She followed suit and took his proffered hand in a limp handshake. "Good luck, it's always important to have a goal in life, although most women are satisfied with catching themselves a good husband."

"Yes, sir, thank you, sir."

She seethed, that was all anybody said but it was not even true. Lots of women made their own lives nowadays. They would even live alone in the city—in special rooms for ladies—and have a job. Rather than argue, she put a smile on her face.

As she turned, Lemuel gave her a little wave and pulled out his pocket watch. He pointed at it. She shook her head. They had agreed to meet later but she was no longer in the mood to sneak out. She caught sight of his frown as she left.

The sound of the analytical was muffled as the door closed behind her. Dieter was still happily drawing, and now there was a considerable pile of paper beside him.

"He ran out," said Mr Prescott. "I restocked him."

"Could I leave him here?" Gilda blurted without thinking, and just as hastily held her breath. Mr Prescott said nothing so she persisted. "I need to go to the Institute library for about half an hour."

Mr Prescott looked surprised but then recovered. He smiled. "Of course, my dear, but if he makes a fuss I shall have to put him out."

"He won't."

She hurried to Dieter's side. "Look, I have to go to the library," she said in *Züridütsch*.

"And you want me to stay, I'm not deaf," he said. She looked at him suspiciously. She had spoken quickly and quietly in English with Mr Prescott. Perhaps Dieter's English was not as bad as he made out.

"You will be good."

"When am I ever anything else?"

She raised her eyebrows. "Just keep drawing."

Gilda hurried to the Institute and pushed her way through the doors. It had been originally constructed to provide education to the masses. However, sometime during its existence, that mandate had been reduced to the occasional public lecture. It had become a private haven for the great and good of Fremantle.

The library remained available to all, though somehow she doubted that a girl who had only recently passed sixteen was included in that definition of "all". But Mrs Holman either saw something in her she approved of, or did not care.

Gilda waved a quick greeting and disappeared into the shelves. The section she wanted contained the John F T Jane Publishing company's annual edition and quarterly updates on air vessels. She picked up the most recent edition of *All the World's Flying Machines*—the original book had been *All the World's Flying Warships* but within two years of that printing the publisher had extended coverage to commercial vessels—and every update since then.

She sat down with the annual and flipped through the pages. She made notes in the back of her notebook on dates and vehicles that resembled the one she had seen. There were so many different designs of Faraday-based vehicles, it was almost bewildering. Dieter would have loved it. Perhaps when she was earning her own living she could arrange a subscription for him.

There were several vehicles that could have been the right one, including an original Brunel design as Dieter had suggested. Once she had been through the whole book, she moved on to the periodicals. There were one or two new vessels and several instances of upgraded and modified designs. Nothing seemed to stay unchanged.

The main thing she noted was that the inclusion of Babbage analyticals—or similar machines—was spreading to smaller and smaller ships as the calculators became more compact.

She wondered whether the vehicle that had crashed had had one. If it had been intended for long distance travel, then it should have. It certainly had not taken off from Fremantle air-dock because, in that case, there would have been no mystery as to its origins.

No, it had just happened to be flying over and its boiler had exploded. She couldn't remember if it had a smoke stack, but she didn't think diesel engines tended to explode. Steam engines, on the other hand, could and did. That was one of her criteria when deciding which ships to include in her list.

She wondered whether it would be possible to develop computations to calculate the likelihood of a steam boiler exploding. You would need to know all sorts of details, but it seemed quite a straightforward sort of thing. But it would have to include both calculus and probabilities. She wasn't sure how that could be achieved with an analytical. That was why she needed to go to a university.

The clock chimed the half hour. She had a few more minutes. She reshelved the volumes and went to the Geography section. This was less familiar territory for her and it took a minute to locate an Ordnance Survey map of Perth, Fremantle and Surrounds.

She unfolded it flat on a table with her notebook from the previous evening open to her notes on the crash. She took out her ruler and measured distances, fitting them into her calculations of the night before. She wrote a number at the bottom, converted it to inches in her head and measured.

The vessel had almost certainly crashed on the scarp. Somewhere near the Swan River up-country.

iv

Gilda ambled along the side of the road. She barely noticed where she was going as her legs followed the path homeward. She paid no attention to Dieter. In her head was a crazy thought that she kept trying to push away, but whenever she attempted to think about something else, it crept back.

"Do all modern flyers have analytical machines?" she said out loud in *Züridütsch*.

"Most of the commercial ones," said Dieter, confirming he had not strayed. "Even some of the smaller private ones."

She heard his footsteps running to close the gap between them.

"You want to find the one that crashed," he said. "You want its analytical."

"I couldn't get it out even if I found it, and I couldn't give it any power," she said. "Anyway, others will find it first. They'll know where it is by now." She sighed. "It will be in the newspapers tomorrow."

But it wasn't.

She found a discarded copy of the newspaper on her way to school. There was a great deal of coverage of the search. Two pilots from the air-dock had taken their planes up and tried to spot the crashed vessel from the air, but without any luck.

There were sketches in the newspaper, supposedly of the ship, but whoever had drawn them had decided it was a Zeppelin. The story also talked about salvage rights; whoever found it would own it, or at least get a reward from the real owner.

Gilda read the accounts carefully. As far as she could tell, the focus of the search was on the coastal lowlands. The planes had overflown some of the Darling Scarp, but if they were looking for a Zeppelin they could have looked straight at the crashed air-plane and not recognised it.

Last summer she and her family had taken a charabanc up onto the scarp. The *jarrah* trees had a lot of space between them, and a downed air-plane could be hidden by the foliage.

As she finished the reports, excitement was growing inside her. If she was right, she knew where it was—and they didn't. She was certain she was. She could even place it on a map, within a certain degree of error, above the Swan River valley as it cut through the hills.

But how could she possibly get out there? It was ten miles to the base of the scarp itself and then a climb, though not a hard one, up to the forest, and even if she got in among the trees how would she navigate to the right place?

She made a mental list of what she would need, making sure to include a compass and food. But she shook her head. It was ridiculous. Her time was occupied at home when she was not at school. There was no way she could get away from home without anyone noticing.

Even if she found it, what could she possibly do? There would be the dead bodies of the people on board. Could she face that? And for what? She had no way to bring the ship back.

She buried the hope she had back down inside. It would be better just to wait for Mr Aronson to agree to let them have their loan for the new boat. Then, when the catch improved, persuade her parents to let her go to university.

That is what she said to herself, but compared to the bright burning hope of finding the downed air-plane, that idea was little more than a flickering candle flame.

On a low brick wall she spied a lizard—a bearded dragon about a foot long—sunning itself in the morning light. She picked up a stone and threw it, but it went low and the stone cracked against the bricks. The lizard vanished in a blur of motion. She chastised herself for wanting to hurt a harmless lizard, but she was just so frustrated.

Why had her father brought them to this place? If they must come to Australia, why couldn't it have been to a city with a university?

"Hey, Gilda!"

She turned at Lemuel's voice. He was in the suit he had to wear to work. "Thought I'd missed you."

"You have caught me."

"What happened last night?"

She shrugged. She was not sure why she had decided not to see him. After her parents had gone to bed, she had spent some time going over her calculations and looking at her notes about the possibly matching ships.

Then she had written out some sequences for code that could change itself—if it could automatically make its own cards. It would work, she thought, but there was no problem she knew of that required it. It was like a kaleidoscope: pretty and clever, but with no practical application.

"I had to do chores and my parents stayed awake talking so I couldn't get out."

He nodded. "Tonight?"

Why not? She smiled. "Yes. Usual place?"

"Usual place," he said. He turned and strode away without even a goodbye.

Gilda felt deflated. This was not going to be a good day.

"Papa would kill Lemuel if he knew about you two," said Dieter. Her assignations were not something she had been able to keep secret from her brother, who also stayed awake at night after their parents had gone to bed. They usually went to bed early because her father always got up before the sun to get out on the lake.

"Well, he's not going to find out," said Gilda. "Is he?"

Dieter shrugged. "I won't tell."

Gilda wondered if her secret would come back to haunt her on the day that Dieter wanted something from her. Probably. Dieter was bright enough not to kill the golden goose while it promised to lay in the future.

The school day contained mathematics and science. She listened dutifully, wrote down what she had to and did the sums. She didn't get them all correct because she wasn't really paying attention.

Rather than thinking about the individual sums, she was always working out the most efficient code that could do the sums for her. Why do it herself a dozen times when she could write one sequence that could do it a hundred times faster? A person just had to understand the method.

She was still the best pupil in the class for those subjects. And that meant both the girls and boys disliked her, for opposite reasons.

Gilda walked home with Dieter though he was perfectly capable of making the journey himself. Mama always worried. She did not like the city and had the idea it was full of criminals and lowlifes. If they were there, Gilda had never seen them.

Papa's boat was drawn up on the beach, which was not usual; he got home in the mid-afternoon. The moment she opened the door she knew that something was indeed wrong. Her parents were not gutting fish or working on the nets but sitting at the table, holding hands across it.

v

"What's wrong?" she said entering in a sudden rush. The daylight that had flooded the dark interior was shut out as Dieter closed the door behind her.

They both seemed to jump at her words as if they hadn't been expecting her.

She saw a letter on the table. The envelope had been sliced open and the single page lay on top of it.

"Our English is not so good, Gilda," said Papa. "Perhaps we did not understand. You read it."

She reached between them, took the letter and carried it to the window. It was from the bank. It started with the usual pleasantries but the second paragraph began with the word "Unfortunately". Gilda went numb as she felt her plans and dreams being pummelled by the blunt words denying their loan. She let her hand drop to her side. "But why?"

"He says your calculations were wrong," said Mama. "I knew it was wrong to let a girl do the figures."

In her state of apathy Gilda did not rise to her mother's unfair attack. She lifted the paper again and read on. It did not say that *her* calculations were incorrect but it said the books supplied had been transcribed into the analytical, the calculations had been made and the results differed from the books.

Naturally he would believe the analytical. Gilda hesitated. Perhaps she had got it wrong, but she did not believe it. She glanced across at her parents.

"I did not get the calculations wrong," she said quietly, in an attempt to suppress the anger she was feeling. Young ladies did not get angry.

Her mother lifted her head and turned towards her. "You are saying you are better than a banker and his machine?"

"Not better, Mama, but not wrong."

"If you are not wrong, Gilda," said her papa. "You are saying that they are wrong."

Gilda tried to clamp her mouth shut. She knew she should not say what she wanted to say but somehow she could not hold it in. "Yes, then I am saying they are wrong. The bank and their analytical are wrong!"

"Go to your room, Gilda," said her mother.

"I didn't make a mistake."

Her mother stood up. "I said go to your room."

Gilda glanced at Dieter, who was pulling back into the shadows. It was not that she expected him to help her—there was nothing he could do—but it still felt like a betrayal. She met her father's sad eyes. For him it meant another year, at least, of working the old boat. It was too small and needed constant care to keep it sound.

"Do I have to take my slipper to you?"

Gilda's attention was dragged back to her mother, who had taken a step towards her. For a moment she braved the anger of her mother's face, then turned and slunk away down the short passage to her room.

Once inside with the door at her back she found herself breathing hard as if she had been running a race. Her pulse pounded in her temple. She dragged her fingers across her cheeks, which felt cold with anger.

She picked up her chair. She had rescued it from a fire; the legs were still blackened but it was serviceable. However, this time she did not want to sit on it. Instead she jammed it against the door, judging the angle to optimise its resistance to the door being opened. Too shallow an angle and it would not resist, too sharp and it would simply fall.

The local church clock rang for the half hour. It was half-past four.

Under her bed was the small case she had used when they had travelled from Switzerland. She wished she was back there. There were so many universities, even one in Zurich itself, where she could have studied. But no, her father had to bring them to the most uncivilised place on the whole planet. Not a single thought for her or her future.

"*Most girls just want to find a husband.*" She spat out the words in imitation of Mr Aronson. He certainly would not think she was a capable computationer now.

She threw a few things into the bag. It was not large but that was a good thing. She needed to travel light. She could make her way up to Darling Scarp, find the air-plane and claim it for salvage. Then they would have enough money to get Papa a new boat and get her to university. And to the very depths of hell with Mr Aronson. He could burn there.

She shut the small case and clicked the locks.

Why would Aronson lie?

The thought struck her like a thunderbolt. If her calculations were correct, that meant his calculations were not, and that Lemuel coded it wrong. Or he was lying deliberately. And if the calculations were purposefully false, then Lemuel must know.

She sat on the bed and stared at her hands. Her fingers were slender and long, her nails just stubs from her chewing them and working around the house. Women who did not work had elegant fingernails and soft skin. Likewise, men who did not work with their hands. Like Aronson, even Lemuel, though she had felt the calluses on his fingers from using the key-punch for his instruction cards.

She had calmed down and was thinking more clearly. Running away right now would not be sensible; very quickly they would find she was gone and be after her.

It was a good enough plan, but she needed to leave during the night when her parents had gone to bed. That way she would be able to reach the scarp and get in among the trees before they even knew she was gone.

And there was now an additional part to her plan.

She lay down to get some sleep before she set off to meet Lemuel.

vi

At about seven in the evening she was woken by her father asking her if she wanted something to eat. He tried the door but found it barred.

"Leave me alone," she said.

"I'll leave you some supper out here."

She heard him put the tray down on the floor and then walk away. She did not open the door right away. Sleep wouldn't return no matter how she tried to coax it.

Instead she watched the light fading and the sounds of the city and houses nearby settling and going quiet. The evening stillness was interrupted only by the occasional dog barking in the distance and the calls of the parakeets.

Only after all movement in the house had ceased did she open the door and pick up the tray of cold food. She took it with her to the kitchen and ate it as she gathered the items for her journey. She had decided to dispense with her travelling bag; she wouldn't need a change of clothes.

Instead she found a drawstring bag. From the pantry she took some dried meat and a couple of tins. The sound of the can-opener hitting the

metal in the bag seemed to shatter the silence, but no one stirred. She was
not sure what else she might need but took a box of matches, one of the
bigger cooking knives, and a roll of twine. Water was unlikely to be a
problem.

Her eyes had become used to the darkness. When she glanced up at the
big clock she could make out the hands indicating it was only ten o'clock.
The enormity of what she was about to do struck her, and she hesitated.
She was running away from home like children did in stories. Everything
that had happened seemed like a fairy story.

She went back to her room with her spoils and laced her feet into her
walking boots. She knew she was pretty safe wandering the Australian
countryside. There were poisonous snakes, of course, but no large
predators. Only dingos, and there were very few in this part of the
continent. Back home in Switzerland there were wolves and bears that
would kill a young girl as soon as look at her, especially in winter. But
dingoes weren't wolves, and it wasn't winter here.

She decided she had better write a note explaining something of what
she was doing. If she was right about the ship, she would have it located
within a few hours of getting up on to the scarp and she did not want to
delay being found.

She wrote a clear explanation of her intentions and a description of the
direction she was heading. Papa would be able to organise some men to
find her; if he was in charge, then he could claim the salvage.

The house had only one floor so slipping out was not difficult. She had
done it many times, even before she had started meeting with Lemuel. The
air was chilly and the night clear, which would be helpful.

It was on the shore of the Swan River, close to some boat huts, that she
usually met Lemuel so she headed that way. On any normal night she would
be excited. She and Lemuel seemed to get on quite well, though mostly he
just wanted to kiss. He wanted to touch her, too, but she put a stop to that.
Aside from the kissing they talked about things, like being a computationer.

She saw his silhouette, dark against the river reflecting the light of the
moon. Perth lay on the other side. The way the geography worked here the
river became very wide, almost like a lake, in the flat coastal region below the
Darling Scarp before it narrowed again and ran into the sea. This was a tidal
area, and the water ran back from the sea into the lake twice a day to fill it up.
That made the bottleneck treacherous. Bridges crossed it at the two
narrowest places.

There was another bridge further upriver before it opened out into the lake. And that was where she was intending to cross; she did not want to walk through the Perth docks in the middle of the night. It might not make sense but she felt safer on the Fremantle side. Perth was a foreign city, while this was her home.

"Lemuel."

He jumped and turned. In the dark she couldn't see his face. "You shouldn't sneak up on a body like that, Gilda."

"Sorry, hope you haven't been waiting too long."

"I was worried you weren't going to turn up again."

She sat down beside him and let the bag drop. It clanked as it hit the ground.

"What have you got there?"

"Just some bits." Normally she let him take the lead with the kissing but she didn't want him questioning her about the bag. So she reached her hand round his neck and pulled his head down so she could press her lips against his.

They stayed like that for a few moments until his arm went round her waist and he pulled her tighter. She usually enjoyed the kissing but tonight her mind was on other things.

She pulled back, though he persisted—the way he always did—but then relented, and they drew apart.

"Sorry, I'm upset," she said.

"Family?"

She hesitated, not sure whether she was more upset about the analytical disagreeing with her figures, or about her parents sending her to her room like a baby.

"I didn't make a mistake, Lemuel." The words exploded out of her even though she had not intended them. His hand that still encircled her waist dropped away.

"You must have." His voice was tight in his throat. "Analyticals don't make mistakes."

"Unless there's something wrong with the code."

"You're accusing me?" Now he actually moved away from her, sliding along the wall but turning to face her. "That's my code. And nobody's ever complained before. If there had been anything wrong you think no one else would have noticed?"

She sighed. "I know, but…"

"But you still think you're right and I'm wrong." He did not shout because, in the night, a loud voice carried across the water—but his temper was like a red-hot poker.

Her own anger was growing and she had trouble keeping it clamped inside.

"The only way there could be a mistake," he said, "is if I put it there."

"Did you?"

He leapt to his feet and loomed over her. "We're finished, Gilda. And, just so you know, you kiss like a baby, and all your code is like—" he seemed to be having trouble thinking of something for a moment, then it came to him "—the rotting fish your father sells."

Her hand lashed out of its own accord and struck him across the cheek with a loud crack. He looked shocked for a moment then gave a sneering laugh and headed back towards Fremantle.

Gilda shook with anger. She hated him.

She stared up at the sky. A sprinkling of high-level clouds glowed in the moonlight, and beyond them a billion stars. She directed her gaze to the star that never moved, close to the horizon, the British Void-station that hung above Ceylon. The British needed computationers for their navy.

Picking up her bag, she set off at a brisk walk along the track that followed the river in the direction of Darling Scarp.

vii

Lemuel hung back in the shadows, nursing his stinging cheek which was hot against the palm of his hand. He wasn't sure what had just happened, except Gilda wasn't his tabbie anymore—even if he hadn't been able to tell anyone about her.

She was prim as a schoolmistress and never let him touch. She said her papa would shoot him if he'd known what they were doing. Lemuel didn't know if that was true but he was not going to take the chance. He had lost nothing. Her pretending to like him was probably just a trick so she could steal his code optimisations.

Why hadn't she got up?

He could see her silhouette still sitting and watching the water. Her head moved; she was looking up at the sky. That was like her, always thinking about things that were far away. Never about him and what *he* wanted. Good riddance.

He continued to watch. Finally she got to her feet and picked up the bag. She had never said what was in it. He moved further back into the shadows so she wouldn't see him when she turned round. But she didn't face back towards the city; she went along the river. Not slowly, either—she moved with purpose.

He watched until her figure slipped among the shadows and was gone. What did that mean? Where could she be off to?

Lemuel pointed his feet back into the city but trod slowly as he tried to understand what she was doing. She wasn't going home, so she was going away and heading inland.

What she had said about him deliberately fixing the computations worried him. She was running away from home after that disappointment for her family, but she had stopped to talk to him and ask him about that.

Mr Aronson needed to know.

Lemuel stopped on a corner. His home was to the right and Gilda's parents' place, the other way. If she had sneaked out of her room by the window as usual, it would be unlocked. He could get in. Maybe she left a note for her parents saying where she'd gone.

The thought of what he was about to do made him nervous, but he headed to Gilda's house. It was eleven at night; nobody was out. Over in Perth he could see the streets lit up with electric lights, but in Fremantle only the streets around the docks had power. Except for the most powerful businesses that provided their own, like the bank.

Yes, Mr Aronson needed to know what she was doing. He would know what to do about it.

Lemuel went through the garden to her window. As he expected, it was unlocked and moments later he was inside. He gave his eyes some time to adjust. The room smelled of her. And fish.

He had two sisters who shared a room. Theirs was decorated with things they had made, instructional texts drawn in capitals, sewing samples, printed flyers from the occasional circus, and drawings of horses. They had three dolls between them that sat on small chairs, and they were not very tidy.

Gilda's room was different, more like his. There was nothing that had been made. The drawings on her walls were fragments of code. He peered at one or two but they didn't make any sense. She had books but they were in some foreign language. Swiss, probably.

There was a letter on the table. There wasn't enough light to read it so he put it in his pocket. Under the letter were ten sheets of sketches torn from a book; he took those as well.

Taking a final glance around the room, he climbed back out the window and closed it down tight.

Feeling considerably happier, he headed back towards home. He even whistled a little to himself. He had been told he couldn't hold a tune to save his life. But it wasn't a tune he needed to save his life now. This information would make Mr Aronson very happy.

"Gilda's not answering, Mama," said Dieter, coming back into the main room. "And I can't open her door."

In her haste, Alys Dettwiler almost dropped the tin plate she was drying. It clattered onto the drainer with a metallic racket. She rushed back to Gilda's door and pounded on it. She turned the handle and pushed. It gave only a little, as if something blocked it.

If Alys had been one of the soft women brought up in the city who did nothing but sew and gossip all day long, she would have been stopped by the door. But she was the wife of a fisherman and she had worked hard all her life. She had the strength a refined woman would have been ashamed of.

She put her shoulder to the door and shoved hard. Something snapped. The door flew open and the chair rattled across the floor. The room was empty. It felt as if something had grabbed her heart and squeezed. Panic threatened to consume her but she took hold of herself.

Even though her husband did not fish in the sea, Alys had lived with the risk of him never returning for over fifteen years. But this was her daughter. She took a deep breath and let it out slowly.

She looked for a note or a letter but there was nothing. Gilda was a tidy girl for the most part, and her room looked as neat as it always did. The bed either had not been slept in, or she had made it before she left.

Then she gasped as her eyes fell on the floorboards. Foot prints. Not dainty prints that Gilda might make, but prints from a man's boots.

She turned to Dieter to tell him to run for to fetch a policeman. But Dieter was clinging to the door frame with a look of guilt on his face that every parent knows.

"Where is she, Dieter?" she said.

Gilda came awake with a jump as a cockatoo screeched directly above her. She rolled over and looked up. Her movement must have scared it. Black wings carried it from the *jarrah* tree and away, still calling its warning.

The sun was up, its rays slanting through the leaves and branches of the forest. Her eyes were filled with the sandman's grit. She pulled herself to a sitting position with her back against the tree and rubbed them.

Her skin felt greasy. She ran her fingers through her hair, knotted and with bits of twig in it. *I must look a sight.* Then she recalled she had filled her water bottle at one of the streams that fed the Swan River once she had got out of the city.

A drink of it made her feel better. She used some to wash her face and dried it with the hem of her dress.

Sleeping on the ground had made her joints stiff. She climbed awkwardly to her feet and stretched. That managed to get some of the kinks out of her arms, back and legs. She rolled her head back and forwards to banish the cramps from her neck.

Picking up the bag, she wandered downhill a little until she came to the rounded edge of the scarp. Perth and Fremantle were laid out before her like a map. The Swan River came down on her left and widened out. She could see the road that had brought her to the base of the hill, about a mile away. When it reached the lower part of the scarp it turned north, to her right. She had left it as soon as she could and climbed up through the undergrowth to the top.

Swamps along the edge of the river before it became the lake reflected the bright blue sky. Boats moved across the sky's reflection; she knew one of them was her father's, but she could not see which from here.

She looked beyond the city to the sea. It was incomprehensibly huge, stretching from the north to the south. There were a few small islands close in, but beyond them nothing but the patterns of waves across the thousands of miles. She wondered what the mathematics were behind the waves. Could she write code that would describe them? Predict them?

Clouds scudded across the sky, their shadows skimming the waves. In the distance a rainstorm blurred the horizon, but in the morning light it reflected orange. She frowned: a red storm?

It was something they talked about in school. Sometimes powerful winds would gather up sand from the desert and blow out to sea, and then return to release it on the land. Rain and red sand mixed together: a red storm.

She felt a pang of guilt. Her mother would be very upset at her leaving, although the letter explained everything. But now Mama would worry about her being out in the storm. Of course they would be coming after her but she would have time to find the air-plane. The storm would probably give her more time.

She looked at the boats again. The memory of her argument with Lemuel the previous evening made her frown. He had not answered her question as to whether he had deliberately made the numbers come out wrong. She was annoyed with herself for becoming angry so easily, but when he had attacked her father she could not hold it in.

It had distracted her.

Dieter always got upset and angry at Mama when she confronted him with something he had done wrong. Just the way Lemuel had.

But why? Could it be because he didn't want her to leave? She was always talking about going off to university. She knew, from listening to the girls at school, that most boys didn't like girls who wanted more in their lives than their customary place.

Was he just trying to make sure she stayed?

But if Mr Aronson found he was using bad code, he would lose his job. Would he risk his job just to keep her here?

A movement on the road caught her attention. It was a steam truck puffing up from Perth. Nothing surprising about that—the road existed to carry traffic. Even so, she pulled back into the shadow of the trees. If she could see them, they could see her.

She studied the truck. It was not hurrying, but then the road was not smooth, and the ride would be very uncomfortable for the men in the back. She could not see the driver or anyone in the cab, but four men clung to the boards round the rear. And all of them were staring up at Darling Scarp.

A pang of fear went through her. Was it possible they were already coming after her? She had expected it to be longer. She did not know the time of day but from the sun's angle it couldn't be more than eight o'clock. Mama and Papa got up early, yes, but they would not have tried to wake her until about now.

She shook her head. She was imagining it. There was no possible way they would be after her yet. Of course she still had time. They were just people heading up north.

The truck reached the long curve that brought it under the eaves of the scarp. As it changed direction, Gilda could see the men were still staring up, turning their heads back and forth, scanning the trees. They had not seen her.

She had allowed a smile to creep onto her face but then the puffing truck juddered to a halt. Fear screamed through her as a baying of dogs arose. One man climbed down from the cab and released the gate on the back. Four dogs piled out and ran about sniffing the ground. The men climbed down and called to the dogs.

Each man was carrying either a rifle or a shotgun.

They might just be hunting, she said to herself in a vain attempt to calm her thumping heart. But every fibre of her body was straining to run. She knew as a certainty they were after her.

The other door of the cab opened and someone got out on the side away from her. His head disappeared but eventually he came around the back, moving nervously and shying away when one of the dogs ran at him.

It was Lemuel. Seeing him shook her to her very core. He must have told someone, and that someone did not want her to do what they thought she was doing. Or know what she knew.

But what could he have said? She had not told him anything about her plans.

He must have watched her. He must have seen her head along the river instead of going home. And he knew she suspected him of deliberately producing a false report.

Aronson. It must be him. It explained everything. Aronson had Lemuel fake the results so her father would be forced to take a bigger loan and pay so much more. And if he had done it to her family, how many other people had he deceived?

The men got themselves organised and put the dogs on leads.

Making sure she kept the tree between herself and the men she stumbled back up the scarp, grabbed her bag and went deeper into the forest.

ix

She headed east. The men would be slow to start with but that would change when the dogs picked up her trail. She did not doubt that would happen. Back in Switzerland a St Bernard could find a man buried beneath the snow.

Somehow she had to escape them, find the air-plane, and return to the city to expose Aronson for his misdeeds—though she would need proof.

She shook her head. There was so much happening she was confused, yet it was a confusion she had experienced more than once when she practised writing code. Sometimes there would be so many elements to a problem the whole was enough to make her head spin.

She had learnt to divide the problem into parts and to solve each part on its own. This was like that. There were many different elements to her problem, but in truth it was several problems—and, while linked, they could be solved in isolation.

And the one problem that must be solved before any other was how to escape the men. So, she must put aside everything else and focus on that one thing.

She felt better.

Clutching her bag tight in one hand, she headed through the forest. The *jarrah* trees were quite widely spaced, just as she remembered, and the undergrowth was not thick. It meant she could make good speed. The ground was too uneven to go fast but she could trot. But the same applied to her pursuers.

The ground opened up beneath her. She stumbled and fell down a slope into a boggy ravine with a small stream bubbling along the bottom of it.

She paused, standing ankle-deep in muddy water. She knew that animals would crisscross their own paths in order to confuse wolves because although they can follow a trail easily enough there was no way of knowing the direction the prey was running when they made the trail.

Dare she take the time to create a false path? Did she have a choice?

There was no sound except the birds, and the brook streaming around her feet. If she did not try they would catch her.

With her decision made, Gilda climbed straight up the opposite bank and continued in the direction she had been going. She counted her footsteps to one hundred and stopped. She took a sharp right and went another hundred paces. She turned back and retraced the path down into the water.

She listened. There was still nothing. With luck they would not be hurrying; as far as they knew, she was ignorant of their approach and no more than a helpless girl in the wilderness. The latter part was almost true.

Gilda waded upstream for twenty paces and then climbed out on the side heading back towards her pursuers. Then she ran in a long arc that eventually brought her back to the stream but further up.

As the final stage she followed the stream back down again, staying in the water. She knew it would lead to the Swan River, joining it before it tumbled down off the scarp. As she reached the place where she had first found the stream, she heard the baying of dogs. It sent a shiver through her. She felt the way a goat on the mountain must feel with the wolves after it.

But she was not a goat.

She continued downstream as quickly as she dared in the treacherous mud, but before she could get round the next bend the baying of dogs abruptly increased in volume. Without taking the time to look back she threw herself into the water among the mud and grasses that grew along its shoreline.

There was barely enough depth to cover her. She could not see what was going on because she was facing in the wrong direction; she did not dare try to turn around, in case her movement attracted their attention. Better to remain completely still.

The dogs had ceased baying and she could hear indistinct words above the sound of the stream. Then a dog gave voice again. She had a moment of terror when she thought they might have found her but, though all the dogs gave cry, they did not get louder. The noise of the pursuit dropped in volume, telling her they had gone over the bank to follow her first trail.

Her plan was working so far, but she would have only minutes. If she was right, her pursuers would charge straight forwards and not realise they had lost the trail at first. Then they would backtrack and find where she had made the sharp turn.

The second time they lost the trail they would think she had turned again and waste time looking for it. After that they would return to the river. With luck they would split up, and the ones going upstream would find her other diversion and call the rest.

That was the weakest part of her plan. They might all come in her direction instead. And even if they did follow her second false trail they would realise that they were dealing with someone who was deliberately trying to evade them and would thereafter be more careful.

She counted to ten to make sure they had gone far enough over the bank that they would not see her. Soaked through, Gilda stood and headed downstream again.

She looked up into the *jarrah* trees as she passed beneath their limbs that stretched out across the stream. If only they weren't spaced so far apart, she could climb them and move across the landscape up high. At this point, even if the trees had been closer together, her clothes were now so heavy with water she would never be able to get up the first one.

The stream was widening and deepening as tributaries ran into it. The banks were steeper now, and she realised it had got to the point where she would not be able to climb out. The air was getting warmer as the sun rose. Insects flitted above the water's surface.

She no longer needed to walk and took a minute to remove her boots as they dragged her down. Though she could still feel the bottom with her feet, if she chose she could float and let the stream carry her. She was almost sure she had outrun them when the sound of baying dogs filtered through the air once more. Gilda almost cried.

They must have realised she was heading downstream and simply followed along the bank. She was very tired and the idea of surrendering crossed her mind. Would that be so bad?

The sound of the dogs grew. They were on the western bank. She manoeuvred herself to that side and brought herself to a halt. Ahead the trees were opening up, but the sky was darkening. The storm must have arrived on shore.

Perhaps they wouldn't see her.

She did not have time to react to the sound of the shotgun going off before something stung her cheek and the water beside her erupted. She should have moved, or dived into the water. Instead, in complete disbelief, she turned to look at the bank opposite.

Twenty feet above her and more than that away were three of the men with their dogs. She was staring into the barrel of a shotgun. Something moved behind the man aiming at her, and he jerked. The shotgun went off but it was no longer pointing in her direction.

Lemuel had spoilt the man's aim.

An incessant pattering filled the air and the surface of the river was suddenly covered in splashes and ripples. The man with the shotgun struck Lemuel with the butt, but the other man, with a rifle, was taking aim.

The storm hit. The air turned orange. The wind whipped air-borne sand into her skin and eyes, flaying her. If the man fired, she never knew because the whole world shrank to five feet around her. She could see nothing beyond that distance and could hear only the thundering downpour.

The river current pulled at her legs. The root she clung to was sinking beneath the surface—no, the surface was rising, fast. The flood dragged at her, pulling her feet from the riverbed and stretching her out.

In moments the root became fully submerged. If she kept holding on to it she would be pulled under. There was nothing else she could see to grab hold of. She had no choice but to let go.

The cold swirling water sucked her out into the current. It rolled her over so she was face up. It was as if she were beneath an orange dome with dim light filtering through.

The water fell away from beneath her and she tumbled into an abyss.

x

Rudger Dettwiler stood at the window and watched the storm rage. The roof's rattling was incessant, but he knew the sheets of corrugated iron were attached firmly; he checked them after every storm.

He had just enough time when the storm appeared on the horizon to pull in his nets. He had furled his sails and strapped them down as soon as he had brought the nets on board then used the oars to return. He arrived back on shore just as the rain began to fall.

The tide was in and with his wife's help they had got the mast down and turned the little boat bottom up. She had said nothing of Gilda's disappearance until they were back in the house.

He knew it was foolish, but he went to look in his daughter's room. He saw the footprints too but could force no further meaning from the scene.

"What does it mean, Papa?" she said.

He shook his head. "I do not know."

The information Dieter had provided was not as helpful as one might have hoped. Rudger was angry, of course, that his daughter had lied to them so completely. Angry that she had been sneaking out of the house at night to meet a boy—the one from the bank, no less. But he blamed himself for not listening to her. She was growing into a woman.

"What is she thinking, Mama?" he said in an effort to understand. "Would you have done this at her age?"

His wife came to his side, threaded her arm with his and took his hand.

"She is such a strange one," she said. "Her head is full of the number machines. How can I say what she is thinking in her head?"

"But she likes the boy," he said. "As you liked me. We had our fair share of secret meetings, did we not?"

She squeezed his arm. "We must find this boy, Lemuel. Find out if he saw her."

"What if it is his footprints on her floor?"

His wife knew what he meant but she shook her head. "She has her head in the clouds, it is true, but she would not make that mistake, Papa."

"It is not just a mistake for her to make," he said. "A man, a young one especially, is not always in control of himself."

"There is no evidence of it, Papa," she said. "No one would make the bed after such a thing."

He did not reply for a while and they continued to watch the wind ripping at the trees—so different from the pines and firs of their home— and the rain beating down. He decided.

"I cannot wait, wife. I must find this fellow, this Lemuel, and discover what he has done with our daughter," he said. "It's only a storm and I will not be on the water."

She did not argue but watched as he donned his waterproof gear along with his most solid boots. "Wait, Papa." Alys dug out the goggles with the wraparound strap his brother had bought for him as a present, for the day they could afford to buy a mechanical. He was likely never to have a machine for travelling, but the goggles would serve against the wind-blown sand.

As he opened the door, the wind ripped it from his grasp and blasted through the room, extinguishing all the lights. His wife was soaked through even though she remained inside. Together they managed to get the door closed again, with him on the outside.

Rain pelted down, driven by the wind. It came at him almost horizontally. He pulled up his collar to protect against the stinging sand. Without the goggles he would have been blinded.

He made his way to the bank, taking care on the roads because if there were any vehicles he would be unable to see them until they were on him. But there were neither people nor carriages on the streets, at least none he saw—though truthfully either could have passed within feet of him unnoticed.

He was not surprised to find the bank closed and locked with shutters drawn across the windows. No one came to the door when he knocked. They would have evacuated as soon as the warning went up about the approaching storm.

But a light caught his eye. It came and went as the rain and sand moved in the wind, but it was there, a little further up the street. He continued along the wooden sidewalk, past the building that housed the electricity generator. The sound of its thumping was a counterpoint to the wind's scream.

The light ahead brightened and he pushed on. More light appeared, glowing through the shuttered windows of the Mechanics Institute. Rudger had never been inside because his sort were seldom invited. He had never taken up such invitations that were offered since he was embarrassed about the quality of his English.

Today was different. He had not been invited and he needed to find his wayward daughter.

He climbed the wooden steps and hammered on the double doors which stood beneath their ornate arch. For a count of twenty there was no response. He hammered again, beating his gloved hand against the wood.

This time there was the sound of heavy bolts being thrown. The door was flung open and electric light poured out. Rudger did not wait to be invited but strode in, dripping rain and orange sand onto the polished wooden floor.

The door closed and the screaming of the wind was reduced to a whine.

Rudger folded down his collar, then removed his leather cap and the goggles. He looked down at the woman in front of him who was staring back with an expression that combined disdain and disgust.

"Greetings, madam," said Rudger. "Is the banker, *Herr* Aronson, here?"

"What if he is?"

Rudger took a moment to decipher the words; English might have some similarities to *Züridütsch* but the differences were also very great. "If he is," he replied with careful placing of the words, "I must speak with him. It is very important."

"And who are you?"

"I am Rudger Dettwiler," he said.

The woman's face softened. "Gilda's father?"

"You know my Gilda?"

"Of course, she comes here often to study in the library," said the woman.

"She comes to the library?"

"A very intelligent and accomplished young lady," she said, and then added, as if she was telling him off, "You should be very proud of her."

Rudger felt a little lost receiving such praise of his errant daughter from someone he did not know. "It is about Gilda I have come," he said, regaining his urgency. "She has gone from our home, and we do not know where."

"And why would Mr Aronson know anything?"

"Because I must find his boy, Lemuel, who works at the bank also. They were…"

He realised he did not know the correct English word to use, so he ended with "…good friends."

Her eyes narrowed. "Good friends?"

He nodded.

"You mean she was his girl?"

"She is *my* girl," he said, then understood and sighed. "*Ja*. His girl. They meet last night. Now she is gone."

She nodded and drew herself up. "I understand entirely. I will fetch Mr Aronson immediately. You," she looked at him dripping water and sand, "you stay there."

xi

She was underwater and her lungs were burning. Her eyes were open and there was faint light above her. In summer in Switzerland she had swum in the lake, but that did not have currents that tried to hold her down.

She struck for the surface. The light had a reddish hue so she knew the storm was still raging.

Why is it so far?

She hit another current. It twisted her around. She did not care which way she was facing as long as she kept heading up. The light was growing, spreading above her. She kicked harder, pulled with her arms, and tried hard not to think about the way her lungs were desperate to suck in the air that was not there.

She fought the muscles in her throat. They strained to open the airways and let the water in. Her legs kicked in time with her arm movements. Gilda's dress held her back and weighed her down but there was no way to get it off in time.

No one would ever find her. Her body would be swept along the Swan River and out to sea. Her strength was failing. Another current swirled about her. She broke its hold and kept moving up.

The redness of the light faded, becoming whiter and brighter. She could see her arms flailing as she clawed towards the surface . . .

. . . and broke through into clean air and rain. She breathed in and coughed. The river current pulled her under again. With renewed strength, she regained the surface and swam hard towards the left bank.

She slammed into a submerged rock and grabbed hold of it in a convulsive movement, coming to an abrupt halt with the water flowing around her and tumbling across her shoulders.

Breathing deeply she clung to the object beneath the surface. It was smoother than she expected rock to be. She needed to get out of the water. The bank was not far but she could see the racing current between her and safety.

Something like a branch protruded from the water a little further out. It was wood but had been weathered and shaped into a slim form. There was something familiar about it.

Being careful not to slip back into the raging torrent that pulled at her, she edged around the submerged rock until she was able to grab the branch. It was completely smooth to the touch and man-made.

It was a long, flat structure that twisted along its length. One of the vanes of a propeller—no, it was too big. This was a rotor. The rock was not a rock; it was the engine casing of the turbine that drove the rotor.

It was little wonder the searchers had not been able to find the ship. She was almost disappointed that she had discovered it by chance instead of through her computations. But still, she would not have been in the right place if not for her skill with numbers.

However, that could wait. She needed to get out of the water. Taking a firm hold of the rotor with both hands, she launched herself into the current. It grabbed her body and dress, almost pulling her hands free.

She clung for dear life and then, hand over hand, moved along its length.

Halfway across, where the current exerted its maximum force, her weight on the rotor made it turn. The concept of levers was not foreign to her. The further she went along the rotor, the stronger the leverage from her weight became.

Every movement she made brought the rotor down further. Her body dipped deeper into the flowing water. It had the beneficial effect of reducing the strain on her arms, and the weight on the rotor, but every time she moved the rotor dropped a little more.

She was almost within arm's reach of the bank when the rotor decided it would turn again and then keep going. Behind her another arm emerged from the river as the one she rode dipped her into it. She managed a breath before it plunged her back into the current.

Hooking her elbow round the wood, she pulled herself along. The rotor arm kept turning, getting deeper, as the one behind lifted, until it finally ran aground and jammed into the stone of the bank. Still holding her breath she managed to get her feet on to the wood and thrust herself upwards.

She burst from the water like a dolphin and threw herself onto dry land, where she lay panting.

The rain reduced to a light patter on her back and finally ceased altogether. She rolled over and stared at the clouds racing across the sky, revealing the blue beyond.

Beside her, the swollen river thundered. She pushed herself up into a sitting position and wrapped her arms around her legs, resting her chin on her knees. Her damp hair fell forwards. Out of the corner of her eye she could see grains of red sand clinging to it.

Somewhere Gilda had lost her bag. She vaguely remembered having it when she was laying the false trail, but sometime after that she had become separated from it. All her food and notes were gone. The notes would not have survived first contact with the water, but the food would have been edible.

But the notes did not really matter; she had found the flyer.

Her cheek ached.

They shot at me, she thought, and it did not seem real. She touched her cheek with the tips of her fingers and they came back with a light covering of blood.

"They shot at me," she said out loud, and the words still did not make any sense.

Then came a voice.

"I reckon you need to get someone to look at that."

It took Gilda a long moment to realise the words she had heard were not her own thoughts.

"My granddad said that when the white man came, the People thought it was the spirits of the ancients come back from the dead."

On the ground beside her, a shadow moved. It was the figure of a person. She turned and looked up but the sun was in her eyes and all she could see was a gangly silhouette.

"They got that bloody wrong."

Aronson did not look pleased as he emerged from the depths of the Institute.

"My decision is final, Mr Dettwiler," he said. "No personal representation can alter a decision once made."

He came to a stop several feet away. To Rudger it seemed too far, as if the air about him was somehow tainted. He shrugged inwardly. His trade did mean he carried the smell of fish with him. Perhaps that was the problem.

"My daughter, Gilda, is missing."

"I'm sorry to hear that."

"She met with your man, Lemuel, last night."

"Did she?" Aronson gave an apologetic smile. "The private activities of my staff are not my concern, of course. If that's everything?"

Rudger took a step forwards. He topped the fellow by almost a foot, causing Aronson to take a step back as he looked up.

"Now see here, Dettwiler…"

"I need to know where he is so I can ask him what he knows of my Gilda."

"Oh. Yes. I see, of course," said Aronson. "That makes sense."

The man offered nothing further. Rudger wondered how someone with such responsibility could seem so … stupid.

"Well?" he said in as pleasant a tone as he could manage.

"Well?" said Aronson.

"If he is not at the bank, and he is not here, then he will be at home in this storm."

"Yes, I expect so."

"And where is that home?"

Aronson looked surprised. "You expect me to tell you?"

Rudger took another step forwards. Aronson retreated again and fetched up against the wall.

"I expect you to tell me."

"I can't reveal the addresses of employees, quite unprofessional."

The anger Rudger had been desperately trying to hold back broke free, and he roared. "My daughter is missing, Aronson, your man knows where she is, maybe. Where is he?"

"Gone!"

Rudger blinked as he tried to absorb this new piece of information.

"He is gone too?" he hesitated. "They have run away together?"

There was a curious pause as if Aronson could not decide whether to agree with him. "No." After that first hesitant answer Aronson seemed to gather himself. "No, you see, young Lemuel came to me last night. He said he had seen your girl."

Rudger opened his mouth to demand to know why Aronson had not mentioned this before, but the man held up his hand. "I did not want to concern you. Lemuel said she had been behaving oddly and after they parted she had headed inland along the river.

"Being a sensible fellow, he came to me and I arranged for him to go with some other chaps to find her, early this morning. Of course we had no idea there was going to be a storm. I'm sure they've found her by now and will shortly be in the process of bringing her home."

Rudger absorbed the news. He had not followed every word but the gist of it was clear enough. He was still uncertain but it seemed as if Mr Aronson had everything under control. He nodded but felt uncomfortable. If this was true then he need do nothing but wait for Aronson's men to return with Gilda. It was simple enough.

"How will I know when they have returned?"

"I will have Lemuel bring her straight round."

Rudger felt deflated, as if all his pent-up energy had been stolen away from him.

xiii

The young man squatted down beside her. His black skin drew tight over muscles like cords. His eyes were dark and he had a wide, flat nose. The hair on his head was black and as messy as hers probably was. He wore trousers that must have been repaired a hundred times from the mends, tucks and patches, and a ragged, unbuttoned shirt.

"David," he said, holding out his hand. Gilda took it in something like a dream. He continued to hold her hand and waited. "And your name is?"

"Gilda."

"Nice name." He looked her over and shook his head. "You're in a right state. I don't know why your lot wear so many clothes. I'm already dry and you'll be wet the rest of the day in all that."

"I'm not taking it off."

He laughed. "There was me hoping you might."

She knew she ought to be offended but the way he spoke was so amiable and good-natured she couldn't take his comments seriously. She barely even flinched when he reached out his hand and took her chin in his fingers. He turned her face to look at her cheek. "It's pretty clean. Probably be all right."

"You speak good English," she said.

"Just 'good'? There was me thinking it was perfect."

"I only started learning it a few years ago. I do not know what perfect is."

He laughed again. "I was brought up on Landy's Farm." He gestured with a thumb over his shoulder in some indistinct direction. "Ma's a good sort, taught all us kids to read and write and," he smiled, "to talk proper."

He stood in a smooth motion and looked across the bay.

"Come on, you better move," he said. "Those fellas with the dogs and guns might decide they need to search for your body."

"I can't leave the plane," she said and looked at the single rotor arm standing out at an angle from the water.

"It's not going anywhere."

"But I need it. It's my future."

He turned and placed his hand on her arm. "You won't be having a future if they catch you, Gilda."

She knew he was right. There was nowhere to hide here. The bank behind them rose straight up another six feet. He must have jumped down to get to her.

"Where shall we go?"

"The farm is just a wander from here," he said. "Ma can take a look at your cheek."

She stared at the almost vertical bank. "I can't climb that."

He smiled, stepped across to it and cupped his hands for her foot.

She heard her mother's voice warning her against men, especially black men, who could not be trusted and only wanted one thing. It hadn't been until she was fourteen she gathered what that 'one thing' might be. She knew that was what Lemuel wanted.

A dog barked in the distance. Whether David wanted that 'one thing' or not, it was preferable to being shot. Although she had a feeling her mother might disagree on that point.

Decision made, she went over to the bank. She no longer had shoes so slipped her stockinged feet into his hand. Using roots sticking out from the surface, she steadied herself and pushed upwards. As she did so David stood up and boosted her over the top of the bank where she collapsed onto prickly grass and more mud.

By the time she had got to her feet, David had climbed up, too.

"Come on," he said. He took her hand and pulled her towards the trees ahead. The skin of his hands was callused, from working hard or perhaps simply living in the open. She allowed herself to be guided into the trees then came to a halt. He tugged her hand for a moment, as if she had simply got caught in the mud and could be pulled free. When that didn't work, he turned to face her but didn't release her hand.

"What?"

"I want to see their faces," she said. "I want to know who's trying to kill me."

He put his head to one side for a moment, then nodded.

He guided her a short distance back through the trees until she could see across to the opposite bank. Then he had her crouch down, hidden by a tree from where she was able to look out through a small bush at the side.

"When they come, don't move," he said, "Especially if you think they're looking at you. People see movement, not stillness."

The sound of barking grew. To Gilda's astonishment, David did not stay with her but stepped out of the trees. He walked to the edge of the bank, upriver from both her and the submerged plane.

He squatted down and fiddled with some grass.

Gilda jumped as five men and the dogs emerged from the trees at a run and pounded up to the edge of the opposite bank, which was a good ten feet higher than this side. But it made her feel safer: There was no way for them to cross.

All five were wet. Their hair, of the four who had hair, was bedraggled and they were all streaked with red sand. Gilda realised she probably looked better than them, since she had taken a wash in the river.

One of the five was Lemuel. He did not look happy. All his movements communicated reluctance. Perhaps he was regretting having told anyone about her intentions and suspicions.

"You! Boy!"

The man at the front looked as if he could go ten rounds with a bear. He had no hair and his huge shoulders stretched the fabric of his shirt. His bare arms were covered in tattoos.

David stood up and looked at the man. Gilda marvelled; he seemed so relaxed.

"You speak English?"

"Little, master."

Gilda's eyes went wide. What a lie. But she understood the lie, as most whites thought the blacks were little more than animals. She had heard talk that they wanted to get rid of them completely.

"You seen a girl?"

"Girl?"

"Yeah, a girl, for Chrissakes. You know what a girl is?"

David grinned. "I know girl, master."

"Have you seen one, a white girl, today?"

David shook his head with great seriousness. "No girl today."

"If you see one we want to know."

"Reward?"

"Oh yeah, of course, reward, you little savage."

"Who give reward? Who I talk?"

"You find me, Jerry Edmundson. You got that?"

"I find you."

"Only if you see the girl."

"If I see the girl."

Gilda watched in horror as one of the other men pulled his rifle off his shoulder and fired at David. The shot ricocheted from the ground at his feet. David did not even flinch.

"Told you they were stupid," shouted the shooter. The men laughed.

The one called Jerry ordered two of his men to head back into the forest until they could cross and then follow the river downstream. The other three, including Lemuel, went up river.

David stood and watched them go then returned to the trees.

"Well, that Jerry's a rum fella."

"Are you all right?"

"Yeah, no worries, couldn't hit a barn door with his mama holding his hand."

Gilda frowned. She had no idea what that meant but she gathered he was implying the man was a bad shot.

David looked up and squinted at the sun. "Let's get moving," he said. "They won't reach a crossing point up stream for a couple of hours. If they do cross, they might go to the farm."

David did not move fast, but his stride ate up the distance. Gilda found herself having to run every few steps just to keep up.

The sun was getting hot and she wished she had a hat. Four years here in Australia had already turned her skin a darker shade but she still tried to keep out of the sun as much as possible, mostly by keeping to her room and working with the books.

She wrote out code sequences, but without an analytical to run them she was forced to pretend to be one herself and work through each instruction one at a time, just as an analytical would. But so much slower.

On the other hand, working that way had given her an insight into how she could miss something obvious and write code that simply didn't do what she intended. An analytical ran the code it was given, regardless of whether it made sense or not—it was one of those mistakes that had given her the idea for code that rewrote itself. However, there was no practical way of achieving that. Analyticals didn't make their own cards.

And that made her think of Lemuel and the bank's assessment of her father's ability to repay a loan. Mr Aronson had calculated it with Lemuel's code, and it had come out lower than it should have.

That shouldn't be hard to do. She had learnt it was important with calculations to do the multiplies before the divides to get the best accuracy. They could never be completely right but doing things in that order was a way to minimise the error. If you did it the other way around you could get a lower result, especially using the silly British coinage system. And if you did that nobody would notice the mistake even if they looked at the way the code performed its calculations.

She tripped over something and landed on her face. She said something rude in *Züridütsch,* pushed herself back into a sitting position, and brushed the dirt from her palms, already stinging from the grazes across the skin. At least her knees would only be bruised, having been protected by her dress.

Gilda realised she was sitting on a stone step. She had been so deep in thought she had not noticed they were on a path. A wave of tiredness went through her; she wanted to just stay here. David loomed over her.

"You all right?"

"Not looking where I was going."

"Old *Wagyl* will catch you if you're not paying attention."

Gilda glanced around and shook her head. "What?"

He grinned. "*Wagyl,* giant snake. You're sitting on him."

Gilda panicked. She threw herself across the path and staggered to her feet. Her dress ripped as one her toes got caught in a tear caused by the fall. David caught her hand and steadied her.

"There's no snake!" she screamed at him, staring at the place she had been sitting. "What kind of stupid joke are you playing on me?"

David sighed. "Sorry, Gilda, really."

"What's this noise? Who's screaming?" The voice of a woman penetrated from some way away. There was a scratching of claws on stone and they were surrounded by dogs … or wolves. Something between a wolf and a dog, with a sandy coat. They sniffed at Gilda and licked David's feet and legs. He scratched one of them under the chin.

"It's all right, Ma!" He shouted back over his shoulder. "No one's dead."

Gilda shut her eyes and felt the world begin to swim. She opened them again. The dogs—she guessed they were dingoes—had started licking her as well. Rough tongues worked their way up and down her calves and across her feet. One of them was trying to lick between her toes.

"Stop it," she said without any conviction.

"Who's this you brought, David?"

"Name's Gilda, Ma," he said. "Some fellas were trying to catch her or shoot her, or something."

"She looks like a drowned rat."

"She was in the river."

"In the storm? Lucky to be alive."

Gilda listened to the words but did not feel as if they had much to do with her. She felt separated from the world. This time everything started to spin even with her eyes open, and there was nothing she could do about it. Strong arms slid round her waist and shoulders.

"Here, have a cuppa." A tin mug was thrust into her hands. It was so hot it almost burned. She found herself sitting at a wooden table. Everything was clean. Sun filtered through the windows and the air glowed with dust. There was the muted buzz of flies.

Gilda was sure she had not passed out but it had still been like a dream. She did not think the farm house was far from where she had sat on the snake.

"What snake?" she said out loud.

"Is she delirious? Might be worse than I thought," said a woman, the same one who had spoken before.

"No, Ma, she just got confused when I said she was sitting on old *Wagyl*."

Gilda sipped the tea and burned her lip. The pain woke her up. The woman was probably in her fifties and she was white (though her skin was wrinkled and brown) but she looked like everyone's grandmother. Gilda resolved to continue to stay indoors as much as possible. She did not want that complexion.

"The poor woman who gave you life would be turning in her grave, ya silly *galah*."

"Sorry, Ma," he said.

"Don't apologise to me—apologise to Gilda."

David turned to her and grinned. His white teeth glowed against his black skin. His was the kind of smile that just made you happy.

"And knock that charm off," said the woman and slapped him round the head. The smile disappeared from his lips, but it was still there in his eyes.

"Sorry about that, Gilda," he said, with only the barest hint of contrition. "I really wasn't trying to scare you."

Mrs Landy—Gilda assumed it must be her though no one had bothered with introductions—went off into the kitchen area and busied herself.

"What snake?"

"*Wagyl*. I suppose your people would call him a god. When he moves he makes all the rivers and valleys and hills of the scarp. That's what I meant when I said you were sitting on him."

"So he made everything?"

"Nah, not everything." He shook his head. "Mostly just the scarp. Can't really explain it. The idea that one god made everything out of nothing seems pretty crazy to me."

"Oh."

"Yeah, well, I go to church and sing the songs like we're supposed to," he said. "I think your Jesus seems like a good bloke, though." He grinned again. "Would have made a good black fella, I reckon."

He received another clip across the back of his head from Mrs Landy. "That's enough of your blasphemy." She put down a plate in front of Gilda. It held three thick slices of fresh buttered bread, a chunk of cheese and some cold sausage. "Don't listen to him. He talks nonsense and lots of it."

If David was upset by her words, he didn't show it. In fact Gilda was
certain he was not in the least concerned.

Mrs Landy sat opposite her across the table but turned to David. "You
go and keep an eye out for those other fellas. We'll have to decide what to
do if they come this way."

"They have dogs."

"How many?"

"Two with them."

Mrs Landy gave a short, barking laugh. "Don't think that'll be much of a
threat."

Without another word David slid out of his chair, padded silently across
the stone-flagged floor and was gone.

"All right, dear, tell me everything."

xv

The flood from the storm up on the scarp hit the lake and spread out. It
had been a torrent pouring from the hills, bursting the river banks. But the
lake gathered up the renegade water and channelled it towards the sea.

The incoming tide did battle with the tumbling flood, raising a tidal bore
that shone red in the afternoon sun.

The rising waters threatened to pour over the sea defences. They rose to
the very top but did not quite make it. Further up the lake they did flow out
across the landscape but all the houses were built on a higher level so even
then the water could not reach them.

Flooding was not uncommon along the coast; every year there would be
three or four huge waves that would pour in from the ocean, driven by
winds. They would crash up the beach and pour into the cities and towns
from Coogee in the south to north of Perth.

But when storm rains filled the river, it came from the other direction.
With the high tide, everything along the coast was at risk.

Rudger was out with Alys bringing their boat to higher ground, along
with a dozen other fishermen doing the same. They had a friendly
community and help was always offered even if it wasn't accepted. The
other option was to simply leave the boat out on the water, but a storm like
this would tear loose any number of branches and tree trunks. They would
be carried down from the scarp and could smash a boat's hull like
matchwood.

Better out of the water.

He sat on the upturned hull of his boat with Alys beside him. They did not speak. He stared up at the scarp and he knew that's what she was doing, too.

"The water won't be good for fishing for a day or two," he said.

His wife said nothing.

"I thought I might head up to the scarp."

"I'll come with you."

"Someone needs to stay with Dieter."

She went quiet for a while and then said, "I'll make you some food."

Back in Switzerland, preparing for a journey in winter was something always done with great care. You never knew when you might be trapped by a blizzard or have your path blocked by an avalanche. Or have to wait for wolves to pass by.

The kind of problems that could arise in Australia, at least here on the coast, did not even approach that level. But that did not stop Alys from ensuring her husband was well supplied with food, or equipment, or both.

She handed him the backpack filled to overflowing, and then his shotgun.

"Why am I carrying the rope?" he said. "There are no mountains here, Alys."

"That may be so, husband, but you never know when a length of rope will come in handy. There is a blanket for the night if you need it."

He kissed his wife on the cheek and smiled. She was right.

"You won't try to cross the Swan, will you?"

He shook his head. None of the bridges were safe during the flood. The ones in the city were closed by official order. He did not know the state of the one further upstream but he would not risk it, at least not until tomorrow.

He set off and did not look back.

The first part of the journey was easy enough. The roads out of Fremantle towards the scarp were good quality. He headed up into Applecross where the Canning River flowed from the east into the Swan. The town was situated where the banks were less than a hundred yards apart. The bridge here was well above the level of the water.

There were plenty of people out and about. Halfway across the bridge he paused to look at the river thundering beneath them. It was terrifying. As a fisherman and sailor he had a respect for the power of water.

Once through Applecross the main road did not go in the direction he needed. He was forced to use tracks as he turned more to the north. A thundering air-plane went over, flying low along the river. Everywhere was mud and he was grateful for the boots. He angled towards the Swan River and kept parallel to it as best he could.

He reached the base of the scarp in the early evening. He was hot and sweating. Flies had decided he was someone of interest and buzzed round him constantly. The area was all fields with farmhouses scattered across the terrain. The ground had a layer of red sand across it. Even the plants had a dusting of it.

After a short stop to eat some pie and take a drink of water, he set off again climbing slowly up the scarp. He looked back across the river. On the road on the other side there was a steam truck, unmoving. Two men lay near it with dogs. He could see their guns leaning up against the truck.

He kept going and reached the top in half an hour. Now all of Fremantle and Perth were laid out beneath him. The sun was low enough that it shone brightly off the sea, rivers and lake. It all looked so serene and calm. So normal.

He sat on a fallen tree and ate more. He finished the supply of water he was carrying, but he was not concerned. Even here he could hear the thundering of the river as it tumbled over the edge of the scarp.

The sun slanted through the *jarrah* trees as he walked on. He thought he could hear dogs in the distance. They did not sound happy. Pausing for a moment, he dug out a couple of cartridges and loaded his shotgun. The dogs were probably nothing to worry about, but better safe than sorry.

He pushed on and stumbled through some undergrowth and out onto a track. It looked well used, though there were no wheel marks since the afternoon downpour. The sound of barking dogs was clearer.

Following the track he rounded a bend to find himself looking at an open area with a farmhouse. In the open space in front were three men with dogs, surrounded by a pack of dingoes.

xvi

Gilda heard dogs—Mrs Landy had told her dingoes don't bark—and ducked deeper into the undergrowth as the farm wife had told her. It was midafternoon and the sun was still very hot. Ma had given her a backpack with food and a blanket. It weighed her down but was easier to carry than the bag she had lost.

She'd been given Mrs Landy's bed for a couple of hours, where she had slept solid and dreamless. Coming awake had been a strange experience since she had only slept in her own bed since coming to Australia—and sleeping in the middle of the day was always confusing.

Mrs Landy had woken her when David had returned. He confirmed her pursuers had crossed the Swan and were making their way back, clearly intent on finding their quarry. He said they were sticking close to the river, though she could not imagine they expected to find her upstream.

With a bit of luck they would think she had drowned.

"If you still had that bag we'd leave it for them to find," Mrs Landy had said. "As it is best you take off."

"But the ship…" Gilda knew she sounded like a whining child. "I came all this way and I found it. I need it for the salvage."

At that Mrs Landy had smiled. "Salvage doesn't work like that, dearie. You have to be able to bring it back and put yourself at risk in the process."

"I was shot at and nearly drowned."

"That's true, of course, but even so the best you could hope for is a reward from the owner for finding it, and nobody knows who that is right now, do they?"

Gilda had to agree. She felt like a balloon that had been ripped open and deflated.

It all happened quickly. Mrs Landy had prepared the backpack while Gilda was asleep and then took her out through the back, away from the river. Behind the farmhouse was a yard with chickens, pigs and goats. Beyond that was a field of wheat bordered by *jarrah* trees.

"I can't send David with you," she said. "I'll be needing him to deal with these lowlifes. All you have to do is follow round the field, stay undercover in case they turn up. Once you get to the far end, head straight until you reach the main track and then turn right, that'll take you down off the scarp towards Applecross. You'll know your way from there."

Gilda thanked her and gave her a kiss on the cheek, and then headed off.

Not a moment too soon, she thought. She had not quite reached the far end of the field when she heard the dogs. She did not want to take anything for granted so crouched behind a tree and peered out carefully—remembering what David had said about people noticing movement.

Directly in front of her was a drainage ditch full to its top with water. Then came the field itself where the wheat had not quite reached full maturity—or so she assumed, as it was tall but did not have the bristly top of seeds. Beyond that was the farm house.

There was nobody in sight. If it was the men approaching, they would be on the other side of the building and wouldn't be able to see her. She drew back and moved a little deeper into the undergrowth. Keeping the field in sight on her left, she moved at a steady pace. She tried to place her feet so that she did not squelch in the mud but it was a losing battle.

If her skin and hair had been as black as David's, she imagined she would be no more than a shadow. Instead she had pale skin and blonde hair. She was probably more like a ghost. She smiled at the thought; perhaps if she caked herself in mud, she could hide better.

The forest looked empty but it was far from silent. The raucous cries of the cockatoos dominated, but there were other animals, too. And the air was full of the buzzing of insects, from the deep drone of the big ones to the high pitched whines of the smaller. There always seemed to be more after the rains. She wondered that they hadn't drowned in the deluge.

She reached the corner of the field and paused. There seemed to be nothing ahead but forest. If there was a trail she couldn't see it. She felt a twinge of fear. People got lost in the outback never to be seen again. Eaten, died of starvation, drowned in rivers, who knew? Or killed by the natives.

The original inhabitants of these lands might have thought the white men were their ancestors at the beginning, but it didn't take long for them to realise their mistake. There were plenty of the natives who did not like people like her. Or so she'd heard. David was the first one she had ever met, and she could not imagine him being dangerous.

But it was not as if she had any choice. She took a deep breath and strode away from the field and the farm.

There was a slight rise in the terrain, and less mud as the water seemed to have drained off—which must be one of the reasons the drainage ditch was so full. She looked back but the foliage prevented her from seeing any better. It seemed she was too far to hear anything from the farm.

But she could hear an engine. It was a flyer of some sort; the constant "thwopping" told her it was one of the British-style machines that could land anywhere. She stared up but could see nothing but hints of blue through the green.

It got louder and then abruptly quieter before fading out completely.

Gilda shrugged and, after checking the direction of her footprints, she pushed on. Mrs Landy had not said anything about the hill. She hoped she had not gone wrong so soon. Though she laughed at that—after all going wrong sooner, when it's easier to correct, was probably better than later.

A minute later she reached the brow of the hill and saw the track ahead. She heaved a sigh of relief and headed the short distance to stand in the middle of it, between the parallel ruts of mud.

The sound of a distant shotgun echoed through the trees.

xvii

The next two minutes were the most difficult Gilda had ever faced.

As the sound of the gunshot echoed and faded, she stood stock still in the middle of the track. The shot must have come from the farm, although determining direction was difficult in this place.

She was only a girl. If there was gunfire at the farm there was nothing she could do about it. Mrs Landy had her own gun, and she had her dingoes. She had David. There was nothing Gilda could do that would help. In fact, since the men were chasing her, going back was simply the worst thing she could do.

But David and Mrs Landy had helped her. What if they were in trouble?

The calculation had an obvious solution: She should not go back. Mrs Landy and David had known they were taking a risk if the men arrived. It was their decision.

There was something else that did not fit so easily into the equation: How would Gilda feel for the rest of her life if she did not go back and either Mrs Landy or David was hurt or killed? She would never know whether she could have prevented it, and the guilt would haunt her.

Like the guilt of lying to her parents about sneaking out at night. Only one hundred thousand times worse. She wasn't a brave person but there was nothing else that she could do. It was an equation that, no matter how heavily one side was weighted, the other side still prevailed.

She faced back into the forest. As the truth of what she was about to do filled her, she shivered. She settled the backpack on her shoulders and plunged back through the trees, following her own trail.

It seemed she covered the distance back to the edge of the field in a fraction of the time it had taken to travel out. But she came to a stop before she reached the field. A man with a dog was coming around the corner of the farm building. She recognised him as the one that had shot at David—even if he hadn't meant to kill him.

The dog would pick up her scent immediately. But she had played this game before and had already laid a false trail all the way to the track. Without having to think about it, she kept moving forwards until she reached the place where she had peered back at the farm. There, she lay down in the mud.

This time she did not stop; she slithered forwards like a snake and slipped into the drainage ditch. It was about four feet deep. She got her feet underneath herself and bent her legs until her mouth was level with the water. The backpack was still on her back. She gathered up handfuls of mud and rubbed it into her hair and across her face.

The dog barked as it headed in her direction. She could imagine it straining against its leash and pulling its owner along. As it got closer, she pulled herself in towards the bank to give herself more cover.

The drainage ditch had the very slightest current, nothing like the river, and tugged her hair in the direction of the farm. Looking over its bank, barely daring to breathe, she watched the dog and man head past. They did not even slow at the point where she had gone into the water.

Gilda liked dogs, but they could be very single-minded.

At the speed he was going she probably only had about ten minutes before he came back. But right now there were only two men back at the farm.

She moved along the drainage ditch but made slow progress. It was clear she would have to get back on dry land. That turned out to be harder than she expected. The banks were slick, and even when she could get a good hold on a root, her waterlogged clothes were too heavy.

The straps of the backpack straining against her shoulders gave her an idea. Taking the thing off was a good first move, but instead of throwing it up on to the bank she pushed it down into the water and stood on it. The reduced weight and additional height gave her what she needed to pull herself up and out like a drowned rat.

Her need to get to the farm before the man with the dog returned galvanised her into action. Dripping water and mud, she set off at a slow run through the trees. The sounds of the farm animals seemed no different to when she had left, barely half an hour before.

As she approached she heard the puffing of a steam engine. The flyer must have landed here at the farm. What did that mean?

She got to the building and pressed her back against the wall. She tried to think. Someone had followed the men up in a flyer. Police? She was not sure, but she did not think they used flyers. Someone that Mrs Landy knew? Perhaps, but that would be a coincidence which she was not keen on.

No one Gilda knew had a flyer, or even had access to one—except Mr Aronson. She didn't know whether he had one but he surely he could get one if he wanted it.

All the computation work she had read about told her that analyticals dealt in absolute values, what you might call certainties. But Ada Lovelace had written that she looked forward to the day when analyticals could be more flexible, even reaching into the field of art. A step towards that would be to let them deal with uncertainties. Probability was a field of mathematics: If it could be described by symbols, then an analytical could be programmed for it.

Which did not help her current situation in the slightest.

Gilda moved to the back door and with great care to avoid any noise got it open a fraction of an inch. She could hear no voices, so judged there was no one inside.

She squeezed through.

xviii

She moved silently through the scullery on bare feet. The door to the kitchen was open, and the room, empty. The kitchen led through to a sitting room with a window looking out on to the front yard.

Making sure she could not see the window, she reached the door and held herself against the wall beside it. The only sound she could make out clearly from the yard was the engine of the flyer turning over with a steady thump-thump-thump.

She played with angles in her mind. If she stepped directly into the room then anyone in the correct position outside would be able to see her. Since she did not know where anyone was, she had to assume there would be someone.

If she was on the floor, only someone right by the window could see her, and anyone there would most likely be looking away. Though, as she remembered David saying, people noticed movement, not stillness.

Waiting would achieve nothing so she ducked down, pulled up her dripping wet skirt and crossed the polished wooden floor. This close to it she noticed the multitude of scratches from dingo claws. She made it to the wall beside the window. In this position it was almost impossible for anyone to see her. But with her back to the wall she could see the damp trail she had left.

"Such sad news. I am so sorry, Mr Dettwiler." The voice of Mr Aronson was raised over the noise of the flyer. Gilda smiled without a hint of humour. She was pleased her estimate of the probabilities had correctly placed him in the machine.

She heard her father. "I do not believe it." His voice was strained and breaking if he was in mortal pain.

"Is this hers?" That was the voice of the leader of the men who had been pursuing her. The only things she had lost were her shoes and the bag. Her shoes could be in the Indian Ocean by now. She was getting familiar with the sounds and was able to block out the engine, but could hear a growling that sent shivers through her spine.

There was a longer pause. She could imagine the man moving to hand over the drawstring bag. Where had they found it?

She wondered why David or Mrs Landy had not said anything. Why they hadn't said they had seen her alive less than half an hour before? Were they dead? Tied up or hurt?

"Is it hers?"

There was no reply from her father (at least none that she heard) for a while, but then: "Where did you find it?"

"My men searching downstream came across it," said Aronson. "The river is in full flood and there are some very bad rapids…" His voice trailed off, leaving the clear impression that the swollen Swan River had dashed her to a pulp against the rocks.

"I'm so very sorry, Mr Dettwiler," he said. "She was a clever girl but with unrealistic dreams. This is what a broken heart can do."

What? thought Gilda.

"What?" said her father, at the same time as a voice she recognised as Lemuel.

"She and Lemuel here had an argument last night," said Aronson. "She wanted him to run away with her, to catch a ship to the east. She dreamed of getting into university. It is so sad."

"She told you this and not me?" said her father.

"She told Lemuel and he has explained it to me. That's right, isn't it, Lemuel?"

There was a long pause. Gilda could imagine the thoughts running through Lemuel's mind—he had seen the men trying to kill her. He knew that she had not wanted to run away with him. And he knew that one of Aronson's men was pursuing her right now.

What would he do?

She did not hear his answer.

"Speak up, boy."

"Yes."

Gilda burned with instant anger. He had lied, he had condemned her to death—or so he thought. He would justify it, of course; he would say he had no choice, or that it was too late anyway. But in the end, it all came down to preserving his job.

"Coward," she muttered under her breath. The whine of a dingo outside increased. She pushed herself into a standing position. Water had puddled around her feet.

With utmost slowness she turned towards the window; she needed to find out how things stood. Her heart was breaking as she thought of the pain her father must be suffering now, thinking she was dead. She felt a slight flash of anger towards Mrs Landy and David for allowing that to happen, though she could guess why.

The first thing that came into view was the side of David's head where he stood only a couple of yards from the window, on the porch area looking out into the yard. At David's feet were two of the dingoes. They were watching the same thing as he, with great intensity.

Beyond him was the flyer, a fairly small machine for perhaps five or six passengers. It had two rotors at the front and a third at the back. They were not turning but smoke drifted up from its stack. The fellow she took to be the pilot stood beside it, smoking a cigarette with an air of disinterest.

"Got you, girlie."

Gilda jumped and turned. The missing pursuer was behind her, the dog silent but straining at the leash. She could see the man's muscles flexing to keep his animal under control.

The grin that came across his face made her courage fail. She threw herself towards the door as he released the slavering dog.

She watched as the dog launched itself at her. She had almost no time to react and nowhere to go—except down. She let her feet slip in the water she had dripped onto the floor and fell. Gravity did not respond as fast she would have liked.

The dog's trajectory was taking him directly to where her chest and neck had been. She slipped sideways. She willed herself to fall faster. It was as if time itself slowed down as the dog's front paws dragged across her body as it raised them to strike where her chest had been.

It had seen her fall, but it was tied to the motion that physics dictated as much as she was. It lowered its head to grab whatever it could of her as it went over. She felt its hot breath as its teeth scraped her skin.

The beast crashed into the wall with a pained yelp exactly where she had been a moment before, just as she hit the ground.

There was no time for her to get out of its way as it fell on top of her. The weight of it slammed into her chest, knocking the wind from her. It scrambled to its feet over her, pausing for a moment to gather its thoughts. The one place dogs could not see was directly beneath them, so in that moment she pulled up her knees to her chest, planted them against its chest and used her leverage to push it up and away.

That move wasn't as effective as she had hoped, as she had failed to knock the dog onto its back or at least its side. Instead it landed by her feet. She yanked them away just in time as it snapped at them.

And then there were dozens of legs and paws around her. A man screamed. The incoming animals swarmed across her attacker, and it disappeared beneath them. Animal cries of pain arose and were just as quickly cut off.

Gilda pushed herself back and away from the melee of dingoes. Two hands reached under her arms and brought her up to her feet. She jammed her elbow into the one who had grabbed her.

"Ow, did I deserve that?"

"David!" She turned to face him. The sounds behind her were grotesque. He took her arm and led her out into the sun.

"Gilda!" She looked up to see her father running across the yard towards her. Another voice echoed her name and she saw Lemuel standing next to Aronson. Lemuel took a half step in her direction then stopped, looking at the dingoes ahead of him. Gilda could not decipher the expression on Mr Aronson's face, but he did not look happy. He turned towards the flyer.

"I wouldn't move if I were you, Aronson, or you other fellas. My pack is a bit on edge right now and they like to chase prey. They'll take you down and munch on your bones before I have a chance to stop them. If I decide I want to."

The tone of Mrs Landy's voice was enough to make the bravest man quail. Gilda had wondered what happened to Mr Landy, but now she was not sure she wanted to ask.

Her father ran into her with the force of a train and smothered her in his arms. He had never been so demonstrative.

"You're alive," he said, and his voice seemed to be cracking.

"No thanks to these fellas, Mr Dettwiler," said Mrs Landy. She moved forwards and put her hand on Gilda's shoulder. "Nice job, Gilda. Looks like you caught quite a big one." She turned to David. "Fetch some rope and let's get these dirt bags tied up so they don't try anything stupid."

"What about the one inside?"

"Does he need tying up?"

"He's dead."

"One less to worry about then," said Mrs Landy. "Though I suppose we'll be sleeping in the barn for a couple of nights."

It took less than ten minutes for David to immobilise Aronson and his men. The pilot said he was just being paid to fly, so they told him to get down into the city and bring back some police. The flyer made a huge racket as it left but soon the farm was back to being quiet except for Aronson's complaints.

Lemuel did not protest when he was bound, but Aronson had to be threatened with gagging before he would shut up.

"I don't understand," said Gilda's father when the fuss had died down and he had stopped clinging to her as if she would melt away in the bush. "Why did you run away?"

"I didn't run away, Papa," she said. "I just came to find the flyer that crashed. I left a letter."

"There was no letter."

"Lemuel took it and gave it to Aronson."

Her father frowned. "But why would Aronson want to hurt you"—it seemed he could not bring himself to say *kill*—"for trying to find the flyer?"

"It wasn't that, Papa," she said. "Aronson has been cheating us and probably other people, too. Lemuel has fixed his code sequences to give the wrong answers. Answers that favour Aronson and the bank."

Her father glanced across at Lemuel. "But you've been meeting with that boy?"

"Sorry, Papa," she said, burying her head in his shoulder. "I didn't know until last night."

She wanted to say *nothing happened* but this was too public. And she would probably have to say it a hundred times to her mother.

It took a further hour before the police turned up in another, larger flyer that had been commandeered for the purpose. The pilot looked well pleased with himself.

With Aronson, Lemuel and his men taken into custody there was no room for Gilda and her father. The light was failing when all the statements had been taken and the police left.

"Looks like we'll all be sleeping in the barn," said Mrs Landy.

Epilogue

Gilda trudged home from school. After three weeks the excitement around her adventures had evaporated like rain after a storm. Investigators for the American company that owned the downed flyer had finally turned up.

She had heard from Mrs Landy they would be bringing in heavy machinery to pull it out of the river so they could recover the bodies and take the machine back to America.

There was no explanation of what it had been doing flying over Perth.

Aronson and Lemuel were in gaol, along with the thugs the banker had employed to find and kill her. Lemuel was likely to get off with a suspended sentence because he was telling the police everything he knew. Gilda had been interviewed again and had confirmed his story about saving her life.

She still never wanted to see him again.

Every piece of news was just another nail in the coffin of her dreams. No money for her parents, no money for salvage (she laughed at herself for having ever thought there might be), and no way to get to university. Her mother had been so angry—after she got over being so happy at Gilda's return—that Gilda had been told she must be at school or at home. Nowhere else. Probably for the rest of her life. Or at least the rest of her mother's life.

She walked past the Mechanics Institute. There was a billboard advertising a lecture by someone from the east. She did not even bother reading it.

The bank still opened as usual. There had been no talk of any changes. Papa could not take the loan that had been offered and still used the same boat.

Nothing had changed. No. It was worse. Now she had no future at all. She would work in the factory making bricks until her hands were callused and hard as leather. She would marry someone and bear him children. Then she would drink gin until she died.

She came around the corner of her street. Swan River was a flat calm. The tide was out and the boats along the shoreline, beached.

A steam taxi sat in front of her parents' house. The driver stood beside it having a smoke. He touched his cap as she walked by.

A visitor? Who did they know that would come around in a taxi? Perhaps it was the police again.

She pushed through the front door and into the gloom. Her father and the bank clerk, Mr Prescott, were seated at the table. Her mother was hovering, ready to make drinks or bring food.

Mr Prescott turned as she came through. "Good afternoon, Gilda."

"Mr Prescott," she said with the uncertainty of confusion.

"Mr Prescott is to be made the bank manager," said her mother barely suppressing an excitement that Gilda could not understand.

"Congratulations, Mr Prescott," she said. She was not sure what to do. She would have gone to her room, but that would be impolite. Perhaps she needed to hover, like her mother.

"Mr Prescott has something to ask you," said her father.

The visitor stood up. He really was very tall, she realised, and he towered over her. "Miss Dettwiler, I wondered whether you might consider coming to work in the bank."

Gilda blinked. She opened her mouth to say something but was at a complete loss.

"I have spoken to your teachers on the matter, and they do not think your education would suffer."

"My teachers?"

"Yes, it was almost unanimous that they had probably taught you as much as you could learn, and that in many instances you are far ahead of the others of your age."

"Really?" was all she could muster in response.

"Of course," he said. "If you would prefer not to, then I quite understand. Your parents, however, also seem to think this would be a good idea."

She looked at her mother in disbelief, but Alys smiled and nodded.

"In what capacity?" Gilda said.

"Ah, an excellent question," he said. "Well, it seems we are without a computationer, and in this modern world one must have someone to operate an analytical."

"But Lemuel…"

Mr Prescott's face fell. "Poor Lemuel, yes. But you see, Gilda, even though he may escape a prison sentence, it would be quite impossible for him to return to his former position. After all, the bank's reputation is already tarnished. Who would trust us if we employed the person who wrote the bad code?"

"But," put in her father, "if they employed the girl who had exposed the trouble…"

"But how do you know I can do it?" she said, with the sudden fear that if she were faced with a real analytical and the need to produce real code that worked properly, she might just as easily fail.

Mr Prescott smiled. "Perhaps because you admitted that you might not know how. There will be a trial period, of course; you will have some time to become acquainted with the machine and learn how to use it."

Gilda looked from Mr Prescott to her mother, who was *still* smiling, and her father, who wore an enigmatic expression.

"Oh, and," said Mr Prescott, "I would expect you to re-evaluate the loan applications and accounts details for at least the previous year to determine which had been calculated incorrectly, so that they can be put right."

It took Gilda a moment to realise what that meant. She looked back at her father with a feeling of excitement exploding inside of her. Then she turned back to Mr Prescott.

"Would I be allowed to use the bank's analytical for my own projects?"

Mr Prescott did not answer straightaway and, for a moment, Gilda was concerned she might have pushed a little too far.

"Within reason, Gilda," he said. "As long as it does not interfere with your proper work."

She almost laughed out loud. "Then yes, Mr Prescott," she said. "I would be delighted to accept your kind offer."

~ end ~

ABOUT THE AUTHOR

Steve Turnbull trained as a computer scientist then spent twenty years as a computer magazine editor and journalist. He ran a design agency for several years then switched back to his first love of computers and is now a contract web developer. He and his (writer) wife have been married for 30 years with two children also pursuing creative careers.

It took him ten years (off and on) to write his fantasy novel "Elona" after which he turned his attention to screenwriting for which he got paid but never produced, which happens a lot in the film business.

Then he switched back to prose and wrote stories set in the steampunk Voidships universe. He started with the 'Maliha Anderson' crime thrillers, then the 'Iron Pegasus' YA series interleaved with the 'Frozen Beauty' stories (a TV series in book form). Plus the action-romance 'Broken Vows'.

He recently began an SF mega-work entitled 'KYMIERA' based on one of his screenplays.

His work (including many more stories set in the Voidships universe) can be found on Amazon:
http://www.amazon.com/Steve-Turnbull/e/B00H20G7P8

Twitter: https://twitter.com/adaddinsane
Facebook: https://www.facebook.com/steveturnbullwriter
Google+: https://plus.google.com/u/0/+SteveTurnbull-Writer/about

Thank you for getting this far. I hope you enjoyed those stories, if you did then please take some time to write a review on Amazon and Goodreads, or your own blog, or indeed anywhere else you can shoe-horn one in under any pretence.

The Faraday Cage anthology has been a work of love for me. A few years ago I was working with a director (Chris Payne by name) on a script for a web series and, while what we were doing was okay, he turned round one day and said "What if it was Steampunk?"

I looked blank. He explained. I said "I can do that."

The result was the script for an eight-part web series called "The Lazarus Machine". It was based on Chris's original premise for the Voidships universe:

In 1843 Sir Michael Faraday demonstrated, to the assembled scientists of the Royal Society in London, his Principle for the Partial Nullification of Gravity.

The rest is alternate history.

From the beginning Chris wanted Voidships to be an open universe attracting all sorts of creatives to help fill it. But, until this book, it had been my work alone, through thirteen books and other stories.

But now it's more than that.

Working with the four other authors, of such varied experience and backgrounds, has been an invigorating experience. Each one brings something new and exciting to the world.

Of course there was some reining in at times. The Voidships universe has its rules and they cannot be broken but, as is true of all creative work, boundaries demand more and make the end result even better.

If you haven't done it yet, join the mailing list to be informed when one of these excellent authors has released another book (not necessarily a Voidships one).

Go to: http://bit.ly/faraday-cage-list

Steve Turnbull
Editor, March 2016

www.ingramcontent.com/pod-product-compliance
Lightning Source LLC
Chambersburg PA
CBHW050346190726
48284CB00007BB/2165